Five-Ring Circus

Five-Ring Circus

Suspense Down Under

JON CLEARY

G.K. Hall & Co. • Chivers Press
Thorndike, Maine USA   Bath, England

This Large Print edition is published by G.K. Hall & Co., USA and by Chivers Press, England.

Published in 1999 in the U.S. by arrangement with Avon Books, A unit of the Hearst Corporation.

Published in 1999 in the U.K. by arrangement with HarperCollins Publishers Ltd.

U.S. Hardcover   0-7838-8617-9   (Core Series Edition)
U.K. Hardcover   0-7540-1313-8   (Windsor Large Print)
U.K. Softcover   0-7540-2233-1   (Paragon Large Print)

The text of this Large Print edition is unabridged.
Other aspects of the book may vary from the original edition.

Set in 16 pt. Plantin.

Printed in the United States on permanent paper.

British Library Cataloguing in Publication Data available

Library of Congress Cataloging in Publication Data

Cleary, Jon, 1917–
    Five-ring circus : suspense Down Under / Jon Cleary.
        p. (large print) cm.
    ISBN 0-7838-8617-9 (lg. print : hc : alk. paper)
    1. Large type books. I. Title.
[PR9619.3.C54F5   1999b]
    823—dc21   99-21862

For Joy

In the first half of 1996 a five-line item appeared in a Sydney newspaper. Two Chinese students were being questioned about the deposit in their bank accounts of some fifty million dollars. The story was not followed up and no more was heard of the students and their sudden fortune.

This book is not a guess at what may have been behind that meagre story. It is fiction and none of the characters is meant to represent anyone living or dead. Anyone who sees himself or herself here has looked in the wrong mirror.

Chapter One

1

'A working mum,' said Tom. 'I can't get used to the idea.'

'I've been a working mum ever since I started having you lot,' said Lisa. 'Watch yourself or you'll be paying for your own dinner.'

'That'll please Old Fishhooks-in-the-Pockets,' said Maureen, patting her father's arm. 'Would you like me and Claire to go Dutch?'

'Speak for yourself,' said Claire. 'I'm being extravagant at his expense tonight. Do Chinese restaurants serve French champagne?'

'If it does,' said Malone, 'I'll have it closed down for extortion.'

He had the benign look that husbands and fathers occasionally achieve when the stars are in their right places in the heavens. Tonight was such an occasion. The family were celebrating Lisa's first month back in the workforce after twenty-one years; an event the children seemed to equate with the introduction of suffragism. He still thought of them as *the children,* or usually *the kids;* but they were kids no longer and he was only slowly coming to terms with the changes in them.

Claire was twenty-one and in her third year of Law at Sydney University, coolly beautiful and with her eyes wide open for the traps that the world and its men might lay for her. Maureen was almost nineteen and doing Communications at New South Wales, dark where her sister was blonde, willing to risk the world and its men. Tom was seventeen and only a year away from university and two years into girls. Malone trusted their independent outlook. He was still coming to terms with Lisa's stated desire for her own independence.

The Golden Gate was not the largest restaurant in Sydney's Chinatown, but it was the ritziest; dim sum and chop suey were unmentionables here. It had a huge chandelier that, it was claimed, had hung in the palace of the Empress Tz'u-Hsi, a lady not known for welcoming foreign guests, gourmets or otherwise. The carpet, it was also claimed, had been woven by the nimble fingers of three hundred small boys working day and night in a village in Sinkiang; there was also a claim, spread by restaurant competitors, that the Chinese characters in one corner of the carpet translated as *Axminster*. Pale green linen covered the tables clustered in the middle of the big room and red velvet-covered banquettes lined the walls, which were in turn covered in green shantung. The waiters, no coolies here, were mandarins-in-training and tips were encouraged to be in ransom terms. On the floor above the restaurant were private dining

8

rooms; the third floor, supposedly the manager's residence, was given over to four gambling rooms that had never known the indignity of a police raid. The Golden Gate was a compulsory pit-stop for all visiting delegations from Communist China, both in the restaurant and the gambling rooms. It had, among all its other claims, class, something that all who came here, including the Communists, appreciated.

'Do you make as much money as Dad?' asked Tom, who was doing Economics in Year 12.

'He doesn't want to know,' said Lisa, 'and neither should you.'

'Right on,' said Maureen, and Claire nodded in agreement.

Tom abruptly looked uncomfortable. He was a big lad, as tall as his father at six feet one, and already starting to bulk out in chest and shoulders. Like his sisters, he had inherited his mother's good looks, though there were hints of his father in them. He had not inherited his mother's cool composure and emotion showed on his face in bold relief. 'Sorry, I didn't mean —'

Lisa, sitting next to him in the banquette, patted his hand. 'It's all right. It's just that the money's not important — What are you grinning at?'

'Was I grinning?' said Malone. 'I thought I was looking pained.'

'Come on,' said Claire. 'Let's order before he starts chewing on his American Express card.'

Malone didn't mind the chi-acking; he couldn't be in a better mood. It had been a quiet week in Sydney for murder: only three, all domestics that had been attended to by local detectives. There had been no call on Homicide and Serial Offenders Unit. There had been appearances in court to give evidence at murder trials; other detectives had been at work on task forces looking into homicides still unsolved; and for Malone, the Co-ordinator in charge of Homicide, there had been the opportunity to catch up on the hated paperwork. This Friday night family dinner was a pleasant end of the week.

Then a tall handsome Chinese got up from a banquette at the rear of the restaurant and came towards them. 'Inspector Malone, it's a pleasure to see you here. A family celebration?'

'Sort of. How are you, Les? You've met my wife. And these are —' He introduced Claire, Maureen and Tom, feeling some of the pride that, a modest man, he occasionally let seep out of him. 'Mr Chung, he's one of the owners.'

Leslie Chung had come to Australia forty years ago, when he was still in his teens. He had walked out of the hills of Yunnan and down to Hong Kong, arriving there just as that city was getting into its stride as a place to coin money. After a couple of months there he had decided there was already too much competition for an ambitious capitalist, especially a teenage penniless one. He had got a job as a deckhand on a

10

freighter plying between Hong Kong and Sydney; on its second trip he had deserted in Sydney, convinced even then that the locals could never match wits with him. His English was negligible, so he took a job as a kitchenhand in a restaurant in Chinatown, changed his name and started saving his money. He won money in the various gambling dens that could be found in every section of Chinatown in those days; he was a careful gambler and a careful saver. He studied English, accountancy and the natives' talent for never taking the long view. He had been born with the long view; he had been poor, but not uneducated in his country's long history. He was never burdened by scruples, since he also learned that a lack of those qualities didn't necessarily hold one back in local business and political circles. He prospered slowly but gradually, not always within the law, but the authorities never troubled him; those who tried went away suitably recompensed for their trouble. He had progressed far enough up the social scale to recognize barbarians when he saw them.

Unlike the majority of his fellow expatriates, he had severed all ties with his family in Yunnan. He set about building his own family. He married the daughter of one of Chinatown's most respected businessmen, now had two daughters, both recent graduates in Law and Medicine respectively. He had a large house in Bellevue Hill, a conservative eastern suburb, he gave handsomely to charity so long as there was a tax rebate and, since Sydney was now an ethnically correct city, he was on all official invitation lists. It was just a pity that he had no scruples. Malone knew about the lack of scruples, but he knew very little else about Les Chung.

'Business is good?'

'Enough to keep the wolf from the door.' Chung looked around the crowded room, then back at Malone and smiled. His sense of humour was not as robust as that of the natives; it was drier, more sardonic. Much like that of the natives of forty years ago, when he had arrived here. Much like Malone's. 'Business is good with you?'

Malone, too, smiled. Part of the pleasure of meeting crims was that, occasionally, you met one whom you had to like, even if you didn't admire him. Les Chung had never been on a police docket, but the police knew, if no one else did, that he consorted with criminals. The difference between him and them was that he was *civilized*. A quality Malone always respected.

'The less business we have, the better.'

'Well, enjoy your dinner. I'll have them bring you some champagne with my compliments.'

Malone was about to say no, but Claire was too quick for him: 'Thank you, Mr Chung. Mum was brought up on champagne.'

'Well, then I'll have them bring you the best, Mrs Malone —'

He looked towards the rear of the restaurant; then abruptly sat down, pushing Tom further

12

into the banquette. 'Move over! Quick — move over, boy!'

Malone, sitting opposite him, looked past him towards the rear of the restaurant. A man in a dark suit, wearing a stocking mask, had come in through the kitchen door. He was carrying a gun. He stopped by the last banquette where three Chinese men were dining. He fired six shots, unheard in the clatter and chatter of the big room, then he turned and, unhurried, went out through the kitchen door, which swung shut behind him.

The killing had taken no more than five or six seconds.

2

'I have no idea who that man was.'

'That wasn't what I asked you, Les. I asked you if you knew who had sent him.'

'No.'

There had been no immediate panic after the shooting. Those people in the banquette next to the last and those at the nearby tables had seemed at first not to have taken in what had happened. Then the bloodied heads slumped forward into the food on the banquette's table had abruptly conjured up horror; one man's hand had convulsed for a moment, like a bird trying to take off, then was still, chopsticks slip-

13

ping out of it like skeletal fingers. Then suddenly panic had set in and, like the starting-up of a washing-machine, turmoil had spun through the restaurant. Screams and shouts shut out the clatter and chatter; chairs were overturned, even a table was sent crashing.

Malone had snapped at Lisa and the children to stay where they were, jumped to his feet and headed for the kitchen. He paused for a moment at the rear banquette, saw at once that the three Chinese men were dead. The booth was a bloody mess; behind him a woman screamed, as if she had only just realized that the men were indeed dead. He went on into the kitchen.

He was not carrying a gun, this was a *night out*. He was in the kitchen, glimpsed the terrified faces of the staff, before he realized he could do nothing if the gunman was not already gone. A miasma of steam hung above the stoves; a huge wok of noodles hissed like a pit of snakes. Kitchen staff and waiters stared at him as if he, too, might be a gunman.

He flashed his badge. 'Police! Where is he?'

For a moment nobody moved; then a chef jerked his head towards the rear and gasped, 'Gone! Through back door!'

'You all okay?' He tried to look concerned; but all he was doing was giving the masked man time to get away. Dead cops never caught killers. He was not a coward, just a cautious hero. He always insisted that his detectives worked on the same principle.

14

The kitchen staff looked at each other, then nodded. They were all Asian (Chinese, Vietnamese, Cambodian: he wouldn't have known the difference till he heard their names) and suddenly they all looked inscrutable. Sweat shone on their bland faces like water on a row of plates. They were going to tell him nothing.

He passed down the narrow aisle between the stoves, pushed open the back door and peered out. He was looking at an alley only wide enough for a car or small truck to back up or down it. A slice of moon hung at one end of the alley, skewwhiff in the sky like a badly hung ornament. Faintly there came the sound of a rock band trying to blow the roof off the nearby Entertainment Centre. A cat snarled somewhere amongst the rubbish bins and cartons along the walls of the alley, but otherwise the narrow lane was empty. He pushed the door wider and stepped out, stood a moment feeling a mixture of relief and frustration. It was a mixture he had experienced many times before.

He took a deep breath, then went back inside to begin work. He saw a phone on the kitchen wall, took off the receiver and dialled 000. 'This is Inspector Malone, from Homicide. There's been a shooting in the Golden Gate in Dixon Street — three bodies. Get the necessary down here quick, police as well as ambulances and the pathology guy.'

He hung up, turned back to the staff, most of whom had already removed their aprons. No

15

customers would be doing any more ordering: what was the point of staying? The Golden Gate didn't pay overtime nor give time off in lieu.

'Nobody leaves, understand?' But he was on his own, he knew as soon as his back was turned they would be gone. He looked at the head chef. 'You're responsible for them.'

The head chef was a man in his fifties, plump and as tough-shelled as Peking duck. 'Yes, sir,' he said, but you could hear the unspoken next words: *You've got to be kidding.*

When Malone re-entered the restaurant, the diners were already flowing towards the front door, not panic-stricken now but certainly in a hurry. Those at the front of the departing crowd were Asians; the Caucasians amongst the diners had been slow off the mark. It was always the same: Asians never wanted to be around trouble. They were not obstructive, just self-effacing.

'Stop!' he yelled. 'Police!'

Those at the rear paused and looked back; it was time enough for him to run between the tables and get close to the front door. He pushed through the crowd, thrusting himself none too gently between people. He reached the door, faced those who remained and held up his badge high above his head. There was a split second when he stepped outside of himself, saw himself being observed by his family. It was the first time they had seen him in action like this and he felt foolishly melodramatic. He lowered the badge.

16

'Back inside, please! Nobody leaves till I say so.'

There were protests. A stout red-faced man, green napkin still stuck in his waistband like an Irish sporran, his arm round a stout woman in a red dress, demanded to be allowed to leave.

Malone stared him down, allowed those behind the man to share the challenge. 'In good time, sir. Now just find a table and sit down. You'll be allowed to go as soon as the police arrive and have talked to you.'

'What about?' demanded the man.

Malone ignored him; nobody in any crowd was ever totally co-operative; it was a police given. The diners he had caught at the front door had reluctantly turned round and, muttering, a woman crying hysterically as if it were she who had lost someone to the killers, were finding tables and chairs and sitting down. One couple sat down at a table for six, saw a bottle of champagne in a bucket, took it out and poured themselves a drink. Two small Chinese children cowered against their mother, while their father stood between them and the ugly sight in the rear banquette.

Across the room Malone saw Lisa and the children still sitting where he had left them in the banquette; there was no sign of Leslie Chung. Malone went across to the banquette, picked up the mobile phone that he had left on his seat and called Russ Clements at home.

'Get down here pronto, Russ. Get John Kagal

17

and Phil Truach. Oh, and Gail Lee — we have some Asians to deal with.'

He switched off the phone, looked at his family. They were still seated in the banquette, all four of them stiff as statues. Then Lisa said, 'Is anyone dead?'

'Three men.' Maureen and Tom flinched; Claire blinked. He was pleased that all three had kept their nerve. 'Where's Les Chung?'

'He just up and went,' said Tom. His voice was steady, as if he were trying to prove something to his father. 'When you went up there to the front door, he went down the back. I'll take Mum and the girls home —'

'Get a cab —'

'Dad, the car's just around the corner in the parking station —'

'Get a cab, I said! You're not going up to that car park while that gunman is loose. Get a cab, go home!'

'Can we do that?' said Lisa. 'You just said that everyone had to stay till the police arrived.'

She and the girls were pale, but composed. Lisa was no stranger to murder at close range, nor were the children; a dead man had once been fished out of the family swimming pool. That murder had been different; Scobie had not been in charge of a crowd scene. She had learned early in their marriage the harness that a policeman's life put on the wife; she often resented it, but only occasionally did she express the resentment. Tonight, she recognized, was not such an occasion. Scobie's job, as witness to a triple murder and not able to apprehend the killer, was going to be difficult enough.

'We'll sit here and be quiet,' she said.

He looked at the four of them for a moment, the crowd behind him forgotten; then he nodded and gently pushed Tom back into the seat. 'Righto, I'll get you out of here as soon as someone arrives.'

He went back down to the last banquette, ripped a cloth off a neighbouring table and threw it over the three dead men as they lay with their faces in their meals. Then he went on out to the kitchen. Only Les Chung and the head chef were there.

'Where is everyone?' he asked, but was unsurprised.

'They've all gone home,' said Chung. 'They were gone before I got in here. That's why I came back, to try and hold them for you. I knew you'd want to talk to them.'

Malone had no trouble hiding his cynical grin; he was in no mood for humour. 'Thanks for trying, Les. How many illegals do you employ?'

'None that I know of.' Chung didn't appear to be in the least upset; murder could have been on the menu. 'We have all their addresses, Inspector. I'll see you can get in touch with them.'

'If I'm lucky. Come back inside. You too, Mr — ?'

'Smith,' said the Chinese chef. 'Wally Smith.'

Another illegal? 'Righto, I'll talk to you both as soon's the police arrive.'

'What about the media? I don't want —'

'I'm afraid they're your problem, Les. But you don't talk to them till you've talked to me, okay?'

The first uniformed police arrived two minutes later; then two ambulances. Fifteen minutes later the Crime Scene team were at work and Clements and the three Homicide detectives had arrived. So had the media, appearing, as Malone thought of them, with the scent of vultures. The uniformed cops were keeping them out in the street, which was now crowded from pavement to pavement. Red and blue roof lights spun, clashing with the street's neon. Two policewomen were running out blue and white Crime Scene tapes, doing the housekeeping.

Malone turned control over to Clements and the senior uniformed officer. Then he got a uniformed man to usher his family out and escort them to the parking station. As they moved towards the front door the stout man stood up and demanded to know why they were being allowed to go.

Lisa stopped opposite him. 'Because I'm married to Inspector Malone. It's one of the few privileges of being a policeman's wife — we're allowed to go home early. Satisfied?'

And now Malone was seated opposite Les Chung in a banquette on the opposite side of the room from the murder booth. 'Les, I asked you if you knew who had sent the killer.'

'I have no idea.'

'Righto, then. Have you any idea why he would come in here and kill your three friends? You were having dinner with them, weren't you? There were four places at that table.'

'Yes.'

'You've told me who the dead men are — they're all respectable businessmen. No Triads, nothing like that?'

It was difficult to tell whether Chung smiled or not. 'No, nothing like that.'

'I've heard of two of them, seen their names in the paper occasionally. But the third feller —' He looked at his notes. 'Mr Shan? Is he a local?'

Chung looked around the room, moving only his eyes, not his head. His hands were folded on the table in front of him and he looked as calm as if this were no more than a social visit on Malone's part. Then he looked back at Malone, who had waited patiently. 'No.'

'From somewhere else? Cabramatta?' Where there was a major Asian community, mainly Vietnamese. 'Or Melbourne or Brisbane?'

Then Clements slid his big bulk into the seat beside Malone, dropped a passport on the table. 'That's from the guy with his back to the wall, the one in the middle. A Chinese passport in the name of Shan Yang.'

Malone picked up the passport, flipped through its pages, then held it out for Chung to look at. 'Shanghai, maybe? Or Beijing?'

Chung's shrug was almost imperceptible.

21

'Okay, from Shanghai.'

Malone looked across the room. The forensic pathologist, a young man who, coincidentally, was Chinese, had looked at the bodies and they were now being wheeled out to the ambulances. Most of the diners had been questioned and allowed to go. Out in the street they would be ambushed by the media reporters: any witness to a triple murder was quotable, even if he made it up. Even as Malone looked, the last diners went out the front door and now there were only police and Les Chung. Wally Smith, the head chef, had been questioned and allowed to go. John Kagal, Phil Truach and Gail Lee were comparing notes, but Malone could tell from their expressions that the notes would not add up to much.

'What was Mr Shan doing here, Les? You were with him, so you must've had him as your guest.'

'He was a visitor. They come here every time they are in Sydney.'

'They?'

'Visitors from China. We Chinese have always been gourmets. Before the French even invented the word or knew anything about cooking.' His lips twitched, but one could not really call it a smile.

'Les, let's not play the Inscrutable Orient game. I know you Chinese claim a monopoly on patience, but you'd be surprised how patient we Irish can be. We have to be, to put up with Irish jokes.'

22

Chung's expression was almost a parody of inscrutability. Then all at once he sat back against the velvet of the booth, as if he had decided the game had gone far enough. 'All right. Mr Shan represented one of our business partners.'

'What in? The restaurant?'

Chung smiled widely this time, shook his head. 'Olympic Tower.'

Malone and Clements looked at each other; then Clements said, 'You're in *that?*'

Olympic Tower had been a huge hole in the ground for seven or eight years, a casualty of union trouble and the recession of a few years back. It had been a monument that was an embarrassment, a great sunken square in which concrete foundations and the odd steel pier had been a derisive reminder of what had been intended. Then six months ago work had recommenced under a new consortium. Malone had read about it, but he had not taken any notice of the names in the consortium. Over the last thirty years developers had come and gone like carpet-baggers. Some of them had built beautiful additions to the city; others had put up eyesores, taken the money and run. It all came under the heading of progress.

'It's a consortium.'

'How many?' Clements was the business expert. He had begun as a punter on the horses and moved on to the stock market.

'Three corporations.' Chung was taking his

23

time squeezing out the answers.

'Mr Feng and Mr Sun —' Malone had looked at his notes. 'They were in it with you?'

'In my partnership, yes.'

'Which is?'

'Lotus Development.'

'Who else? You said three.'

'The Bund Corporation.'

'The Bond Corporation? You're kidding.' The Bond Corporation had been the *Titanic* of the eighties. Its captain had spent several years trying to dodge the iceberg, but was now doing time.

Chung smiled. He now appeared completely unperturbed by what had happened in his restaurant. Yet Malone had a sudden flash of memory, saw the look of fear that had stricken Chung as he had pushed into the banquette against Tom. If he was still afraid, it was now well hidden. 'No, no. The *Bund* Corporation. Named after the famous Bund on Shanghai's waterfront.'

The Bund's fame hadn't spread as far as Homicide; but the two detectives nodded. 'Who's the third partner?' said Malone. 'Someone else from China?'

Chung looked around the restaurant again. The Crime Scene team had come through from the kitchen and the back alley; the sergeant in charge glanced across at Malone and shook his head: *nothing*.

The big room was still brightly lit, the huge

chandelier hung like a frozen explosion, a glare that was obtrusive. Chung abruptly stood up, crossed the room and flicked a switch. Everyone looked up as the glare disappeared; it was a moment before the yellow lamps on the walls asserted themselves. Chung came back, sat down, said nothing.

'Les,' said Malone patiently, 'who's the third partner?'

'It's in the application at the Town Hall,' Chung said at last. 'Kelly Investments.'

'And who,' said Malone, patience threadbare now, 'are Kelly Investments?'

'One of Jack Aldwych's companies.'

'One of Jack's? Named after Ned Kelly?' A national hero, a bushranger. Perhaps it was the convict beginnings of the nation, but part of the heritage seemed to be a reverence for crims. Jack Aldwych had been a leading crim for years; but, so he claimed, was now retired. He also claimed he was trying to slide into respectability, but even he found the idea risible. Respectability was not a difficult achievement, not in Sydney; but it must not be treated as a joke, which was what Aldwych was doing. He was also co-owner with Les Chung of the Golden Gate and he was one of Malone's best acquaintances, if not best friends. 'Les, if you and Jack are partners in Olympic Tower, would you blame me if I thought some of your old mates were trying to muscle in?'

'I have no old mates who do that sort of thing.'

Malone refrained from naming some of them; Les Chung, too, was now into respectability. 'Well, with your Shanghai friends involved, do you think the Triads might have arranged these killings?'

'The Triads?' Chung's expression suggested that Malone might have named the Jesuits or the Masons.

Exasperation was seeping out of Malone like perspiration. 'Les, Russ and I are trying to get to the bottom of this. That feller would've done you if you'd been in that booth — he didn't look as if he were being selective. You were on his list —'

'I don't think so.'

'Well, *I* think so. And so does Russ, right?' Clements nodded. 'Now we can take you back to Homicide and talk to you till you come to your senses. Or you can go home, talk to your wife and kids and your lawyer and your mother, if need be —'

'I'm not Jewish.'

Malone had to smile. 'Righto, Les, you've still got your sense of humour. Now use it, see the sense in what I'm saying and come and see me and Russ in the morning and give us the full picture. But we're not going to let it lie, Les, understand?' He stood up, pushing Clements ahead of him out of the booth. 'In the meantime we'll talk to Jack Aldwych. What I know of Jack, he never liked his business partners being bumped off.'

Chung didn't move from the booth. Hands

26

folded on the table in front of him, he looked up at the two big detectives. 'I'll talk to you in the morning. Without talking to my mother, just to my lawyer.'

'Do that, Les. In the meantime I'm going to get a court order to close down the Golden Gate till we know what's going on. Next time some innocent customers might get in the way.'

3

The street outside was still crowded; those that had lingered had been augmented by the crowd spilling out from the Entertainment Centre round the corner. The police cars, the media vans, the Crime Scene tapes: more entertainment, hey guys, let's hang around. The windows on both sides of the narrow street were stuffed with people; close to Malone and the other police expectant faces leaned forward, as if hoping that the score had gone up. Half a dozen reporters, recorders held up like guns, rushed Malone, but he waved them away, drew his detectives around him.

'What'd you get?'

Phil Truach, the sergeant, shook his head. An habitual smoker, he had had three cigarettes while in the restaurant; he knew the Chinese, civilized people, were the last ones to condemn smokers. But he never smoked in front of

Malone, a lifelong non-smoker. 'Nothing, Scobie. We've got six descriptions of the guy who did the shooting — all different.'

'Was he Asian? Chinese?'

'Three said Asian, three said Caucasian.' Gail Lee had a Chinese father and an Australian mother. It was usually the Chinese heritage that prevailed in her, but Malone put that down to her having decided that was the best way of handling the Australians who surrounded her. She was close to being beautiful, but a certain coldness, perhaps suspicion, turned one off her before one could look at her in impartial appreciation. She was a good detective.

'What about Wally Smith, the head chef? The killer would've gone right past him in the kitchen, coming and going.'

'Said he saw nothing, he had his head buried in a pot of chop suey.' John Kagal was in black tie and dinner jacket; he had been on call but had obviously hoped not to be called. He saw Malone look at his outfit and he smiled. 'My mother and father's fortieth wedding anniversary. They like to dress up.'

So do you, thought Malone unkindly; Kagal was the fashion plate of Homicide. 'Not chop suey, John, not at the Golden Gate. Okay, that's it for the night. Who's in charge here from Day Street?'

On cue a lean, medium-height man in an open-necked shirt and a lightweight golf jacket stepped forward. He was Ralph Higgins, the

28

senior sergeant in charge of the local detectives. Malone had worked with him before, knew his worth. He had a constantly harried look, but it was never apparent in his work.

'G'day, Scobie. We'll handle it, do the donkey-work —' Even his grin looked harried, as if he were unsure of his jokes. 'But I gather you were the principal witness?'

'Don't remind me. This'll need a task force, Ralph. You set it up and we'll co-operate. I'll check it out with Greg Random and you do the same with your patrol commander. Russ here will be our liaison man. Phil will exchange notes with you. We've got bugger-all so far.'

'What else is new?' said Higgins. 'This is Chinatown, mate. The day I walk into an open-and-shut case around here will be time for me to retire.'

Malone glanced at Gail Lee out of the corner of his eye, but her face was a closed-and-shut case. 'Righto, Ralph, it's all yours. Russ and I are going out to have a chat with Jack Aldwych.'

'Are we?' Clements looked at his watch. 'He'll be in bed.'

'If he is, he'll be wide awake. He'll have just had a phone call from Les Chung.' Malone explained to the other detectives the set-up at Olympic Tower. 'John, you and Gail find out what you can about —' he looked at his notes — 'the Bund Corporation, a Shanghai outfit. See if it's registered here. Phil, you look into Lotus Development. Ten o'clock tomorrow morning I want to know all there is to know.' He grinned at Kagal. 'Dress will be informal.'

The younger man smiled in return; there was rivalry between them, but also respect. Some day Kagal would hold Malone's job or even a higher one; he could wait. 'I'll wear thongs.'

Driving over the Harbour Bridge in his family Volvo, Clements said, 'I've got the feeling we're putting our toe into a very big pool.'

'What do you know about Olympic Tower?'

'No more than I've read in the papers.' He always read the financial pages before he read the rest of the news; the last thing he read were the crime reports. Homicide and Fraud were the only two Police Service units that subscribed to the *Financial Review*, and the *FR* was purely for Clements' benefit. Big and slow-moving, almost ox-like, he had a brain that could juggle figures like the marbles in a lottery barrel; except that his results were never left to chance. Malone had no idea how successful Clements was in his stock market bets, but the odds were that he made more from them than he made as a senior sergeant, the Supervisor of Homicide. 'Get Lisa to look into it. She's at the Town Hall.'

'She's on the council's Olympic committee, not in council planning.'

'Okay, but she'd know who to ask. Watch it, you stupid bastard!' as a car cut in front of them to take the Pacific Highway turn-off.

'I don't like asking my wife to do police business.'

'You ask my wife to do it.' Romy Clements was deputy-director of Forensic Medicine stationed at the city morgue.

Malone gave up. 'Righto, I'll ask her. But from what she tells me of council politics, I don't want her getting bumped around.'

Twenty minutes later they were approaching Harbord. Jack Aldwych lived high on a hill in the small seaside suburb. The house was two-storeyed, with wide verandahs on both levels and all four sides. Standing on an eastern verandah, its owner had a 180-degree view of the sea, a domain that had never provided any return, since he had never dealt in drugs, either by sea or any other entry. He had only just been getting into crime when Sydney had been a halfway house for illegal gold shipments between Middle East ports and Hong Kong; he had missed out on that lucrative industry, but had graduated into robbing banks of gold, a much more dangerous pursuit. Standing on a western verandah he looked back on slopes and valleys lined with modest mortgage-mortared houses and blocks of flats as alike as slices of plain cake. This, too, was not the sort of territory where he had made his money; he had never been a petty criminal, at least not since his teen years. He had once boasted that he had never robbed the battlers; but only because the battlers weren't worth robbing. He had his principles, but only for amusement.

Every morning, summer and winter, although

he was now in his late seventies, he went down to Harbord beach to swim. Once upon a time sharks had cruised off the beach and there had been one or two fatalities. But, whether it was coincidental or not, from the day Jack Aldwych entered the surf no more sharks had been seen. Perhaps the grey nurses and the hammerheads and the great whites knew a bigger shark when they saw one.

When Malone and Clements rang the bell at the big iron gates that led to the short gravel driveway, two Dobermans came round the corner of the house, salivating at the prospect of a night-time snack. Two minutes later Blackie Ovens, in striped pyjamas and polka-dotted dressing gown, came out of the house and, after snapping at the dogs to back off, opened the gates. 'The boss is expecting you.'

'I thought he might be. Nice gown, Blackie.'

'The boss give it to me. He thought me last one looked too much like a jail uniform.' The dogs barked and he barked back at them and they slunk away. 'I'll get you some coffee while you're talking to the boss.'

It was characteristic of him that he didn't ask what had brought the two detectives here at this time of night. He had worked for Jack Aldwych for thirty years, an iron-bar man as rigid in his allegiance to the boss as his favourite tool of trade. He no longer wielded the iron bar as a profession, but Malone had no doubt that it was kept handy for emergency use.

Aldwych was waiting for them in the big living room, in his pyjamas and dressing gown. Each time Malone saw him he marvelled at the dignity and handsome looks of the old crim; he could have passed for a man who owned banks rather than robbed them. He now lolled against the upholstery of wealth, taking on some of its sheen. Even the roughness of his voice had been smoothed out, though it could harden with threat when needed. He was, as he had often told Malone, retired but not reformed.

'Soon's Les Chung told me he'd talked to you, I knew you'd be over to see me. What d'you think I can tell you he hasn't already told you?'

'How do you know what he's told us?' said Malone.

Aldwych smiled, showing expensive dental work: a banker's smile. 'I don't think Les would of told you much.'

'What about these partners from China, the Bund Corporation? One of them, Mr Shan, is dead.'

Aldwych wasn't disturbed by the news; he had ordered at least a dozen deaths. He waited while Blackie brought in coffee and biscuits; then when Blackie had gone out of the room, he said, 'I hadn't made up my mind about him. Jack Junior's going to have another look at him.' Jack Aldwych Junior ran the Aldwych enterprises; he was the front, respectable and more than competent. 'There's a woman, too — Mrs Tzu. Calls herself Madame Tzu. T-Z-U. She comes in from

Hong Kong every month or so. I've never dealt with partners as blank as those two.'

'Dumb?' said Clements.

'Christ, no. Smart as they come. Always polite, but sometimes it's like talking to the Great Wall of China.'

'It used to be like that talking to you, Jack,' said Malone, and the old man gave him a Chinese smile. 'How much have you got in this venture?'

Aldwych sipped his coffee, nibbled on a Monte Carlo biscuit; then: 'A hundred and twenty million.'

The two detectives looked at each other and Clements shook his head in wonder. Then Malone, who thought a two-hundred-dollar suit was an investment, said, 'That's a lot of money, Jack. You're as solvent as that?'

'You're not being very polite,' said Aldwych with a grin. 'Yeah, we've got it . . . Scobie, d'you know what Olympic Tower is gunna be? It'll be almost a small city on its own. A five-star hotel, offices, shops, restaurants — the lot. It's gotta be up and running eighteen months before the Olympics. The main part of the hotel is already booked — the International Olympic Committee, the IOC you're always hearing about, they've booked it for all their top delegates. The rest of the hotel, we're aiming for top-of-the-market bookings, no package deals, no prize-winners from *Wheel of Fortune* or *The Price is Right*. The cream, that's what we're after and

34

what we're gunna get. The IOC booking guarantees that.'

'All this time ahead, the project nowhere near finished,' said Clements, 'how did you manage to collar the IOC booking?'

'Strings, Russ, strings. I wouldn't of gone into this deal unless I knew there were strings to pull. There are more strings in this town, Russ, than there are in a trawler net. All you have to do is find out which ones to pull.'

'And you knew?' said Malone; then held up a hand. 'Don't tell me. All we'll want to know is if strings were pulled in these three murders . . . Don't be offended, Jack — but would you bump somebody off to protect your investment?'

'Scobie, I'm not offended, just surprised you asked. Of course I would.'

Malone looked at Clements and the two of them smiled. 'He's on his own, isn't he?' said Clements. 'They don't make 'em like him any more.'

'Of course they don't,' said Aldwych, joining in the humour.

The three of them were silent a while in contemplation of his uniqueness.

Then Malone said, 'Jack, what about the Triads? I mean, you're in this with all Chinese partners —'

This time the smile was that of a kindly uncle towards a not-very-bright nephew. 'Scobie, all the time I was in the game I never met a Chink said he was in a Triad. But then —' the smile widened — 'I never met a Dago said he belonged to the Mafia or the Camorra or what's this new one, the Ndrangheta?' He used the terms Chink and Dago without embarrassment or apology, the back of his big tough hand to political correctness. 'But that ain't to say all of 'em don't exist.'

'Let's stick with the Triads. Would they be in this?'

Aldwych shook his head. 'They've been here for years, they were going when I was in the game. The Sun Yee Ho, 14K, Wo Hop, Wo Yee Tong —' He knew the names like a racecourse punter might know the names of champion racehorses. 'They were and still are the biggest importers of heroin into this country. I never had anything to do with them, because I never had anything to do with drugs.' For a moment he succeeded in looking pious, even though it was a mask. 'Back in the eighties some heroin syndicates were run by local mugs, blokes like Neddy Smith and a lot of small-time no-hopers. Then some of 'em got greedy and they started killing each other off. Then the Lebanese and the Vietnamese moved in — but you know all this.'

'Go on,' said Malone. 'We're talking about the Triads.'

Like all retired men, criminals can't help reciting history: memories are as sweet as an acquittal. 'Then there were the Dagoes and the Roumanians and the Colombians and the Russians and now the yakuza are here. This is virgin

36

territory for a lot of 'em — they couldn't believe we were so ripe. But then they had their donnybrooks, started killing each other. But all the time that's been going on, the Triads have just sat back and played wily buggers. Any problem came up, they sat down and talked it out. They're in the game for money, not war.'

'So you think we can wipe them from tonight's killings?'

'Forget them. If they'd wanted to muscle in on Olympic Tower, they'd of talked to Les Chung and he'd of talked to us.'

'And what would you have done?'

Again the smile, not pious this time. 'Told 'em to get stuffed.'

'Would they take any notice of you?'

'I dunno. They're a ruthless lotta bastards, but they're sensible. I think they'd of listened to me.'

'Okay,' said Clements, 'have there been any threats from any other direction?'

'Meaning who?'

'Come on, Jack,' said Malone, 'don't play the Great Wall of China with us.'

Aldwych grinned. 'Okay. No, there's been no death threats, none that I know of. Maybe on the site, union stuff, but none against me or Jack Junior. You sure the hitman was Chinese?'

'Well — no. He was wearing a stocking mask.'

'Everyone looks Chinese in one of those.'

'I guess so. Did you wear one when you were holding up banks?'

'They weren't fashionable in my day. The wife

found one of them, a stocking, in my pocket, and she'd of cut my balls off. Even though she was a lady. More coffee?' He poured three more cups. 'Look, I dunno everything there is to know about our Chinese partners, the ones from Shanghai. Jack Junior did all the due diligence on them and he's pretty thorough. But we discovered pretty early in the piece we were dealing with another culture.' Since his retirement he had not sat around reading only old newspaper clippings of his misdeeds; he was halfway into a belated education. 'These blokes are hard-headed about money, for instance. But superstitious — Christ, I wanna laugh at 'em sometimes, only I'm too polite. They have this thing feng shui — they won't shit unless the dunny is pointed in the right direction. They caused headaches for the architects. Even the starting date had to be — what's the word?'

'Propitious?' said Malone.

'That's it. We hung around for three days till the fucking wind or the stars or the sun were in the right place.'

'What about Les Chung and his partners in Lotus? Mr Feng and Mr Sun. Any superstition there?'

'They've been in Australia as long as Les — they were both born here. They knew better than to bugger me about with superstition.'

'What were they like?'

Aldwych shrugged. 'Les vouched for them. They seemed straight enough. If they were any

38

sort of problem, they were his problem, his partners.'

'What about the unions? The original project had a lot of trouble with them, just as they did on World Square.'

Aldwych nodded his head ruefully. World Square had been another vast hole in the ground for a number of years, but it, too, had been saved and the project was now close to completion. 'Them days are gone — I hope. There's a union election coming up, but we aren't expecting any trouble from that. I had Blackie go down and talk to some of the organizers.'

'Carrying his iron bar?' said Clements.

'I don't think so. He just took a coupla heavies with him. He says he's like me, the old days are over.'

'Who invited the Shanghai people into the consortium?'

'Les. There's plenty of Asians putting money into property here — Indonesians, Malaysians, Chinese from Hong Kong — the Chinks who got outa Hong Kong before it was taken back. I dunno when Les first got in touch with the Shanghai lot, but he's, you know, still *Chinese*. Mainland Chinese. It's in their blood, I guess.'

Malone stood up. 'Righto, I guess that's all for now. How do you get on with your neighbours, Jack?'

Aldwych gave him a quizzical look. 'You think they wish I wasn't here? I don't think so, Scobie. One of 'em told me, since I been living here there's never any trouble in the neighbourhood. No break-ins, no domestics, no car-stealing. Even the hoons from down on the beaches never come up here.' He smiled, a guardian angel. 'I think I've got 'em all scared. Another thing — you notice I got practically a whole block to myself, surrounded on three sides by streets? Nobody hanging over the side fences sticky-beaking.'

'What's on the fourth side?'

'At the back there's a retirement home for old nuns. Blackie goes over every couple weeks, mows their lawns for 'em. Every afternoon they go for a walk, see me sitting out on the verandah, they wave their beads and tell me they're praying for me. They're a harmless lotta old ducks, God bless 'em — I don't like to tell 'em they're wasting their prayers.' He smiled again, a pope this time.

'Will you go and live in Olympic Tower when it's built?' asked Clements.

'Shirl would come back and haunt me if I ever moved outa here. She made this my retreat, she used to call it.'

He looked around the big high-ceilinged room. It was furnished to his dead wife's taste. Laura Ashley prints, a floral carpet, Dresden-ware on the mantelpiece, *nice* landscape paintings on the walls: no arid Outback stuff, no Whiteleys with sexual trees. It had surprised Aldwych that, after his wife had died, he had found, hidden away in a wardrobe, novels by

40

Judith Krantz, Erica Jong. He wondered how he had let her down in their love life. His marriage had been the one honourable thing in his life and maybe he had honoured her too much.

'No, I'll die here.'

He escorted them to the front door, pushed open the screen door. 'Blackie put this on yesterday. The summer flies are starting to buzz.'

Malone turned as the screen door closed. 'Jack, what would you do if these killers came after you?'

The hall light was behind him; he looked big and menacing behind the wire screen. 'I'd come outa retirement.'

4

When Malone got home Lisa was in bed but still awake. 'How'd it go?'

'Dead ends, so far.'

'That's what you like. You look disappointed when it's an open-and-shut case.'

He was folding his trousers and putting them on a hanger as she, with her Dutch neatness, had taught him. 'You're kidding.'

'Maybe. But sometimes . . .' Her hair was pulled up under a net, her face creamed. A woman lost half her looks with her preparations to stay beautiful. But he would never say that, not with three women in the family. 'Darling, let someone else handle this one. Russ.'

He slid into bed beside her, naked; he gave up pyjamas the middle of spring the way some people put on tweeds the beginning of autumn. 'I can't give it up. I was *there* —'

'So were we.' She sat up against the pillows. 'I saw it happen. I looked down towards the back of the restaurant when Mr Chung looked down there — I saw the expression on his face, he was scared stiff. I didn't see the men in the booth, the ones who died, but I saw the man fire his gun —' If she shuddered, it was inwardly; she always seemed to be in control of her emotions. 'I was just glad that Tom and the girls didn't see any of it.'

'How are they?'

'Quiet. They said practically nothing all the way home, you'd have thought we were on the way to a funeral. Or driving away from one . . . Maureen drove. You know what she's like, talks all the time at the wheel. Not a word tonight.'

'You want me to discuss it with them in the morning?'

'No, not unless they bring it up.' She turned her head. 'Be careful, darling.'

'Nobody's going to come after me. For Crissake, darl —' He put a hand on her thigh under the sheet, pressed it. 'I've got to handle it, but I'm going to be perfectly safe.'

She kissed him. 'Like you say to everyone, take care.'

He turned out the bedside lamp, put his arms

round her, licked his lips. 'What's that? Ella Baché?'

'Who else? She's been coming to bed with us ever since I started to lose my looks.'

'Tell her she needn't have bothered.'

He put his leg between hers, the love-lock.

Chapter Two

1

Saturday was not normally a work day at Homicide, though there were always detectives on call and usually one or two came into the office to catch up on paperwork. Expecting the office to be practically deserted this morning Malone had chosen to call in a probationary detective and sack him.

'I'm giving you a week's notice, Harold —'

Harold Boston was in his middle-thirties, a senior constable, had been in uniform fifteen years and three months in plainclothes. He was already two weeks behind on his paperwork. He worked at the frenetic pace of a hospital cleaner and could stretch Monday into Wednesday without effort. Worst of all, he had neglected paperwork on a particular homicide and the Director of Public Prosecutions had sent a blast to Malone.

'I'm recommending you for Police Archives, Harold. There'll be no pay disadvantage and you can work at your own pace. History was never meant to catch up with the present —'

'With respect, you're being pretty bloody sarcastic —'

'I mean to be, Harold. You've got me a blast from the DPP like I've never had before — I'm proud of this unit. Here in Homicide we rarely catch a murderer red-handed, but we do like to get him before he dies of old age and leaves a confession in his will —'

Boston rose. He was of medium height and bony, with a square-jawed face, calculating eyes and slanting eyebrows that gave him a malevolent look. He looked particularly malevolent at the moment. 'I won't forget this —'

'Don't,' said Malone. 'You had the opportunity here and you buggered it. Learn a lesson, Harold.'

Clements came into the big outer office as Boston went out to it. The two men looked at each other, but said nothing; it was Clements, as Supervisor, who had had to assess Boston's work and finally turned thumbs down on it. Clements put some papers on his own desk, then came into Malone's small office, slumped down in his usual position on the couch beneath the window. He was dressed in a blue skivvy, slacks and a double-breasted navy blazer with gold buttons; anyone else might have looked like an elegant yachtsman, but somehow he gave the impression that he had been hauled out of the drink and allowed to dry in the sun. Neither he nor Malone would have got nods of approval from Armani or Zegna.

Clements held up the front pages of two newspapers. 'Seen these?'

It had been a slow week for political news, both State and Federal; overseas nothing had happened that would increase sales amongst the immigrant population. So the Chinatown murders got the Page One treatment; Malone, though not quoted, was featured as a principal witness to the killings.

'Yeah, I've seen them. The *Australian* makes me sound as if I ran the other way. Greg Random called me at home, and Bob Grenville.' Random was the chief superintendent in charge of the Homicide and Serial Offenders Unit; Grenville was the new Assistant Commissioner, Crime. When Malone got calls from them at home he knew his spot was warming up. 'All I need now is a call from the Commissioner.'

'Has he spoken to you since his beatification?' Clements was an agnostic, but he had heard Malone, an indifferent Catholic, talk of beatification and sanctification and other promotions unknown to the public service.

The new Commissioner, William Zanuch, had groomed himself for the post since his probationary constable days; no one, in Malone's experience, had had such an inexorable rise. 'Not yet. But he will . . . I told Harold he has to go.'

'I think we're well rid of him — he's got a nasty streak in him. Why'd we ever take him on?'

'Because we were told to. Administration is not going to like it when they get your report on him.'

'*My* report?'

'You're the Supervisor, sport. I did the dirty work — you do the paperwork.' He stood up. Out in the office five detectives had arrived. 'Let's go out and see what the troops have come up with.'

Chairs had been arranged in a semi-circle; Malone sat on a desk and addressed the three men and two women; Clements sat at his own desk. Boston was against a far wall, already an outsider.

'Righto, let's get the basics first. They're setting up an incident room down at Day Street — their Ds are handling the legwork. I want you, Sheryl, to put up a flow chart for us here, so we'll have a reference.'

Sheryl Dallen was in her late twenties, another newcomer to the unit but no longer on probation. She was broad-faced and broad-beamed, a gym enthusiast desperately fighting a battle against the crime of avoirdupois. She was also an enthusiastic worker and in the four months she had been with Homicide she had established a future for herself. 'It'll be on the wall by lunchtime, boss.'

Malone looked at the others. 'What have you come up with?'

'I've been down to Day Street,' said Phil Truach. 'They've come up with bugger-all as far as evidence goes. Ballistics has the bullets — a couple of them must've gone through the victims, they were in the upholstery of the booth. The rest are in the corpses and we'll get them from the morgue. Physical Evidence found nothing, no fingerprints. There were some shoe-prints out in the alley at the back, but there were dozens of them — they could've been the kitchen staff stampeding.'

'I was out in the alley myself,' said Malone.

'From what I read in the papers this morning, you were the principal witness.'

'Thanks,' said Malone, but he grinned; Truach's humour could be dry but it was never malicious. 'Andy?'

Andy Graham had been with Homicide five years. For too long he had exhausted everyone with his galloping zeal; sometimes he had rushed right by clues and had had to come back to them. He had been the unit's Airedale pup; now he had become its bloodhound. 'I've tracked down all the kitchen staff. Well, all but two — they were illegals and they'd shot through by the time I got to their boarding-house. The others, they all said they were headfirst into their pots and woks. Nobody heard the shots. One guy said he thought the killer was a health inspector.'

'With a stocking mask?' said Clements. 'That's real undercover stuff.'

'Gail? John?'

'I tried the Chinese consulate,' said Gail Lee. 'Then the embassy in Canberra. Both of them told me they didn't work on Saturday, they said call back Monday.'

'They've been too long in Australia,' said John Kagal. 'The Great Leap Backwards. Chairman

48

Mao must be spinning in his grave.'

'What did you learn?'

Kagal took out his notes. 'The Bund Corporation is a private outfit, not a Chinese government body. It claims it has capital assets of two hundred million dollars, but that's a dicey figure.'

'Where do you get all your info?' said Malone in wonderment. 'On a Saturday, too?'

'Don't ask.' Even when he thought he was unobserved, Kagal always looked smug; he looked that way now. He had more connections in the financial world than an Internet computer, but he never divulged them. There was money in the family background, but he never mentioned the background and Malone and the others never asked. It was known he had gone to Cranbrook, one of the more expensive private schools, and to Macquarie University, where he had taken two degrees. He lived in a flat in one of the better blocks in Double Bay, otherwise known as Double Pay because of its prices, and he drove a Honda Accord. However, though smug, he was discreet. Two attributes, Malone knew, that did not always go together. 'These figures are what's public, but I think I need to do some further checking. The company is registered in Hong Kong, but I'll have to find out whether it was registered there before the Brits left or after China took over.'

'Is there much private capital in China today?' Phil Truach was bouncing his lighter up and down in his hand: time for another smoke.

'What do the old men in Beijing think about it?'

'Millionaires are springing up like rice shoots,' said Kagal, whose reports always had a little more decoration than the others'. 'There's not much the old men can do about it. Gail would know more about it than I do.'

'Why would I?' Conversationally, Malone had noticed, Gail Lee could leave a high-diver two feet off the board with no water in the pool.

'Well —' Kagal gestured, left airborne.

'My father won't let us discuss modern China. For him China stopped the day the Communists took over.'

So much, Malone thought, for Jack Aldwych's theory that China was always in the blood of mainland-born Chinese.

'Righto,' he said, 'what about Lotus Development?'

'It was registered eighteen months ago,' said Kagal. 'It was a two-dollar shelf company that Les Chung bought. So far I haven't been able to find out what its capital is now. But when the present consortium took over the Olympic Tower hole in the ground, they assumed a seventy-million-dollar debt. *Someone* put up the seed money.'

Malone looked at Clements. 'Jack Aldwych?'

Clements shook his head. 'If Jack's true to his old form, he wouldn't put seed money into a bank hold-up. He and his son are worth Christ knows how much, but they don't *start* projects.

50

They come in when all the groundwork's been done.'

'I think we're getting into one of those Chinese box puzzles,' said Malone.

'Jack said last night there'd been some union trouble. Do we talk to them? Maybe we'll pick up something there.'

'Let Day Street do that. Union Hall is on their turf. We don't have anyone to spare, not yet anyway.'

'I can do it,' said Boston from his distant seat. 'I worked out of Day Street, I know everyone at Union Hall.'

Malone didn't want any help from Boston; he was not interested in allowing him to rehabilitate himself. Yet if the ex-uniformed man had contacts amongst the union officials, a lot of time could be saved. Homicide had little or nothing to do with union troubles; lately, aside from some election rorts, the unions had been relatively law-abiding. The old days, in which his own father, Con, had been one of the principal troublemakers, always straddling not only the picket line but also the line of the law, had gone. Industrial reform, long coming and still with only one foot in the door, had brought a more pragmatic union official, one who had at last realized that the writing on the wall was more than just graffiti. Perhaps Boston *could* help.

'It's yours, Harold. I'd like to know something by lunchtime Monday.' Meaning: *not lunchtime Wednesday or Thursday.*

Boston caught the hint; his face stiffened. 'It'll be here. Lunchtime Monday.'

Malone looked at the other detectives. 'You, Andy, can go home, but you're on call. Phil, you and John go out and talk to the Sun family, see if they know anything. Gail and I'll go out later and talk to the Feng family . . . Russ, ring Les Chung, see if he's going to drop in. If not, tell him we'll be out to his house, flashing lights, siren, the lot. He mightn't like that, not out in Bellevue Hill. He lives just up the road from Kerry Packer, doesn't he?'

'Kerry wouldn't like it, either.'

Malone went back into his office, sat down and looked at his phone. Breakfast with the family had been an uncomfortable meal; for once on a Saturday morning the girls and Tom had got themselves out of bed and eaten with him and Lisa. There had been no discomfort on their part; or none that had been apparent. It had all been on his part. When Claire had casually remarked that last night's murders had been pretty brutal — 'doesn't a killer like that think of other people? Those in the restaurant, innocent people just having a night out?' he had snapped, 'Professional killers aren't interested in innocent people.'

The sharpness in his voice made Lisa look up from her toast, but he had ignored her. He knew he was wrong in his attitude. He was a cop and this was a cop's family; he couldn't go on protecting them from everything for ever. But he was unwilling, could not bring himself to the fact, to let them be part of his job. The murder of strangers was not a subject that bound a family together.

He said as much and Lisa said, 'May we quote you? We were *there*, we saw what happened. We're not blaming you for taking us there — it was the girls' suggestion.'

'Yes,' said the girls, looking at him over their cereal with the eyes of a biassed jury.

'Mine, too,' said Tom. 'Incidentally, we never got to eat.'

'Stay out of this,' Maureen told him. 'You're not helping the argument.'

'That's exactly what I'm trying to do. Lighten things up.'

'It's not an argument,' said Malone defensively.

'All right, then,' said Lisa. 'It's not an argument. But you don't want it to be a discussion, either. So we'll drop it.'

'But —' said Claire.

'I said, drop it!'

The milk had turned sour on his cereal, his toast had tasted like brittle brick. When he had left to come to the office, had kissed Lisa, her cheek had tasted as if she had been out in a cold wind.

He was still looking at the phone, wanting to call her, when Clements said from the doorway, 'Les Chung is already here, he's on his way up.'

He put away the thought of the call to home,

said, 'Let's hope he's decided to loosen up. I'm fed up with Oriental inscrutability.' Then he saw Gail Lee just behind the big man. 'Not you, Gail.'

'Of course not. I'm saved by my in-your-face Aussie side.' Then she blinked, a small-girl expression that was out of character with her. 'Sorry. I didn't mean to be rude.'

He grinned, though it was an effort. 'Gail, the day your Aussie side becomes subtle or inscrutable, we're done for. Come in and sit down. Make Mr Chung feel at home.'

Chung was dressed almost exactly like Clements; unlike the big man, he looked like the yacht squadron commodore. He sat down opposite Malone, crossing one leg over the other, showing a black loafer that looked as if it had been hand-polished three times a day by a coolie bootblack. He looked around at the three detectives. 'I'm here against my will,' he announced.

'So many of our visitors are, Les,' said Malone, relaxing back in his chair, ready for the patience game if it was to be played again. 'But we always try to make you welcome.'

Chung smiled. 'I'm sure you do. So what do you want to know?'

'What've you got to tell us?' said Clements.

Chung looked at Gail. 'Do you find it difficult, dealing with the local bluntness?'

'One gets used to it, Mr Chung.'

Malone was watching her; it was difficult to tell whether the Chinese or the Australian side of

54

her was working. Then he said, 'Les, tell us about the Bund Corporation.'

'Can I speak off the record?'

Malone gestured. 'No notebooks, Les, no tape recorder. Go ahead.'

'Why off the record?' Clements asked, blunt as ever. 'Are you afraid of them?'

Chung put both feet flat on the floor, seemed to lose some of his relaxed air. 'I could be. It's only a suspicion . . . I said I'm here against my will. I'm also here against my good judgement.'

'Let us be the judge of that,' said Malone, still sitting back in his chair. 'Tell us exactly who the Bund Corporation are.'

Chung took his time; he might be giving evidence that could be used against him. 'They are a private company — a proprietary limited one, just like mine and Jack Aldwych's, no public investors. It's not listed on the stock exchange here.'

'What about the Chinese government?' said Clements. 'Are they in it?'

'No-o. I was led to believe —' He stopped.

'Go on, Les. I find it hard to believe that you were *led* to to believe . . .' Malone smiled. 'No offence. I'm paying you a compliment.'

Chung smiled in return, appeared to relax. 'I think I *wanted* to believe . . . When someone comes to you and offers you seventy million dollars for openers . . .' He gave an elegant shrug. 'I took them at face value.'

'One would,' said Malone. 'Wouldn't you, Russ?'

'Only up to a point,' said Clements. 'But then, I take it, you did some due diligence.'

'Ye-es.' It was like a soft hiss. 'Things weren't quite what I was told.'

'We've been to see Jack Aldwych,' said Malone. 'He said his son had done due diligence on Bund. Did he come up with what you discovered?'

Chung nodded.

Malone and Clements looked at each other. 'Jack wasn't telling us the truth.'

'It wouldn't be the first time,' said Malone.

'Maybe he's become a Taoist,' said Chung. 'They believe all truth is relative.'

'Do you?' Malone knew nothing of Taoism.

'If it suits me.'

'Let's not be relative now, Les. What did you find out about Bund that they hadn't told you? Who was Mr Shan? Some Shanghai buccaneer?'

'Oh yes, I guess he was that, all right.' Now that he had started to open up, Chung seemed more relaxed. 'But he was also a senior government official in the Central China Department of Trade. So he said.'

'So he said?'

'It took us some time to check. Communist government offices don't exactly open up to you when you ask questions.'

'The Great Wall of China approach?'

'Jack has been talking to you? Yes. Mr Shan

had been only a consultant to the department, but he'd left them more than a year ago.'

Malone switched tack: 'What about Madame Tzu?'

Chung raised an eyebrow. 'Jack's told you about her?'

'Just in passing. You tell us something about her.'

'Madame Tzu — she likes to be called Madame — is a throwback. I'm not sure how old she is — she looks about forty, but I think she might have been at the court of the Last Empress. She acts like that at times. She's not a government official, but she seems to know everyone in government. She lives in Hong Kong, but she comes and goes — to Canton, Shanghai, Beijing. She's a remarkable woman.'

'And you don't like her?' said Clements.

'Oh, I like her. I just don't trust her.'

'How long did it take you to find that out?' said Malone. 'That you don't trust her?'

'Some time, a few months.'

'Is she in Sydney now?'

'Not that I know of.'

'Not that you know of?' said Clements. 'She's your partner and she doesn't let you know when she's in town?'

Chung spread his hands, almost a Gallic gesture. 'That's Madame Tzu. She might have come to Sydney with Shan — he arrived yesterday morning — but he didn't mention her.'

'Check with Immigration,' Malone said to

Gail. Then to Chung: 'Are you Chinese inscrutable with each other?'

'Are we?' Chung smiled at Gail.

'My father tells me I'm an open book,' she said. 'That's the Australian side of me. I'll check on Madame Tzu, sir, find out if she is in town. Where does she usually stay, Mr Chung?'

'The Bund Corporation has an apartment in the Vanderbilt.'

The three detectives looked at each other: no inscrutability there. 'Do the comrades back home know about this luxury?'

'The comrades back home don't know the half of it about the Bund Corporation,' said Chung.

Out in the main room a phone rang. Sheryl Dallen turned away from her wall chart and picked it up. She listened, then hung up and came to Malone's doorway. 'Excuse me, sir. That was Bondi. There's been another homicide.'

'Do they want us?' asked Malone.

'It's another Chinese. They thought we might be interested.'

Malone looked at Chung. 'Do you know anyone at Bondi, Les?'

Chung shook his head. 'I never go near Bondi, Inspector, even though I live only a mile or two from it.'

'A bit below your idea of class?' said Clements.

Chung smiled. 'No, I'm afraid of sun cancers. Leave me out of this homicide. As you must occasionally say, I haven't a clue.'

2

Bondi has one of the most magnificent of Sydney's twenty-two surf beaches. It is a long shallow curve of white sand between two headlands; it has two life-saving clubs. The southern end is the topless end, where male eyeballs are as susceptible to melanomas as the bosoms they are staring at; the northern end is populated mainly by youngsters waiting to grow up and migrate to the southern end. Behind the beach is a wide esplanade, neglected for so long that it grew to look like a wasteland staked with parking meters; recently the local council had raised enough energy and money to turn it into a broad attractive plaza. In the middle was a pavilion that had started out to be a Greek temple for the surf gods and goddesses on the sands in front of it; somehow, along the way, the philosophy and plot had been lost and for years it had been no more than a columned eyesore. Behind the esplanade was a breakwater of surf shops, cafés and restaurants, a hotel that looked as if it had drifted ashore from Miami and, at the southern end, a drinkers' hotel that had been a Saturday night blood bin till the police had at last asserted their authority. Behind the shops and hotels a shallow valley sloped upwards, its streets lined with modest houses and cheap blocks of flats. Bondi had once been a suburb that had its pride, but over the years the pride had been stained and badly dented. Drugs had been freely available; New Year's Eve celebrations had turned into riots; women had been afraid to walk alone down certain streets. Now, however, with Sydney being told that it had to be an exemplary city by the time of the Olympics, like a child being dressed up for the visit of some rich relatives, Bondi had a certain shine to it, even if it was only veneer.

'Homicide sent two *women?*' The detective sergeant from the Bondi station was stocky, overweight and had the weary air of a chauvinist who knew the war between the sexes was lost.

'You have a problem with that?' Gail Lee looked at Sheryl Dallen; they nodded at each other, they were on familiar turf. 'We're here just to do the housekeeping.'

Sergeant Napolani's smile was unexpectedly friendly. 'Girls, you couldn't be more welcome. There's a pile of dirty dishes in the kitchen . . . Only kidding. Actually, the dead guy kept a very neat pad. Almost too neat. Or else someone's been through the place and tidied it up.'

Zhang Yong had lived in a one-bedroom flat in a drab block halfway up the southern hill from the valley. His body had been taken away, but Crime Scene tapes hung across the front door

60

like an auctioneer's invitation. The Physical Evidence team were still at work, but showing no excitement, as if they had already decided that whatever they unearthed here was not going to be of much value. The flat was typical rent-stuff: cheap carpet, cheap furniture, a faded print of a bush scene on one wall, the bare essentials in the kitchen. Zhang's body, fully clothed, had been found huddled in the shower-stall, the shower drenching him like a last benediction.

'The water seeped down into the flat below,' said Napolani. 'A coupla Maoris. They came up to complain, so they said — they look more like they would of beat the shit outa him. When he didn't answer the door, they kicked it in — they tell us they play rugby for Easts. They found him and, like good citizens, they phoned us.'

'What have you found?' asked Sheryl.

'Nothing. The place is so bloody neat, you wonder if he actually lived here. There's some clothes in the wardrobe and stuff in the bathroom cupboard, but nothing to identify him. It was the Maoris who gave us his name, told us he was a student.'

'No passport, no bank book, credit card?' said Gail.

'Nothing. The Maoris think he was at UTS, we're gunna check.'

'What killed him?'

'A bullet in the left temporal, another one practically dead centre in the heart. Our guess is they used a silencer — nobody heard any shots.

He'd been dead eight to ten hours was the pathologist's guess — that would of been about midnight last night. They'll tell us more when they do the autopsy Monday.'

Gail Lee looked around the small bedroom: a featureless box in which an almost anonymous man had lived and died. The bed had not been slept in, so Zhang had either been up at midnight expecting visitors or had come home with them. 'I noticed there are no books or newspapers out in the living room.'

'If there were, they'd all been taken away,' said Napolani.

'What about the TV set?' asked Sheryl. 'There's a VCR on top of it.'

'No videos.'

'So he was sitting up till almost midnight, looking at TV, or he'd come home with the guys who killed him?'

'Looks like it,' said Napolani.

'What made you think this homicide has anything to do with the ones last night in Chinatown?'

Napolani shrugged. He was a cop who had learned his trade the hard way: never behind a desk, always on the beat or, once he had become a detective, out doing the legwork on an investigation. He had worked his way through robbery, assault, drugs and murder. He had developed an instinct: 'It was a guess, a wild one. You don't get four Chinese murders in twelve hours . . . Is that why they sent you?'

'No.' Gail gave him a thin smile. 'Sheryl just drags me along to read the tea leaves.'

'You win.' Napolani's smile was wider than hers.

'Okay,' said Sheryl, 'now we've got the cross-cultural bit out of the way, do you want us to hang around or do you want us out of the way?'

'Before we go,' said Gail, 'I think we should talk to the Maoris.'

'They're downstairs. Kip and Keith, friendly as a coupla buffaloes.' Napolani led them out of the flat, ducking under the tapes, and down a narrow flight of stairs where their heels click-clacked on the cheap tiles. 'I had a check run on them. They've both got records — assault, battery, that sorta thing. Saturday-night wreckers, probably after they've been playing rugby.'

'You're not a rugby man?' said Sheryl, who occasionally dated footballers. 'Not rah-rah?'

'Golf. A gentleman's game.' He grinned again as he knocked on the door of the flat immediately below that of the murdered man. 'Don't mention we know their records.'

The door was opened by a handsome dark-skinned man who filled the doorway. 'G'day. What's the problem now?'

'A few more questions, Kip.' Napolani introduced Gail and Sheryl. 'They're from Homicide.'

'Women?'

'I'm afraid so,' said Gail. 'We'll try to be as genderless as possible.'

Kip had a smile like a truck headlight. 'Come in. Me mate handles women better'n I do.'

Sheryl and Gail exchanged looks. 'Ain't we the lucky ones?'

Keith, the delicate handler of women, was slightly less dark than his flatmate and only slightly less huge. The five people seemed to push back the walls of the small living room. 'Siddown,' said Keith, and cleared a couch of what looked like a month's laundry. 'Sat'day's cleaning-up day.'

'When did Mr Zhang move in upstairs?' asked Gail.

Keith looked at Kip. 'I dunno — what? Six months ago?' *Six* sounded like *sex*. 'He always kept to himself.'

'He ever have any visitors?'

'Occasionally,' said Kip. 'Always Chinese. They were a quiet lot.'

'How do you know he was a student?' asked Sheryl.

'I asked him straight out one day what he was doing here.'

'He didn't tell you to mind your own business?'

Kip and Keith exchanged smiles, as if no one had ever been foolish enough to tell them to mind their own business. 'Man, he saw I was just trying to be friendly. We're a friendly lot, us Kiwis. Right, mate?'

'Nobody friendlier,' said Keith; and you'd better believe it or else, said his smile.

'He said he was doing computers at the University of Technology, Sydney. He spelled it right out, like I was dumb or something.'

'Friendly but dumb, that's us,' said Keith, the truck light gleaming again.

Gail looked at Napolani. 'I didn't see a computer in his flat. Surely he'd have one at home to work on?'

'There was none.'

'Oh, he had one, all right,' said Keith. 'I saw him carting it up there just after he moved in. What's going on up there? We've had trouble in these flats, but never a fucking murder.'

'What sort of trouble?' said Sheryl.

Both men shrugged, a major tremor of bone and muscle. 'You *know*, a party getting outa hand, some guy and his girl having a fight, the usual stuff. But someone being *shot* —' Keith shook his head. He had a flat-top haircut with shaven sides and when he frowned it seemed to start up a vein, like a lizard, in his right temple. 'The landlord's gunna be outa his fucking mind when he hears about it.'

'Who is the landlord?'

'We dunno. All we ever see is the agent, he comes knocking on the door, we don't pay the rent.'

'How often don't you pay the rent?' said Sheryl, but smiled.

'We miss occasionally,' said Kip. 'But it's never a big deal.'

'What do you do?' said Napolani, although

65

from their record he knew.

'We're dole bludgers. Ain't that what all Maoris are supposed to be? We only come over here to bludge on the Aussie system. You got a better class of welfare here.' For a moment Kip's broad face went a shade darker. Then he grinned. 'No, we both got jobs. I work at a service station up on Bondi Road, Keith's a public relations officer at a club up the Cross.'

'A bouncer?'

'Yeah,' said Keith.

'You'd be good at it,' said Napolani.

'Yeah, I got a diploma in bouncing. From UTS.' He was all smile, it would be a pleasure to be bounced by him.

'If you saw someone coming into the flats with a gun,' said Gail, 'what would you do? Bounce them?'

'I'd close the door. They don't pay you for being a hero. Welfare doesn't stretch that far.'

'It's been a pleasure meeting you two gentlemen,' said Sheryl, rising. 'If anyone comes around asking questions about Mr Zhang, get in touch with Sergeant Napolani, will you? In the meantime, who are the agents for the flats?'

Kip named them. 'They're just off Campbell Parade. They've probably already got the flat listed for rent again.'

'You're a cynical lot, you Maoris,' said Napolani.

'We learned it from the *pakeha*.'

Gail and Sheryl, in an unmarked car, followed

Napolani in his unmarked car down the hill and to a street that ran off the esplanade. Napolani pulled into a zone reserved for disabled drivers and Sheryl squeezed the second car in behind it. At once, as always, a parking officer, another Maori by the look of him, was standing at the kerb, charge-book in hand.

'I take it youse can read?' He nodded at the sign.

Sheryl produced her badge. 'We've got to get our daily quota, just like you. You want us to pinch you?'

He held up both hands in surrender. 'I was just standing here minding my own business, officer . . . How long you gunna be?'

'Ten minutes, the most,' said Napolani, coming up behind the parking officer. 'G'day, Charlie, we've got some business across the road. We'll limp across there if you want us to be disabled.'

'What'm I gunna do if some little old lady on crutches turns up? Okay, but make it quick.'

The man behind the counter in the estate agency was more welcoming; he thought they were prospective buyers till Napolani showed him his badge. 'There's been *what?* A murder? In one of our properties? Oh Jesus, that's going to be a dead loss for a coupla months.'

Napolani gave him the bare details.

'I can't remember everyone on our books — what'd you say his name was? Zhang?'

'You have a lot of Chinese tenants?' said Gail.

67

'Well, no, not a lot.' He was a young man who looked as if he might never sit down; he kept moving from foot to foot, his hands played a noiseless tune on the counter. He wore a bright white shirt and a tie that lay on his chest like a limp bouquet. Behind him two girls at computers had stopped to listen to the talk of, migod, murder! They couldn't wait to put it on the real estate Internet. 'We got thirty or forty blocks of flats on our books, Chinese tenants come and go. Bondi, you know, it's sorta transient, people come and go.'

'All the blocks of flats,' said Gail, 'who owns them? Particularly Mr Zhang's block?'

The young man looked over his shoulder at one of the girls, who instantly punched her computer keys. Then she said, 'It's one of half a dozen blocks owned by the same man. Mr Feng. Mr Charles Feng.'

'Where does Mr Feng live?'

The girl glanced at her computer again. 'He has two addresses. One in Chinatown and the other out at Drummoyne. We send the rent cheques to Drummoyne.' She gave a street address.

Gail Lee and Sheryl Dallen exchanged glances and Napolani caught the look. But he asked no question, just said to the young man, 'I'll be back in a minute —'

'Look, I'm busy —'

'So'm I.' Napolani followed the two women out of the agency. 'What's on? Who's Mr Feng?'

'He was one of the three men shot last night at the Golden Gate,' said Gail.

3

'Maybe it's the wrong time,' said Gail Lee.

'There's never a right time for this sort of thing,' said Malone.

Gail and Sheryl Dallen had reported back to Homicide from Bondi. Sheryl had been told to go off duty but to remain on call. Malone and Gail had driven out to Drummoyne.

The suburb lies halfway between the affluent of the eastern suburbs and the battlers on the western front, where all is seldom quiet. It curves along the southern bank of the Parramatta River, the main artery flowing out of the harbour. Originally it was a land grant to an Irish military surgeon, presumably for not making too many blunders with the knife. He then, illustrating the affinity between the Irish and the Jews under English rule, sold the land to a Jewish convict tailor. The tailor had already been granted a pardon for providing two pairs of pants with each suit he made for the Governor. Raising enough capital to buy the land, he then turned from cutting cloth to cutting up lots. He sold to the aspiring gentry, a class already blossoming in the colony. Ever since the area has clung to a presence of respectability, even though it once

69

had a rugby team known to other rugby teams as the Dirty Reds. It is solid, conservative and, along the shoreline of its several small bays, suggestive of mild affluence.

Now Malone and Gail were in this dead-end street lined with solid houses, some dating back to the last century; a few looked as if they had been built only yesterday, angular blocks of concrete and glass. The Feng residence was in the latter category, an ultra-modern mausoleum. Its double driveway was packed with seven cars, three were parked on the wide footpath, three others were double-parked alongside those at the kerb. A marked police car was double-parked on the opposite side of the road.

Gail pulled their unmarked car in behind the police car and she and Malone got out. A uniformed cop opened the door of the police car and looked back at them. 'Not there, sir.'

Malone showed his badge, introduced himself and Gail. The young cop instantly slid out of the car, put on his cap. 'Sorry, Inspector. But you can see the schemozzle we've got here — I've been instructed to give everyone twenty minutes, the most. But I haven't the heart —'

'Any of your men in with the Feng family?'

'No, sir. I'm just playing traffic cop, but it's hopeless. One or two of the neighbours complained —'

'Ignore them, at least for another hour or so. Give whoever's in there time to pass on their condolences. Then clear 'em out. Nicely, of course.'

'Of course, sir,' said the young cop as if he ever acted in any other way.

'Do you know the Fengs?'

'Only by repute.' He was tall and slim with sharp quizzical eyes and there were already faint lines in his face, as if age was waiting to pounce. Malone had seen a growing number of officers like him, men who, disappointed, would leave the Service long before their time was up. Corruption, public apathy or resentment: the ills had worn away at them. Corruption was now almost stamped out, the public had become a little more appreciative of the fact that cops were human, not supermen: but for some, like this young man, the tide had turned too late.

'He's a big number,' he said, 'in the local council, the rowing club, things like that. He *was*, I mean.'

'The family?'

'I dunno much about them. The Chinese —' Then he looked at Gail. 'No disrespect, ma'am, but Chinese families keep pretty much to themselves. As families, I mean.'

Gail just nodded, made no comment. She turned away and crossed the road towards the Feng house. The young cop looked at Malone. 'Have I offended her, sir?'

'I don't think so. But you never know.'

The double front doors were wide open to a wide entrance hall in which people seemed to be

71

coming and going in slow motion; not all of them, Malone noted, Chinese. A girl dressed in a high-necked black dress came towards Malone and Gail. 'Yes?'

Malone introduced himself and Gail again. 'We'd like a word with someone from the family.'

'I am Camilla Feng — it was my father who was shot. Did you have to come *now?*'

Malone, perhaps because of his own height, always thought of Chinese women as small. Camilla Feng, however, was an inch or two taller than Gail, who was of medium height. Her slimness was accentuated by the simple black dress; she moved with the elegance of an older model, no angularity to her at all. She wore no jewellery or make-up; her black hair was cut in a gamine bob that complemented the bonework of her attractive face. Malone decided that, with make-up, she would turn the heads of a lot of men, not all of them Asian.

'Can we go somewhere quiet?' he asked, aware that people were now turning to stare at them. He looked up the stairs that led to a gallery on the second floor. Les Chung was at the head of the stairs; he looked down at Malone and gave a slight shake of his head: *why now?* But Malone had answered that question too many times before. 'Miss Feng — somewhere where we won't be disturbed?'

She had turned her head, following Malone's gaze up at Chung. Nothing seemed to pass between her and Chung, or if it did Malone did not catch it. 'Has Mr Chung told you he has been to see us?' Malone asked.

'No.'

Then without a further word she led the two detectives down a flight of stairs. The house turned out to be three-storeyed; the bottom level was below the street. She led them out onto a deserted terrace, where a swimming pool threw back a glare like blue glass. Below the terrace there was a sharp drop to the waters of a small bay; some yachts floated there, their owners doing weekend work on them. Above the bay, like a concrete grey rainbow, was the long arch of the Gladesville Bridge.

'There's been a fourth murder,' said Malone, plunging straight in. 'Someone besides your father and his friends. A Chinese student named Zhang Yong.'

Camilla Feng frowned. 'We don't know anyone of that name.'

'Perhaps your father did. Mr Zhang rented a flat in a block owned by your father in Bondi.'

'What has that to do with us?'

'You don't think it a coincidence, four Chinese men murdered within a couple of hours? Your father owning the flat where one of the victims lived? We tend to link coincidences like that, Miss Feng. Did your father sponsor students from Hong Kong or Singapore or China?'

'Hong Kong *is* China now.'

He didn't want a lesson in political history; but

saw that she was playing for time. She put on dark glasses against the glare; Gail followed suit. Malone had left his own glasses at home, so that he was the one left barefaced.

'Yes, my father did sponsor the occasional student.'

'Any of the refugees from China?' asked Gail.

'Possibly. We're all refugees of some sort, aren't we? Refugees from poverty, prejudice, whatever.'

'I was being specific,' said Gail patiently. '*Political* refugees.'

Camilla Feng had seemed remarkably composed for someone whose father had been murdered. But now she turned her head away to look towards the bridge and in her profile Malone saw the sudden tightening of her jaw as if she were stopping it from dropping. She said nothing, seemingly ignoring them, and at last Malone said, 'Miss Feng, did your father visit China, mainland China?'

Only then did she look back at them. 'He never mentioned that he did. Why do you ask?'

'At this stage we're asking a lot of questions that may be irrelevant, but we often get unexpected answers. Did he visit Hong Kong, Taipei, Singapore? Places where money, finance, is readily available? He was a wealthy man, Miss Feng. He and Mr Sun and Mr Chung put together a lot of money, millions, for their share of Olympic Tower —'

'My father would go to Hong Kong three or

74

four times a year. Taipei and Singapore — no.'

'Never to the mainland?' said Gail. 'Shanghai, for instance?'

'Not as far as I know. My mother comes from Shanghai. She went with him to Hong Kong, before it was handed back, but she would never cross the border back into China. She has never mentioned that my father did.'

'Was she a political refugee?'

Her jaw loosened, but she did not smile. 'Good God, no! She was only ten years old when she came out here with my grandparents. I suppose you could say *they* were political refugees, but they weren't called that in those days. My grandfather was a major in the Kuomintang. When Chiang Kai-shek fled to Formosa, my grandfather chose to come out here.'

'What did your grandfather do?'

'Here? He became an importer, silks, that sort of thing. My grandmother's father had been a silk merchant in Shanghai.'

'Did your grandfather keep up his contacts with the Kuomintang?'

'I wouldn't know, Inspector. What happened in China in the thirties and forties was never discussed, not in my presence.'

Malone glanced at Gail, hoping for some comment; he was lost in any map of China. But Gail was looking up towards the terrace above them and Malone followed her gaze. A woman stood there staring down at them, her face half-hidden by dark glasses.

'Is that your mother?' said Malone.

No,' said Camilla Feng. 'It's my mother's cousin, Tzu Chao.'

'Madame Tzu?'

Even the dark glasses could not hide Camilla Feng's surprise. 'You know her?'

'We hope to. Ask her to come down.'

4

'What d'you reckon?' said Malone.

'Madame Tzu? She's every other inch a charmer,' said Gail Lee. 'It's the in-between bits I wouldn't trust.'

They were driving back to Homicide through a bright gold day; summer was promising to be hot and long. The beaches would be thronged this weekend; it would be murder trying to get a parking space at Bondi or Coogee or Maroubra. In his youth, when he had had no money, Malone had spent a lot of time at the beach: there was no cheaper exercise and relaxation. But now, with the pool in the back garden at the home at Randwick, with the constant search for a parking space, he never went near the surf. But he would go down to Coogee this afternoon, to the oval, and watch Tom play cricket and maybe close his eyes and see himself in those summers of long ago when, a year or two older than Tom was now, he had been what the cricket writers had called *promising*. The time when, as a cadet constable, he had just been entering the playing fields of murder.

'I wonder if Tzu is her real name,' said Gail, not turning her head but keeping her eyes on the road. She drove with calm precision, a little faster than Malone, a nervous passenger, liked, but always with room to spare between her and the other traffic. 'She has the name of two empresses, two of the worst China ever had. One named Wu Chao, who lived in the seventh century — Christian century, that is —' For a moment she took her eyes off the road as she smiled at him. 'Only yesterday, in Chinese history.'

'Are you Confucian or Buddhist or what?' He had no idea of what religion had prevailed in China before Communism.

'I'm Christian, actually. Roman Catholic, like you.'

'Not like me. I'm Irish Catholic. We're a breed apart. Was this Empress Wu Chao a Christian?'

'I hardly think so. She was one of the most murderous bitches of all time — she would have made Lucrezia Borgia look like Mother Teresa.'

'The other one?'

'The Last Empress, Tz'u-Hsi. She put her nephew on the throne, then had fifty-three of his servants executed when he tried to assert himself. She had his favourite concubine wrapped in a rug and thrown down a well and then for good

77

measure she poisoned her sister. Both those ladies made a pastime of murder, like needlework, and I'm sure Madame Tzu is the sort who would know every detail of their history. I'll find out if there's a Mr Tzu.'

'If it's not her real name, why would she adopt it?'

'The Chinese revere the past, even the bitches and sons-of-bitches. They're not so different from Westerners. The state religion of England was founded by a king who cut off the head of one of his wives to get rid of her.'

'Like I told you, I'm an Irish Catholic,' said Malone piously.

While Camilla Feng had been collecting Madame Tzu, Malone and Gail had admired the tranquil view. A rowing eight, on a practice run, came under the towering leap of the bridge; the shell's wake was as delicate as a Chinese fan. A small yacht, under power, chugged out of the bay beneath the Feng house; a laugh floated up, light and careless. On the terrace above, from which Madame Tzu had now disappeared, there came a soft wail, ululating till it died away in a sob.

Then Camilla Feng and Madame Tzu came out onto the lower terrace. Madame Tzu was as tall as the girl, carried herself like a woman whose back had never been bent under any burden. Her black hair was cut in soft waves, a grey streak like a feather angling away from the centre parting. She was wearing dark glasses, so that her eyes were not visible, but the features round the glasses were regular and well cared for. It was Gail who recognized how expensively the older woman was dressed: the Chanel summer suit, the silk blouse, the Ferragamo shoes. But even Malone, who would have had trouble distinguishing a Karl Lagerfeld label from a K-Mart tab, remarked that Madame Tzu looked like a woman who, even if she had been a peasant, would have had her field pyjamas custom-made. He guessed she was the face of the New China, the face that the Old Guard in Beijing hated and feared.

'Do you speak English, Madame Tzu?'

'Reasonably well.' She had a soft but clipped voice. 'I spent four years at Oxford. I may be a little pedantic at times, but that's Oxford for you.'

'Our questions are a little pedantic at times, but that's Homicide for you.' He hadn't meant to joke, but if she was put out by his remark it did not show. 'You understand why we're here?'

'My niece has explained.'

'Your niece?'

'Well, second cousin or whatever the relationship is — does one ever work these things out? Does it matter? I always think of her as my niece.' She gave Camilla a smile like a bequest. 'Almost as my daughter.'

If Camilla was pleased or honoured by the adoption, she gave no sign. As he often had, Malone damned dark glasses. They might guard against cataracts or glaucoma, but they put a screen over communication.

'So you've known each other for some time?'

Madame Tzu took off her glasses, blinked in the bright sunlight, and put them back on. Malone recognized the ploy; she had stumbled and wanted to get back in step. Suddenly she smiled, was all expensive caps, friendliness and good humour. 'I tend to exaggerate. That was something else I learned at Oxford. Some of the dons there were professional eccentrics.'

She's dodged the question, thought Malone; but let it go. 'Had you known Mr Shan long?'

'Oh yes, we were students together.'

'How well have you known him since, say over the last few years? Would you know if he had any enemies?'

'We all have enemies, haven't we? Even the police.'

'Very true. We just try not to cold-bloodedly murder them.' That was untrue: there had been several cases of cold-blooded killings by cops. But he reckoned on Madame Tzu's not being too well versed in the history of the New South Wales Police Service.

She was silent a moment; behind the dark glasses she was studying him. 'I could quote some saying by Confucius about enemies, but he was a misogynist and I prefer to ignore him.'

'I'm glad of that. I sometimes have trouble separating Confucius from Charlie Chan, they're such wiseacres.'

80

'Charlie Chan?' All three women looked at him.

'Forget it.' None of them, obviously, was a fan of late-night movies. 'Do *you* have any enemies?'

'Possibly. Probably. Yes, Mr Shan had enemies. Our generation grew up in that sort of climate.' She shrugged, as if the past was too familiar; then she looked at Camilla. 'But I don't think your father had any enemies, did he? He was a dear man.'

'If he had any,' said Camilla, 'he never spoke of them.'

'Did you know Mr Sun?'

'No,' said Madame Tzu. 'I met him once, that was all.'

'What about Zhang Yong?'

'Who?' She looked genuinely puzzled.

Malone put the dead student on the back burner for the moment; he went on: 'Did you work with Mr Shan?'

'We were together for a while in the Central China Department of Trade — before I left.'

'To do what?'

'I'm an economic consultant. A new breed in China.' Again the smile.

'Is that what you did at Oxford — Economics?'

'Oh no. History. I went on to Harvard to do Economics.'

'You've been very fortunate,' said Gail. 'All that foreign study. Was it condoned — I mean, say twenty years ago?'

81

The smile this time almost ate Gail. 'You're guessing at my age.' But she didn't give it. 'There were some people in power then who didn't have closed minds about what the West could teach us. As you say, I was fortunate.'

'Are you a consultant to the Bund Corporation?' asked Malone. 'Or a partner?'

There was a barely discernible hesitation. 'I'm registered as a partner.'

'Here and in Shanghai?' said Gail, who had done her homework. 'The corporation is registered here in Sydney and in Hong Kong. What about Shanghai?'

Again there was the slightest hesitation. 'No, it is not registered there.'

'So,' said Gail, 'it is a private company?'

'Yes,' said Madame Tzu, and she was now beginning to look less at ease. 'Overseas investment is being encouraged. A quid pro quo for the foreign investment in China.'

'Seventy or eighty million dollars,' said Malone. 'Quite a quid pro quo.'

'I think it incredible,' she said, finding the smile again, 'but such sums are common currency these days. But would you excuse us now? Camilla and I should get back to her mother. She is absolutely devastated by what has happened.'

'You'll be staying in Sydney?' said Malone. 'At the Vanderbilt?'

An eyebrow went up above the dark glasses, but she made no comment on the fact that they already had a trace on her. All she said was, 'You must come and have tea with me.'

'We'd like that,' said Malone, and matched his smile with hers, though it hurt. 'Perhaps we can talk history. Corporation history.'

He and Gail followed the two women into the house and up to the street floor. As they went out into the street Les Chung followed them. 'Thanks for being discreet, Inspector. You caused no comment in there.'

'We try not to, Les. Your friend Madame Tzu is a charmer.'

'You think so?'

'There's another side to her?'

'There always is, isn't there?'

'You mean, to women?' said Gail.

'Oh, I wouldn't say that. I just don't believe that, with anyone, what you see is what you get. You police would know that better than I.'

He left them, walked along the street and stopped by a large green car. 'A Bentley Turbo,' said Gail. 'Half a million dollars' worth.'

'You envious?'

She shook her head. 'No. With money like that — as Madame Tzu said, everyone has enemies.'

Then they had driven back to Strawberry Hills and now as they drew into the yard where Homicide and the other police units parked their cars, Gail said, 'Do we follow up Madame?'

'We do, but let her sweat for a while. Although —' he grinned — 'I don't think Madame Tzu would ever sweat. Just see she doesn't try leaving the country before we talk to her again — get on to Immigration. Also, keep digging into the Bund Corporation. There's nothing much we can do over the weekend — let Day Street and Bondi do the legwork, they'll call us if something breaks. First thing Monday look into Zhang Yong, find out who and what he was.'

'First thing.' She got out of the car, then looked at him across the roof. 'This is my biggest case so far. Thanks.'

'You're very necessary on this one, Gail. We may need you to get behind all the inscrutability we're going to come up against.' She looked disappointed and he hurried on, 'That's only part of it. You do your homework and that's what counts in my book.'

He knew he would never have to sack her as he had Harold Boston.

5

That afternoon, forgoing his usual tennis, Malone went down to Coogee oval to watch Tom play for Randwick seconds. At the tea interval father and son sat with their sandwiches and cups of tea on a seat by the picket fence. Anyone passing by would have recognized them for father and son: the same build, the same way their dark hair grew in a widow's peak, the boy better-looking than his father but with similar features. What was still undefined was whether the boy would have his father's pragmatism in an emergency.

'You're pitching the ball too short,' said Malone. 'If you were a yard or two quicker, it would be okay. But you're giving them time to get on the back foot and play you.'

'I can bowl faster.'

'No, there's time for that later on.' He didn't want Tom plagued in later life by back and hip trouble, brought on by too much fast bowling too young.

'How quick were you?' Tom never seemed to resent his father's advice.

'It's hard to tell, yourself. But they reckoned I was as fast as Dennis Lillee.'

'Why didn't you play for Australia?'

'I never had the killer instinct. Have you got it? D'you hate batsmen?'

Tom sipped his tea, thought a moment, then grinned. 'Not really. I hate the guys who hit me around the paddock, but no, I guess I'm not a killer.'

Malone changed the subject, abruptly; the worry had been with him all day: 'Did that killer upset you last night?'

Tom took his time swallowing a mouthful of sandwich; then he nodded. 'It was so bloody cold-blooded.'

'Fifty per cent of the time, murder is.'

Tom looked sideways at him. 'Dad, are you

worried that Claire and Maureen and me saw what happened?'

'Of course. Any father would be. It doesn't make it any better that I'm a cop.'

'We were worried, too.' Tom looked out at the empty oval now. 'When you ran after that guy. I had to hold Mum back from going after you.'

'I'm glad you did.'

Then the players were filing back onto the field: men dressed all in white, no fancy colour costumes, no logos spattering them like birdshit: it was the sort of cricket in which he had grown up but which was fast disappearing.

Tom stood up. 'I guess we all worry for each other, right?'

Malone nodded, words stuck in his throat.

The rest of the afternoon was a father's delight; the son took five wickets. Malone sat there and saw himself in every pace that Tom took, every ball he bowled. Memory mixed with pride and turned the afternoon golden.

Murder was an aberration on another planet.

Chapter Three

1

But it wasn't, of course; it was right here in Harbour City. The playwright Williamson had called it Emerald City; but Malone had never seen it as anything but a cracked and flawed jewel. Violence was on the rise, racial tension was increasing, the gap between poor and rich was growing. The cracks in the jewel were widening.

Sunday there had been two more homicides, both domestics: men and women who had snapped in the condition of living together. Monday morning Malone did paperwork at his desk, then went out into the main room for the ten o'clock conference.

He glanced towards the wall where Sheryl Dallen's flow chart had been mounted, a neat collage of murder. Then he sat on a desk and looked around. 'Well?'

Boston was in the circle of chairs this morning. 'I was at Union Hall eight o'clock this morning, got in early before they got too busy to talk to me.'

'They tell you anything?'

'There's been trouble on the Olympic Tower

site. Nothing, I gather, to do with the bosses. It's inter-union stuff, the Construction mob against Allied Trades, the usual argument about whose turf it is. There was the building slump a coupla years ago, now they're fighting about who's gunna get the jobs.'

'It's not dirty enough, is it,' asked Clements, 'for them to start hiring hitmen?'

'I suggested it to Albie Krips, the assistant sec. down at Union Hall, and you'd of thought I'd suggested his mother had done it. They're so pious, these days, they've never heard of what used to go on.'

'We'll look into it,' said Malone, and in the moment before he shifted his gaze saw the resentment in Boston's face; the latter had thought he was on his way to rehabilitation. 'John?'

'I'll tread water a while,' said Kagal. 'Kate is coming over from Fraud. She has some information I think you'd like to hear. I'll let her tell you.'

Kate Arletti had left Homicide a year ago to work for Fraud, which was on the same floor but in another wing. She and Kagal had been both police partners and lovers till, during the hunt for a gay serial killer, he had confessed to her that he was bisexual. She had instantly asked for a transfer from Homicide and Malone had reluctantly but wisely let her go, recommending her for a vacant post in Fraud, where she had done well. Over the past year, however, she and Kagal

88

had patched up their differences and were now living together in Kagal's flat, an arrangement that had Kate's mother, an ardent Catholic, on her knees morning and night. Malone said his own prayers for Kate, not for the present but for the future.

'Righto, we'll wait for her. What's happening at Day Street and out at Bondi?'

'No progress,' said Phil Truach.

'The post-mortems?'

'I've just talked to Romy,' said Clements, and managed not to make it sound like a husband-to-wife chat. 'They did the PMs on all four Chinese this morning. Ballistics picked up the bullets half an hour ago. If they get their finger out, we should have their report pretty soon. I rang Clarrie Binyan and asked him to make it a priority.'

'What's the betting the Golden Gate job and Mr Zhang were all done by the same gun?'

'I wouldn't take money on it,' said Clements the punter, 'not if I was a bookie.'

'What more do we know about the corporations in Olympic Tower?'

'Sheryl and I have an appointment with a nice young man from the Securities Commission,' said Gail. 'He does weights with her at gym.'

'Where are you talking to him?' said Malone.

'At the gym, at lunchtime,' said Sheryl. 'If we turn up at his office, questions might be asked. We don't want that yet, do we?'

'Not if they want us to be official — that just

wastes time. Can he get his breath to answer questions while he's lying on his back pumping iron or whatever it is you fitness fanatics do?'

'He can when I lie beside him,' said Sheryl.

'What are you going to do, Gail? Pump iron or just make notes?'

'I think I'll just watch.'

Then Kate Arletti was knocking at the glass panel of the security door. Kagal got up, went across and admitted her; Malone waited for him to kiss her on the cheek, but they were as formal as strangers. Except for Kate's smile. She's still in love with him, thought Malone.

'Tell us what you know, Kate.'

She sat in Kagal's chair and he stood behind her, like a guardian. 'The Feds got in touch with us a week ago — they asked us to look into it, they were up to their necks in something and couldn't afford the staff. It's not strictly our line of work, but things are slow with us —'

'Swindlers turned honest all of a sudden?'

'Could be. Anyhow, I looked into it. The Commonwealth Bank and a few other bods were worried about a couple of deposits in two of their accounts, one at Bondi, the other at Cronulla. Cheque accounts held by two Chinese students.'

'The plot thickens,' said Andy Graham, and instantly looked embarrassed. 'I read that somewhere.'

'Go on, Kate,' said Malone, and could feel the familiar rising of adrenaline that always came when another piece of the jigsaw fell into place.

90

'These two are *students,* mind. Overseas students, from China. Their names are —' she glanced at her notebook — 'Zhang Yong, he's the one from Bondi. The other is a girl, Li Ping, she banks at Cronulla. Zhang opened an account with the Commonwealth six months ago, with modest transfers from Hong Kong. Three weeks ago he had twenty-eight million deposited in the account —'

'Twenty-eight *million?*' The amount registered on everyone's faces as if it had been rung up on a cash register; except there was no cash register that could flash up that amount. Its till would fly open like Andy Graham's mouth.

'Wait,' said Kate, 'there's more. The girl at Cronulla had twenty-three million deposited in her account on the same day.'

'The bank branches must of thought they'd won the lottery,' said Clements. 'It would make head office look sick. Can you imagine a branch manager having that much handed to him in one whack?'

'Where did the money come from?' asked Malone.

'They're still tracing that, the actual sender. But both amounts came through a bank in Hong Kong. And Hong Kong banks are like what Swiss banks used to be. Hear no money, see no money, speak no money.'

'Whoever sent it must be bloody dumb,' said Clements. 'Did they think amounts like that wouldn't raise suspicion? Could you imagine the

91

commotion there'd be if someone sent amounts like that *into* China, deposited in some student's account?'

'Is the money still in the accounts?' asked Gail.

'The bank's frozen them — they invented some excuse about foreign credit control,' said Kate. She was obviously enjoying her visit and her information: she was back in Homicide, even if only for the moment. 'There's an act called the Cash Transactions Reporting Act. Any transaction involving more than ten thousand dollars has to be reported if there's a suspicion there might be money laundering. We used it earlier this year to put the Drug Squad on to a gang.'

'What currency were the transfers in?' asked Clements.

'That's the intriguing part — or part of it. It was in American dollars. So someone at the Hong Kong bank had to be in the scam. If that's what it is.'

'Righto, John, you and Gail go out to Cronulla, get Miss Li Ping's address from the bank and have a talk with her.'

'If she's still there,' said Kagal sceptically.

Malone nodded. 'If she's still there . . . Thanks, Kate.' He escorted her to the security door, opened it for her, said quietly, 'Everything still okay?'

She understood the question. 'So far. Don't worry about me, boss. I'm a big girl now.'

'You're neater, too,' he said with a grin, noting that every button on her shirt was done up.

'That's John's influence. He does a beautiful job with the ironing.'

'Glad to hear it,' said Malone, who wouldn't have known the front end from the back end of an iron. He had been blessed with a mother and a wife who had protected him from the drudgery of everyday life.

He watched her go down the hallway and wondered how he would feel if some day Claire or Maureen came home with a bisexual lover. Probably throw an iron at him. Then Kagal said behind him: 'She should still be working for us.'

Malone took his time. 'I know that. But you two put the kibosh on that.'

'Office romances, you mean? I've seen them work.'

'Not in our job. I couldn't send you two out as partners on, say, a domestic. You walk in, a feller has killed his wife, or vice versa. You're a husband-and-wife team investigating *that?*' He shook his head.

Kagal didn't split hairs by saying that they were not husband and wife. 'We wouldn't have to work as partners.'

'John, sooner or later you'd be rostered together —' He was dodging the real question in his mind: how long was Kagal going to remain faithful? He had no idea if the temptation for a bisexual man was double that of a heterosexual; he was not going to enquire, least of all of Kagal. 'I'm sorry, John. It's just not on.'

Then Gail Lee came across the room towards

them. 'Boss, I was going with Sheryl —'

'Now you're not —' He couldn't help the sharpness in his voice; but it wasn't really meant for her. 'You're going out to Cronulla with John, find that girl student. You may be needed to translate.' He looked past her at Sheryl Dallen, who had joined them. 'You can handle that young man from Securities on your own. Do some push-ups, pump iron, do whatever you like, but get some info out of him.'

He walked across and into his office; Clements followed him. The big man stared at him a moment, then said, 'I heard all of that. You've really got shit on the liver. If you're going any-where this morning, I'd better come with you or we're gunna have a lot of unhappy troops in Homicide. What's biting you?'

Malone slumped down in his chair. 'I don't know. Watching Kate with John got me started — d'you think I'm trying to play father to her?'

Clements remained standing in the doorway, as if blocking out the troops. This was something between the two senior men: the guardians. 'Maybe. I don't think about Kate and what she's got herself into —'

'That's because your daughter is only a year old. Mine are older.'

'Okay, I'll give you that. But I worry when I send Gail and Sheryl out on a job, if it's a messy one and the killer's still loose. That makes me a chauvinist, I guess, and the feminists would tell me to mind my own business, that women can

94

look after themselves. Maybe Gail and Sheryl would, too, if they knew how I felt.'

'So what are we supposed to do? Be like the British generals in World War One?' Con, his father, the anti-imperialist, had told him about that. 'Don't give a stuff for the troops?'

'Come on,' said Clements, giving up the argument, 'let's go in and talk to Union Hall.'

Malone stood up, reached for his hat and jacket. He always wore his pork-pie, even if it made him look like a detective out of the fifties; but he was not going to fall victim to sun cancers. Clements never wore a hat, which was just as well: *two* images from the fifties would have been too much. No crim would have taken them seriously.

'Let's go in first to Olympic Tower, to the site. That's at the centre of all this and I've never looked at it, bar when I'm driving past.'

It was only five minutes' drive from Strawberry Hills, in to George Street, the city's main street, and only a long stone's throw from Town Hall. They were pulled up at the main gate by a security guard. They asked to see the site manager and were directed to a parking space beside a demountable administration hut. 'But put these on soon's you get outa your car,' said the guard and handed them two safety helmets.

Malone put his on, looked across at Clements. 'Why does everyone look such a boofhead in these things?'

'I always have to laugh whenever I see politi-

95

cians wandering around wearing these. It only makes 'em look more at a loss than usual.'

'Let's hope none of 'em comes down here asking for a helmet.'

The site manager was in his thirties, professional written all over him. White shirt, striped tie, mobile hanging from his waist like a weapon: he wore a different badge from the workers. He was not happy to be interrupted by a couple of boofheaded detectives.

'Look, you should be talking to the bosses, not me —'

'Actually, we don't want to talk to you,' said Malone. 'We're just doing you a courtesy. We want to talk to the chief union delegate.'

'What about?'

'That's confidential, unless the union man wants to tell you. Now may we see him?'

'Okay. At least you're less demanding than the other cop who was down here.'

'Oh. Who was that?'

'Thin guy. Foster, Fosgate — no, Boston.'

'He won't be troubling you again,' said Malone, not looking at Clements. 'The union delegate?'

The manager rang his mobile and the two detectives moved away. 'Boston?' said Clements. 'What was he doing here?'

'Maybe we'll find out when we meet the union bloke.'

'You've got shit on the liver again.'

'Do you blame me?' Malone nodded at the

manager. 'I can't remember when I was last on a case where everyone was so bloody uncooperative.'

'Maybe he's just concerned for our safety,' said Clements, and adjusted his helmet which had slipped sideways on his head.

'He's coming down,' the site manager called out and went back into his office.

The two detectives stood under the honeycomb of the many storeys that had already gone up. Noise reverberated through the shell of the building, sounds that had their own mark, that of modern construction. Jackhammers pummelled the nerves; steel clanged against steel; the drum of a nearby cement truck whirled like a lottery barrel spilling pulverized marbles. Men came and went, all under the white or yellow toadstools of their helmets. A whistle blew and a huge girder was swept up into the sky like an exclamation mark that had broken loose.

Then a voice said, 'G'day, Scobie, you wanted to see me?'

Malone turned round. 'Roley! What're you doing here?'

Roley Bremner was a small hard ball of a man; his mother might have hand-rolled him when he was an infant. His white helmet sat so high on his head it could only have withstood a hit from directly above; ginger hair stuck out from beneath it like thin dry weed. He was dressed in a white boiler suit that gaped at his prominent beer belly.

'Ah, I left the Wharfies. They brought in all this waterfront reform, I seen there was no future for me — enterprise bargaining don't do no good for old union blokes like me. I come across to the Construction mob — I'm the site delegate, they know I got years of experience with bosses. It's tougher. Back on the wharves we had the bosses in our hand — here, it's a different kettle of fish. Especially —' He leaned closer, his gravelly voice dropping back into his throat; against the noise of the site Malone and Clements had to lean down to hear him; they looked like two uncles listening to the secret of a short fat nephew. 'Especially when you're dealing with Asians. Kee-rist, some of 'em think we're fucking peasants, you know what I mean? So what can I do for you?'

Malone explained the circumstances of what had brought him and Clements here. 'We heard you'd had some union trouble —'

'What's that gotta do with these murders you're talking about?'

'Maybe nothing, Roley. But which union would profit, you or the other blokes, if the current bosses were eliminated?'

'Depends who we had to deal with. Jack Aldwych's got his finger in the pie — we could deal with him. He'd be tough, but he'd be fair, we reckon. He might try a bit more of the stand-over stuff, but in the end he'd talk turkey. Jack's never been against the workers.'

'Only because you weren't worth robbing,'

98

said Clements. 'When did you have dealings with him?'

'When I was on the wharves. He was running a gold smuggling racket for a while — came to me and offered me dough to turn a blind eye.'

'Did you?'

'None of your business, mate . . . But you're barking up the wrong tree, you think anyone here had anything to do with the murders. The other crowd wouldn't have ten per cent of the workers on this site, though they're trying their hardest to get guys to move across to them. See that big guy over there?'

Malone and Clements looked towards the man supervising the unloading of the cement truck. He was tall and all muscle: dressed only in tight jeans and a skimpy blue singlet, he displayed shoulders and pectorals that would have been an advertisement for any gym. Under his helmet his long black hair was pulled back in a pony-tail that hung down his back like the tail of an animal hidden under his helmet. He looked across at Bremner and the two detectives and made no attempt to hide his stare. There was an arrogance about him that seemed to upset Roley Bremner. His hat wobbled on his head and he had to steady it.

'He's with Allied Trades — he likes to think of himself as their enforcer.' The bile in the roly-poly man's voice was like spit on the air. *He* had seen what real enforcers could do on the wharves in the old days: the swung hook, the packing-case suddenly dropped, the blow on the back of the head and the push into the harbour. He had survived all that. 'I've never seen him try the rough stuff, but the size of him, that build, he just stands over some of the guys, then they come and tell me maybe they'll join Allied Trades —'

'All that muscle,' said Clements, who had allowed most of his muscle to sink beneath softer flesh. 'Stick a pin in him and he'd squirt steroids. Is he into body-building?'

'He was on *The Warriors*, that TV show where they whack each other over the head and call it entertainment.'

'He gave up that for this?' said Malone.

'He didn't give it up — they just sacked him. Told him his IQ wasn't high enough for such an intellectual show — I got that from another guy who tried out for the show. Don't ask him two questions in a row — his eyes'll glaze over.'

Malone shook his head in mock admiration. 'You live amongst such interesting types, Roley — life is nothing like this in Homicide. What types have you got in *your* union? Any standover men?'

'Amongst ourselves it gets a bit rough at times — but you expect that, you're in union business. But it ain't like the old times, mate. The politicians are less interested in us than they used to be, there ain't the pressures. How's your old man?' Roley Bremner and Con Malone had once worked on the waterfront together. Malone was just glad that, as a cop, he had never been called on to face the two of them when there had been trouble on the wharves. 'He was a great union man, hated the bosses. He'd go stark raving mad, he was working on this job.'

'So there's a lot of hatred of the bosses?' said Malone.

Bremner shrugged, so hard that his helmet wobbled again. He steadied it, but said nothing. Malone had come to know that the only rival to a hardened crim in the tight-lipped stakes was a hard union man.

'Six or seven years ago,' said Clements, 'on the original job, before it closed down, there was trouble. A couple guys disappeared, right? We were never called in, there was no proof of homicide, but the guys never reappeared, did they? They go interstate or what?'

Bremner considered a moment, as if he had had enough of the detectives and their search for information; then he said, 'I wasn't here, right? I was still on the wharves. All I know is hearsay. You know, things get talked about, it's like telling funny stories. The two guys, they're foundation members.'

Both detectives looked quizzical. 'You mean —'

'Sure. They're buried in the foundations.' Bremner jerked his thumb downwards. 'Five storeys down, the bottom level. You gunna start digging?'

'Roley,' said Malone deliberately, 'we didn't

hear what you just said and don't bother to repeat it.'

'You shouldn't of asked,' said Bremner, and grinned.

'Do you have any Asians working here?' said Clements.

'Half a dozen — Vietnamese. And there's two Chinese on the white-collar staff.'

'Locals?'

Bremner shook his head; the helmet wobbled again, 'From China. They're engineers, they work for the Hong Kong crowd, the Bund Corporation. I think they're here to keep an eye on things, day to day.'

'They trouble you?'

'They're uppity buggers, a pain in the arse. But I take no notice of 'em.' Roley Bremner had been doing that all his working life, taking no notice of those over him. Con Malone would have been the same: two stalwarts at the barricades. Another world, another time, when unions had been a force, had controlled seventy-five per cent of the workers, instead of thirty-five per cent as now. Things would never be the same again.

'Where are they now?'

Bremner nodded towards the administration hut. 'Give 'em my regards.' He raised his middle finger.

'I'll tell my old man you haven't changed. He'd love to be here with you.'

Bremner shook his head again; his helmet fell

off this time and he held it to his chest like a knight who knew the battle was over. 'No, he wouldn't, mate. The old days are gone, for ever. He's just lucky he's retired.'

I'll never be able to tell him that.

Bremner was about to walk away when Clements said, 'Have you had a detective named Boston down here talking to you?'

Bremner turned back. 'Yeah. Why?'

'What did he want?'

'He's got a bee in his bonnet that it's union in-fighting that caused these murders. He used to work outa Day Street station, I remember him when I was on the wharves. He's always been anti-union.'

'What did you tell him?'

'To get stuffed and piss off.'

'What'd he say to that?' said Malone with malice towards Boston.

'Nothing. He just walked over and talked to our mate over there.' Another nod towards the Allied Trades man. 'Look, forget we had anything to do with these murders. Talk to the Chinese, all of 'em.'

'What makes you say that?'

'There's nobody hates like brothers. That's one of the things you learn in union politics. We all call each other Brother This and Brother That, but Christ, when we fall out it's the old Cain and Abel thing. Look at the Chinese, Scobie, don't waste your time with us.'

He walked away into the depths of the concrete honeycomb. The two detectives looked at each other. 'Maybe he has a point,' said Clements.

'If he's right, then I don't fancy our chances.'

They walked across to the administration hut, asked for the site manager and he came to the door, looking as irritated as before.

'Yes, what is it?'

'We'd like to talk to the two Chinese gentlemen, the engineers, on your staff.'

'They're not here. They phoned in and said they were going to the funeral of their boss.'

'Their boss being Mr Shan Yang?' said Malone, and the site manager nodded. 'There's no funeral today. Mr Shan's body hasn't been released from the morgue yet. Have these two fellers ever discussed Mr Shan with you?'

'Look —'

'No, *you* look, Mr . . . ?'

The site manager hesitated, then stepped back. 'Come inside. I'm Ron Fadiman. I'm sorry — things are in a mess this morning — I've got shit on the liver —'

'Join the club,' said Malone.

Fadiman looked over his shoulder at them and Clements said, 'Every second day. He's getting worse as he gets older.'

Fadiman grinned and led them down the long narrow room to his desk. All along one wall were slanting desk-tops holding drawings; half a dozen men sat at or leaned on the desks. They looked curiously at the two detectives, but just nodded and said nothing. Malone was abruptly aware of the atmosphere, a familiar one: the unease of people who found themselves, unexpectedly, on the outskirts of murder.

The site manager was showing the same unease. He gestured to the two detectives to sit down on a couple of folding metal chairs, sat down on a swivel chair and leaned forward with his elbows on his flat-top desk. 'What happened Friday night, those murders — it's shaken this place from top to bottom. I tried to get in touch with Tong and Guo first thing Saturday morning, but there was no answer. Same thing Sunday. I was beginning to wonder if they'd been done in, too —'

'Why'd you think that?' said Clements.

'I dunno. I dunno why the other three guys were killed . . . Then Guo Yi called in this morning, said they were going to the funeral and hung up.'

'What were their names?' Clements had his notebook out.

'Tong Haifeng and Guo Yi. We called them Harry and Joe.'

'Where did they live?'

'Tong lived at Bondi and Guo at Cronulla.'

The two detectives looked at each other; then Malone said, 'They have families?'

'Not as far as I know, not here anyway. Guo sometimes mentioned a girlfriend, but we never saw her. He was always more outgoing than his mate, at least as far as we were concerned. They never really told us anything about themselves.'

'Did they like being here? In Sydney, I mean.'

'Oh sure. But even then they were cautious, as if they were afraid of someone telling them to pull their heads in.'

'So they weren't dissidents? Political, I mean.'

'I wouldn't say so. They were both engineers, up to the mark in technical knowledge, but lacking practical experience, I'd say. This was their first time abroad. They didn't know how to deal with the guys on the job, that was their main trouble.'

'So Roley Bremner's told us,' said Clements. 'We understand there are three partners in the consortium building Olympic Tower. Has there been a dominant partner?'

Fadiman looked beyond the two detectives. Malone half-turned and saw that the other men in the long hut had stopped work; one could almost see their ears standing out from their heads like pink antennae. 'Any comment, fellers?' he said. 'Whatever you say doesn't go out of this room.'

The man nearest, a curly-haired man in his fifties with a beer belly and tired rheumy eyes, looked at his colleagues, then back at Malone. 'No, Ron can say it all.'

'Thanks,' said Ron drily.

Malone turned back to him. 'Say it, Ron.'

'Well —' Fadiman picked with one finger at the paper on his desk, as if pecking out his words on an invisible word processor: 'Well, yes. Bund, the Hong Kong people, have tried to run things. Right from the jump they've acted as if they're the senior partner.'

'Are they?' asked Clements.

'Forty per cent. The others own thirty per cent each. Darrel —' he nodded at the beer-bellied man — 'Darrel looked them up when things got stroppy once. They were pushing us, wanting us to get ahead of schedule.'

'Did you get any support from the other partners or did they just sit back?'

Fadiman nodded. 'I dunno who organized it, but one day half a dozen heavies came down here. They just walked on the site, said they represented Kelly Investments and there was to be no more pressure and we were to stick to schedule and to budget. Mr Shan and Madame Tzu were here that day. They just stood off and watched, said nothing. I don't think they understood how capitalism works.' He grinned and some of the men laughed.

'Madame Tzu,' said Malone, 'had she been interfering much?'

Fadiman looked along at his colleagues, then back at Malone and Clements. 'Who knows? She'd come out from China or Hong Kong, we were never sure where she came from — she'd come out maybe once a month, sometimes twice, her and Shan, and every time that was when the pressure started. She was the Dragon Lady, as far as we were concerned. Women are always a pain on projects like this, but she was worse than most.'

All the other chauvinists in the hut nodded.

'Have you had a visit from any of the partners this morning?'

'Yeah, Madame Tzu was here. I guess she's taking over from Mr Shan — she said she would be here for a month.'

'What about the other partners? They come down here?'

'Not so far. I got the impression the Tzu woman was speaking for all of them. Maybe she wasn't, but you don't question Madame Tzu.'

'Okay,' said Clements, 'let's have the addresses of Mr Tong and Mr Guo.'

Fadiman flipped open a notebook, wrote the addresses on a slip of drawing paper and handed it to Clements. 'If you contact them, tell 'em I want them here tomorrow morning seven sharp. They've left some work undone.'

'Righto,' said Malone. 'That'll do for now. If Madame Tzu or anyone from Lotus or Kelly comes down here, let 'em know we've been here.'

Fadiman stood up. 'At the moment we're all wondering if this site is jinxed. It was a hole in the ground for seven years, now *this*.'

'I think you're safe. Kelly Investments and their heavies aren't going to let murder get in their way.'

Fadiman looked at them quizzically. 'You seem to know them.'

'We're old friends,' said Malone.

Outside the administration hut Malone and Clements went looking for the muscleman from Allied Trades.

'Jason?' said a workman. 'Nah, he's gone. Said he had to go down to Union Hall on business. He left in a hurry.'

2

The gilt lettering said the door led to the offices of seven companies. Top of the list was Landfall Holdings Proprietary Limited, the sort of title that could own half a continent and still tell the casual enquirer to mind his own business. At the bottom of the list was Kelly Investments Pty Ltd, the gilt fresher than that above it. The Aldwych companies did not encourage shareholders it didn't know or control. Jack Aldwych had run his gangs the same way. He had never believed in democracy, which only held up progress and company meetings.

The suite of offices was a long way from the seedy room above a delicatessen in Darlinghurst from which Aldwych had run his old empire. They were on an upper floor of the AMP Tower, a fifty-storey fortress owned by one of the biggest insurance companies in the nation; rock-solid conservatism surrounded the Aldwyches, father and son, and the only hint of blood sport, an occupational hazard with gang leaders, were the old English hunting prints on the dark green walls. The attractive brunette on the reception desk, soft-spoken and genteel, at least on the surface, was a distant reminder of Aldwych's past: she was the granddaughter of a brothel madam who had worked for him. The four other girls and the two men who worked for Landfall were all products of private schools and strangers to commercial sex, not needing the money and keeping their amateur status. The legal and stockbroking firms in the building were raffish compared to Jack Aldwych in his corporation identity.

He, his son and Les Chung sat in the main office that looked out to the harbour, the Opera House and the Bridge. Jack Junior, seated behind the big leather-topped desk, was as distinguished-looking as his father; there was none, however, of the soiled edges that occasionally showed in his father. As were showing now.

'Les, if any of your Hong Kong friends are thinking of muscling in on us, tell 'em to forget it. I haven't forgotten how to play dirty —'

'Dad —' Jack Junior could still feel afraid when the gangster side of his father broke through the veneer of the recent years.

'It's all right, Jack,' said Les Chung, addressing Junior. Like Jack Senior he looked like a banker: dark suit, wide-spread collar, a dark blue tie decorated with tiny shields. He had learned long ago how attention had to be paid to understatement. The tie suggested a university or an exclusive club; but he wore it with such modesty that nobody ever asked its connection. He had a dozen of them, made for him by a tailor in a back street of Hong Kong who had a talent for design but thought Oxford was a type of cloth. Chung had learned, too, the value of a quiet voice; he would never have been heard in the clamour of the back streets of Kunming and Hong Kong; but here in Sydney he was heard and listened to. Now he was addressing Jack Senior.

'My Hong Kong friends, as you call them, had nothing to do with what happened Friday night —'

'How d'you know?' The rough edges were still showing.

'I made some calls as soon as I got home Friday night. It worries people if you call them in the middle of the night, it sharpens their perceptions. They called me back Saturday morning. What happened Friday night didn't originate in Hong Kong. Take my word for it, Jack.'

'Then who? You think it's our Bund mates?'

'I don't know.' Les Chung sounded chagrined; his whole life had been built on knowing the next step, whether forwards or backwards, and the next and the next. He felt at the moment that he was in iron boots and calf-deep in thick mud. 'The unions, for instance, wouldn't go in for this sort of thing.'

'I'd soon straighten 'em out if they did. Anyhow, it ain't — isn't their method, killing bosses. They used to do each other, but not the bosses.

The thing is — they were after you too, Les. If they'd got you, Jack and I would of been next on the list.'

'You think I hadn't thought of that? But we still don't know why.'

'Have you talked to your Triad mates? They know anything?'

'They know nothing nor do they want to know. Or if they do, they're not telling me.' Les Chung knew it was useless denying to Aldwych that he had contacts with the Triads. He never did business with them, but he paid his compliments to the network. 'They would never get involved in a messy business like this one.'

Aldwych stared out the window. A helicopter, like a huge fly, swooped by; a cameraman hung out of its open door, photographing — what? Aldwych turned back into the room, as if dodging the camera. He had hated photographers as much as rival gang leaders.

'There's a lot of opposition,' said Jack Junior, 'to overseas investors. Selling off the farm, that sort of thing.'

'I'm not an overseas investor,' said Les Chung, digging out some national pride, though he wondered where it came from. 'Neither were Sam Feng and Norman Sun. We are — were — all homegrown.'

'I didn't mean you. As soon as we announced the consortium, when we bought up Olympic, there were a couple of Town Hall councillors who got up on their hind legs and did the usual barking. And there were some MPs in parliament, here and down in Canberra. They all know it's good for some votes with the usual xenophobes.'

'I was one of them once,' said Aldwych.

Les Chung smiled at him. 'What changed your mind?'

'Money. What else? It's always more bankable than patriotism.'

Jack Junior smiled weakly. He was every bit as commercial-minded as his father, but the blood of his mother still flowed in him, sometimes uncomfortably. Shirl Aldwych had always had a little weep on Anzac Day and often stopped in mid-stride when the radio played 'Advance Australia Fair'.

'The feller who did these murders,' said Les Chung, 'wasn't a nutter issuing a warning to overseas investors. I *saw* it, the whole thing. It was — *calculated.* The nuts with causes — greenies, the anti-immigration lot, the anti-abortionists — they make a song and dance about their protests — but they always make sure there are cameras present, otherwise what's the point of a demonstration? This feller didn't want anything like that. He fired six shots, as calmly and deliberately as I'm talking to you now, then just walked out through the kitchen and disappeared.'

'Didn't any of your staff try to stop him?' said Jack Junior.

The two older men looked at each other.

Aldwych shrugged: *the boy doesn't know any better.*

Chung said, 'You don't have to be a hero to be a chef or a kitchenhand. The killer just nodded to them, walked straight through the kitchen and out the back door. Wally Smith, our head chef, said he didn't even hurry.'

'Jesus!'

Aldwych rarely sounded exasperated, but he was losing patience with this situation. In the past members of his gang had been murdered and there had been three attempts on his own life; but he had always known who the killers or would-be killers were and had dealt with them. He had never been the meticulous planner that Les Chung was, but he would not have been out of place on any military staff, except for his one-time lack of polish. He had always had a professional grasp of strategy and tactics. In twenty-five years only one of his planned hold-ups had been bungled and that because one of the gang members had turned up high on cocaine; a week later the man had disappeared, never to be seen again, victim of another strategy, one that had no time for fools who believed you had to be on a high to rob a bank. Aldwych had always been a down-to-earth, no-fuss leader. Sometimes, in thoughts he would never have confessed to anyone, he had visions of himself as Prime Minister.

He looked out again at the harbour. The helicopter was now on the other side of the water, cruising past Kirribilli. There, under the eastern shadow of the Harbour Bridge, Asian money had come in and begun buying up the water-front, building luxury apartments that had been bought up by Asian buyers. He did not resent them, neither the developers nor the residents. Now that he had given up robbing it, he had come to love Sydney. Anything that enhanced its value got no objection from him. He had had no reservations when Les Chung had first come to him with the suggestion that they should go into partnership with the Shanghai lot. Jack Junior had done due diligence and the Bund Corporation, at first, had come through with solid credentials. Only later had the Aldwyches come to realize that every breeze that blew out of China brought another smokescreen. It was no wonder, said Jack Junior, who had done a quick course in Chinese history, that Confucius had died a disappointed old man.

Aldwych turned back to look at his son and Les Chung. 'We get this thing under control. We see the Olympic delegation don't cancel — that would be throwing shit at us. You better see your mate at Town Hall, Les, tell him to get his finger out and see this doesn't spoil our picture with the Olympic mob.'

Chung nodded. 'We may have to oil his palm a bit more, but he'll do it.'

Aldwych went on: 'We take control now. Between us we've got the whip-handle.' Or, in past terms, the iron bar. 'Our sixty per cent says

115

we run things from now on. Nobody does nothing —' the old rough edges were showing again '— without our say-so. Everybody — the architects, the engineers, the union blokes — they're all gunna be responsible to Jack here. Okay?'

Les Chung came from a land of emperors; he knew one when he saw one. He just nodded.

'What about Madame Tzu?' asked Jack Junior.

'We get rid of her.'

Jack Junior said nothing, afraid to ask the next question.

3

When Malone and Clements returned to Homicide, Clarrie Binyan was waiting for them. As always he looked serene, as if while waiting he had taken a trip back through the Dreamtime and found it to be everything he had been told. He had once remarked to Malone that there was more comfort in myth and legend than in religion. Tribal elders were less trouble than priests.

He pointed to two plastic envelopes on Malone's desk. 'Six bullets and fired cartridge cases out of gun A. One of each out of gun B. Gun A was used in the Chinatown job, gun B did the one at Bondi.'

'What sort of pieces?' asked Malone.

116

'The Bondi gun was a standard Thirty-two, could of been a Fabrique Nationale. You know, the old Browning. As for the other —' He shook his head. 'I won't guess at this stage. The fired cartridge cases are all 7.65 millimetres by 17. That's not a common calibre.'

'Do the Chinese, mainland Chinese, make their own brand of weapon?'

'Yeah, they do. I've got one of my blokes looking into the details. They didn't have a great deal of their own handguns before World War Two and most of their early stuff was based on Russian models. There was a lot of gun-running by foreigners in the middle of the nineteenth century, but the Chinese didn't try to copy much of what they bought. Most of it was sold to war-lords who weren't interested in manufacturing. Now things have opened up in China they make copies of everything but catapults. Bloody awful stuff.'

'Where did you learn all this?'

'I'm supposed to be an expert on guns, aren't I? I could give you a history lesson on bows and arrows and boomerangs, too.' He grinned. 'I boned up on the Chinese because they invented gunpowder. They're pretty hip on weaponry of all sorts, these days, though they wouldn't win any quality control awards. You're pretty sure the murders were done by Chinks?'

The one true native, he used all the politically incorrect terms — Chinks, wogs, slopeheads — without apology. Yet, if asked, he would have

117

said he meant no offence. He had been a target, coon or Abo or darky, for so long he was past offence.

'We think so,' said Clements. 'But it's all guesses at the moment.'

'Especially now you've told us the Bondi job was done by a different gun,' said Malone. 'The only connection is that they were all Chinese.'

'And the Bondi guy lived in a flat owned by one of the Chinatown guys,' said Clements.

'So there could be two hitmen running around?' said Binyan.

Then Kagal and Gail Lee came into the big room and Malone beckoned them into his office. Clements shifted to one side on the couch, his usual rest, and Gail sat down beside him. Kagal leaned against the door jamb.

'No luck at Cronulla,' he said. 'The bird had flown. Looks as if she had a boyfriend — he'd flown, too.'

'A guy named Guo Yi?' said Clements.

Kagal and Gail looked at each other in surprise; then Gail said, 'You've heard of him?'

'He worked on Olympic Tower, him and a guy named Tong Haifeng, who lived out at Bondi, just around the corner from Mr Zhang, Saturday's hit victim.'

'What did you find out?' said Malone.

'The girl, evidently, was friendly with the neighbours, but the guy kept to himself. They lived in one of the new blocks of flats near the beach, a furnished two-bedroomer that was costing them three-fifty a week. Not bad for a student,' said Kagal, who, as a student, had lived at home in a house that had since sold for a million and a quarter. He supported double standards: they made conscience much easier.

'Not with twenty-five million in her account,' said Malone, and looked at Binyan. 'You just went pale, Clarrie.'

'I always do when you mention white fellers' money.'

'This is Chinese money,' said Malone, and explained.

'You find anything in the flat?' asked Clements.

'Nothing that would identify them,' said Gail. 'It was just like the flat out at Bondi, the Zhang flat. It had been cleaned out.'

Malone, out of the corner of his eye, saw that Clarrie Binyan was watching Gail Lee, observing how she fitted in here. The old and the new: the two outsiders on the banks of the mainstream. Eighteen months ago a newly elected woman MP had sparked off a debate about immigration and race; old prejudices and bigotry had been revived. The furore had since quietened down, but there were still patches of thin ice everywhere.

If Gail had noticed Binyan's study of her, she gave no indication of it. Except: 'So far we're chasing Chinese shadows. But what if Jack Aldwych had something to do with all this?'

'I don't think so,' said Malone. 'This looks like

119

one occasion when Jack is lily white.'

'If the killer was Chinese,' said Clements, 'Jack would never have used him. His hitmen were always homegrown.'

Malone could feel the thin ice beginning to crack. He stood up. 'I'm going out to Bondi to look at Mr Tong's place. You come with me, Gail.'

As he and Gail went out of his office he heard Clarrie Binyan say with his dry chuckle, 'I'm homegrown, Russ. You think Jack would of used me?'

'Shit,' said Clements, and looked after Gail, his tongue between his teeth as if he wanted to bite it.

Then Malone and Gail were out of earshot at the front door. As he slipped his card into the security slot he looked at her; he was surprised to see she was smiling. She said, 'Some day they'll learn.'

'Russ?'

'Everybody. You have no idea how superior my father can be about the — the homegrown. Yet he goes to football matches and he stands up straighter than anyone else and sings louder when they play "Advance Australia Fair".'

'What about you?'

'I'm half and half. They've never written anthems for us.' She was smiling still, but it looked a little forced now.

They drove out to Bondi through one of those days when Sydney looks like a glossy advertisement for itself. In the bright sunlight everything looked so *clean;* the city and its suburbs on some days had a way of putting a gloss on its shabbiness. The purple smoke of an occasional jacaranda showed in a garden; an Illawarra flame tree demanded attention. The sky was flawless; because they were driving eastwards, towards the sea, there was no pollution haze on the horizon. A good day to be alive, not to be looking into the possibility of another murder.

Clements had been wrong when he had said that Tong Haifeng lived just round the corner from Zhang Yong. He lived in a block of expensive apartments at the southern end of the beach; if he was keen-sighted he wouldn't have needed binoculars to admire the bare bosoms on the sands below. Whatever his background in China, he had treated himself well in Australia.

Gail parked the car in a No Parking zone, got out and looked down at the bodies on the beach. 'What do you think attracted him here? The boobs or the surf?'

It was the first time in all the months she had been with Homicide that she had been less than formal. 'Aren't the Chinese supposed to be straitlaced about —' He gestured at the bodies below where all the laces were undone.

'The old ones, maybe. I don't know about the young ones. I see pictures of them, on TV, the ones who can afford it are all wearing Armani, Gucci, stuff like that. I don't think Italians ever designed anything to be straitlaced.'

121

He grinned, suddenly warming to her. 'I'd like you to meet my daughters some time.'

'Thank you,' she said, but he wasn't sure whether she welcomed the invitation or not.

They found a woman cleaner who, after they had produced their badges, used a master key to let them into a flat on the third floor. 'I dunno I should be doing this — I don't clean for this guy —'

'Did you ever speak to him?'

'Never. You wanna know anything about him, you better ask someone else. There. Close the door when you come out. Don't tell anyone who let you in.'

'We'll say we used a sledgehammer,' said Malone.

'I seen youse do it on TV. Very effective.' She went away, convinced sledgehammers were everyday equipment for cops.

She was about to step into the lift when Gail went after her. 'Does he own the flat or rent it?'

'Rents it, I think. This whole block is owned by a Chinese gentleman. People who live here ain't short of a dollar. Don't tell anyone I said that.' She was in her forties, but her face had the look of someone who had been that age for the past twenty years. If she looked up into the sun it was to look for clouds: she had suffered that sort of life. 'He's the only Chinese living here. What's he done, anyway?'

'Nothing, as far as we know. Thanks, we'll close up when we leave.'

122

The lift door closed on the woman and Gail came back to Malone. 'Owned by a Chinese gentleman. Mr Feng, maybe?'

When they were in the apartment Malone looked around. 'Looks like he didn't want to be reminded of home.'

If Tong Haifeng had been nostalgic for China he had not relieved his homesickness with the apartment's furnishings. Everything was starkly modern: black leather couch and chairs, glass tables, thick white rugs on the black-stained floor. The stark white walls held no scrolls, no painted silks; a Hockney California print faced a Leroy Neiman print of a baseballer; Mr Tong seemed America-oriented. The view from the apartment's wide balcony would have brought no memories of home.

'You reckon this stuff is his or comes with the apartment?' said Malone. 'What would a place like this cost?'

'To rent? Four or five hundred unfurnished, maybe seven-fifty furnished like this. Not bad for a junior engineer.'

'Unless he, too, had twenty million in the bank. Righto, let's start looking.'

As far as they knew no crime had been committed here, so Physical Evidence could not be called in. If Mr Tong came back while they were here, there could be ructions; they had no warrant to search. But Malone was not the first cop who had learned that if you lagged one step behind civil rights you would never catch up. If conscience worried you, you put it on hold till you were caught out. Pragmatism was never based on conscience.

If Gail Lee was worried, there was no sign of it. She went through the flat with the thoroughness of a second wife inspecting a first wife's house-work. Malone followed her, empty-handed: if Tong Haifeng had left anything of himself in the flat it could only be a fingerprint and they had no equipment to register that.

'I thought there might be something in the bathroom cabinet,' said Gail. 'But nothing, no medicine, not even toothpaste. He's taken all his toilet things.' She looked around. 'There's something missing.'

'What?'

'In the flat out at Cronulla there was a phone connection but no phone. Same here. They must have used mobiles.'

'You got yours?'

She produced it from her handbag, handed it to him.

He dialled Homicide: 'Russ? Our feller's gone. Get on to Immigration, I want a watch on all air-ports. He may be scooting back to China.'

'What've we got on him?'

'Nothing. Tell them we just want him for questioning. The same time, tell them to look for the Cronulla pair, the girl and Mr Guo. I want 'em all, the quicker the sooner.'

'You sound as if you've got shit on the liver again.'

'I've got a feeling we're going to have to take the Great Wall of China apart brick by brick . . . When you've finished with Immigration, get on to Telephone Intercepts. Get them to contact Telstra or Optus, we want a trace on two mobiles. Tong Haifeng, Guo Yi or the girl. They made that call this morning to the site manager at Olympic, that would've been on a mobile, I'd guess. Ask Intercepts to get on to it right away.'

He hung up as there was a ring at the front doorbell. He looked at Gail. 'It can't be Mr Tong. Open it.'

She opened the door. Jack Aldwych and Blackie Ovens stood there, no surprise at all on the two faces that had learned long ago never to show surprise when faced by cops.

'Hello, Scobie. Are we looking for the same bloke?'

Chapter Four

1

Queen Victoria, a lady not renowned for taste, would possibly have been proud of Sydney's Town Hall. Located in the heart of the city it is built on a graveyard; it could be mistaken for the outsize mausoleum of some mad emperor. It has all the style of Victorian bad taste, carbuncled and columned till one's eyes cross in reluctant admiration of the architectural excesses. Its tower rises like a stone wedding cake; one would not be surprised to see stone kewpies of a mayoral couple at the very top. Only the clock in the tower has managed to escape ornamentation: someone appreciated the simplicity of Time.

Its interior, however, has some dignity, even if heavy. Decorative tiled floors, vaulted ceilings, magnificent panelling: Lisa enjoyed wandering through the building in her spare moments. In an odd way it brought back memories of her days on the diplomatic circuit in London, where the interiors of many buildings had been better than the exteriors.

Though she had been working at Town Hall a month this was only the second committee meeting she had attended. She was still getting

126

to know the councillors and their affiliations: the Labor councillors, the left-of-centre Democrats, the Reform conservatives, the green-hued Independents. Though she had been only twenty-one she had spent enough time on the diplomatic circuit to appreciate that politics, at whatever level, was a swamp where webbed feet were essential. She had been the High Commissioner's private secretary, despite her youth; she had been resented by older public servants, but she had managed to stay afloat. Public service was often politics at its lowest level.

'We've got to do something about the poor bloody battlers down in South Ward. We're always hearing about the poor bloody battlers out west, but we've got our own right here on our doorstep.' He was a thin intense man with a beard; someone had once told him he looked Christlike and he'd been striving ever since for the image. He wore his sympathies like a hair shirt, one that scratched and irritated his fellow Democrats.

'The battlers, the poor bloody battlers,' said the Deputy Lord Mayor and made it sound like his daily mantra; with the talent of the truly hypocritical, he even made it sound sincere. 'The Bible says they're always with us.'

'They're a fucking nuisance,' said the chairman of the works committee, a Reform councillor. 'Our job would be much easier if everyone was rich.'

'Like you,' said an Independent, a grey-haired, blunt-faced man who had travelled the spectrum of politics and finished up adrift.

Lisa sometimes marvelled at the gems of wit and wisdom that dropped on the table at the two meetings she had attended. The public was not admitted to these gatherings, as it was to general council meetings; here behaviour was unrestrained, knives flashed, abuse smoked like fuses that never actually set off an explosion. Labor, the Democrats and the Reform party had an equal number of councillors; the balance of power was held by three Independents, all independent of each other and all as unpredictable in their flights of fancy as blind birds. Lisa had come to wonder how the city survived its council.

'Let's get down to business,' said the Deputy Lord Mayor. He had all the usual authority of a compromise candidate; he looked for friends, for supporters, in a wilderness of his own making. He was big and fat and could convince himself that a slush fund was an environment contribution towards protecting a wetland; bribes were alms offering by concerned developers. Those citizens who knew him hoped he would be gone before the Olympics year. 'What's on the agenda?'

'It's not on the agenda,' said a Democrat, a once sensible and honest man worn down by disillusion, 'but these murders of top businessmen don't say much for our image. I believe you were there, Mrs Malone, when it was all happening, as the cricket commentators say.'

'Yes,' said Lisa. 'But the last thing on my mind was the city's image.'

'But we *must* think of it,' said the Deputy Lord Mayor, concerned for image, since he had none of his own.

'Your husband is handling the case?' That was the chairman of the works committee.

'Yes, Mr Brode.'

'How's it going? Any suspects?'

'I couldn't say. We don't exchange views on our respective jobs.'

'I'm glad to hear it.' Brode was a large fair man who would run to fat when he slowed down. He had thinning wavy hair, a large nose and a mouth in which the lips were constantly moving, as if practicing what he was about to say next. Despite his fairness he had very dark brown eyes that, like his lips, were never still. Lisa knew that nobody at Town Hall liked him, but popularity, it seemed, was never one of his ambitions.

'Why has that project always been such a bloody headache?' asked another councillor, an Independent who always wore green shirts as a token of his leanings. 'We should've put a park there.'

'Grow up,' said Brode. 'Parks never brought in revenue.'

'Money. That's all you think of.'

'I've been looking into who's building Olympic Tower,' said a second Independent, a middle-aged woman with a shark's smile and a talent for tearing budgets to shreds. 'Two men with criminal records are linked with the two Australian companies and God knows what sort of record the Chinese company has. Who okayed the project?'

Lisa saw all heads turn towards Brode. He ignored the stares, gave his flinty attention to Mrs Harrity, the Independent. 'I did. What of it?'

She looked at the notebook in front of her; she carried it everywhere with her, like a weapon. 'You were on the council several years ago when the original project was okayed. Did you have anything to do with that one?'

'Yes. What's all this leading to?'

'My notes say that you were a director of the company that did the feasibility study on the project. You were on the town planning committee at the same time.'

'I stood aside from the committee so there'd be no conflict of interest.'

'I'm sure you did.' The shark's smile had all the good humour of a set of butcher's knives. 'I just happen to believe that "conflict of interest" is as empty a phrase as "see you later". Which one invariably does. Did you stand aside when it was decided that the present project could increase its height by four levels?'

'Hold on a minute,' said the Deputy Lord Mayor, whose name was Goodenough, one that fell short of his aspirations. 'What extra four levels?'

'I'm going on Mrs Malone's report —'

The atmosphere in the committee room, never warm, had abruptly chilled. Lisa felt a certain amount of the chill directed towards her.

'My report was not meant to be a critical one — I just assumed the extra four levels had been approved. I was asked to give the latest assessment on hotel accommodation, present and future —' She was not flustered, but she was suddenly aware that she had been left holding someone else's can. 'The extra four levels in the hotel section of Olympic Tower will give another sixty rooms.'

'Well, well,' said Goodenough. 'Looks like you have some explaining to do, Raymond, old chap.'

'Who gets the extra revenue this time?' said Yagovitch in the green shirt. 'You should've let it be a park, mate.'

'I'm not your fucking mate,' said Brode. 'This was decided down in the planning department.'

'It may well have been,' said Mrs Harrity, 'but nobody on committee appears to have heard of it. If it hadn't been for Mrs Malone's diligence —'

'Thank you,' said Lisa, 'but don't blame me.'

'I'm not, my dear — we're grateful to you.' Due to an unfortunate array of dental work Mrs Harrity was unable to give a warm smile; but she tried. 'Something smells. I think we should have the head of the planning department up here, maybe he can enlighten us.'

There were seven councillors present; no final decisions were made here but went before the full council. The seventh member, Brode's fellow Reform councillor, at last spoke up. He was a squat portly man with a florid face and a bouffant crop of white hair; his name was Pascal, he was the head of the biggest legal firm in the city and he had been a city councillor for fifteen years. He could smell scandal at a hundred paces.

'Don't let's open doors till we are sure what's on the other side. I think we should have a closed discussion on this — and I mean *closed*. Would you ladies mind leaving us?'

A secretary and Lisa were the only two non-committee members present. They both stood up and without a word went out of the big room, closing the door behind them.

'That's the last we'll hear of that.' The secretary was a slim woman in her mid-thirties with enough hair to have got a starring role in *The Bold and the Beautiful*; unlike the players in that soap opera she never let any crisis trouble her. 'We can close our notebooks.'

'What do you mean?'

There were half a dozen people in the hallway, sitting on chairs as they waited to be called to report to the committee. The secretary, whom Lisa knew only as Rosalie, as if secretaries didn't have surnames, jerked her head and led Lisa along the hall and out into the main vestibule. Here there was traffic, but no one, as in the hallway, had their ears cocked.

'Look, Lisa, you're on the Olympic advisory staff, right? From now on that's all this council is going to think about — the Olympics.' She took out a compact, made sure her auburn mane had not blown away. 'I dunno what went on down at Olympic Tower, but whatever it was, that lot back in that room aren't going to broadcast it. Not even Mr Yagovitch to his Greenie mates. Someone obviously copped a handout —'

'Mr Brode?'

'No names, Lisa, please. I've kept this job for seventeen years by never hearing or mentioning a name, okay? Sydney is the squeaky clean city for the next eighteen months and nobody is going to be allowed to rub any dirt into it. You, me, Mrs Harrity, Mr Yagovitch, anybody. You better believe it. Mr Pascal will give them legal advice, for which he'll charge the council, or his firm will, and we'll go back in there and it will be "any further business?" '

Lisa smiled. 'You know, I worked on the diplomatic circuit in London when I was young — I keep hearing echoes.'

'Was it much different?'

'Only the language. Foreign ministers and ambassadors didn't use four-letter words — not to each other. In private, probably.'

'It'd be different if we women ran the world.' Rosalie put away her compact, hair still intact. 'But then, who am I kidding?'

2

'I only met Tong and Guo once,' said Jack Aldwych. 'Les Chung gave a reception on the day we started the job. They'd just arrived from China. They were supposed to be Shan's protégés, but they were a couple uppity young bastards. Like Blackie here used to be.'

Blackie Ovens grinned, his face crumbling like a soft muffin; all the hard-baked toughness of his earlier days had gone. 'You'd of done me, I ever got uppity with you.'

'How were they with Madame Tzu?' asked Malone.

'You've met her? Stainless steel right through, eh? I never saw 'em with her, but they wouldn't of got uppity with her. Not her.'

Blackie had found coffee, biscuits and some fresh milk in the kitchen and now the four of them were sitting out on the balcony, as relaxed as tenants. Below them the Monday leisure class dotted the beach: waiters, drug couriers, retirees, young mothers and hookers. A dozen or more bosoms were bared to the sun, nipples on their way to melanoma; bare buttocks invited the

134

sun to zero in on twin targets. Sun cancers were what happened to other people.

'What brought you here?' said Malone. 'Did you think Tong or Guo might be the feller in the stocking mask on Friday night?'

'It's a thought.' Aldwych this morning wore a blue linen shirt and slacks, a light blue cardigan and a Panama hat. He had been a rough-and-ready dresser in his early days, but Shirl, over the years, had groomed him. Left to his own taste he would have reverted to those early days, but Blackie, an unlikely valet who had revered the late Mrs Aldwych, saw to it that standards were kept up. 'If Tong had been here, Blackie was gunna ask him a question or two. He'd of soon told us if he'd been there Friday night.'

'Jack, I asked you to leave this to us —'

'So you did. I must of forgot.' Aldwych smiled above his coffee.

'You're never going to impress young cops like Gail if you keep going back on your word. Stay out of it, Jack . . . Who brought the original capital for the Bund Corporation into Australia? Mr Shan or Madame Tzu?'

'Either. We weren't able to check on that. The money was already here when they came to us.'

'Were you and the other locals asking for another injection of capital?'

'Why?'

'There's fifty-one million frozen in the accounts of two Chinese students brought in through a Hong Kong bank. One of the students lived over there —' Malone nodded inland. 'He was murdered Friday night or Saturday morning, early.'

'Same gun?' Aldwych never missed a trick in the murder game.

'No-o.'

'So where's the connection?'

'The other student was a girl who lived out in Cronulla with Mr Guo. She and Guo and Tong have disappeared. Do you know anything about the fifty-one million? You or Jack Junior?'

Blackie Ovens had screwed up his eyes at the sum mentioned, as if trying to count it up in his mind; but Aldwych had remained impassive: 'No, we know nothing. Go on. Thanks, Miss Lee,' as Gail offered him more coffee.

'If Les Chung had copped it on Friday night along with Mr Feng and Mr Sun, who'd take over Lotus Corporation?'

'The families, I guess. Les and I never discussed it.'

'How much would it take to buy out Lotus?'

'I see what you're getting at. More than fifty million. The stage we've got to now, nobody would sell out under a hundred million. More — two hundred and fifty.'

'What would you do if you found the Bund Corporation was your only partner?'

'I'd be very careful. I might send Blackie to do some due diligence.'

Blackie shook his head. 'I'm too old, boss, to take on any big stuff.'

'You'd need more than an iron bar and a couple of heavies, Jack,' said Malone. He looked at Gail. 'Go and knock on a few doors, see what you can find out about Mr Tong.'

As Gail disappeared into the flat Aldwych looked after her. 'Is she any help, being Chinese?'

'Half-Chinese, Jack. She's a mongrel, as one of our enlightened mayors over in South Australia once called them. But anyone will tell you, mongrels are tougher than pure breds.'

'Oh, I dunno,' said Aldwych with a grin. 'Blackie and me are pure breds. That true-blue Aussie mayor would of been proud of us.'

Malone turned to look out at the beach, not seeing the bare bosoms, just the waves rolling in with the inevitability of government interference. At last he said, 'Jack, the government is going to poke its nose into this sooner or later. It's been flat out for overseas investors — selling off the farm hasn't worried them. I dunno that it wanted Chinese investment, but it's got it and it hasn't squawked. Civil rights, all that sort of stuff, never worries a government when you wave money at it.'

'It didn't worry me, either,' said Aldwych, honesty glimmering out of him like a flickering candle. 'If that's what you're getting at?'

'Jack, I'd never accuse you of being a civil rights militant.'

'You had me worried for a minute.'

'*I'm* worried. If I don't get on top of this pretty soon, Homicide is going to be in a bigger hole than the one you took over when you started this project. We have eight unsolved murders on our books — the Opposition was asking questions about us last week in parliament. Not us specifically, but the Service in general. Now that we've rooted out most of the corruption, they want to know if we're now playing Boy Scouts. It's all political bullshit, but the media make the most of it. And sooner or later the government — in particular the Premier and our Police Minister, The Dutchman — will respond to it, as they always do, and we'll be booted up the arse. Now what I'm getting at, Jack, is this —'

'I thought we were getting to something,' said Aldwych, but offering no encouragement.

'You know more than you've told me. Right?'

Aldwych considered for a long moment. Then he said, 'Scobie, if you mean do I know who the killer is — no. I dunno any more than you do. But if you mean do I know what I'm gunna do from now on — yes, I do.'

'Are you going to tell me?'

'Not unless it pays me to tell you. I once told you I wasn't reformed, I'm just retired. I might come outa retirement, I dunno. If I do, you and me mightn't be friends any more. We'd be back on opposite sides of the fence again.'

The two men stared at each other; then Malone said quietly, 'I'd be sorry if it happened, Jack.'

'So would I.' The old crim sounded sincere. 'But nobody's ever taken anything away from me and I'm not gunna let it happen now.'

Malone looked at Blackie Ovens. 'What about you, Blackie? You going to come out of retirement?'

'Whatever the boss says,' said Blackie.

Malone sat back and sighed, stared out at the beach in silence. A breeze blew in from across the water; a thin curtain in the balcony doors shivered. A gull flew past, mewing like a lost child. Blackie gathered up the coffee cups and went back inside.

Then Gail came back. 'The only one home was the woman two doors along. She had nothing but good to say about Mr Tong. Friendly, helpful — a good neighbour, she said. Went to dinner a couple of times in her flat, had her and her husband in here for drinks. I just checked — there's good stuff in the drinks cabinet. Scotch, vodka, Aussie champagne. But —'

'But?' said Malone.

'About a week ago he suddenly changed. Passed her on the stairs, just nodded. She bailed him up eventually, she's the sort who would and asked him what was the matter. He was pretty short with her, but he said he would probably have to go back to China. She got the idea that didn't appeal to him at all.'

'Did he ever have any visitors?'

'Yes, a young Chinese couple used to come here — that could have been Guo and the Cronulla girl. And once or twice a middle-aged Chinese lady — very much the lady, the woman said. From the description, I'd say it was Madame Tzu. She was here Friday night, the last time the neighbour saw Mr Tong.'

3

The Chinese vice-consul did not appear to welcome Malone and Gail Lee. He was a tall thin young man, his mouth a hyphen between the parentheses of his hollow cheeks. He did not offer to shake hands, just stood behind his desk and said, 'Yes? You are police?'

Malone wondered how welcome police were in China. 'We'd like to ask some questions about some recent arrivals from your country.'

'People claiming to be political refugees?'

He knows bloody well that's not why we're here; State Police had nothing to do with political refugees. 'No. We're investigating murders, Mr Chen, not politics.'

Chen relaxed almost visibly. 'Sit down, sit down.' His thin narrow mouth had some difficulty in getting out the words; they came out as if he were blowing bubbles. 'Oh yes, we've read about those. Most regrettable. One doesn't expect that sort of thing in such a wonderful city as Sydney.'

Why not? Malone wanted to ask him.

'Do students who come in here,' said Gail, 'do they have to register with the consulate?'

'Of course. They like to keep in touch. You are referring to the unfortunate student Zhang?'

'He and another student named Li Ping.'

Chen opened his narrow eyes. 'She has been also murdered?'

'We don't know,' said Malone. 'She has disappeared, along with two other people, not students. Mr Tong and Mr Guo — are they registered with the consulate?'

'Yes.' He appeared to have a computer list in his head. Or perhaps the names were in the papers on his cluttered desk. 'They have disappeared also? That is very disturbing.'

'Yes, you could say that.'

Chen unexpectedly smiled, an unexpectedly sweet smile. 'We are not reluctant to co-operate, Inspector. But it is not in our character to fling the door wide open as soon as you knock.' Then somehow the small mouth widened further. 'You expect us to talk in aphorisms, don't you?'

Malone was aware that Gail, sitting beside him, was sharing Chen's smile. 'I have to tell you, Mr Chen, I am still working on Constable Lee's character.'

The Chinese consulate was in Woollahra, a habitat for consuls who had a yen for tree-lined streets, trendy cafés and smart restaurants; one worked better for one's country if one could leave the visas and go out and flash a Visa. The Chinese consulate had moved here after the taking over of Hong Kong, into a small mansion where the red flag hung from a flagpole in the garden like something that had blown in from another era.

Driving back from Bondi Gail had suggested dropping in at the consulate, which was on the way back to Strawberry Hills. Normally, when working on a case, she had a cool detachment; on this one there was an involvement, a *determination,* that he had not remarked before. As if she had stepped into an examination she had to pass.

'Persistence,' she said now to the two men, 'it's the secret of every woman's character.'

Chen and Malone exchanged male smiles; then Chen said, 'To be serious, we are very much disturbed about the young people you have mentioned.' Though he had to be less than thirty, he spoke as if the missing student and engineers were mere children. 'The Fraud Squad have already been to interview us about those extraordinary amounts in Zhang's and Li Ping's bank accounts.' Now that he was relaxed his words came out less explosively. 'That sort of thing is a great embarrassment.'

Malone had not expected such an admission. 'Can you explain how such an embarrassment was allowed to happen?'

'Mr Deng, our consul-general, is down in Canberra —'

'Deng?' said Gail. 'As in Deng Xiaoping?'

Again the sweet smile. 'No relation.'

'That must be fortunate for you. No nepotism so far south. My father told me nepotism rules

142

the roost in China.'

'Where does he come from?'

'Oh, he was born here. But my grandparents came from Hunan.'

'Whereabouts?'

'Changsha.'

The smile widened, was almost joyous. 'Where I come from! How remarkable!'

Nice work, Gail, thought Malone. She had Mr Chen completely relaxed.

'Does Mr Deng work out of Canberra?' asked Malone.

'Oh no, he is down there at a conference at the embassy. That is why I am holding the fort.'

Malone wondered if Deng would be as expansive as Chen now appeared to be. 'A conference on the murders we are investigating? On Mr Shan in particular?'

'We now have problems, just as you did in the 1980s. Entrepreneurs —' He shook his head.

'What do you do with them?'

Chen smiled again, less sweetly this time. 'We don't let them flee to Spain or Poland. We keep an eye on them, but they are slippery customers.'

'Was Mr Shan a slippery customer?' said Gail. 'He seemed to have an awful lot of money at his call.'

Suddenly the mouth was a hyphen again. 'Mr Shan was not who he claimed to be.'

'Who was he then?'

A moment's hesitation; but he was still relatively relaxed: 'He was General Huang Piao.

Ex-general, I should say.'

'Then he never worked for the Central China Department of Trade?' said Gail.

'Not as far as we know. He was retired from the army five years ago —'

'Retired?' said Malone. 'Or sacked?'

Chen shrugged. 'He had an honourable record. But —' Then he stopped: he had said too much.

'Go on, Mr Chen.'

'No, I think it best that I wait till Mr Deng comes back from Canberra.'

'I'm an ordinary Australian voter, Mr Chen — we take everything that comes out of Canberra with a grain of salt. Whether from our government or foreign embassies. Reality never bites down there.'

'You can be so free with your opinions of your government.' Chen sounded almost wistful. 'Do you think Mr Deng will not come back with the truth?'

'Oh, I'm sure he'll come back with the truth. Whether he'll pass it on to us — well, what d'you think?'

He was no longer smiling. 'As soon as Mr Deng returns I shall call you.'

'Before we go,' said Malone, 'what do you know about a woman named Tzu Chao? Madame Tzu, as she likes to be called.'

'I think Mr Deng should answer that.' He had retreated behind his own Great Wall. 'I shall call you as soon as he returns.'

Outside in the street Gail Lee said, 'Where to now?'

'I think we'd better go and see Madame Tzu before *she* bolts.'

4

The Vanderbilt was one of the oldest apartment blocks in the central business district, built right after World War One. There were few Australian millionaires then, so such style and luxury had to be named after the American super-rich; the American invasion has been around much longer than the cap-on-backwards, basketballing, guys-and-gals generation know. Nobody bought off the plan; that sort of gamble came later. But as soon as the building was finished, buyers fell over each other to be amongst the chosen few. For the next seventy-five years living in the Vanderbilt retained its cachet. It was in Macquarie Street, the finest street in the city. It rose twelve storeys above the Botanical Gardens and was halfway between the Opera House and Parliament House, equidistant from harmony and discord.

The concierge was missing from his cubicle and Malone and Gail Lee walked straight through the foyer to the lifts. The timber panelling of the lift looked as if it was polished every week; the button-panel was a brass mirror.

'I like luxury,' said Gail. 'This old-fashioned kind.'

'Notice how slowly the lift travels? Nobody in this building has to rush to earn a dollar.'

'I wonder how the other tenants feel about having Communists as neighbours?'

'*Rich* Communists — there's a difference. Anyhow, do you think Madame Tzu is a Communist?'

The Bund apartment took in all the tenth floor. It was expensively furnished, with only the occasional Oriental piece, as if the interior decorator had been given a nudge. The big living room did have a large silk rug laid over the plain white carpet. The pictures on the walls were Oriental scenes, but none of them suggested anything that might remotely resemble Chairman Mao's philosophy. The Great Leader had faded from the scene, at least here.

Madame Tzu hadn't bolted. She received Malone and Gail Lee with the impeccable charm of a professional hostess. The smile, perhaps, was put on like make-up; she showed them to chairs as if seating them at ringside. If she was wary of them she gave no sign of it. She was absolutely at home in the Vanderbilt.

Malone, as soon as he had stepped into the apartment, had a feeling of familiarity. He must have betrayed it in some way because Madame Tzu said, 'You are looking for something, Inspector?'

146

'No,' he said, suddenly remembering, 'I was here in this apartment eight or nine years ago. The woman who owned it was murdered.'

She showed no shock, gave no shudder. 'How interesting. I haven't noticed any ghost. Were you expecting to see one?'

'Homicide detectives never look for ghosts. We'd never sleep if we did.'

She offered them tea, rang a bell on a side table and an elderly woman in a blue smock appeared from a rear door. Madame Tzu said something in Chinese and the woman disappeared. Then she sat down, arranging herself in a gilt-armed chair as if granting them an audience. She was wearing a grey silk dress and a single strand of black pearls. This morning she was not wearing sunglasses and Malone, for the first time, saw the calculation in her eyes. Ghosts would never disturb her.

'So how can I help you?'

Malone plunged straight in: 'Madame Tzu, on Saturday you told us that you and Mr Shan had known each other since student days. You also told us you had once worked together in the Central China Department of Trade. Would you care to alter your story?'

There was a sudden remoteness in the dark eyes. 'In what way?'

'Well, for one thing, Madame Tzu, Mr Shan never worked in the Department of Trade. For another, I doubt if you were ever students together. He must have been older than we thought — when he was retired from the army five years ago, he was a general — General Huang Piao. You knew that, of course?'

She sat very still, saying nothing.

Malone went on, 'Even in the Chinese army I don't think they have generals who are barely middle-aged.'

Her smile was white lacquer. 'You are guessing at my age again.'

She's playing for time. 'We're guessing at a lot of things.'

They were interrupted by the maid bringing in a tray; Malone wondered if a kettle was kept on constant boil out in the kitchen. Tea was poured from a china pot into thin china cups: it was pale tea with a slice of lemon, take it or leave it. But the biscuits offered with it were Aussie icons: Monte Carlos.

'Do I have to answer your questions, Inspector?' Madame Tzu sipped her tea, nodded her approval at the maid, who slipped out of sight again. 'Perhaps I should have a lawyer here with me? I seem to be under suspicion of some sort. You like your tea?'

'It's fine, thanks. You can have a lawyer, if you wish, but I think you can handle our questions without any outside help.'

Madame Tzu looked at Gail. 'Is he flattering me?'

'I've never known him to do it before,' said Gail, not looking at her boss.

Madame Tzu seemed to be searching for

answers in her tea leaves; then she said, 'Yes, Mr Shan was an army general. But we did know each other as students — he came to Oxford to study History. History as the West has written it, that is.'

'He was older than you?'

'Yes, he was a colonel at the time. A mature student, I think they are called these days.'

'Did *you* ever work for the Department of Trade?'

'Yes, I did. So did Mr Shan after he left the army — he was an outside consultant. I take it you think I lied to you?'

'I think you believe all truth is relative.'

Madame Tzu looked at Gail again. 'You have taught him Taoism?'

'He's a quick learner,' said Gail.

Malone said, 'Madame Tzu, let's cut out the —'

'Bullshit?' The word hung on her lips like a cold sore.

'That wasn't the word I was going to use, but okay, it'll do. I take it you knew the two young engineers who worked at Olympic Tower? Tong and Guo?'

'Worked? They still do, as far as I know.'

'I don't think so. They didn't report in this morning and we've been to their flats. They're both gone.'

She took refuge in her teacup again, considered, then said, 'Yes, I know them. I have no idea why they have disappeared.'

'A student named Zhang and a girl student Li Ping — did you know them?'

'No.'

But she had hesitated. 'You're sure? We asked you about Zhang on Saturday morning — you didn't appear surprised that he had been murdered.'

'If I didn't know him, why should I be surprised? You are a homicide detective — are you surprised by murder?'

'It's our trade.'

'Inspector, I'm old enough to have seen a thousand murders. My country went through a terrible period . . .' She put down her cup; there was just the slightest agitation in her hand. 'No, I am not surprised by murder.'

'Not Mr Shan's?' said Gail.

The older woman looked at her. 'You are one of the lucky ones. You have our heritage but none of our tragedy. Don't start judging what you've never experienced.'

'Were you a Red Guard?'

'No, I was not!' All the composure was gone; she was consumed with hatred, anger that made her ugly. But not at us, thought Malone: 'Those idiot fanatics murdered my parents and my brother!'

Thirty years on was a little too late to offer sympathy; both detectives remained silent. Madame Tzu faced away from them for a long moment; then she slowly turned back. Her face was expressionless; it was as if nothing had happened. 'Do you have any more questions?'

'Not at the moment,' said Malone, rising. He was no fisherman, but he had learned the value of a long line. 'But I'm sure there'll be more questions. Thank you for the tea.'

At the door he turned back. 'Do you have any contact with the media, Madame?'

'None at all. I've never found them necessary.'

Oh, if only we could have that attitude. 'Keep it that way. As a favour.'

'Tell me when you're coming next time,' she said, 'and we'll do it with a little more ceremony.'

'That'll be nice,' he said. 'Why did you visit Mr Tong on Friday night?'

He had jerked on the line: she stiffened. 'I thought you said Tong had disappeared?'

'He has. But someone saw you at the door of his flat on Friday night. They described you to a T, Madame Tzu.' A little exaggeration never got in the way when questioning. 'Was he still alive then?'

Her mouth was tight, she looked as if she would refuse to answer; then: 'Yes, he was alive. He gave me no hint that he was going to — to *disappear*. We talked about how Olympic Tower was coming along, then I left. I wasn't there more than half an hour.'

She's too glib. 'Was anyone else there? Mr Guo?'

'No. I got there at eighty-thirty and left at

nine.' *Precisely:* he waited for her to show a timesheet.

'Well, thank you. We had to ask.'

'Of course. You wouldn't be doing your job if you didn't. I hope you find Tong and Guo.'

Malone opened the door, ushered Gail out ahead of him. 'Oh, we'll find them. We always do. Dead or alive.'

She didn't blink, showed no expression at all; just said, 'You mentioned that the woman who owned this apartment was murdered. By her husband or a lover?'

'No, by a business partner.'

5

'Something is rotten in the State of Denmark.'

When Lisa got pompous, which was rarely, Malone knew they were in for serious discussion. Monday night, now that television was in the non-ratings seasons, was a poor night for entertainment. Maureen had gone out to a girl friend's, Tom was in his room weaving strings on the Internet, and Claire and her parents were in the living room, each with a book.

Malone put down his book, a paperback by Carl Hiassen. He rarely read crime novels, most of which seemed to him to be written by the Muscle Beach school of writing; but Hiassen and Elmore Leonard made him laugh at the crime they invented. Lately he had found that, more and more, he was looking for humour in his reading. He had recently discovered Gwyn Thomas, a dead dyspeptic Welsh humorist, who, as far as he could gather, no one else in Australia had read. Thomas' sour humour had begun to appeal to him.

Lisa had closed her own book, a history of the Olympic Games. It was her homework, but she had confessed it was boring her; when she had applied for the job at Town Hall no one had thought to ask her if she was interested in sport. Claire closed her book, a David Malouf paperback. None of them would have remarked it, but three books open in the same room at the same time was an oasis in a gradually growing desert.

'I'm talking about the Town Hall,' said Lisa. 'I was at a meeting today. Something came up about Olympic Tower and suddenly I and the secretary, Rosalie, were asked to leave.'

Malone knew about exclusion from committees; corrupt cops, especially senior ones, had never wanted an honest one in attendance. 'Go on.'

'Raymond Brode was going to be asked some questions that outsiders, like Rosalie and me, weren't supposed to hear. There was a hint there might have been a handout, a bribe. There are four more floors due on Olympic Tower that none of the works and planning committees knew about.'

'What would happen,' said Malone, 'when the

tower is finished and someone looks up and starts counting?'

'That would depend, according to Rosalie, who seems to know about these things. Probably nothing, unless some architects or builders who missed out on the job decided to get nasty and ask questions.'

'How did they find out?' asked Claire.

'Through me. I put in a report that gave the game away.' Lisa explained what had happened.

'You should follow it up,' said Claire, already half a lawyer.

'No,' said Malone. 'Let it lie. This Olympic Tower business looks dirty.'

'But how can they get away with it? What if the building is unsafe with the extra floors on it? I mean, surely *someone* can spill the beans?'

'Self-protection,' said Malone with the weariness of long experience. 'It's the skin on every committee. If someone does add up the new level and compares it with the original plans and then asks questions, the committee will say the extra floors were approved. They are not going to admit they were asleep or hadn't been near the site since the plans were first approved. It's called survival of the slickest.'

'Oh my God, how can you be so cynical?'

'You'll learn, when you become a lawyer.'

'Rosalie explained it all,' said Lisa. 'From now till the Olympics we're the squeaky clean city. No scandal, nothing.'

She was not naïve. She knew that corruption

was part of the body politic, that in most of the world it was the aspirin that kept the circulation going. She had been isolated in a happy marriage, where there was only the sweet corruption of love. It was not enough just to read about venality, as one did almost every day. In newsprint one did not get the smell.

'You still haven't said whether it will make the building unsafe.' Claire had a lawyer's persistence: in another year or two, thought Malone, she's going to be a real pain in the arse.

'I don't know,' said Lisa. 'I could ask one of the council engineers —'

'Stay out of it.' Malone was adamant. 'I told you, this could be a really dirty business.'

'Explain yourself,' said the trainee lawyer.

'Pull your head in,' said her father. 'I'm not in court. Just accept what I'm saying — it's going to get dirty. There have been four murders so far, three people are missing —' He saw the shine in Claire's eyes, a sort of madness that he had seen grip young legal eagles; eventually, as cynicism set in, the infection would subside. 'Calm down. You've got a long way to go before you're a Crown prosecutor.'

'Well, *someone* should find out if the building's going to be safe. Sydney won't be squeaky clean if a five-star hotel collapses and kills a load of tourists.'

'I'll talk to someone. In the meantime, don't you talk to any of your mates at law school —'

'As if I would —'

'As if you wouldn't. Women were the first gossips, lawyers were the second —'

Both women threw their books at him. The Olympic Games history, a hardback, hurt the most.

Chapter Five

1

Tuesday morning Boston came to Malone after the morning conference. He had always been neat in appearance, but now he seemed even neater, as if his wife had run an iron over him before he had left home and he had come to work on foot so as not to disturb the creases. There was also a newly ironed look to his demeanour. He had thrown out last week's sullenness, looked keen to impress. Too late, mate, thought Malone; but made no comment.

'I went back to Union Hall this morning — *early*.' As if to underline his new git-up-and-go. 'I talked to a mate there. Not one of the officials like Albie Lloyd, just one of the clerks. They're worried about what's going on at Olympic Tower.'

'In what way? The murders have nothing to do with them. I hope,' he added. Union strife was always something to be avoided if you were a cop: you were always on the wrong side.

'The Chinese are trying to split the two unions by offering enterprise agreements. The Construction mob don't want to have anything to do with it — they think it'll lead to too many risks being taken.'

'Are risks being taken now?' *Do the unions know about the extra levels?*

'My mate wasn't sure about that. But he says the Allied Trades lot are willing to listen — anything that'll shift the Construction mob off the site.'

'Which Chinese?'

'Why, the Hong Kong crowd. The Communists.' He spoke with the bile of the Far Right, but Malone had always made it a principle never to ask any of his detectives their political opinion. They could be anti-politics, but not pro-party.

'Does Union Hall think the Hong Kong crowd did the murders?'

'Of course. They think it's cut-and-dried.'

'I wish I had that cut-and-dried attitude that everyone but cops seems to have. It's too pat, Harold. Why would they kill one of their own? Mr Shan. Ex-General Huang Piao?'

Boston shrugged. 'Who understands the Chinese? Or Communists, for that matter?'

This feller is out of the 1950s. But Malone knew that some of those attitudes were still more widespread than was generally admitted. 'Is that your thinking or Union Hall's?'

'Mine, I guess,' Boston admitted. 'They're still pretty Leftish down there.'

'Righto, let's stick with your thinking. If we don't understand the Chinese, where does that put Les Chung?'

'He's a capitalist, a developer — there's no

158

problem understanding them.'

'Are you for or against developers?'

Boston all at once seemed to become aware that he was straying into territory he hadn't previously explored. He had no idea what Malone's political inclinations were. Police were supposed to stay out of political waters, but that was like asking fish to sunbake.

He hedged: 'Why would Les Chung try to complicate things for himself? Another thing — he was in that booth with the three guys who were shot. If he hadn't come up to talk to you, like you told us, they'd have done him.'

'But he wasn't in the booth when the shooting started. What if he'd known the killer was coming?' Malone had considered this, but rejected it. Lisa said there had been real fear on Chung's face when he had seen what was happening in the rear booth. 'There's Jack Aldwych to think about, too. Jack used to hire killers.'

Boston nodded. 'I know that. I once found the body of a guy Jack got rid of — I was a new cop, a year on the beat. The finger pointed at Jack, we all knew he'd ordered it, but we never laid a hand on him. Those were the days when he had cops on his payroll. You know him pretty well, don't you?'

'What does that mean?' He had to squash down his sudden temper.

'Nothing. I was just asking.' Boston's insolence was what-are-you-going-to-do-about-it?

Malone managed to keep cool. 'I use him for

information, that's all. Forget him — he had nothing to do with the killings. The hitman was Chinese, we're pretty sure of that, and Jack's a racist when it comes to hiring killers.'

'We're talking in circles, aren't we?' Boston was making no attempt to hide his arrogance now; creases were starting to show in him.

Malone sat back. 'I guess we are. Don't get yourself too involved in this, Harold. You'll be gone next week.'

Boston flushed, the old malevolence back in his face. 'With all due respect to your rank, you're a real shit.'

'So I've been told.' He was not going to let the other man see him lose his temper. 'It comes with the rank. Maybe you'll do better in Archives. There's only a senior constable in charge there.'

'You may be wrong about Archives.'

He stood up abruptly, almost knocking over his chair, left the office with quick strides, grabbed his jacket from his chair in the far corner of the office and stalked out of the big room, fumbling at the security door in his anger and haste. A moment passed, then Clements, as Malone expected, came in and slumped down on the couch beneath the window.

'Problems?'

'I dunno. He just said we could be wrong about Archives. I don't think Administration would go against my recommendation and insist he had to stay here.'

'If they do, I'll see he does only paperwork, never moves out of the office. He's a mean bastard, I wouldn't trust him, and he's bone lazy.'

'He says he has contacts at Union Hall.'

'Forget them. We'll make our own — I'll get Phil Truach down there.'

Boston obviously had the contacts at Union Hall, something not easily obtainable, and he might have proved useful. Malone himself, not through any stiff-necked morality but because he hated debts of any kind, had always trodden warily with contacts. Like all cops he had his informants; cops and crims were two sides of the same coin and it couldn't be flipped without calling the odds. He had no informant in government politics and he wanted none in union politics. In both those circles favours were always demanded in return.

He explained what Boston had told him about Union Hall. 'There may be something to it, but I think it's bigger than that. This is more than a union stoush to see who runs the site.' Then he looked at the doorway. 'Hello, Clarrie.'

Clarrie Binyan came into the office, sat down and laid a manual on Malone's desk. 'I get outa the office as much as I can — I like showing off the uniform.' Recently many of the Service's plainclothes officers had been put back into uniform, part of the plan to make the Service more visible to a public that had become suspicious of too many of the detective force. Malone was waiting for the day when Homicide would have to put on a uniform, a possibility he was ambivalent about. The voters had little time for uniforms: they had even been known to attack bus conductors. Binyan put a finger to his shoulder. 'Especially now I'm an inspector. You wanna stand up and salute me, Sergeant?'

'Not particularly,' said Clements, lolling like a sea lion or an overweight civilian on the couch. 'What've you got for us?'

Binyan opened the manual, took out a black-and-white photo. 'I'm pretty sure that's the type of gun did the Chinatown killings.'

Malone studied the photograph, then passed it to Clements. 'What is it?'

'It's a Chinese Type 67,' said Binyan. 'One of my blokes looked it up, but we haven't been able to find an actual piece. All we have is that photo. The calibre, 7.65 millimetres by 17 millimetres, started me thinking — it's not one we come across at all. The Chinese army use that particular gun for covert operations.'

'Covert?' said Clements. 'You mean espionage hits, stuff like that?'

'Or bumping each other off,' said Malone, and told Binyan that one of Friday night's victims was not Mr Shan but General Huang Piao. 'Where did you get this information?'

Binyan winked. 'I have my gigs, just like you blokes.'

Malone took the photo back from Clements and studied it again. 'Friday night's killer used a silencer. There's none on this.'

'It's built in, that's why it's so good for covert work — you don't have to screw on the hush-puppy before you do the job. It's a very sophisticated piece. He just made one mistake.'

'What's that?'

'If he'd used a standard piece we'd still be in the dark where the action is coming from.'

'You think this is a Chinese army hit?' said Clements. 'Killing off one of their own?'

'He killed off two outsiders, Mr Feng and Mr Sun,' said Malone.

'There's the Bondi kid,' said Binyan. 'Done with a standard piece. What's he got to do with this?' Binyan's interest was only academic. That way, he had once told Malone, he was interested only in the machine, not the feelings that drove it. In a way he was connected to murder more than any detectives: all murder weapons finished up in Ballistics' exhibit-room. 'Was the kid army, too?'

Malone spread his hands: who knows? 'I'm beginning to think we're going to need a China expert. Gail understands the language, but she doesn't understand what's happening in China itself.'

'What about Les Chung?' said Clements.

'He's a vested interest. You think he's going to explain China to us?'

'If he stands a chance of getting his head blown off, he might open up.'

'Les has been in shady deals all his life. I'm not

saying this is a shady deal — though it may well be — but the two honest men in this were Feng and Sun. I think we should be talking to someone from their families.' Then he looked up. 'Yes, Gail?'

She stood in the doorway. 'Mr Deng, the Chinese consul-general, is here.'

2

'What you must remember,' said Madame Tzu, 'is that we Chinese, like the Italians and the Spanish, have a talent for revenge.'

'What had my father done that called for revenge?' asked Camilla Feng.

'Probably nothing. He just happened to be *there*. When my parents were murdered during the so-called Cultural Revolution, I'd have been dead, too, if I'd been there. It just so happened that I wasn't and so I was spared.'

'It's different now.'

'You think so? When you were in China last year you saw only what you wanted to see, you were a tourist. I don't know about Sydney, I don't know it well enough, but I assume the tourists who come here don't go looking for the ugly side. Each time I've gone to New York I haven't gone up to the Bronx or down to those parts of New York where people sleep in the streets and the subways — I go to the stores on

Madison Avenue and to the Metropolitan Museum of Art and I stay at the Hotel Pierre. The same when I go to London or Paris —'

'You're a very fortunate woman.'

Madame Tzu ignored that. 'I'm not interested in America's or Britain's shame — nor Sydney's, for that matter. And you weren't looking for what's still wrong with China.'

'Which is?'

'The die-hards who are afraid of what's happening, who don't believe in a free economy. The men who'll kill in the name of Mao.'

'Deng Xiaoping is dead. The other old men must all be gone soon.'

'They don't have to be old to cling to the past.' The scorn in her voice was harsh. 'That's been our trouble. We are always looking back.'

They were seated in the Fengs' Mercedes in the parking area under the half-fleshed skeleton of Olympic Tower. Here was comparative quiet, but noise sluiced down from above. Both wore the compulsory hard hats and looked slightly ridiculous in the car, like ladies on their way to some construction workers' garden party. At Camilla's insistence, Madame Tzu had brought her here to introduce her as her father's heiress and successor.

'Men think they hold the power,' Madame Tzu had said, 'but it is we women who count the money.'

'Which is what I intend to do,' Camilla had said. 'Mother has folded up completely, I doubt if she'll ever get over the way Dad died. So I'll be running things.' She had three siblings, but they were all teenagers. 'So I'd like to see where our money is invested.'

She said now, 'You mentioned revenge — do you know who killed Mr Shan and my father and Mr Sun?'

Madame Tzu adjusted her hat. 'No.'

'Are you afraid he may come back for you?'

'Yes.'

'Revenge?'

'You ask too many questions, Camilla.'

'That's all I have — questions. No answers.'

Madame Tzu turned her head carefully, as if afraid her hat might fall off. 'You will be safe, that's all you have to worry about.'

Camilla tapped her fingers on the steering wheel, thought a moment, then said, 'Meaning that your company, the Bund Corporation, is the honey-pot in this awful mess?'

Madame Tzu opened the door of the car. 'Let's go and I'll introduce you to the engineers.'

As the two women moved across towards the administration hut a tall, well-muscled man in a blue singlet, tight shorts and a hard hat approached them. 'G'day, Mrs Tzu, how're things going?'

'As well as can be expected, Jason. This is Miss Feng.'

He put a thick finger to the brim of the hard hat. 'Pleased to meetcha.'

Camilla was not particularly attracted to muscular athletes; she had always thought Bruce Lee or Jackie Chan would be a tiring lover. She was not attracted to this man, who seemed intent on displaying every muscle he had, including that in his shorts. She just nodded, her eyes as blank as the dark glasses she held in her hand.

Jason recognized the rebuff; he put his hand behind his head as if he intended to pull off his pony-tail and slap her with it. Then he gave her a smile that said, *Up yours,* and looked back at Madame Tzu.

'Things gunna be different now? I mean, after Friday night?'

'Possibly. I'll let you know.'

'You run into any trouble, Mrs Tzu, you know where to come. We'll look after you.'

'I'm not expecting any trouble, Jason.'

'You never know.' He spoke slowly, as if he had to examine every word before he delivered it. 'Looks like things're getting nasty. You know where to come. Nice meeting you, Miss Feng.'

He walked away, his tight shorts offering an invitation to any woman who got excited over buttocks.

'Can he pass a mirror without stopping?' asked Camilla. 'Who is he?'

'He's just a go-between — Mr Shan was talking with his particular union. Jason's not the brightest man on this site, he's the muscle, I think they call it.'

'He's all that. He probably takes his girlfriends on guided tours of himself.'

Madame Tzu smiled; she hadn't expected any humour from Camilla. 'I'm glad you have taste.'

'What did he mean — if things get nasty, you know where to come?'

Madame Tzu adjusted her hard hat again, looked away and said, 'Oh, there's Mr Fadiman. Come, I'll introduce you to him. He's brainy, no muscle at all as far as I can see.'

For the second time in two minutes Madame Tzu had dodged a question. Camilla tucked both questions away for future use. She had only a fraction of the older woman's experience, but there was nothing between them in intelligence. She was also maturing in something else: persistence. She would be asking a lot of questions in the future.

Fadiman was obviously impressed by the good-looking young Chinese woman, but his look was not challenging, as Jason's had been. Though she was Australian-born Camilla always scanned men with a foreigner's eye; they have no subtlety, her mother had warned her. She had had boyfriends, all Chinese, and it was expected that she would marry one of them; but, secret to herself, she was still looking for an Australian man who would meet her and her mother's standards. At first glance Fadiman was not the man, but she exchanged his friendly smile with one of her own. Which was more than Jason had got.

'You'll be coming down here regularly?' Despite the fact that he was looking favourably on her, there was no real invitation in his voice.

Bosses, especially women bosses, were never welcome on a building site.

'No,' said Madame Tzu. 'Isn't it enough to have one woman interfering?' Her smile said, *Answer that if you dare.*

'I'll come occasionally,' said Camilla, speaking directly to Fadiman. 'Not necessarily to interfere.'

Fadiman looked uncomfortable, caught in cross-fire against which his hard hat offered no protection.

Madame Tzu, after a bland-eyed glance at Camilla, retreated; or anyway, changed tack. 'Have Mr Tong and Mr Guo reported back?'

'No,' said Fadiman. 'We haven't seen them since Friday. We were wondering — have they gone back to China?'

'Possibly.' If Madame Tzu was concerned, there was no sign of it. 'Have we lost any time this week?'

'An hour this morning, a union meeting.'

'About what?'

Fadiman shrugged. 'Union business. They never tell us, we never ask.'

'We'll ask in future. We can't have them stopping work just because they want to discuss union business.'

'Madame Tzu —' Fadiman was visibly uncomfortable. He wished that, like an old-time dogman, he was riding the girder that had just started its trip to the upper levels — 'these people aren't coolies —'

169

Watch it, thought Camilla, amused.

Madame Tzu was not amused. 'Don't be impertinent, Mr Fadiman. You're not dealing with some stupid farmer's wife —'

Fadiman had realized his blunder as soon as he had spoken. 'I'm sorry — I didn't mean to be rude —'

'You were very rude, without even trying.' She was not going to let him off lightly; had there been a rug and a well handy she would have wrapped him in one and thrown him down the other. She was giving him the empress treatment, something of which Fadiman had had no experience. 'I am in charge here —'

'And I,' said Camilla quietly.

It took the older woman a moment to change gears; then she nodded. 'And Miss Feng. Neither of us treats people as coolies. Not even trade unionists,' she added with the thin blade of her tongue.

'I'll try to remember that,' said Fadiman, finding some backbone. 'Do we take any notice of Mr Chung and Mr Aldwych if they come down here?'

She gave him a look that put him at the bottom of a well, then turned and walked back to the Mercedes.

'There goes my job,' said Fadiman, and didn't sound particularly downcast.

'I don't think so,' said Camilla. 'Do you have any idea who killed my father?'

Fadiman had not expected the question.

170

'Why should I know?'

Camilla studied him; then nodded. 'Of course. Why should you? But if you should learn anything, anything at all, please let me know, will you?'

He was out of his depth with these two Chinese women; but he was not obtuse. 'Do I let Madame Tzu know?'

Camilla looked across at the Mercedes where Madame Tzu sat in stiff arrogance, as in a steel palanquin.

Camilla turned back to Fadiman. 'No, don't tell her.'

3

Deng Liang, the consul-general, was dapper, a fashionplate. He wore an Italian high-buttoned jacket that encased him as if he were trying to escape from it; a button-down white shirt; and a tie like a shattered rainbow. Armani or Zegna or Versace had followed Marco Polo to the Middle Kingdom; traffic was going the other way on the old Silk Road. All that spoiled him were the round horn-rimmed glasses which Malone had seen in so many newsreel shots of Chinese officials, as if they were government issue, designed to keep everything in official focus.

He sat down in the chair Clarrie Binyan had vacated, looked at the three male detectives, ignoring Gail Lee, who still stood in the doorway. 'You are all working on the Chinatown murders?'

'And the murder of a Chinese student at Bondi,' said Malone, and nodded at Binyan, who had moved to join Clements on the couch. 'Inspector Binyan is our ballistics expert. He is pretty sure that the gun used in the Chinatown murders was Chinese army issue.'

Fast bowlers know when to bowl a bean ball; Deng hadn't expected it, but he didn't duck under it. 'You are sure of that?'

'Sure enough,' said Binyan. 'Type 67. Do you know it?'

'I was never an army man.' Said almost as if he had been insulted.

'But you know weapons?' Binyan persisted.

It was obvious that the consul-general had never had to deal with an Aboriginal officer, not one with Binyan's rank. Gail, still in the door-way, remembered something her father had once told her: We Chinese were racists long before anyone else.

'Well — yes,' said Deng. 'One learns about them.'

'In the diplomatic game?' said Malone. 'Spies, that sort of thing? Inspector Binyan says the Type 67 is used for covert operations.'

Deng displayed a good set of teeth. 'Not by consuls-general.'

'Do all visitors from China report to your consulate when they come to Sydney?'

'Not necessarily. Senior visitors, trade delegations, people like that don't come to us. Why?'

'The covert operator is probably a recent arrival.'

Deng was taking his time now. He was not hostile, but he was cautious. 'I understand Mr Chen, my colleague, has told you all we know?'

'Not quite. We don't know what you learned down in Canberra at your embassy.'

'Oh, I can't disclose that.' Deng was affable but firm. 'The embassy would have my head. I'm sure you understand. You would not expect to tell me all you might learn in a conference with the Police Commissioner.'

All four detectives looked at each other: at their rank you learned practically nothing at a conference with the Police Commissioner. Clements said, 'Okay, then tell us about General Huang Piao. How much money did he bring out to Australia?'

Deng took his time; then: 'We are still checking that — he had so many sources. Our guess is ninety million dollars. Australian dollars, that is.'

'Including the fifty-one million deposited in the accounts of the students Zhang Yong and Li Ping?' asked Gail.

'You are very thorough,' said Deng admiringly, and seemed to see Gail for the first time. 'You are the financial expert in this case?'

'No,' said Gail, 'just an all-round expert.'

Smiles flitted around the four males like white

butterflies. *Women!* the smiles said.

'Tell us how General Huang managed to get that much money out of China,' said Malone. 'Did it come out of Hong Kong, all of it, or Shanghai or where?'

Deng took his time again; it seemed that he had all the patience in the world. Clements was the only one of the four detectives who stirred impatiently: 'Come on, Mr Deng, for Crissakes. We're trying to solve the murder of four men, including one of your ex-generals —'

'I don't think General Huang will be missed,' Deng said at last. 'But the others —' He turned over a hand in what could have been a gesture of sympathy. 'Yes, we owe you some information . . .' Another pause before the plunge: 'China, as you may know, is going through a difficult period. We have problems that you have never experienced here in Australia. And Shanghai, where General Huang came from, is the centre of our problems. Shanghai citizens have always been famous for their financial sense. It was once our most advanced city — it still is. But don't quote me to Beijing.' He managed a smile. 'Last year foreign investors poured over a hundred *billion* dollars, US dollars, into China. The major part of it went to Shanghai or what Shanghai controls. General Huang was one of those who decided some of those dollars should be siphoned off.'

'One of *those?*' said Malone. 'Who are the others?'

174

Deng undid another button of his jacket, like a bound man trying to loosen a knot. 'They are being attended to in China.'

'Other generals?' said Clements. 'Or ex-generals?'

'Some of them.'

'The money for Zhang Yong and Li Ping came through a Hong Kong bank,' said Gail Lee. 'Did the original money that went into Olympic Tower come through the same bank?'

Deng was beginning to look unhappy. 'Unfortunately when we took back control of Hong Kong we allowed them too much latitude. Hong Kong still leaks like a sieve.'

'The capitalists are still running loose?' asked Clements.

'Are you anti-capitalist?'

'Are you kidding?' said Malone. 'Let's talk about someone else — Madame Tzu. She is a partner in Bund Corporation?'

'A formidable lady.'

'So we gather. But does her capital in Olympic Tower come from the same source as General Huang's?'

Deng shook his head. 'We don't think so. As far as we can make out, her capital is her own.'

'How much?' asked the capitalist on the couch.

'Ten million,' said Gail, and all the men looked at her. 'Sheryl has been back to see our nice young man at the Securities Commission. He gave her a breakdown on the partners.' She

175

smiled at the men. 'He's not supposed to do that, but when you're all sweaty and up close and personal in the gym, things slip out. He leaks like a sieve when he's around Sheryl.'

'Where does she get her money, then?' asked Malone. 'Ten million? Is there that sort of capital lying around for individuals in China?'

'Unfortunately, yes.' Deng took off his glasses, wiped them with a silk handkerchief, looked suddenly careless of what he was paid to defend. What, perhaps, he no longer believed in. Malone suddenly recognized that most personal of possessions: his tone of voice. 'It is very difficult these days to defend a lot of our people. You went through your greed decade, we are going through ours. Madame Tzu is a very rich lady by our standards.'

'There are a couple other characters in this who have disappeared,' said Clements. 'Tong and Guo. What do you know about them?'

'They were once army cadets. They were protégés of General Huang. Incidentally, is anything to be released to the media about Huang?'

'No, he's still on our books as Mr Shan.'

'Can we keep it that way? At least for the time being?'

Malone was always willing to keep sensation out of the headlines. 'I'll talk to my superiors, suggest it to them. The dead student Zhang and the girl Li Ping. All that money in their bank accounts — were they protégés of General Huang?'

'Don't you know?'

'What?'

'They are — were — General Huang's son and daughter.'

4

'The crotch of the matter,' said the Premier, 'is it does bugger-all for Sydney's image.'

He's at it again, thought Ladbroke, his press minder. He had been with Hans Vanderberg almost twenty years now and still the Old Man managed to surprise him with yet another mangled metaphor. Yet The Dutchman, despite what he did to the English language, never failed to get across the gist of his message. He might send junketing MPs to the Parthenon to see the Acropolis or advise backbenchers not to put the horse behind the cart or tell Ladbroke himself to turn a blind ear to criticism. But no one ever missed the point.

The Premier had called this meeting in his office this morning to read the Riot Act to several of the councillors from Town Hall. There were three of them, two men and a woman, plus Lisa.

'Who're you?' Vanderberg had asked her when she entered his office.

'Lisa Malone. I'm handling the Olympics PR for the council.'

Ladbroke had leaned forward and whispered in the Premier's ear. Vanderberg had twisted his mouth, shifting his dental plate as if he were about to spit dice. His hooded eyes, like those of an eagle that had spent years picking at bones, stared at Lisa. Then he nodded, but said nothing further to her.

'I been hearing about what's going on at that building site,' he told the councillors. 'Union strife, extra floors that weren't okayed —'

'Where do you get all this information?' said Councillor Brode, who knew his question was only rhetorical. There was nothing that went on anywhere in the State that The Dutchman didn't know. Every breeze that blew carried whispers into this office.

The old man gave him a grin that had more malevolence than humour in it. 'Mr Brode, you're a politician, you know better than to ask a question like that. I hear things about Town Hall before you do.'

'With all due respect, Mr Premier —' Pascal, bouffant hair rising like froth: his hair seemed to rise with his blood pressure — 'you have no right to interfere in council's affairs.'

'Simmer down, Mr Pascal. Don't trot out the Local Government Act — I been too long in this game to worry about what the rules say. All I got ta do to pull you people into line is cut off the State's contribution to Olympics funds.'

'You can't do that!' Mrs Harrity bared her teeth, but not in a smile.

'You wanna try me?' Hans Vanderberg, like Jack Aldwych, had no fear of sharks. 'What d'you reckon, Nick?'

He looked sideways at Agaroff, his Sports Minister and the man responsible for overseeing the State's part in the Olympics. He was a youngish man, prematurely bald, with a long face that looked permanently mournful. As well it might, since he had had nothing but trouble since he had been appointed to his job. He had gone to the Atlanta Games and been carried away by the atmosphere. He had been thrilled by the closing ceremony in which Sydney had accepted the honour of handling the next Games. Aboriginal musicians had cavorted; little boys had cycled madly away from paedo-philic kangaroos; Sydney had been put on the map and he was the pin holding it there. Then, on his return, the reality of organizing a modern Olympics had hit him. He had begun to think of himself as the shuttlecock in a badminton game of anagrams. IOC, AOC, SOCOG: he was bat-tered and bruised by the alphabet. And all the time the coach, the cranky old man now looking at him, was there on the sidelines offering advice. Advice that was never to be ignored.

'What worries me most,' he said after some thought, 'is the racial angle to all this. I mean the murders.'

'The murders have got nothing to do with the Olympics,' said Brode. 'For Crissake, stop stretching this —'

'Keep talking, Nick,' said the Premier, not even looking at Brode.

'Only Chinese have been bumped off. That's going to do nothing for our image in Asia.'

'Especially since Beijing wanted these particular Olympics,' said Mrs Harrity. She was a large lady who liked bright colours; this morning she was in vivid red and yellow, a human bushfire. Lisa, sitting behind her in beige, looked like a smudge. 'They'll make hay out of this, mark my words.'

Lisa raised a hand. 'May I say something?'

Vanderberg examined her again, then nodded. 'Go ahead.'

'I think the Chinese authorities will be doing their best *not* to make a big thing of this. So far it hasn't been released to the media, but the mainland Chinese gentleman who was murdered was an ex-army general.'

'Where'd you get this?' said Vanderberg. 'Your husband?'

Lisa hesitated, then nodded. 'Yes. But I'd rather that wasn't mentioned.'

The Premier looked around, threat in the hooded eyes. 'You all get that? We don't get Mrs Malone into trouble with her husband.'

'That wasn't what I meant,' protested Lisa.

He gave her a grin that was meant to be friendly and sympathetic but could have sent an infant into shock. 'I know that, Mrs Malone. Maybe the councillors didn't know what you've just told us, but I got that information from the

180

Police Commissioner yesterday.'

'Why weren't we told?' demanded Mrs Harrity, all ablaze.

'I think Councillor Brode knew who he was, didn't you, Councillor?'

'Well —' Brode was too brash and arrogant to look uncomfortable, but he did look as if he would rather be elsewhere. 'Yes, I knew. But I thought it was irrelevant. He's been out of the army five years. I took him to be a perfectly respectable private investor.'

'If you did, you're naïve. Or a liar.' The Dutchman never mangled his insults.

Brode flushed and half rose from his chair. 'I don't have to take that from you —'

The Dutchman pushed him back in his chair from ten feet away. 'Siddown. Getting high on your horse isn't gunna solve this problem. We've gotta put our heads together and mix some thoughts. Would you leave us alone for a while, Mrs Malone?'

'Perhaps I can make a suggestion or two, Mr Premier. I'm sworn not to divulge any decisions at a meeting —'

His grin looked like a slit in a sack of wheat. 'Ain't we all? But what you dunno, Mrs Malone, won't harm us. Outside — please?'

Lisa got up, took her time about collecting her handbag and notebook, and went out of the room. Ladbroke followed her, led her to a window away from the two secretaries at their desks in the outer office. Beyond the windows was the Domain, the city common, where at weekends free speech burned the air like cordite and nobody was excluded from hearing it.

'Don't be offended by him, Mrs Malone.'

Ladbroke had spent years apologizing for his boss; sometimes it was no more than political spin, sometimes out of pure sympathy. He was in his mid-forties, lunch-plump and cynically relaxed about life in general and life in politics in particular. He had once been a junior political roundsman for the *Herald*, getting high on what he learned each day, and he had been like a deprived addict each time he had to go back to the office, and the sub-editors, wearing rubber gloves against libel, had pulled out the needle. When Vanderberg had offered him the job as press officer he had stepped into it as if into a bath of drug. He would never be cured and he had no desire to be. He had a wife and three children, but he was married to the Premier and this life.

'I don't know what they'll hatch up in there, but you'll be happier for not knowing.'

'This is the second time in a couple of days I've been asked to leave the room,' said Lisa. 'I'm beginning to feel like a ten-year-old.'

'There'll be some skullduggery, as the Old Man calls it, and you and I will be told to write a press release that says nothing, not even between the lines. And in five, ten years' time, no one will care a damn about what's been cooked up. That's the nature of the voter, Mrs Malone, his *conditioned* nature, and no one knows it better than my boss. We're breeding them to have short memories. When television came along, politicians greeted it like it was manna from heaven. If the voters look at pollies at all on TV, they see only the faces, they don't hear a word that's said.'

'Does your cynicism keep you awake at night?'

He looked out the window. The big lake of green grass bordered by its shore of trees was almost deserted; an elderly couple limped along the path leading to the art gallery beyond the trees and two youths threw a frisbee back and forth with the lazy grace of slow-motion athletes. Ladbroke knew the history of the Domain and wished he had been born early enough to have witnessed more of it. In his historical eye he saw a regimental band playing while carriages rolled and ladies strolled under parasols. He was there in spirit a hundred and fifty years ago when a French balloonist, after weeks of hoop-la and hot air, failed to get his balloon off the ground and an angry crowd had set fire to the balloon. There had been another crowd sixty-six years ago that had gathered out there on the sward to yell defiance at the British governor who had sacked a premier. Now, as he gazed out the window, a crocodile of small children crossed the park, heading for the art gallery, all in orderly line like a string of rosary beads. The Domain was no longer a battleground.

'I sometimes lie awake, but only because I

wonder at the apathy of the voters. They get stirred up occasionally, like they did after the Port Arthur massacre, but do you think political skullduggery keeps *them* awake at night?' He shook his head. 'If it's not wearing football boots or cricket boots or basketball shoes, it ain't happening. I'll write a press release and the Old Man will go out there under the trees and after the TV cameramen have finished photographing each other, they'll turn the cameras on him and he'll make a fifteen-second soundbite and it'll be on TV tonight and that's when Mr and Mrs Sydney will go to the toilet or the fridge or the stove and the charade will be the same as last night and tomorrow night and every night till Parliament goes into recess. Ninety per cent of the voters will be in the toilet or at the fridge when it's announced that tomorrow is Judgement Day.'

Lisa looked out at the Domain. A few more people were appearing: the lunchtime netball players, half a dozen joggers, a street musician playing empty tunes to the empty air, the passers-by ignoring him as if he were no more than a treestump. At last she turned back to Ladbroke. 'Do you think they'll tell the police to stop looking for the murderers?'

'I shouldn't be surprised. Not tell them to stop looking, just not to look so hard. The Old Man wouldn't know a javelin-thrower from a pole-vaulter, but he doesn't want his Olympics spoiled.'

'*His* Olympics?'

Ladbroke smiled. 'You don't think he's going to let the Lord Mayor or the IOC or the AOC or SOCOG claim the Games as theirs? He'll be eighty-four in Olympics year. If his prayers are answered, he'll drop dead in the VIP seats just as the Olympic flame is lit. He'll get a posthumous gold medal for timing.'

Chapter Six

1

The Sun family had been visited by Phil Truach and Sheryl Dallen on Saturday morning; the two detectives had come back to report that the family, devastated by the tragedy, could offer no help at all. When Deng, the consul-general, had left, Malone called Gail Lee back into his office.

'We're going over to see the Sun family, Gail. I've looked up Phil's notes — there are two sons in the family about the same age as General Huang's son and daughter. Maybe the Sun boys knew them.'

'What about Camilla Feng? Maybe she knew them, too.'

'We'll try her, too. But first . . .'

'Phil showed me his notes. The two sons work in the father's office — it might be better to try there first.'

'Do you know where the office is?' *Why do I bother to ask?*

She looked at her own notebook. 'In the Optus building in North Sydney.'

'Gail, are Chinese women all as thorough as you?' He said it with a smile to make it politically correct.

'Of course. The most efficient rulers of China have always been women.'

'I thought you said those two women, Tzu and the other one, were cruel and brutal?'

'So?' she said with her own smile.

'I'm going to have to watch out for you.'

'No,' she said without a smile. 'I have too much respect for you.'

He could accept praise and respect; he had just not expected her to offer it. 'Thank you.'

On the way out of the main office he spoke to Sheryl Dallen. 'Ask Immigration for a list of all arrivals in the past two weeks travelling on Chinese passports. Eliminate the women and old men. I'm guessing, but we're looking for a man in the twenty-five-to-forty-five age group. It's a long shot, but try it. How are we going on the mobile phone trace?'

'Nothing so far. The media may have stuffed it up for us. There's a piece in the paper this morning about how Telephone Intercepts was used to trace a rapist. If our missing guys read it, they could be shrewd enough to stay off their mobiles.'

He said nothing, frustration choking him.

He and Gail drove through the city and over the Harbour Bridge through a humid day that threatened a late afternoon storm. Haze hung like the thinnest of veils and already out west, towards the mountains, clouds were piling on top of each other like another, higher range. Up ahead an illuminated sign on top of an office building said the temperature was 34°C, but that was up where the pigeons flew. Down in the narrow streets of North Sydney Malone knew it would be much more uncomfortable.

North Sydney lies at the northern approach to the Bridge, no more than a couple of kilometres from the main city. It is a post-World War Two development, an inner suburb of terraced houses and a few mansions that was now a jumble of office high-rises. The jumble had sprouted before town planners had grown to have influence. Houses and small shops had been pulled down, high-rise buildings had gone up like controlled explosions. Belatedly there had been efforts to control planning and development, but the damage was done thirty or forty years ago. The largest open space is its busiest cross-intersection.

Gail parked the car in the Optus building underground car park and the two detectives rode up to a middle-level floor where the Sun family company had its offices. It was a modest establishment behind two large glass doors: an outer office and two inner offices. The gold letters on the glass doors said no more than *Sun Limited*, like a cautious weather forecast.

There were two girls at separate desks in the outer office, a bottle-blonde Caucasian and a blue-black Chinese. They had almost identical hairstyles and looked like a positive and negative image of the same girl.

Malone produced his badge. 'We'd like to see Mr Sun.'

'Certainly, sir. Mr Darren or Mr Troy?'

I don't believe this: Chinese Rugby league players? 'Both.'

Both Sun sons were in the same inner office, at desks on opposite sides of the room. Through an open door there was a glimpse of a large corner office with a view down to the Bridge and across the water to the main city. Evidently it had not yet been decided which heir would move in there.

Darren was the taller and older of the two brothers, Troy the plumper. Both were without their jackets, wore uncrumpled white shirts with plain black ties, were stiff and formal: starched either with grief or at this intrusion on their grief.

'Has your father been buried yet?' Malone asked.

'Not yet. He is being cremated tomorrow.' Darren appeared to be the spokesman: Troy stood to one side, on the bench as it were. 'I hope you have not been worrying our mother?'

'We try not to worry anyone, Mr Sun, but we do have to ask questions if you want us to find the man who murdered your father.' It was an explanation cops had to make time and time again. It was extraordinary the number of people who seemed to believe that a murder could be investigated without any input from them, no matter how close they might be to the victim. 'I'll be as brief as possible. Did your father confide much in you?'

The brothers glanced at each other; then Darren said, 'Yes. We're partners — junior partners — in the family company.'

'The sign on the door,' said Gail Lee, 'says Sun Limited. You're not a proprietary company?'

'We're a public company, but not a listed one. It was my father's whim — he wanted people to think the family company was publicly listed on the stock exchange.'

'Quite a whim,' said Gail. 'Not Chinese at all.'

I'm glad you said it, thought Malone.

'It's the Australian in us,' said Darren. 'Everything out in the open.'

'If you are partners,' said Malone, stepping into what looked like the beginning of a civil war, 'you'll have some idea of what was going on at Olympic Tower?'

'In what way?'

Uh-uh, we're suddenly Chinese now. 'Did your father know Mr Shan's true identity? Did you?'

Again a glance between the brothers; then: 'Our father knew who he was. He didn't tell us till about a month ago.'

'Why then?'

It suddenly appeared to dawn on the brothers that this questioning might go on; up till now they had remained on their feet and had not invited the two detectives to sit down. Now Troy said, 'Perhaps we should go into the other room — it's more comfortable there.'

He led the way, waved Malone and Gail to two chairs, sat down beside the large carved teak table that served as a desk. Darren followed, sat down behind the desk. The heir had been decided.

'About a month ago,' said Darren, 'Mr Shan — General Huang, if you like — looked to be having money problems. The Bund Corporation's progress payments on the construction weren't coming through on time. That was when our father explained General Huang's connections, when he suspected that the Bund set-up wasn't kosher.'

'Kosher?' Malone grinned.

The grin seemed to take some of the starch out of the brothers. 'We have a Jewish accountant.'

'Chinese and Jewish?' said Gail. 'You must be unbeatable.'

The brothers said nothing and the joke fell flat. *Back off, Gail:* Malone said, 'Did the money situation improve?'

Both brothers had their eyes on Gail, as if trying to place why a half-Chinese woman detective should be here. Then Darren looked back at Malone. 'Not immediately, no.'

'Was the Bund Corporation still behind on its payments when General Huang was killed?'

'Yes.'

'What about Madame Tzu? She's a director of Bund.'

'Madame Tzu came good, yes.' Darren looked at his brother: 'How much?'

Troy felt obliged to explain himself: 'I'm the finance officer. Madame Tzu came up with thirty per cent of the progress payment.'

'How much?' said Gail.

'Five million.'

'That leaves quite a lot short,' said Malone. 'Did you know General Huang's son and daughter?'

The brothers seemed surprised at how much the detectives knew.

'We thought that had been kept very quiet,' said Troy. 'We met them for the first time about two or three weeks ago. General Huang brought them to our parents' house.'

'Did you get to know them?'

'We took them out to dinner,' said Darren. 'To the Golden Gate, as it happened. Just the once. They were not easy to know.'

'In what way?'

Another glance between the brothers, then Troy said, 'We thought they were scared.'

'So they should've been,' said Malone. 'They were sitting on the money that should've been going into Olympic Tower.'

A moment, then Troy said, 'We know. Investigators from the government were here — they told us they were investigating infractions of the Cash Transactions Reporting Act.' He recited the title as if he were familiar with it and Malone wondered if Sun Limited had occasionally been guilty of an infraction or two. 'There was money here in certain accounts that they thought might have been meant for Chinese investment in Sydney. We were on the list as possible targets. They didn't tell us how much money was involved, but they did tell us it was in two students' bank accounts. Dad and us, we put two and two together. We guessed who the students were.'

'The investigators didn't tell you how much was involved?' said Gail.

The Sun brothers shook their heads.

'Fifty-one million. US dollars.'

If Gail had expected any reaction from the brothers, she was disappointed; they were suddenly inscrutable. 'Well!' said Darren, and that was the only reaction from either of them.

'Why were the two of them scared?' asked Malone.

'We don't know,' said Darren. He had a habit of wiping one hand across the other, as if washing his hands of something; now it looked to be more a hint of panicky nerves. 'Maybe they were unused to such large amounts of money —'

'People do get afraid of large amounts of money,' said Troy, who looked as if it would take the national debt to frighten him. 'That's why so many lottery and casino winners blow the lot, soon's they get it. They're scared of it.'

Malone, who never bought a lottery ticket or paid a bet, said nothing, just nodded to Darren to go on. Who did: 'The other thing that may have scared them was because they suspected someone other than the government investigators knew about it.'

'Such as someone from China?' said Malone.

Both brothers nodded, Darren wiped his hands furiously, and Malone went on: 'Are *you* scared?'

Darren looked down at the arms of the heavy teak chair in which he sat, as if he half-expected to see the ghostly hands of his father clutching at them. He's not sure he wants to sit in that chair, thought Malone.

Then Darren said, 'Wouldn't you be scared?'

'Yes, I think I would be. It might be an idea if you hired a coupla security guards. You know that the son is dead. Li Ping, the daughter, is missing — she may be dead, too. The two Chinese engineers who were working on Olympic Tower — they're missing, too. Did you know them?'

Troy nodded. 'Madame Tzu brought them to our house once. Nice guys, very clued up.'

'Clued up about what?'

Troy raised his shoulders, spread his hands. 'Everything. These guys weren't *peasants*.'

'Were they Communists?' asked Gail.

'I doubt it. I don't think any young people in China today are Communists, not the old-fashioned sort. These guys were into fashion —' He unexpectedly laughed, a pleasant sound. 'Darren and I were square compared to them. They were into all the Italian gear. I didn't get any idea that they believed in spreading the wealth.'

194

'But well-dressed as they were,' said Malone, 'you still got the idea they were scared?'

'Not them, no,' said Darren. 'They acted as if they had the world made.'

'Till Friday night,' said Malone. 'They were gone Saturday morning.'

The phone on the desk rang and Darren picked it up. He frowned, then said, 'Tell her to come back later.'

Malone was on his feet ready to leave. Something in Darren's face made him pause; the young Chinese this time was not inscrutable or had not practiced enough. 'Madame Tzu?' Malone said.

Darren frowned again. 'No.'

Malone turned swiftly, crossed to the door that led to the outer office and opened it. 'Miss Feng?'

Camilla Feng turned back from the main doors. 'Inspector Malone! Why, what a nice surprise.'

I'll bet. 'Care to come in and join us? Better than coming back later, as Mr Sun advised.'

She went past him into the corner office. She was dressed in a black suit with a single strand of pearls and matching ear-rings; she wore black crocodile shoes and carried a matching bag. She looked most elegant, but if animal welfare activists had fired on her Malone was sure she would have fired back.

Both Sun brothers came forward to kiss her on the cheek; it was obvious all three were old friends. Then she turned to the two detectives and did her best to look on them as friends. She certainly looked more at ease than the Suns.

'Were you expecting me?' she asked.

'No,' said Malone. 'To be honest, you weren't on my mind at all — someone else was. But now you're here . . .' He recounted the conversation he and Gail Lee had had with the Sun brothers. 'Did you know all this?'

The hesitation was almost imperceptible; but Malone caught it. 'Yes.'

'Why didn't you tell us when we came to see you at your home?'

'I didn't know it then.'

If she was lying, it was difficult to tell. Malone sighed, an act he was good at. 'Seems that everyone around here arrived at a lot of information pretty late in the piece. Wouldn't you say so, Constable Lee?'

Gail nodded; she hadn't yet learned the change-the-bowler act that Malone had developed with Clements. But she wasn't entirely clueless: 'Exactly why are you here, Miss Feng?'

'Ms Feng,' Camilla corrected her; it was the first time Malone had heard one woman correct another on the title. 'For the moment I am running my father's company. And he was in partnership with Darren and Troy's father on a number of other things besides Olympic Tower.'

'Good,' said Malone, deciding for the moment to leave out what the number of other things might be. 'We're starting to get some focus here. So what are you planning to do? The three of you?'

The three of them looked at each other; then Darren said, 'Continue with Olympic Tower.'

'What are you going to do about the shortage of capital?' said Gail.

Good on you, thought Malone. A Chinese woman counting the money.

Camilla turned to the Sun brothers. 'Haven't you told them?'

'Not yet,' said Darren, anything but inscrutable this time.

'Told us what?' said Malone.

The brothers were distinctly uncomfortable; then Troy said, 'We are trying to negotiate something with General Wang-Te.'

'And who the hell is General Wang-Te?' Malone's patience was now paper thin. Even Gail Lee looked exasperated.

The three Chinese were silent a moment; then Camilla, the most composed, said, 'He arrived yesterday from Shanghai. He is the financial comptroller of the Southern Command army. He is here to try and have the money in those frozen bank accounts returned to China.'

'And you think he might be seduced into putting the money into Olympic Tower?'

Camilla smiled, still more at ease than the Sun brothers. 'Seduced is hardly the word, Inspector — I wouldn't go that far.'

Malone returned her smile, keeping her in good humour. 'Not for fifty-one million?'

'If it was for myself . . .' She gave her smile this time to the Sun brothers, who both looked even more uncomfortable. 'No, Inspector, we are trying to talk to General Wang purely on commercial terms.'

'Does the Chinese army go in for commercial deals?' asked Gail.

'That's what we are hoping to find out.'

'Where is General Wang now?'

'Staying with Madame Tzu.'

2

'Gail, you stay here with these gentlemen, see they don't make any phone calls to Madame Tzu or General Wang.'

Darren was highly offended. 'Don't you trust us?'

'Absolutely,' said Malone. 'It's just that we cops are so damned suspicious. May I use your phone?'

'Have we any choice?'

'No, but we always like to ask.' He picked up the phone, dialled Homicide. 'Russ? Meet me down at the Vanderbilt, wait for me in the lobby.'

'When?' said Clements. 'I'm up to my navel in paperwork —'

'*Now.*' He hung up. 'Do you have a car, Ms Feng?'

'It's down in the garage. Are you going to borrow it?'

'No, I'm asking you to drive me in to see Madame Tzu and General Wang.'

'As Darren asked, do I have any choice?'

Malone grinned. 'Of course you do. But you wouldn't like to be suspected of complicity in theft, fifty-one million dollars, would you? That money General Wang is trying to retrieve was stolen, wasn't it?'

'Put like that —'

'There's no other way to put it.' He turned to Gail: 'Think up some more questions for the gentlemen, Gail.' He looked back at the brothers: 'Who knows who Mr Shan really was?'

'Only us and Camilla,' said Darren. 'And of course our fathers knew.'

'And Madame Tzu. Keep it that way. Anyone comes to talk to you, General Huang is still Mr Shan.'

Going down in the lift Camilla said, 'Are you any closer to finding out who murdered my father?'

'A little closer,' was all Malone would tell her.

Then two girls got into the lift, discussing some male yahoo who made Bruce Willis look like Prince Charming, and Camilla and Malone rode the rest of the way in silence. When they got out in the garage she led him to a blue Mercedes.

'I thought you'd be a BMW girl.'

She slid in behind the wheel. 'This was my

father's car. I do have a BMW, but not for business. This is a fringe benefit.'

She drove out of the garage, handling the heavy car expertly, found her way on to the approach to the Bridge. 'Do you have the toll?'

He glanced sideways at her. 'You mean a car like this doesn't have a piggy-bank?'

'It does, but I'm not here by choice. Two dollars, please.'

He fished in his pocket, gave her two dollars. 'You'd have paid two bucks to get home to Drummoyne.'

'I go home by way of Gladesville Bridge — there's no toll.'

'My family think I'm tight-fisted. I think you'd give me a run for the money.'

Her gaze was intent on her driving. 'My father began life mixing and selling herbs in the old Paddy's Markets. He built his fortune by saving pennies.'

'You're going to do the same?'

She turned her head for a moment. 'No, I'm saving bigger denominations than that.'

'Do you and Madame Tzu have much in common?'

'What sort of question is that?' But she gave him an answer after driving some distance in silence: 'Yes, we possibly do. Does that worry you?'

'It might — some time,' he said.

She turned her head again. 'That's an enigmatic answer.'

'It's the Irish in me,' he said, and she threw back her head and gave a full-throated laugh. She looked all at once a different girl. *How many sides are there to her?*

'Are you married, Inspector?'

'With three kids.'

'What a pity.'

When they achieved a parking space in Macquarie Street right opposite the Vanderbilt Malone felt his luck might be in. General Wang might prove more co-operative than anyone else involved in Olympic Tower. But he made no immediate attempt to get out of the car.

'Last Saturday you said Madame Tzu was your mother's cousin.'

'Second cousin, actually.'

'How long have you known her?'

She appeared co-operative, almost too friendly. She had turned in her seat, leaning back against the car door, facing him squarely. 'She just turned up out of the blue about a year ago. She sort of adopted us.'

'How did your father get on with her?'

'Dad would fall over like a puppy if a good-looking woman looked at him.'

'How did your mother feel about her second cousin?'

'She didn't trust her.'

'Is there a Mr Tzu?'

'There was. She says he's dead. He was a banker or something in Hong Kong. But we have only her word for it.'

'You're like your mother — you don't trust her?'

'I can handle her.'

'I'm sure you can.'

As they got out of the car Malone looked up; the sky was black, clouds spewing up like oil smoke. Then there was a deafening crash of thunder and a blaze of lightning in which the buildings across the road seemed to tremble.

'Do you believe in omens?' Camilla said as they crossed the street.

'All the time.'

He had taken her arm as they dodged the traffic and now she squeezed his hand between her arm and ribs. *Cut it out;* but he didn't take away his hand.

Clements was waiting for them in the lobby. 'You haven't met Ms Feng?' said Malone, removing his hand now.

'No,' said Clements, impressed but cautious. Then to Malone: 'What are we doing here?'

Malone explained what he had learned at the Sun office. 'The madame doesn't know we're coming. Let's hope the general is still with her.'

'He will be,' said Camilla. 'He's expecting me. This was to be my next call.'

'Then you owe me two bucks,' said Malone.

She opened her handbag, gave him two dollars with a smile and led the way to the lift. Clements raised his eyebrows enquiringly, but Malone just shook his head. He could smell a Chinese stew on the menu.

There was no doorman in sight to announce them to Madame Tzu and as they stepped into the lift Malone said, 'If they ask who you are over the intercom, don't mention us. We'll just follow you in when they open the door.'

'You may get a blast from Madame Tzu,' said Camilla.

'Just so long as it's not from a gun,' said Malone, and was instantly sorry when he saw her wince. Even Clements, used to Malone's sometimes loose tongue, looked at him.

The door was opened by the maid, who looked at the two detectives in surprise, then scurried away into the apartment, saying something in Chinese. Only a moment or two passed before Malone and Clements followed Camilla into the big living room, but Madame Tzu, it seemed, had already prepared herself.

'Why, Inspector, how unexpected! The gentleman with you is also a policeman?'

She's warning the general. 'Sergeant Clements, our Supervisor at Homicide. And this gentleman is . . . ?'

'General Wang-Te.'

Malone had had no experience of Chinese generals. He had a dim image of Chiang Kai-shek from a documentary he had seen months ago on the Soong sisters; the generalissimo had appeared to have more than the usual straight-backed arrogance of Western generals. Wang-Te was thin, stoop-backed and wore glasses; he was in a black suit and stiff white collar and looked like the cliché bookkeeper. Perhaps that was why he was the financial comptroller. He just smiled a big-toothed smile at the two detectives, but said nothing.

'Does the general speak English?' Malone asked.

'Fluently,' said Madama Tzu. 'And French and German.'

'We'll stick to English, our French and German are a little rusty. May we sit down?'

'Of course, how rude of me.' She said something in Mandarin to the general.

'What did Madame Tzu say?' Malone, rudely, asked Camilla.

Camilla looked at the older woman, who said, 'I told the general, one can forget one's manners after a day or two amongst Australians.'

Malone ducked his head in mock acknowledgement. 'Take no notice of her, General. We're not really rude, it's just our rough-and-ready ways —'

There was another tremendous crack of thunder and the building seemed to shake. Then beyond the windows the rain fell down in a thick curtain, silvered by lightning.

There was silence in the room for a moment, as if everyone was waiting for another avalanche of thunder; then Malone said, 'I understand you are here to try and recover some millions of dollars that ex-General Huang seems to have misappropriated?'

'That is correct.' Wang had a soft precise

voice. 'Fifty-one million. A large amount.'

'When did you find out the money was missing?' said Clements, taking over the bowling.

Wang-Te might look like a bookkeeper, but he had a general's appreciation of rank. 'You are only a sergeant?'

'A senior sergeant, actually,' said Clements. 'Licensed to ask questions of anyone of any rank.'

Good for you, thought Malone; but looked at Madame Tzu. 'Madame, I think things will go better if we stop trying to score points off each other.'

The general and Madame Tzu exchanged glances; then she nodded. 'As you wish, Inspector.'

Wang-Te looked at Camilla Feng. 'What have you told the gentlemen, Miss Feng?'

She didn't correct him to *Ms;* she knew an irredeemable chauvinist when she saw one. 'Nothing they didn't already know.'

Nice one, thought Malone: looks like we're in for a little prevarication.

'Inspector —' said Wang-Te, ignoring the senior sergeant. 'We only learned of the missing money three weeks ago. It had, of course, been coming here for some months — not *here,* exactly, but into Hong Kong on its way here.'

'I don't mean to be rude, General, but I understand you are the financial comptroller — wouldn't you have noticed such a large sum of money missing from your army accounts?'

'You are naïve, Inspector —' There was another clap of thunder, as if to underline the insult. Wang-Te waited, then went on, 'The money didn't come from army accounts — not all of it.'

'Then where from?' said Clements.

It seemed to pain Wang-Te that he had to answer someone so far down the totem pole in rank. 'Investments.'

'*Army* investments?'

The general ignored the question, looked back at Malone. 'The army has a bureaucracy like everything else. Scandal takes a long time to float to the top.'

'When you did learn it was missing, did you send someone out here to Sydney to, well, influence General Huang?'

'In what way?'

'I'm going to be rough-and-ready — by threatening him?'

Wang-Te looked at Madame Tzu, who was ready for her cue: 'Are you accusing the general of ordering the murder of General Huang?'

There was another clap of thunder, further away; the rain abruptly ceased. There was a weak blaze of sheet lightning and a moment later a bedraggled pigeon, an orphan of the storm, stumbled onto the windowsill, flapping its wings furiously.

'Poor bird,' said Camilla, but no one else seemed at all interested in the sodden pigeon.

Malone said, 'He may not have ordered the murders, but if he sent someone out here, things got out of hand. The gun that killed General Huang, Mr Sun and Miss Feng's father was the sort of weapon that's used by the Chinese army in covert operations. A Type 67,' he told Wang-Te.

'I know the gun,' said the general, 'but I am not an ordnance man — that is not my field. Neither are, as you call them, covert operations. I did not send anyone out here to see Huang, with or without a gun.'

'He must of had accomplices in China,' said Clements, too long out of the attack. 'Have you discovered them and dealt with them?'

'Yes.'

'Executed?'

'They are still awaiting trial. Our legal system is not as rough-and-ready as you seem to suggest, Sergeant.' The rank was emphasized, a put-down.

Malone turned to Madame Tzu. 'If the fifty-one million dollars goes home to China, is your investment in Olympic Tower in trouble?'

'What have you told them?' Madame Tzu snapped at Camilla.

'I told you — nothing they don't already know.'

Another brick in the Great Wall: *keep it up, Camilla.* Malone waited patiently till Madame Tzu looked back at him.

'Yes,' she said in a flat tone. 'It will place the

whole project in jeopardy.'

'Not quite,' said Camilla quietly. She had been sitting between Malone and Clements, demure as an old-fashioned convent girl: one who would think nothing of cheating at exams after three Hail Marys. Malone had remarked how totally self-contained she appeared to be, as if the two older Chinese did not in the least awe her. 'There are half a dozen corporations around town that will jump in if we invite them. The trouble is if we do that, then our investment goes out the window. You and I and the Sun brothers will be told to get lost.'

The older woman's face was suddenly as hard as ivory. Malone wondered if anyone, even the Red Guards, had ever told her to get lost. Camilla's pragmatism, it seemed, was devastatingly offensive.

'What about the Aldwyches and Les Chung?' asked Clements.

'They have more clout than we have,' said Camilla. 'They would stay.'

She was businesslike to a degree that Malone had to admire; he was beginning to be on her side. But there was a coolness, almost a coldness, to her that took the edge off his admiration. Did she weep for her dead father when she was alone? Was she more concerned for her legacy than for him?

Malone said, 'While the money is still here, General, would your army command be interested in putting the money into Olympic Tower?

You mentioned army investment.'

Wang-Te might have been asked if the army command should be asked to declare war. 'Inspector, I wouldn't ask a question like that from here.'

'But you might ask it when you get back to Shanghai?'

Wang-Te shrugged. 'It wouldn't be an army command decision. Do your defence forces throw money around?'

'We civilians think so,' said Clements. 'They're the only ones who never suffer a cut in their budget.'

'Whom are they afraid of? China?' Wang-Te almost smiled as he threw the bait.

Clements didn't bite. 'While you're here, why don't you ask them?'

Madame Tzu had been on the sidelines too long. Her models were Mei-ling Soong and Margaret Thatcher; she was not a by-stander. 'Olympic Tower is a solid investment with a guaranteed return. It is not like some of the schemes some of your con men, your *entrepreneurs* —' she gave the word a swipe of acid — 'the schemes they launched a few years ago. Do you think Mr Aldwych would have put money into this if he thought it was a risk? I know his past record —'

'You did homework on him?' said Clements.

'Of course.'

'You told him?'

'Yes. It didn't upset him. He told me he had

retired from his old line of work —'

'Did he tell you that he'd retired but not reformed?' asked Malone.

'Yes, he told me that. Every country has its retired criminals, doesn't it? You accept their money at face value.'

Malone grinned, shook his head. 'Do you voice that sort of opinion in China?'

Madame Tzu looked at Wang-Te; he gave a thin smile and she took that as approval of what she was about to say: 'In Shanghai, yes. If one doesn't take money at face value in Shanghai, one never attracts it.'

Malone looked at Wang-Te. 'So will you recommend the investment of the fifty-one million in Olympic Tower?'

'That will depend,' said the general. 'First, your authorities have to release the money, then it has to be transferred back to China. But why do you ask? Aren't you interested only in the murders?'

'You look in every mirror you find,' said Malone, and smiled at Madame Tzu. 'Old Homicide aphorism.'

'In the meantime,' said Camilla Feng, 'you appear to be getting no nearer to finding who killed my father and Mr Sun.'

Malone remarked that she hadn't mentioned General Huang: the disposable one? 'Oh, we've come some way, much further than we were last Friday night.'

Clements came in: 'You are quite sure, General, that no one came here from China to kill General Huang?'

'I didn't say that. I said *I* didn't send anyone on such a mission.'

'So the killer could of come from China?'

'Possibly. Huang had many enemies.'

'Did you know any of them, Madame Tzu? You were in business with him.'

'In business, Sergeant, one makes and needs enemies. Friends never sharpen your wits the way enemies do.' She looked at Malone. 'Old commercial aphorism.'

He grinned and got to his feet. 'When this is over, I'll come for tea . . . When are you going back to China, General?'

'As soon as possible.'

'Before you go, I hope to be able to tell you who committed the murders.' It was a dim hope, but the credo had to be demonstrated: *the police are hopeful of an early arrest.* 'May I use your phone, Madame Tzu?'

She waved her hand towards the entrance hall and he went out there; then had to put his head round the door: 'Miss Feng, what is the Sun office number?'

She took a small Filofax from her handbag, but before she could flip it open Madame Tzu gave the number.

Clements said, 'You have a good memory.'

'One needs it,' she said but didn't explain why.

Malone, out in the hall, dialled the number,

asked for Gail Lee, who came on the line almost at once. 'You can go back to the office, Gail. How'd you go with the brothers? Learn anything more?'

'Yes,' she said, and he could hear the undercurrent of excitement in her voice: 'Li Ping, the missing girl, was not Huang's daughter — she was adopted. She and Zhang, who was Huang's natural son, didn't get on. They hated each other.'

3

'He used to play one against the other.'

'Splitting heirs?' said Clements.

Malone and Gail didn't get it at first; then Malone groaned and Gail rolled her eyes. Clements grinned and went on, 'What sort of bastard was he? Anyhow, an *adopted* daughter? I thought sons were the first priority with Chinese fathers?'

'My father would dispute that,' said Gail with a smile.

They were back at Homicide, in Malone's office. Clements was going through the print-out of the running sheets. He looked to Malone like the Clements of old: the bloodhound that smelled blood. For a while, since he had become a father, he had been only going through the motions of being a detective. His daughter,

Amanda, was now a year old and to all intents and purposes he had seemed concerned only to protect her against the rapists, robbers and romeos converging on her from the future. Yet even on automatic he was the best detective on Malone's staff and the latter had never complained.

'How many suspects have we?' Clements held up the sheets. 'Madame Tzu, General Wang, the two missing engineers —' He looked at the sheets again; the Chinese names did not seem to lodge in his memory. 'Tong Haifeng and Guo Yi. And the missing daughter, Li Ping. And Les Chung and Jack Aldwych.'

'Cross Jack off the list. But why Les Chung? What would he have to gain by bumping off two of his partners besides General Huang? While I think of it —' He looked up, gestured at Sheryl Dallen in the outer room. She got up and came to the doorway of his office. 'Sheryl, get on to Immigration. If General Wang-Te attempts to leave the country without getting in touch with me, I want him held. Tell 'em I want every airport covered from Cairns to Perth.'

'Sure, boss.' She was all aglow, as if she had just come from a session at the gym. He had never seen anyone who looked so damned *healthy*. He could feel the fat growing by the minute round his waist.

'Has your sweaty friend at the gym come up with anything new?' She looked puzzled and he went on, 'The feller at the Securities Commission?'

She grinned. 'All my friends at the gym are sweaty. It's one of the things we have in common. Yes, Boris has told me a few more things — I'm putting them into the computer now.'

'Such as?'

'The Feng family companies are in trouble with the Taxation Office. And the banks are threatening to foreclose.'

'For Crissakes!' Clements almost crumpled the print-out in exasperation. 'Aren't there any cleanskins in this Olympic set-up?'

'Jack Aldwych,' said Malone; but he, too, wondered at the nest of snakes in the basement of Olympic Tower. And that Aldwych, of all people, should look like the only untainted one. 'How deep's the trouble with the Fengs?'

'Enough to bankrupt them,' said Sheryl. 'Which would mean they would have to withdraw from the consortium with Les Chung and the Sun family.'

'What about the Sun companies?' asked Malone.

'My friend Boris didn't say anything about them. They apparently are clean.'

Malone looked at Gail Lee. 'I think we'd better have Ms Feng in here. She's not telling us as much as she knows.'

'What if she refuses to come in?' said Clements. 'She's not the one in trouble with the

Tax guys. Let Gail and Sheryl go out to Drum-moyne and talk to her. Get cracking, girls.'

He waited till the girls had gone out of the small office, then he stood up, laid the print-out on Malone's desk. 'I've got ten more like that on my desk outside. I'm up to my balls in paper-work and you aren't helping, mate. We've also got a problem with our friend Boston. He's not going to Archives, as you recommended. He's going to Headquarters.'

'How'd he manage that? What sort of report did you put in?'

'As dirty as I could make it without being sued for libel. But someone at Headquarters is on his side. Guess who was his patrol commander when he first worked out of Day Street?'

'I've run out of guesses on this Olympic case. I'm not trying for any more. Who?'

'Commissioner Zanuch. I dunno whether Zanuch asked for him or not, but Boston's going over there tomorrow morning.'

'He's got no rank. What the hell use will he be over there?'

'Mate, half the establishment in Headquarters are no bloody use.'

Malone nodded and they both pondered this terrible state of affairs. In every uniformed ser-vice it was a given that deadheads were the airbags round the brass. Troops from Caesar's day to the Gulf War had chewed on the subject.

'I couldn't care less what use he'll be over there. It's the harm he might do us that worries me. He hates our guts — or anyway, yours. I just got sideswiped with the shit he feels towards you.'

Malone looked out into the main room. Boston had just come in, had sat down at his desk, which was completely clear of any paper. He swung his chair round and sat staring out the big windows at the sky that had now started to clear. Malone, watching him, saw a man who, suddenly and unexpectedly, exuded self-confidence. He had put one foot in heaven's gate, going to Headquarters.

'Send him in to me.'

'Don't blow your top, mate. Even though we don't like where he's going, we're glad to be rid of him.'

Clements gathered up the pile of letters Malone pushed towards him, grimaced at them, then went out into the main room and across to speak to Boston.

The latter looked across at Malone's office, then rose unhurriedly and came to stand in Malone's doorway. 'You wanted to see me?'

Yes, you arrogant bugger. 'I hear you managed to dodge my recommended transfer and you're going to Headquarters. They haven't told me.'

'I'm sure they will — it only happened yesterday afternoon.' He had sat down in the chair opposite Malone without being invited; but Malone was determined to keep his cool. 'You don't mind, you know, not so long as I'm gone from here.'

Stay calm, Scobie. 'How did you manage it?'

Boston pursed his lips, as if deciding whether to give away a secret; then he said, 'The Commissioner and I go back a long way.'

'So do he and I, but I don't think he'd do me any favours.'

'Maybe you wear the wrong colours. The Irish green.'

Malone frowned, but said nothing.

Again Boston pursed his lips; then he gave away the secret: 'He and I belong to the same lodge.'

For a moment Malone didn't make the connection; then his frown deepened, disbelieving: 'The Masons?' Boston nodded, as smug as a Grand Master. 'For Crissakes, that sort of thing went out ages ago. In the old days, yes — but *now?*'

In the old days, thirty or more years ago, Catholics ran up against barriers in certain sections of the Public Service; there had been certain large firms that would not employ Masons. But that sort of bigotry had disappeared; or so he had thought.

'He knows me better than you do,' said Boston. 'He remembers the work I did under him when he was my patrol commander. There's a vacancy at Headquarters, I heard about it and I spoke to him at a lodge meeting. I'm going into the security unit that is being built up for the Olympics. As a sergeant.'

Malone didn't stand up or put out his hand.

'Righto, good luck. You may as well sign off now.'

Boston took his time about getting to his feet; his rank could have been equal to that of Malone's. 'I can't say it's been a pleasure working here.'

'Don't even try.'

When Boston had gone Malone leaned back in his chair and stared out the window. A pigeon strutted on the windowsill, full of importance. It turned an incurious eye on him; man and bird stared at each other. Then it spread its wings, shook them at him almost derisively, and flew away. He would have wrung its neck if he could have reached it.

Gail Lee had taken the precaution of calling the Feng home at Drummoyne. No, Ms Feng was at the family offices in Chinatown. The two women detectives drove into the city, parking in a lane in a Loading zone and walked round into Dixon Street, the heart of Chinatown. A slow surf of white hair was spilling out of a tourist bus; senior citizens had come for a Chinese lunch at a restaurant opposite the Golden Gate. The group paused for a moment and looked across at the Golden Gate as if it still had an aura of murder. But the Crime Scene tapes were gone and inside the restaurant the bloodstained velvet of the back booth had been replaced. It was business as usual, though its prices were above the pockets of the senior citizens.

The Feng offices were in a modest four-storeyed building diagonally opposite the Golden Gate. The ground floor was occupied by a store that appeared to sell everything from sharks' fins to firecrackers and elaborate kites: the window was almost a parody of Chinese commerce. A narrow flight of stairs at the side led up to the Feng offices.

'I love all those spicy smells,' said Sheryl Dallen as they climbed the stairs.

Gail wrinkled her nose. 'I'm a steak-and-kidney pie girl, myself.'

'So am I,' said Sheryl. 'But just a look at a pie and I put on three kilos.'

There was no hint about the Feng offices that the family went in for multimillion-dollar investments. There was no reception area; the stairs ended on a narrow landing off which there were three small rooms. Camilla Feng was in the front room.

She stood up as the two detectives were ushered in by the very young Chinese girl who had intercepted them at the head of the stairs. 'I've been expecting you. My mother said you had phoned me at home.'

'What made you expect us?' said Gail.

Camilla waved them to the only two spare chairs in the small office. It was a room in which expense had been spared to a spartan degree; Samuel Feng had been able to work without luxury or the need to impress. There were no pictures on the walls, just a framed certificate of a degree in Economics from the University of New South Wales. There was no air-conditioning and the two narrow windows were closed against the noise in the street outside. Sheryl, who had more boyfriends than Gail, thought the room smelled like a bachelor's microwave oven.

'What made you expect us?' Gail repeated.

Camilla looked weary, not at all like the girl Gail had seen in the Sun offices in North Sydney only an hour or two before. Her make-up was washed out, the full lips no longer bright red. 'You don't sit on your hands on a murder case, do you?'

'Would you expect that of us?'

Camilla sighed, picked at some papers on the table that passed for a desk. 'No . . . Look, I want the murderer of my father found — I appreciate everything you are doing in that regard. But . . .' She picked at the papers again, then looked up at the two detectives. 'The roof has fallen in on us — my mother and my two sisters and me. Not just Dad's murder, but other things —'

'What other things?' said Gail, for the moment playing ignorant.

Sheryl sat quietly, the outsider, leaving the two Chinese girls to play the game. She was at ease with other ethnics, the Italians, the Greeks, the Lebanese; but she was always cautious with

Asians. Especially with the Chinese, who made her feel — immature? Whatever it was she felt, she was glad that Gail was here now.

'What other things?' Camilla stared at the two of them for a moment and looked as if she would keep those things to herself. Then she flung up her hands in despair; she was definitely not the girl of a couple of hours ago. All her composure was gone; in its place was something that even Sheryl recognized as fear. 'Half an hour ago, just after I got back here, a man called and told me to do the right thing or I'd be dead like my father.'

'The right thing?' asked Sheryl, feeling she could now come into the game. 'What did he mean by that?'

'I can't tell you that —'

'I think you'd better, Camilla,' said Gail. 'Is it to do with the tax charge that's hanging over you? And the bank debt? That if you can't pay it and you go into receivership you'll have to draw out of the Olympic Tower project? Is that what they want you to do?'

'How much *don't* you know?' Camilla was surprised; she had been slumped in her chair, but now she sat up. 'Who's been talking? Madame Tzu?'

'How much does she know?'

Camilla gestured in frustration. 'I don't know. But knowing her, she'd know everything . . . Have you talked to her?'

'Not about these matters, no. We have our own sources —' Gail glanced at Sheryl and gave her a tiny smile. 'Have you any idea who was the man who called you up? Was he Chinese?'

'I think so — he spoke perfect Mandarin. Foreigners always sound different when they speak it. But he was pedantic, like a scholar.'

'How many men do you know who speak Mandarin?'

Camilla spread her hands; still sitting forward, she was nervous. 'I don't know — maybe a dozen, maybe more. Mostly the older men, friends of my father. But I don't think this man was someone I know — you know when a stranger's speaking to you —'

'Mandarin?' Sheryl looked at Gail for enlightenment.

'It's the main Chinese language, but a lot of them here in Sydney speak Cantonese.' Gail turned back to Camilla. 'What are you going to do? Do the right thing, like he asked? Drop out of the project?'

Camilla sat back, was silent for a long moment; she picked at the papers on her desk again, then she said, 'I don't want to give up. Olympic Tower was my father's dream, to be involved in something as big as that. To be part of a landmark of Sydney. He was out of his league, that was how he got into trouble with the tax people. He put everything he had into the project, just ignored his tax and bank debts, which got bigger and bigger . . . I'm not naïve and romantic. I don't want to stay in the project for Dad's sake, to build his dream. If I can somehow stay in it, it will be because I can see the pay-off when it's completed. I'm not greedy, but I *am* ambitious. If I let our company go into bankruptcy it could be years before I get it out of it.'

There was silence in the room for a while; faint noises came from the street, but there was no definition to them. Gail wondered if Camilla had unburdened herself to anyone else as she had to the two strangers. She thought not: Camilla, up till now, would have been self-contained. But police, Gail was learning, were often a sounding board.

'So how do you avoid it?' asked Sheryl.

Camilla looked steadily at her. 'I ask someone to bail us out.'

'Who, for instance? A Hong Kong bank?'

Camilla hesitated. 'No-o. Jack Aldwych.'

The two detectives looked at each other, then Gail said, 'I don't know Jack Aldwych, but from what Inspector Malone and Sergeant Clements tell us, Mr Aldwych wouldn't lend the Pope a dollar.'

'Or even the Queen,' said Sheryl, a royalist and a non-Catholic.

'What about Madame Tzu?' said Gail. 'She seems to be the queen bee in all this.'

Camilla shook her head. 'She's got her own problems.'

'Such as?'

'Ask her.'

Gail considered a moment, then nodded.

'Okay, we will. But whoever threatened you wants the whole Olympic Tower business to collapse. Why?'

'I don't know. If it was something more closely connected to the Games, there might be a reason. There are some people in China who are still pissed off that Beijing didn't get the 2000 Games — they might be happy to see, say, the stadium or the Olympic village in trouble. But the Tower? Sure, it's already booked solid for Games delegations, but . . .' She shook her head again.

'What about the competition? Other developers who wanted that site and that project?'

'The others who missed out were all local developers, Australians. The man who threatened me was Chinese, I'm sure of it. The man who killed my father was Chinese. Why would Australians hire a Chinese to do their dirty work? If there's any local influence, it's only indirect. Everything to do with this is coming out of China.'

'Or Hong Kong,' said Sheryl.

'The same thing these days.'

Gail stood up. 'I think you should get some protection, Camilla. Get a security firm to give you twenty-four-hour protection. We'll let the Day Street police know you've been threatened. And the Drummoyne police — they can keep an eye on your home. Just sit tight and don't do anything till we've got this cleared up.'

'When will that be?' Camilla looked too

exhausted to stand up to show them out. 'I have just a week to try and stall off the banks and the tax office.'

Gail was standing by the framed degree certificate on the wall. 'This yours? You're a Bachelor of Economics?'

'I also have an MBA. Fat lot of good they're worth right now.' Then she stood up, but did not move out from behind the desk. 'Thanks. I know you're trying to help, but —'

'We'll do everything we can,' said Gail.

When they got down into Dixon Street Sheryl said, 'I've always envied the rich. But I wouldn't fancy being in her shoes.'

'All she has to do is not be killed,' said Gail. 'She'll be rich in another five years. She's got Shanghai blood in her.'

'How do you know?'

'Those who haven't got it always recognize it.'

'You Chinese,' said Sheryl, but smiled as she said it.

When they approached their car in the Loading zone in the rear lane, a young Chinese was waiting for them, his van parked alongside the unmarked police car. He immediately began yelling at Gail in Cantonese.

'Do you speak Mandarin?'

'Yes,' he said, spittle at the corners of his mouth. 'A little —'

Mandarin for centuries was a stately, elegant language. Then in the 1920s the woodworm of colloquialism crept in: 'Then get stuffed,' said

Gail, but managed to sound decorous.

'Was that Mandarin?' asked Sheryl as they got into their car.

'Yes,' said Gail. 'Word perfect.'

5

Malone waited for Lisa in the vestibule of the Town Hall. Once a week, since she had started back at work, they had lunch together; their only meal alone. They were both waiting for the two girls to move out to share flats with their friends; neither of them looked forward to the prospect, but they knew it was inevitable. Tom was more of a homebody than his two sisters, but even he would eventually move out. Until the general exodus began the meals at home were a family affair and Malone always enjoyed them. But, like all parents, he and Lisa had learned that, as their family grew older, their own privacy lessened. Their love-making, for instance, had its own rhythm method: the rhythm of the children's absences. He would have shouted them all to the movies seven nights a week, except that he knew the girls' sly smiles would have embarrassed him.

Lisa came towards him with the Lord Mayor. Rupert Amberton had been a fixture in Sydney civic affairs for almost a generation. He was in his early fifties, but looked younger. He had a mane of dark hair that was his pride and a cartoonist's joy; he was handsome, as any mirror, and he looked at several a day, told him. He leaped onto any charity bandwagon that rolled past, always ready with a cheque and a tear or two or three. He wore his heart on his sleeve, only because the usual cavity was chock-a-block with ego, and nothing would please him more, in the year 2000, than to see his heart up there on the flag with the five rings. He lived for Sydney and liked to think it lived for him.

'Inspector! I've only just learned you are Mrs Malone's husband. You're a very lucky man!' He always spoke in exclamations, as if at a rowdy council meeting. 'You're conducting this dreadful business connected with Olympic Tower!'

Malone wouldn't have put it that way. 'We have the matter in hand, but there's a long way to go.'

He had kept his voice low, but Amberton couldn't be anything less than operatic: 'Good luck! The last thing we want is a spate of racist murders!'

Malone looked around without moving his head: *why doesn't someone murder this loudmouth?* People passing through the vestibule, which had never been designed to stifle secrets, an oversight on the part of the architect, were slowing their steps, waiting for more details. Malone, voice still low, said, 'It's not as bad as that, Mr Amberton.'

The Lord Mayor all at once seemed to become

aware that the passing traffic was in slow motion as if underwater; all heads were turned towards him and the Malones. He threw out a glittering smile, like a royal salute, his head swivelling round so that he missed no one. Then he looked back at Malone, dropped his voice and the exclamation marks: 'Of course, of course. Well, good luck. The sooner you clear it up, you know, the better for us.'

'Us?' Malone couldn't resist it, the old tongue getting away from him again.

'Of course!' The operatic voice was back. 'The city! Sydney!'

'Of course,' said Malone, and tried to show some civic pride; he even threw in an exclamation: 'Keep the flag flying! The Olympic flag!'

Amberton raised his fist, like an Olympic winner, tossed his mane and went back across the vestibule, his smile lassoing bystanders whether they wanted it or not. The year 2000 couldn't come soon enough.

As they crossed the road to the Queen Victoria Building, the QVB as it was called, Lisa said, 'You'll have me fired.'

Malone shook his head. 'Look at his record. He wouldn't have sacked Judas Iscariot, for fear of making waves. You're a good-looking woman, too. He's a closet lecher.'

'What do I do if he makes a pass? Make a civilian arrest?'

They climbed the stairs to an upper gallery, found a table in one of the restaurants. They sat by the big window that looked out into the heart of the old restored building. For years it had been an almost empty shell; it was foreign money that had rescued it from demolition. All the local developers had passed it by, their hands stuck in their pockets.

Window-shoppers cruised the galleries, balancing their credit cards against what the boutiques offered. The economy had been slow all year and the store owners, atheists and believers alike, were on their knees hoping Christ and Christmas would bring buyers from the East, preferably Japanese, with gold and Diners frankincense and American Express myrrh. Father Christmas, two weeks early, wandered by outside the window, eyes dull and tired above the froth of white beard.

'You look worried,' said Lisa when they were settled.

Malone glanced up from the menu. 'Gail and Sheryl came back to the office just before I left. The Feng girl, she's taken over from her dad, she's been threatened. By a Chinese, she thought.'

'Do you have to protect her?'

'We'll have to keep an eye on her, but we can't give her round-the-clock protection. She's not in the Witness Protection scheme. How are things at Town Hall?'

Lisa waited till the waitress had taken their order and gone away. Then: 'I've been instructed to tell lies.'

229

He wasn't sure whether she was joking or not. 'Like the old days? That was what diplomacy was all about, wasn't it? Still is.'

In her two years as the High Commissioner's secretary in London, where she had first met Malone, Lisa had recognized that diplomacy and hypocrisy were partners in the trade; the honesty lay in the simultaneous recognition of the fact. She, for her part, had always tried to avoid the cynicism of the diplomatic profession. Diplomacy was the art of telling lies for one's country. Telling lies for one's city somehow did not have the same cachet.

'The murder of those men connected with Olympic Tower is uncovering a lot of dirt. I've been told I have to put a spin on it, somehow disguise it as top dressing. I'm out of practice at that sort of thing.'

'No!' With an exclamation mark. Two girls at a nearby table turned their heads.

'Keep your voice down,' said Lisa. 'No what?'

'No, you don't get involved in this.' Now that he knew she wasn't joking, he was afraid for her. More than dirt had been uncovered in Olympic Tower; blood, a lot of it, was showing. 'We don't know how far these people will go.'

'Which people?'

He sat back in his chair, shrugged with frustration. 'I wish I knew.' He glanced out of the big window, saw two Asian women come out of a boutique on the opposite gallery. He leaned forward, almost pressing his nose against the glass.

Then he shook his head and sat back.

'What's the matter? See someone you know?'

'I thought it was Madame Tzu. I've got her on the brain.'

Lisa stared out through the glass at the two women who had now paused outside another boutique. Each of them held three fancy shopping bags; there was always room on the arm for another. 'They are Japanese.'

He nodded. 'I know. But at first glance . . . Like I said, I've got her on the brain.'

'Why?'

'I don't know. She just seems central to all this.'

Lisa waited while the waitress put the smoked salmon salad in front of her. When the waitress had gone she said, 'I think she might have been over the road this morning.'

'Madame Tzu? At the Town Hall?'

'Yes. From the way you described her to me, it could have been her. Just as I was getting to work. She was coming out of Councillor Brode's office with a Chinese man.'

'What did he look like?'

'Medium height, thin, middle-aged. With glasses, not designer ones.'

He grinned, though he felt no humour. 'You can come and work at Homicide any time you like . . . Madame Tzu and General Wang-Te.'

She sipped her glass of white wine, reached for a wheatmeal roll and buttered it. He had ordered a small steak, a salad and a glass of red; anything heavier and she would have re-ordered for him. He knew that if he were not married to her, he would be as big as Russ Clements.

'I could find out what they were doing in Brode's office.'

'No.' He was chewing on a roll, so there was no exclamation this time. He cleared his mouth. 'Stay out of it. One cop in the family is enough.'

'Are you going to tell that to Claire when she graduates? She still wants to join the police.' She ate a mouthful of smoked salmon, then said, 'I'm on good terms with Rosalie, who acts as Brode's secretary. We exchange bits and pieces.'

The restaurant had filled up, chatter chipped away at any silence. Father Christmas rolled slowly by out on the gallery, this time tolling a bell; somehow it had no merry sound to it. Malone leaned forward, keeping his voice low. 'Darl, this Olympic job is a bloody mess, in more ways than one.'

'I know that. I'm not going to act stupidly. I'm not going to play at Joan of Arc storming some citadel —'

'You'd be good at that.' He tried to divert her by being facetious, a frayed marital ploy.

She ignored it. 'I'd forgotten there's a girls' network as well as a boys' network. Private secretaries aren't always so private when someone else has some gossip to exchange. Rosalie isn't a private secretary to Mr Brode, she's just someone who attends to his council business. She works for the council, for the *city*. She's a public servant, like you and me.'

'I'm a little more public than either of you. And I say stay out of this.'

She took another sip of her wine. 'I'll think about it.'

He knew there was no point in further argument. She had told him more than once that it was only Dutch stubbornness that had kept the North Sea from flooding the Lowlands.

Chapter Seven

1

'Someone at Town Hall is lining his pockets,' said the Premier.

He was honest as the day is long, depending on the season and daylight saving. He couldn't be bought, but he could be rented: a favour for a favour. He had thought of changing his name from Hans to Jan, but somehow Honest Jan didn't have the right ring to it. Neither did Honest Hans, according to his critics, who were many.

'Who, for instance?'

Since becoming Commissioner three months ago Bill Zanuch had trodden warily with the Premier and his *alter ego,* Police Minister. As an Assistant Commissioner he had had some contact with Vanderberg, but he had done his best to avoid him. He was an arch-conservative in his voting habits, but not naïve; he would have voted for Machiavelli, except that one couldn't trust Italians. He knew that the Premier was Machiavellian, but one always expected that of the Labor Right.

'Ray Brode.'

'Careful,' said Ladbroke, his minder. 'No

names, no pack drill.'

'Who's gunna give me any pack drill — Bill here? Police Commissioners never sack their Minister, do they, Bill? Or their Premier?' The bone-picking smile was at its widest.

'Never.' Zanuch almost tore a muscle forcing a return smile. 'But what do you want me to do? It's not a police job.'

'It's connected. Explain it to him, Roger.'

The three of them were in the Premier's office, the door shut against interference and passing ears. Zanuch was in his silver braid and Ladbroke in his Cutler double-breasted; the sartorial ruin was the Premier. He was in his shirt-sleeves, his white shirt already wrinkled, his standard plain red tie, one that he had worn for ten years, caught sideways across his chest under his black braces. There was no doubt, though, who was Caesar.

'It's Olympic Tower,' said Ladbroke. 'Ray Brode has prospered out of it, how much we don't know. The Tower project —'

Zanuch interrupted. 'How did it get the name Olympic? I thought all Olympic logos were the property of the organizing committee.'

'Only since Sydney got the Games. There was Olympic tyres, remember? There are fifty-two Olympic this-that-and-the-other in the phone book, but none of them uses the logos. Brode was in on the original project, the one that went broke. He knew Sydney was going to bid for the 2000 Games and he got the original developers to get in early, register the name. When the present consortium took over, Brode set about taking advantage of the name. It was he who sold the accommodation in the hotel to SOCOG.'

'He got the Chinese in, too,' said The Dutchman, who always kept a foot in the door of every conversation.

'It was common knowledge,' said Ladbroke, 'that several of the top guys in the IOC wanted Beijing to have the Games. Brode thought it might be a sop if he could persuade Beijing to invest money in Olympic Tower — make money out of *our* Games. He went to Beijing to sell the idea. But Beijing wasn't interested, not then. All the old men up there are a lot of stiff-necked bastards.'

The old man behind the desk nodded; none knew better how to stiffen a neck.

'Now Beijing has changed its tune,' said Ladbroke.

The Premier had been quiet long enough: 'The Chinese consul-general's been to see me. Shrewd feller, got his slanty little eyes wide open.' Out on the hustings he was every ethnic's best friend and patron; but he never had to look for votes in his own office. 'Beijing's just discovered it's got some corrupt generals in its army, fellers willing to use army money to make a dollar or two for themselves. Or a million or two. Beijing doesn't like the picture and they'd rather we didn't frame it.'

He'll be writing his own speeches next,

thought Ladbroke.

'I'm not quite with you,' said Zanuch, though he was well ahead of them. He hadn't risen through the ranks by looking backwards.

'You know who's involved in this. Les Chung, coupla other Chinese families, the —' He looked at Ladbroke.

'The Sun family and the Fengs.' The Dutchman would have known their names if they had been big Labor contributors. Ladbroke knew the Suns and the Fengs were Opposition backers.

'The Suns and the Fengs,' Vanderberg went on. 'And a General Huang. Your fellers aren't even close to finding who murdered Sun, Feng and Huang. Beijing couldn't care less about Sun and Feng, they're just locals. But they'd rather you forget about General Huang. They'd like us to forget the whole thing.'

'They're not serious!'

'I've shocked you, eh?' The Premier couldn't stand the Police Commissioner, but Cabinet, for once, had overruled him when the appointment had to be made. 'They're dead serious.'

'Are you?'

The Dutchman looked at Ladbroke. 'Am I?'

'There are advantages,' Ladbroke told Zanuch. 'We don't know how big this mess is. As it is, it's already getting us bad publicity overseas. Fleet Street, which wanted Manchester to get the Games, have gone back to their old ploy of painting us as The Land of the Long White Con. Brash Sydney, where anything goes, all that crap. They keep bringing up Bond, Connell, Skase — none of them was a Sydney-sider. They forget all about the shonky deals in the City of London. So far we've kept the Chinese connection out of the news —'

'Police PR have done that,' Zanuch corrected him. 'The media knows nothing because we've told them nothing.'

'Correction, Commissioner. The media does know and they're going to blow it any minute. They know part of the Tower development capital came out of China. They know there's been some wheeling and dealing with Town Hall. The one thing they don't know is that Mr Shan was General Huang.'

'Why do we have to protect the Chinese army's good name?'

Ladbroke managed to suppress a sigh. He knew that Zanuch saw the whole picture, framed or unframed, but that he had to play dumb. Commissioners of Police were not supposed to pay lip service to political skulduggery.

Vanderberg took over again: 'Bill, we couldn't give two hooters for the Chinks and their army. But if it gets out about them, it's all gunna spread like diarrhoea on a blanket —'

Zanuch, a fastidious man, shut his mind against the image.

'— and in no time at all Sydney's name will be mud.'

'Shit,' said his adviser.

The Dutchman nodded. 'Yes. We've had

enough crap thrown at us already. The Greens abusing us because the Games aren't gunna be green enough — Jesus, they think the world is gunna turn on their TV to count how many trees we've planted, how clean the Parramatta River is? Then there's the Abos threatening to demonstrate if they don't get their land claims —'

'Have you made any statement about those claims? You'd have a legitimate answer.' Zanuch knew what a storm such a statement would make.

'Nah, not worth it.' He was wise enough not to appear wise: the voters suspected wisdom, unless it came from radio talkback hosts. 'I had my way, I'd take the Olympics out of the media for a while.'

Zanuch was ambivalent in his attitude towards the Games. As Commissioner he knew there would be godalmighty headaches for the police: traffic problems, just for starters. And threats from demonstrators, security against terrorists: the list was already filed in his office and would grow. Yet there was the irresistible attraction: himself in full uniform up there on the official platform with the VIPs. Standing tall and proud, even through the smoke of a terrorist's bomb, the star of ten billion television screens. His one handicap, his wife, an iconoclast, had told him was that he would be wearing silver instead of gold. Still, better silver than bronze.

'We'd like the whole Olympic Tower business to die quietly,' said Ladbroke. 'Cancel the IOC accommodation, get it out of the picture entirely. But it's too late for that, there's already talk we're going to be short of accommodation. So all we can hope for is that you solve the murders quickly — or not at all. Just get them out of the media as soon as possible. From now on Sydney has to be pure as Shangri-la.'

'Or the Garden of Eden,' said the serpent behind the desk.

Zanuch stood up, ran a polishing finger along the braid on his cap. 'We'll do what we can. But these sort of things are never easy.'

When he had gone the Premier looked at Ladbroke. 'Well, will he play balls with us?'

I hope not. 'He will. The last thing he wants is to be known as the Commissioner of Murder City.'

'You should of been a politician, son,' said the Premier with grudging admiration.

'Every man to his last.'

'Nobody ever got anywhere, son, running last.'

Almost twenty years, thought Ladbroke, and I still don't know when the Old Man is fair dinkum with his aphorisms.

2

'It's official,' said Chief Superintendent Greg Random. 'General Huang never came near

Sydney. It was Mr Shan. He's the corpse, not the general.'

He and Malone were in his office at Police Centre in Surry Hills. Long and lean, he was a throwback to the disappearing laconic man from the bush; he had come out of the western plains thirty-five years ago and understatement still clung to him like plains dust. He never used words like *incredible* or *fantastic*. He had seen too much of human nature to know that nothing was incredible or fantastic, so he never wasted hyperbole the way the young did. He was sure, however, that hyperbole would burst out of this case.

'The media are going to get on to it sooner or later,' said Malone.

'Not from us, it won't. If anyone from Homicide gives any hint to anyone from the press, they're suspended, okay?'

'Greg, when we first learned who Mr Shan really was, it went into the computer. I've since put nothing new into it and I've had Sheryl Dallen recall the back-ups. But nothing leaks like a computer.'

Random pondered a while; Malone was accustomed to his long pauses. He had been commander of the Major Crime Squad, South Region, but recent reorganization, a growing disease in the Police Service, had made him the officer responsible for the Homicide and Serial Offenders Unit; it was rumoured there was a secret group at Police Headquarters who did nothing but dream up new names, a ploy also

241

rumoured to be financed by the stationery suppliers. The titles changed, but the work never.

He knew as well as anyone that secrecy in the Service, as in any bureaucracy, was an impossibility; even the corruption in certain sections, which had now been almost wiped out, had not been as secret as the corrupt had thought. He knew the truth of the old Hebrew proverb: Do not speak of secret measures in a field of little hills. Or a field of computers.

'Okay, we just play dumb. Anyone asks questions, you just refer them to the Commissioner. Let him carry the can.'

Malone looked out the window at the gathering clouds. 'I'm not getting very far, Greg. I've got twelve people working on this, including the fellers from Day Street. I want to find the three young Chinese who are missing, but they could be back in China for all I know.'

'Why don't you try and contact someone from the Triads?'

'You think that's easy? I've had a tail on Les Chung for the past coupla days, but he's not leading us anywhere.'

'What about Madame Whatshername? Tzu?'

The woman hovered like a shadow through the case; she was on his mind all the time. 'She's being tailed, too. By my wife.' He explained what Lisa had told him at lunch. 'I think she might be shaking hands with Councillor Brode.'

'Money changing hands?'

'Could be, but that's none of our business . . . I

told my wife to stay out of it and I've got Andy Graham tailing her and General Wang-Te. But the kids are the ones I want to talk to, they must know something or they wouldn't have shot through. I want the girl, Huang's adopted daughter.' He stood up, an eye on the clouds, which were black now. 'Suppose we find out the three Chinatown murders were organized from China, by the army?'

Random indulged himself in another long pause; then he grinned. 'Blame it on the CIA. They are always good as patsies.'

'You're a great help, Greg.'

'Scobie, someday you'll be sitting here in this chair. When the wind blows from the top it blows right through this chair. The thing you learn is that chief superintendents are just wind-breaks. All you can do is see that inspectors and other inferior ranks aren't bowled over by it. Our gods have suddenly become Olympian, all we can do is what they think is best. Which, more often than not, is the worst. But that's politics, right?'

Malone drove back to Strawberry Hills through a thunderstorm, which exactly suited his mood. Lightning scratched threatening mes- sages on a blackboard of cloud; a thick mesh of rain tried to bring him to a standstill. Pedestrians floated across the windscreen, saved from drowning by their umbrellas; a fire engine, looking for a fire, went by on a surf of dirty water. He was tempted to drive on through the rain, out into the clear weather of home.

'Get wet?' asked Clements as Malone came into the main office, his pork-pie hat dripping like a guttering, his jacket dark with water.

'Don't ask stupid bloody questions!'

'Oh-oh, bad news?' Clements followed him into the small office. 'I've got more bad news.'

Malone didn't answer, just took off his sodden jacket.

'Or maybe it's not so bad.' Clements sat down, in the visitor's chair this time, not the couch. 'It adds a bit more to our puzzle.'

'And that's good?' Malone took a towel out of a desk drawer, dried his face and hair. 'Come on, Russ, for Crissake, quit buggering about!'

'Sit down and simmer down,' said the big man. He waited while Malone combed his hair and then sat down behind his desk. Then: 'Okay? Four months ago two insurance policies were taken out, one on Mr Sun and the other on Mr Feng, each for ten million dollars. John Kagal has been doing some ferreting.'

'Each man took it out on himself or on each other?'

'No. The kids took it out on their respective fathers. The Sun boys on their dad, Camilla Feng on hers. The policies are on the fathers, but it's the kids who supposedly have paid the premiums and benefit from their fathers' deaths.'

'The rest of the families, the mothers and the other kids, don't get a look in?'

'No.'

Malone sat back; he felt he was drying out by the minute. 'Ten million? Can you take out that much life insurance in this country?'

Clements nodded. 'According to John, yes. One of the big companies here will issue the policy, then lay it off around the world.'

'What would the premium be on a policy that size?'

'John's been on to AMP. Just on $23,000 a year.'

'I dunno about the Sun brothers, but would Camilla have that sort of money? Her own, I mean?'

'We don't know if it was her money — it could of been her old man's. The whole thing could of been his idea. Four months ago he wasn't in trouble — well, he was, but only he knew it. He arranges a ten-million-dollar policy, more than enough to look after his family when the bad news breaks —'

'You said the family didn't figure as beneficiaries.'

'Okay, so they don't. Maybe he wants Camilla to stay in the consortium, pay off his debts and still be part of Olympic Tower. So he arranges his own murder.'

'And Mr Sun? He does the same? There's no evidence he was in financial trouble.'

'Feng persuades him to take out a similar policy, so his — Feng's — plan won't be too obvious.'

'Then he does the dirty on Sun and arranges

his murder, too? You're getting soft in the head, sport.'

Clements knocked his knuckles on his big head. 'Solid as a rock . . . No, our girl Camilla learns about Dad's financial black hole, decides Dad's gotta go anyway. So *she* arranges the murder.'

'And Mr Sun's? Or are the brothers supposed to be in it with Camilla?'

'No, that's the clever bit. She arranges for the killer to do her dad, Mr Sun and General Huang —'

'Mr Shan. There never was any General Huang. I'll explain in a minute. Go ahead.'

'Maybe Les Chung was to be bumped off, too — I dunno. But with a triple murder, it would look less like a put-up job to get the Feng insurance pay-out.'

'Are the insurance companies going to pay out?'

'When John went to see them, they decided to stall.'

'Don't they always?' Malone tapped his fingers on his desk. 'It's a good scenario, Russ, but —'

'But what?'

'I just have the feeling that the murders weren't homegrown. Don't ask me why — it's just a feeling.' Then his phone rang. 'Malone.'

'This is Sergeant Clover, sir. Telephone Intercepts.' He had a soft whispering voice, as if there was secrecy in his blood or he had been overwhelmed by the conversations he had heard on a thousand tapped wires. 'We've traced one of those mobiles you wanted. They are Telstra customers. They made a call this morning, to the Town Hall.'

'Where are they now?' Malone could feel the adrenaline starting up again. Even the sky was lightening outside.

'The call was made from an apartment in The Mount in Chinatown. Apartment 24C on the twenty-fourth floor. We'll meet you in the lobby.'

3

'Les,' Jack Aldwych had said yesterday, 'everything in this fucking business has got a Chinese name to it. Pretty soon the Chinese community is gunna have shit smeared all over it. The loony right-wingers are already making noises about Asian shenanigans. They called up Landfall Holdings asking why we're in cahoots with Asians —'

'Do they know *you* are Landfall Holdings?' Les Chung had said.

'I dunno. It don't matter whether they do or not.' The rough edges were showing, like a rock that had been washed clean of the moss that had softened it. 'So long as I'm not Asian, I'm lily white as far as they're concerned.'

'So what do you want?' Les Chung was not afraid of the old man, but he knew when to give and not take. He still woke at night in a sweat, the hitman coming back for him in a dream.

'I want to see some of the Triad leaders. I wanna find those three kids who've disappeared. They haven't shot through because all of a sudden they wanted a holiday on the Barrier Reef. They *know* something and I wanna know what it is.'

'What makes you think the Triad guys know where they are?'

'Maybe they dunno now — why should they? It's been none of their business up till now. Unless they're your silent partners?'

'Jack, why are you always so suspicious?'

'Because I spent bloody near sixty years learning trust is something I'd never put money on. Okay, they're not your partners. But you ask 'em where those kids are and I'll bet they'll have an answer in twenty-four hours — or sooner. Then I wanna meet 'em. Anywhere they name.'

'I don't think I'll be able to persuade them, Jack —'

'Les, tell 'em they can trust me.' His grin would have impressed Confucius.

So now he was sitting in one of the gambling rooms above the Golden Gate. With the advent of the Sydney Casino and the proliferation of poker machines in clubs and pubs, business had fallen off in these rooms; State governments encouraged gambling as a new religion and the voters had fallen on their knees in prayerful thanks. But old patrons still came here to these rooms, comfortable with the atmosphere and the odds. Luck, they knew, was a deity who would be no more favourable across the water in the casino glitz.

The heavy red curtains had been drawn and the only light came from a standard lamp aimed at Aldwych. Beyond the lamp, sitting behind one of the gambling tables, were the dim figures of four of the Triad leaders. Aldwych was amused by the theatricals, but he knew there was no one as secretive about their identity as the four who had agreed to meet him.

'Mr Chung vouched for you.' If there was a leader amongst the leaders it was the man sitting second from the right. 'He explained your reasons for wanting to meet us.'

Aldwych took his time, establishing his own position; he, too, had been a leader. 'With some politicians talking about Asians the way they are, you Chinese blokes don't want any bad publicity. I could of asked the business leaders from around here to help me find these kids, but they don't have the contacts you blokes have.'

The dark heads turned to look at each other; there could have been hidden smiles. They were heirs to a society that had been founded in the seventeenth century by a monastery abbot; they still had all the paraphernalia of religion but no religion. They paid homage to the Five Ancestors, the only survivors of the original society, which had been betrayed by one of its senior members. They paid their respects to the three Triad elements: Heaven, Earth and Man, aware always that Man was the most unreliable of the elements. Perhaps the abbot of Shao-Lin, looking down from Heaven, if he is there, ponders on how a company of 128 warrior-monks, formed to put down a small Tibetan rebellion, had grown to a conglomerate wherever Chinese are to be found. These four men in this darkened room thousands of miles from Shao-Lin were captains of their own peculiar industry; Aldwych knew they had more power than he had ever had. But they had never had his independence.

Then the spokesman said, 'You flatter us, Mr Aldwych, but we accept it — we don't get much of it.' One of them gave a short cough of a laugh. 'Do you think these young people have something to do with the murders downstairs?'

'I dunno. But you know, like I do, that the girl had twenty-three million deposited in her bank account. You'd be suspicious of her, wouldn't you?'

No heads nodded: they wouldn't spoil any of their own children that way. 'What about the two young men?'

'Suspicion again. Why did they suddenly skip the morning after the murders? Maybe they're all just shit-scared, but I wanna find out why. Les Chung and I've got a lotta money tied up in Olympic Tower.'

'What will you do to them if you find out they

did have something to do with the murders?'

Aldwych knew his answer would be important to them. He smiled. 'I might turn 'em over to you.'

'Not to the police?' This from the man seated on the far left, a man with a very narrow head and a sibilant hiss to his voice.

'Would you want me to? Suppose we dunno what would come out in court?'

'What are you afraid of that would come out in court?'

'Nothing that would hurt me or Les Chung. But you've got connections in China —'

'How do you know what connections we have, Mr Aldwych?' This from the spokesman.

'I know what connections you had forty years ago — things haven't changed. They don't change with you blokes — and I mean that as a compliment. You're conservatives like me, you know the value in no change.'

'We've known all about you for forty years, but I don't think we ever thought of you as a con-servative, Mr Aldwych. But go on . . .'

'Maybe back home in China there are a lotta high-ups who wouldn't want it broadcast that one of their ex-generals had been smuggling money out of China into the accounts of his son and daughter.'

None of the heads moved, no shoulders twitched: Aldwych knew then that they knew as much as he did, maybe even more. The spokes-man said, 'What happens if the third partner in

251

your consortium goes bust?'

'Les Chung and I will buy them out.'

'Would you consider us as partners?' This had obviously been discussed; nobody looked at the spokesman in surprise.

He could guess at the extent of their investments in Sydney: all money like his own that had been laundered, folded and accepted by stockbrokers who could turn a blind eye as neatly as they could turn a dollar. 'All local money or cash out of China?'

'Would more cash out of China matter?'

'It would if we were gunna have the same trouble as we had with General Huang.'

'We've never met before, Mr Aldwych, but you are much more scrupulous than we expected.'

Aldwych grinned, unoffended. 'Once bitten, twice shy, that's all. I'm sure you run your businesses the same way.'

'Is the money deposited in the bank accounts of General Huang's children, is it still here in Australia?'

'I dunno. It could be. But I'll bet it's not available. I thought you'd know what was happening to it.'

'Why us? We don't have any influence with the banks here. Or the government.'

'You know the new bloke who's just arrived, General Wang-Te.'

'What makes you think we know him?'

'You've just given yourself away. If you didn't

know him, you'd of asked who he was.'

Despite their vague forms Aldwych had now identified the four men. They came regularly to the Golden Gate, to the restaurant downstairs and to these gambling rooms; never together, but each with members of his own Triad. Aldwych had never questioned Les Chung about them; he knew Chung would give him no answers. They had been no part of his other life, there had been no battles with them; ethnicity had drawn the lines, the Great Wall had been built from both sides. Later there had been the Italians and the Greeks and, still later, the Lebanese; now there were the Vietnamese and recently the Koreans; the Russians still had to arrive. Aldwych had had nothing to do with the later arrivals and he knew the Triad leaders had the same reservations. Small empires set their own boundaries and their own rules.

The four men sat in silence; they looked at each other, but said nothing. Then the spokesman said, 'The three young people you are looking for are in The Mount. Apartment 24C.'

'Anybody with them?'

'No.'

'Who owns the apartment?'

'An offshore company. Hoop Investments.'

'Who owns Hoop Investments?' He knew they would know.

'Mr Raymond Brode. Councillor Brode.' A moment, then: 'You don't seem surprised.'

'The last time I was surprised I was nine years old. I'd just won the Under-Sevens race at the Water Board picnic for the third year running. I was surprised the organizers hadn't woken up to me.'

'You should have been Chinese,' said the spokesman, and all five of them, including the Caucasian, laughed.

4

The Mount was a steel-and-concrete high-rise that rose like a phallus out of the otherwise flat belly of Chinatown. It had been the first joint venture between Les Chung and Jack Aldwych and its thirty floors had been sold off the plan, mostly to Chinese buyers: Singaporeans, Hong Kong and locals. Aldwych had not been near the project since it had been built. Development for him was like a bank hold-up: take the money and run. It amused him that there were so many honest men with the same philosophy.

Malone knew nothing of Aldwych's connection with the building. With only a lukewarm interest in heritage preservation and conservation, he had never paid any attention to developers, never read the property pages in the newspapers. He was continually surprised at how the city's skyline kept changing; high-rise office and apartment buildings seemed to erupt like peaks thrust up out of the tectonic plates of the city. Sometimes he worried that one day he would find himself a stranger in a city that he had once known as intimately as his own back yard.

He and Clements and Gail Lee parked their car in the taxi zone right outside the entrance to The Mount. A taxi driver instantly fell out of his cab; he stabbed a finger at the sign: 'Can't you buggers read?'

Clements wearily produced his badge. There were advantages to having an unmarked police car, but sometimes he thought it would be better to have a disabled driver sticker on the windscreen. 'We're picking up a fare.'

'Oh, sure.' But the driver shook his head. 'But you got no idea — this is taxi territory, but buggers all the time —'

'I know just how you feel,' said Clements. 'It's the same in our territory.'

He followed Malone and Gail into the lobby of the building. It was not large, but it suggested you were entering luxury. The floors were marble, the furniture was glass, brass and leather; the two Chinese girls behind the reception desk were expensively groomed. Nobody dropped in here looking for a twenty-five-dollars-a-night bed.

A tall thin man in blue overalls came towards the three detectives.

'Sergeant Clover, sir.' His voice had a little more resonance than it had had on the phone. He gestured at his clothing. 'I'm supposed to be from Telstra. Only the manager knows why we're here and he's not happy.'

'They never are,' said Malone. 'You've got someone else with you?'

'He's up on the twenty-fourth floor. Are these people going to cause trouble? I don't want my bloke getting winged.'

'We dunno. They may, so we'll get your feller out of the way first. We've got a SPG team on the way —'

'They're here now,' said Clements.

They came into the lobby, six men in dark caps and tactical vests, their Remington 12-gauge shotguns held across their chests as if presenting arms. Behind the reception desk the two Chinese girls were suddenly round-eyed; an elderly Chinese woman stopped dead halfway across the lobby, her head moving awkwardly like a street mime's. Then the manager came out of his office, hands flapping, looking anything but managerial.

'I hope you're not going to do any *damage!*' He looked at the shotguns as if they were howitzers.

'No,' said Malone. 'This is just a precaution, in case —'

'In case of what?' He was short and tubby and all the police, with the exception of Gail Lee, towered over him. But he was the gatekeeper to this castle and, though he was not happy, he was not standing back.

But Malone had turned away from him, was speaking to the sergeant in charge of the State

Protection Group: 'We're not sure whether they're armed —'

'The lift's coming down from the twenty-fourth floor,' said Clements.

All eyes turned up towards the line of figures above the lifts. The light ran backwards across the line: 21–20–19. 'Righto,' said Malone, 'get everyone out of the lobby. Quick!'

Everyone was cleared from the lobby in a moment, Gail taking the elderly Chinese woman into the manager's office. The SPG men lined up three to either side of the descending lift; Malone and Clements stood behind them, as behind human fences. Malone, watching the light running across the line of figures, as under an invisible finger, felt his nerves beginning to tighten. There was no evidence at all that the missing Chinese girl and the two engineers, if they were in the lift, were armed and murderous. But Malone, awash in the puzzle of the case, was taking no chances.

3–2–1: the shotguns came up, the men in front of Malone and Clements stiffened. The doors of the lift slid open. Three young Chinese stood there, a girl and two men. And Jack Aldwych and Blackie Ovens.

'A guard of honour?' said Aldwych; on Judgement Day he would meet the Devil as an equal, ask the same question. 'Your idea, Inspector Malone?'

Malone somehow managed to stifle the laugh that, like a nervous tic, threatened to make a fool of him. He had a sense of the farcical; this was mockery with shotguns. The SPG men lowered their weapons, looked at each other and shook their heads.

'How do we report this?' the sergeant asked Malone.

'With restraint,' said Malone, and allowed the laugh to escape. 'Coming with us, Jack?'

'Of course,' said Aldwych. 'I was bringing these young people to see you.'

Chapter Eight

1

'Cut out the bullshit, Jack,' said Malone. 'What were you going to do with them?'

He, Clements and Aldwych were in Malone's office at Homicide. Li Ping, the young Chinese girl, was out in the main room, seated at a desk with Sheryl Dallen keeping an eye on her. Tong Haifeng and Guo Yi were being held separately in the two interview rooms. Blackie Ovens, a veteran of police questioning and therefore to be trusted as an old acquaintance, sat at an empty desk by a window in the main room, reading the *Telegraph-Mirror*'s sports pages.

Aldwych, perfectly at ease, considered a moment. He wore a dark blue summer suit and what could have been a regimental tie: any regiment, it made no difference to him. He was every inch the businessman and all he had been about was business.

'Scobie, all I was gunna do was ask them a few questions.'

'Why was Blackie carrying a piece?'

'You had *six* blokes carrying guns. And you and Russ here had your own pieces.'

'We have licences to carry them.'

259

'So has Blackie.' He grinned, still at ease. 'It may be ten years outa date, but he still has it. Come on, you two. I wasn't gunna blast those three kids. I was there for the same reason as you, to ask 'em some questions. You were the ones with all the artillery.'

As if on cue Gail Lee, who had stayed behind at The Mount, came into the main room and crossed to Malone's doorway. 'Nothing, boss. I went through the flat with a toothcomb. Not a gun, nothing.'

'Bank books, passports?'

'Nothing, just a couple of suitcases with a change of clothing.'

Malone looked at Aldwych. 'Did you or Blackie take anything off them?'

Aldwych shook his head. 'No, but we didn't search the place. We just knocked on the door, they opened it and we walked in.'

'They opened it, just like that? They didn't ask who you were?'

'Oh sure. Blackie said he was the house maintenance man. They're not very smart, those kids. The girl opened the door right away and, like I say, we just walked in.'

'Were they surprised? Scared?'

'Yeah, I think they might of been. They recognized me, the two young blokes. They might of been upset, too, when they saw Blackie with his gun.'

'It'd upset me,' said Clements, then looked at Gail. 'Okay, Gail, have a few words with Li Ping.

Tell her she's got nothing to worry about.'

'Has she?' asked Gail.

Clements looked at Malone, then back at Gail. 'That depends what Scobie's gunna ask her when he gets around to her.'

Gail nodded appreciatively, smiled at her two seniors, then went out and across to Sheryl and the young Chinese girl.

Aldwych said, 'I can't get used to women Ds. They wouldn't of lasted a week in my day.'

'Some of them are tougher than we are,' said Malone. 'I might give Constable Lee half an hour with you.'

'How'd you get on to the kids, Jack?' asked Clements.

'I'm sworn to secrecy.' Aldwych was enjoying himself, though disappointed. He was certain he would have got more out of Li Ping and her boy friends than the police would.

'Who rents them the apartment?' said Malone. 'The manager said they just moved in there, no reference to him. It's owned by some firm called Hoop Investments. That wouldn't be you, would it?'

'You're barking up the wrong tree, Scobie.'

'We do that quite a lot, but sooner or later we find the right tree. Come on, Jack, it won't take us long to find out who Hoop Investments are.'

Aldwych took his time; then: 'Ray Brode.'

'Councillor Brode?' said Malone, and looked at Clements. 'Why ain't I surprised?'

Aldwych was surprised. 'You mean you knew

261

he was mixed up in all this?'

'No, Jack. It's just that I feel we're in a circus and circuses are full of surprises. Don't you feel like that, Russ?'

'Oh, indubitably.'

'Indubitably?' Aldwych had a little difficulty with the word.

'It's the new Service policy,' said Clements. 'We're supposed to sound as if we had a tertiary education.'

'All the lawyers who tried to send me to jail had tertiary education. Last count, three of *them* were in jail.'

The small exchange had relaxed the atmosphere. Malone, almost against his will and certainly against his training, had over the past few years come to accept Jack Aldwych. But he was under no illusion: the relationship was a cobweb spun over the past, but which still had menace for the present. If it came to a crunch, Aldwych would take care of Number One; others, including Malone, would be taken care of in another sense. It was politics of the personal, which can be just as self-serving as the other sort.

'Have you spoken to Brode?'

'No.' He had, but that had been months ago on the matter of the four extra levels on Olympic Tower. Madame Tzu had done most of the talking, but it was Aldwych's and Les Chung's money that had had the final word.

'Leave him to us, Jack.' Malone stood up, eased his back. This case was like cold weather, stiffening his joints. 'We'll let you know if we get anything out of the Chinese kids. Oh, and tell Blackie to put his gun away in a drawer and throw away the key. Why didn't he hand it in during the gun amnesty?'

'He must of forgot. He ain't as young as he used to be.'

'Are you?'

'Oh, indubitably.' His grin, if nothing else, was youthful.

When he and Blackie Ovens had gone, Malone said, 'Why do I like the old bugger so much?'

'He's an honest crim,' said Clements. 'If he was gunna stab you in the back, he'd turn you around first and tell you. This city's full of bastards who wouldn't do that.'

'I like you, too. You're such a comfort.'

He went out into the big room and across to where Gail, Sheryl and Li Ping sat at the desk. One or two other detectives were at their desks, but most of Homicide were out on other cases or, the dread of all cops, in court awaiting their call.

The two women detectives went to stand up, but Malone waved them down, took a chair and sat down with them, across from Li Ping.

'Have you told our two ladies anything, Miss Li?'

She was pretty in a flat-featured sort of way that only lately had he come to appreciate. Most of his life, from the time he had discovered girls, he had looked for fine bones, expressive eyes,

263

preferably heavy-lidded, and a full sensual mouth. Not all the girls he had known had had those qualities, though most of them had been sensual in other places. Then Lisa, who had all the qualities, had come along and established his standard for all time. It was she, running Asian movies on SBS, the multicultural channel, who had pointed out to him that not all beauties were Western.

'What should I tell them?' It hadn't occurred to him to ask whether she spoke English; he chided himself for his stupid, narrow outlook. Her English was careful, though; or maybe it was just she who was careful. 'I do not have anything to tell.'

Malone looked at Gail and Sheryl. 'What have you asked her?'

'Only why she and her boy friends suddenly disappeared,' said Sheryl.

'And what did you say, Miss Li?'

'We were frightened. Very much afraid.' She did not appear very frightened at the moment, though she was not totally relaxed.

'What of?'

'The murders.'

'The Chinatown murders? Or the murder of your brother Zhang Yong?'

She looked sideways at him: carefully. 'Who told you he was my brother?'

'Okay, not your blood brother. You were the adopted one. By General Huang. Right?'

'Who told you all this?' As if police were not

entitled to pry into family matters.

'We told each other,' said Malone, and Gail and Sheryl smiled. 'When did the general adopt you?'

'When I was very small, a baby. His wife wanted a girl. She was very good to me, till she died.'

'And things haven't been so good since then?'

She didn't answer, just sat staring at him: *decide your own answer.* He said, 'Do you know who your natural mother was?'

'No.'

He fired an arrow wildly into the air: 'Was it Madame Tzu?'

Gail and Sheryl raised their eyebrows, but he ignored their look. Aimless arrows occasionally hit a target.

But not this time: Li Ping shook her head at his stupid imagination. 'You must be joking!'

'Righto, let's say I am.' Then he stopped joking: 'Where were you when your brother was murdered?'

It hit home; she flinched. 'I — I was with my boyfriend.'

'Who is?' But he knew.

'Guo Yi.'

'And where were the two of you?'

'In Chinatown. At —' She named the largest restaurant in the area, one that could seat a thousand diners.

'A pretty big place. I don't suppose you would have been noticed by anyone? Not by the waiters?'

'I do not know. Why should we wish to be noticed?'

This girl is smart: too smart. 'Where did you spend the rest of the night?'

'We went home to our flat at Cronulla. We slept together, if that is your next question.'

'When did you learn your brother had been murdered?'

She did not flinch this time. 'We heard it on the radio.'

'And that was when you decided to disappear? When did Tong Haifeng join you?'

'We met him at the apartment in The Mount. He arranged it all.'

'With Mr Brode?' Her face remained blank. 'The owner of the apartment.'

'I suppose so.'

Malone changed tack: 'What was to be done with all the millions in your and Zhang's accounts?'

'I don't know.'

'You don't know? Twenty-three million dollars in your account and no one told you what it was for. Come *on*, Miss Li. You were stupid —'
She looked up sharply at that. 'Well, you were, weren't you? You and whoever sent the money. Didn't you think so much money would instantly make the bank suspicious?'

She was wearing slacks, a white shirt and a sleeveless brocaded vest. She fumbled in her pockets, but came up empty-handed; then murmured *Thanks* as Sheryl handed her a tissue. She blew her nose, looked at the tissue, then folded it neatly and put it in her pocket. She's stalling, thought Malone and waited patiently.

'I had nothing to do with the transfer of the money,' she said at last. 'It just arrived.'

'And the bank rang you to tell you?'

'No. I happened to go to the bank the day it arrived.'

Malone looked at Sheryl, who said, 'We've been in touch with your bank, Ping. You went to the bank three days in a row, asking if money had arrived.'

Li Ping sat very still. She had a slim figure and long legs; there was nothing of the squat peasant about her. She came from the north, she had told Gail Lee, but she had not named a town or village where her natural mother had borne her: because, she had said, she did not know. As the questioning had proceeded she had sat up straighter; there was now an air to her almost of defiance. As if to say that, after all, she was a general's daughter. Adopted, sure, but that meant she had been chosen.

'Why wasn't the money sent to General Huang?' Malone asked. 'He had the Bund Corporation account.'

'I do not know.' Her English had suddenly become careful again. 'He was not here in Sydney when they told me the money was in my account.'

'And in Zhang's?'

'I suppose so. Zhang and I were not speaking

267

to each other.' She was prim.

'And General Huang didn't come to see you when he arrived?'

'No.'

'Did he go to see Zhang?'

'Probably. He always saw him first.'

'When was he to see you?'

'We were to meet on Saturday morning. He was murdered on Friday night.'

'Did your boy friends know about the money?'

'I do not discuss everything with them.' Even primmer.

'Miss Li, we know Guo Yi is your live-in boy-friend. You mean to tell us you suddenly have twenty-three million dollars in your bank account and you don't mention it to him?'

She stared at him, said nothing. All at once Malone had had enough of her; she would keep. He stood up. 'I'll talk to Guo, maybe he'll be a bit more co-operative.'

'May I go now?' She seemed totally uncon-cerned about her boyfriend or how co-operative he might be.

'You don't want to wait for your friends?'

'They will know where to find me.'

'But we mightn't. Stay a little longer, Miss Li. Detective Lee will make you some tea.'

She looked at Gail. 'I'd prefer coffee.'

Another section of the Great Wall. But Malone just grinned at her and walked across to the first interview room where Andy Graham was keeping Guo Yi company. As soon as Malone walked into the room the young Chinese looked up at the video camera that recorded interviews.

Malone shook his head. 'It's not turned on, Mr Guo. We only do that when we have a suspect. Do you think you're a suspect?'

'No.'

'Good. What have you told Detective Graham?'

Guo gestured. 'Nothing. But he's been very friendly.'

Andy Graham grinned and Malone said, 'He's the friendliest man on my staff. I'll try and be friendly, too.' He sat down opposite the young Chinese. 'Why did you disappear at the weekend?'

Guo Yi was just above medium height with more weight and muscle than Malone, still trapped by image, expected in a Chinese. He was handsome, almost Western in his looks (again the prejudiced image), with long black hair brushed straight back and a small pearl ear-ring in his left ear. He was dressed in blue jeans, a black Mambo T-shirt and brown deck shoes. After his initial glance at the video camera, he was now composed. Almost coldly so.

Oh Christ, thought Malone, another Great Wall. 'Why did you run away, Mr Guo?'

'We were scared.' His English was more relaxed than Li Ping's. 'Wouldn't you be? Four murders, all Chinese? All people we knew.'

'There are other Chinese involved in this case. Mr Chung, Madame Tzu, Miss Feng, the Sun brothers. They didn't run away.'

Guo shrugged, sitting back in his chair. 'None of them come from China.'

'Madame Tzu does.'

He nodded. 'Except Madame Tzu.'

'Is she friendly? I mean, with you?'

'She is very —' he paused for the word '— gracious.'

'But not friendly?'

'She is older. They expect respect, older women.'

'Does she get it? From you?'

'Of course.'

'Do you think all four murders were committed by someone who came from China for that specific purpose? We would call him a hitman.'

'I don't know what to think. But it's probable, don't you think?'

'I'm like you, I don't know what to think. What do you think, Detective Graham?'

Andy Graham shifted his bulk in his chair. He was an amiable young man who had been five years with Homicide and still had his initial enthusiasm. He was clumsy in his movements, a danger to children and fragile women. But he was never clumsy in his thoughts, not when a clear mind counted.

'I think Mr Guo is lying.'

'There you are, Mr Guo. Detective Graham doesn't believe in lateral thinking, he goes straight for the obvious.'

Guo stared at both of them, then he nodded at the camera. 'Are you going to turn it on now? Am I suddenly a suspect?'

'Suspected of what?'

Guo shrugged. 'I don't know. So far all you've accused me of is running away. I've explained why.'

'Do you own a gun?' said Malone.

'Why should I own a gun?'

'Were you ever in the army?'

'Yes. I was in the engineers corps.'

'Did you know General Huang then?'

Guo laughed: it sounded genuine. 'I was a very junior lieutenant. I didn't know he existed.'

'When did you know he existed?'

'When I met Li Ping. About a year ago.'

'Did you get on with him? Was he friendly towards you?'

Guo seemed to give the question sincere thought. 'No, not *friendly*. He was very rank-conscious. I was still very junior.'

'You were still in the army then?'

'No, I had been out a year.'

'So he resented you being Li Ping's boy-friend?'

'I don't think he cared one way or the other. He was not a very caring parent.'

Malone sat back in his chair. 'Like Detective Graham, I think you're lying, Mr Guo. We have it on good authority that you and Mr Tong were protégés of General Huang.'

Guo ran his tongue round his teeth. 'That was

after we went to work for his development company. He recognized that Tong and I were good engineers. The best, he said.'

'So actually you got on well with him? As a protégé?'

Guo was ill at ease now but only just. 'No. Once Li Ping and I started going together, things changed.'

'I wonder how many more lies you're going to tell us?' Then Malone changed tack: 'Do you know what a Type 67 is?'

Guo shook his head. 'No. I haven't a clue, isn't that what you police say?'

Smartarses are international. 'Occasionally. Are you going back to work on Olympic Tower?'

Guo hesitated, then nodded. 'I think so. Mr Aldwych told us we'd better.'

Malone grinned. 'Then I'd take his advice.'

'Do you think the murders have stopped?'

'I haven't a clue,' said Malone and stood up. 'You can go out and join Miss Li. We want you to wait till we've talked to your friend Tong Haifeng. Would you like some coffee?'

'Tea,' said Guo.

'Will you oblige, Andy? Loose leaves, no tea-bags. Right, Mr Guo?'

'You're a civilized man, Inspector.'

'We still have a few barbarians running around loose.'

Why do I get into these smartarse exchanges with the Chinese? They're not all sons and daughters of Confucius.

He went out and into the next interview room, where Tong Haifeng sat with Phil Truach. 'Things okay, Phil?'

'We're both dying for a smoke. Mr Tong smokes fifty a day, he tells me.'

'Nerves, Mr Tong?' Malone looked at the young Chinese, who was cigarette-thin and tobacco-sallow. 'I'm a non-smoker and heartless. No smoking till you're out of this building.'

Tong coughed, then smiled, showing tobacco-stained teeth. 'Why are we here?'

'I told him,' said Truach, 'but he thinks it's a joke.'

'Why would we waste our time joking, Mr Tong, when we have four murders on our hands? Do you speak Mandarin?' Gail Lee had told him about the threat to Camilla Feng.

Tong frowned. 'Of course. And Cantonese.'

'And Mr Guo — does he speak Mandarin?'

'Yes. Am I going to be questioned in Mandarin?'

'Hardly, Mr Tong.' Malone sat down opposite him. Truach looked imploringly at him (can't I just step outside for a smoke?), but it was standard procedure that when questioning anyone two detectives had to be present. 'If you give quick answers to our questions, you and Sergeant Truach can soon be out on the street having a smoke. Who suggested the three of you should disappear Saturday morning? Or was it Friday night?'

Tong coughed again, but didn't smile this

time. He appeared to be all skin and bone under the white shirt and tan trousers he wore; but he had big, strong-looking hands that kept moving one within the other like coupling crabs. 'Li Ping was the frightened one. Women always are, aren't they?'

'What would Madame Tzu say to that?'

Tong wrinkled his thin nose. 'She's different.'

'Did you know her before you came to Australia?'

Tong coughed again; it was a stalling ploy. 'Yes.' He took his time before going on: 'General Huang introduced us to her, recommended we be brought out here for Bund Corporation.'

'You were one of the general's protégés?'

He hesitated, then nodded. 'Yes.'

'Did you know Zhang Yong?'

'No.'

'You didn't know he was Li Ping's brother?'

'Well, yes.' Again the cough. 'But I never met him.'

'Do you own a gun, Mr Tong?'

Once more the cough: it was too obvious a ploy now and Malone was irritated. 'Why should I own a gun? I'm an engineer.'

These bastards have rehearsed their answers. 'You were in the army with Guo. Do you know what a Type 67 is?'

'There is a Type 67 theodolite, an old model. Some surveyors still use it.'

Malone looked at Truach, who had remained expressionless during the questioning. 'Never

274

lost for an answer . . . Righto, Mr Tong, you can go. Don't smoke till you're outside the building — you might be arrested.'

'For smoking?' He had stood up, was taller than Malone had thought.

Malone just grinned. 'See them out, Phil, right down to the front door.' Where Phil Truach could have his own smoke. 'Go back to the apartment in The Mount, Mr Guo, not back to Bondi. We want the three of you to stay together. We'll be in touch again.'

'What have we done?' Now he was on his feet he sounded more confident; or just closer to a smoke. 'Have we done something wrong by being afraid?'

'We just want to keep an eye on you. We don't want three more murders. Bullets kill you quicker than cigarettes.'

He grinned at Phil Truach, then went out of the room and crossed to his office. Clements got up from his desk and followed him. 'We're letting them go?'

'We've got nothing to hold them on. But I want them kept under surveillance. Ring Day Street, let them do the legwork.'

'Do you think the girl and these two young guys know something?'

'They know more than we do, but we're not going to get it out of them today. We'll try the Chinese water torture. We'll have 'em in again.'

Clements nodded appreciatively. 'You're getting more and more Oriental by the day.'

275

'Most of my life I found trouble with three things. Plastic kitchen wrap, putting a ribbon into a typewriter and passionate virgins who wanted to remain virgins. But these bloody Orientals . . .' He shook his head in frustration.

'What are we gunna do about Councillor Brode? Try some water torture on him?'

Malone looked at his watch. 'We'll talk to him tomorrow. I'm going home.'

Then his phone rang. It was Phil Truach on his mobile. 'I'm downstairs, Scobie. The kids have just been picked up by a woman who was waiting in the car park for them. In a Mercedes.'

'What did she look like?' But he knew.

'Chinese. Middle-aged. Well dressed.'

'Madame Tzu.' He hung up and looked at Clements. 'I think I'm beginning to feel the water torture myself.'

2

'Are you awake?'

'Yes. But I've got a headache.'

Lisa dug him in the ribs. 'I'm serious — *that's* the last thing on my mind.'

He rolled over on his back, switched on the bedside lamp. 'Righto, what *is* on your mind?'

'Ray Brode went home sick today. Suddenly.'

He had not discussed the case with her this evening. He had come home, glad as always to walk in the front door. He had paused by the two camellia bushes: no, *trees*. He had planted them when they had moved into the house in Randwick North, as the locals called it, as if the extra designation gave it some sort of cachet. The camellias had been bushes then, but now they were trees. He was not a dedicated gardener (Lisa was that) and occasionally he was surprised at the growth of what had been planted: the azaleas, the roses, the gardenias: somehow Lisa managed to get them all to flourish in the same soil. But he did remember planting the camellias; somehow it was almost as if he had forgotten to watch their growth. And now they hung over him, an awning that led to his house, his home. He wondered how many men marked their own years by the growth of the bushes they planted.

He had stopped and looked to the west, above the houses on the opposite side of the street. The setting sun had exposed a gold reef in a cliff of cloud, promising a better tomorrow. But his mood was low, he knew it was fool's gold, tomorrow would be no better. So tonight he had not discussed the case, had kept it to himself like a disease he didn't want to spread.

'Why did you have to wait till now to tell me?'

'You told me at lunch to mind my own business.'

He felt for her hand. 'Darl, don't get involved —'

'I'm not. I didn't go asking Rosalie why Brode

277

had left so suddenly — I didn't know he'd gone. She came into my office to give me some papers and she just remarked on it. Said it wasn't like him, he was always boasting how fit he was . . . He's not, he's overweight —'

'Go on,' he said patiently.

She dug him in the ribs again. 'Brode comes in two days a week to Town Hall. He was dictating to Rosalie today when he got a phone call. He listened to it, evidently it was quite short, then he hung up and told Rosalie he suddenly felt unwell and he was going home. He was gone before she could ask if she could help him.'

'I think I know where the phone call came from.' He told her about Brode's owning the apartment in The Mount. 'Tomorrow you go in and you mind your own business, okay?'

'I'm not going to act all girlish and stupid like the girl in that stupid Woody Allen murder film. But if I hear things —'

'Darl —' He turned his head on the pillow to look at her. 'This is *my* case. I'll do my own investigating.'

She turned her head. 'Do you have any idea how it's going to end up?'

'No. I'm having so much pressure put on me —' He had been almost on the point of sleep when she had first spoken. Now he was wide awake. He put his hand on her belly, felt the warmth of her. 'Now I'm awake, my headache's gone.'

She lay a moment, then she raised herself and

kissed him. 'You know where it is . . .'

In the morning at breakfast Claire said, 'You had the State Protection Group out yesterday. You didn't tell us.'

'There was nothing to tell. Where'd you hear it?'

'It was on 2UE this morning, half an hour ago. They said it was some sort of balls-up.'

'They use that sort of language on 2UE?'

'Was it a balls-up?'

'It was just an exercise. You don't want to believe everything you hear on radio.'

'So it was a balls-up?' said Maureen, the student in Communications.

Malone looked at Lisa. 'Let's buy a flat and move out. We don't need this lot.'

'I'll come with you,' said Tom. 'You can teach me how to organize a balls-up.'

'Better still, you all move out.' But he would hate the day they did.

3

Madame Tzu was furious with the man. She had never had any time for army officers; even the corrupt ones had no imagination. 'You have to move! The other two, Chung and Aldwych, are waiting to take us over!'

General Wang-Te was unmoved by her fury. He sat sipping the tea that Tzu's maid had brought in when he had arrived. He was not staying at the Vanderbilt, but had booked into a three-star hotel as Mr Wang-Te, a lecturer from Shanghai University. The less advertisement for himself, the army and the current problem the better.

'You will have to be patient —'

'Patience be damned!' Anger made her look older. As it always does with women, thought Wang-Te, a misogynist.

He took another sip of tea, the very image of patience. 'We can do nothing about your project —'

'Not *my* project! Not just mine — there are others in this —'

'*Were* in it,' he corrected her. 'Your two friends in Shanghai are in jail awaiting trial. They may be executed. As Huang would have been if he had come back to China.' He sipped his tea. 'The thinking in Beijing is that a lesson must be taught. There is enough corruption at home — soon we'll be as bad as the Russians —' He shook his head at the prospect. 'The worst of it is that I knew your partners. All good officers till —'

'Till I what? Seduced them?'

He smiled at her. 'Is that how you persuaded them?'

'Don't be ridiculous!' For a moment she looked as if she might throw her own cup of tea at him.

'There are too many irons in the fire.' He was

not an aphorist, but he had a fondness for clichés, which in many cases started life as aphorisms. 'Some will have to be taken out.'

'Who? What?'

'Huang's daughter and your two young engineers.'

'Taken out? You mean killed?' She was a devotee of American films, especially Scorsese's gangster films. They showed the uses of ruthlessness.

They were speaking Mandarin and he had used the phrase *taken out* in its literal meaning. 'Killed? Do you want that?'

The idea seemed to cool her; her anger died down. 'Another three killings here in Sydney? No, that would be too much.'

But the idea hasn't repelled her, he thought. He was a married man, but he had spent all his life since his youth amongst men. Ruthless women were as unfamiliar to him as nymphomaniacs; his wife, educated by American missionaries, had kept him protected from both. 'I want to take them back to China.'

'All three?'

'No, but the girl must be taken back. Our embassy in Canberra is working on that.'

'How?'

He ignored the question; as he had, for sake of peace and quiet, learned to ignore his wife. 'The main problem has to do with the money.'

'Of course the problem is the money!' She had little patience with him. He was an accountant,

281

despite his rank: General Profit-and-Loss. Her partners had been generals, but they had never thought of loss, being generals of the old school. They had been stupid about the outside world, but stupid partners were always more manageable than smart ones. Till General Huang had tried to be smart . . . 'Are the Australians going to release it?'

'Who knows what Australians will do? Often, they don't know themselves. But our embassy is working on them.'

'The embassy! Don't you know that diplomatic channels are streams that run uphill?' She was an aphorist, though her wit and wisdom were often borrowed. 'We need the money *now!* Tell your army friends in Shanghai the money will be returned double in five years. It's here — leave it here and use it!'

He knew she was probably the smartest woman he had ever met, but greed had made her naïve. 'How do we tell that story to the Australians? They are not interested in *our* profits.'

'You find the right men to talk to —'

'Our embassy are doing that. But whatever understanding is arrived at, it won't be between Canberra and Shanghai. It will be between Canberra and Beijing.'

'Beijing!' The scorn in her voice would have curdled milk, if any had been served with the tea. 'What do they know?'

Wang-Te had been born in Shanghai and raised there. His father had worked for a foreign bank and had stood and watched the night Chiang Kai-shek's men had come to the bank and removed all the gold in the vaults. Mr Wang-Te had stayed on and survived; the Communists had needed his expertise in international banking; those had been the pragmatic days before the mass stupidity of the Cultural Revolution. Mr Wang's son had been brought up not to question Communism, though not necessarily to believe in it. The Wang-Te family had had their own pragmatism.

'They know nothing. When it was Peking they knew nothing. The same now it is Beijing. When London ruled half the globe, do you think it understood those it ruled? Do you think Washington understands us Chinese or the Arabs or even the Jews? Capitals are the same everywhere. They are just halls of mirrors.'

'Who said that?'

'Why, I did,' he said and looked surprised; an aphorism had crept up on him.

'Things are getting desperate,' she said; and he knew she meant she was getting desperate. 'Without the money . . .'

'Fifty-one million dollars,' he said with an accountant's wistfulness, a rare state of mind; then he said in English, 'Just lying there in limbo.'

She wasn't mission-educated, but she knew a non-interest paying bank when she heard it. 'It's Bund Corporation money — if Huang hadn't stolen it —'

'It was already stolen money,' he said. 'It was army money.'

'If we hadn't used it, someone else would have.' She had the simple logic of the thief. 'Don't preach morality to me. That money has to stay here in Sydney. Somehow . . .'

'I'll see what I can do. But no more killings.'

'Not unless necessary,' she said.

4

Annandale is no more than five or six kilometres from the heart of the city, once a workers' suburb, now on its way to gentrification. It is part of the larger municipality of Leichhardt, whose town hall has seen more battles than the Western Front in World War One. Raymond Brode began his local government career there and the scars still showed.

Like so many inner areas in the early colony, Annandale was a land grant, in this case to a Colonel Johnston. He distinguished himself and temporarily lost the grant, by assembling his troops and marching into Government House and arresting William Bligh, the Governor. Bligh was not the first nor the last to make the mistake of angering the citizens by thinking that tyranny was an acceptable form of administration. He was held in jail, then placed on board a ship and told to get out of town. Some time later

Johnston himself was placed aboard ship, under arrest, and sent back to England. He eventually returned to the colony and his land grant was restored. Offering further proof that in those days anything, if you weren't a convict, was forgivable.

Raymond Brode lived in Johnston Street, the extremely wide thoroughfare that is the spine of Annandale. The street still has several of the Gothic Revival houses built in the 1880s and Brode lived in the grandest of them. It was a four-storeyed mansion that, like several of the other survivors, had a steeple on its roof, suggesting the original owner had had churchly ambitions. Under the Brode roof, however, no choirs sang and if the plate was passed around it was for the resident sinner.

The house looked top-heavy, as if at any moment it might topple over on to the modest one-storey houses on either side. It had been built by a wool merchant who thought he was looking ahead but somehow didn't see the Great Depression of the 1890s. It had originally stood in three acres of garden; now a bank of hydrangeas and a square of lawn that wouldn't have fed two sheep were its only complement. Those and a fence of six-foot ornamental spikes. A large mail-box just inside the spiked gate said in large letters: 'NO JUNK MAIL'.

'You think that's a warning to his Town Hall mates?' said Clements.

Malone had phoned Lisa at her office to find

out if Brode had reported for council duty this morning. No, he was still at home, still supposedly unwell.

'Would he be at his offices?' Malone had asked.

'He works from home, Rosalie tells me. He's a wheeler-dealer, he doesn't need offices.'

'You've been too long at Town Hall, you're starting to sound cynical.'

'It's educational, if nothing else. It beats doing the laundry.'

Now he and Clements pushed open the ornamental gate and went up the half a dozen marble steps that led up to the thick security door guarding the ornamental front door. The windows on either side of the door, fronting on to the wide marbled verandah, were heavily barred. A hundred years ago the wool merchant, unprotected, had felt safe even in those depressed times.

The front door was opened; a slim-figured woman stood behind the security door. 'Yes?'

Malone introduced himself and Clements, showed his badge. 'We'd like a word with Mr Brode.'

'My husband is not well. He's not seeing anyone this morning.'

'I think he'll see us, Mrs Brode.'

She continued to stare at them through the wire screen that covered the grille of the door. Malone, staring back at her, had the sudden image that they were two faces on a computer screen. All that was missing was the text below the faces; neither knew anything of the other. But at last Mrs Brode seemed prepared to take a chance: 'Wait there.'

She disappeared and Clements said, 'This isn't the first time she's had cops at her front door.'

The two detectives waited patiently. Out on the broad street an ambulance came along, did a U-turn and slowed in front of the Brode house. Then it moved along and pulled up half a dozen houses along.

'Shall I ask 'em to wait?' said Clements.

Then Mrs Brode came back, opened the security door. 'My husband will see you. But he's not well, so please don't stay too long.'

They followed her down the long wide hall. She was in her forties, Malone guessed, smaller than she had looked through the security door. But she walked with the squared shoulders and firm step of an army sergeant-major. The sort of wife, Malone thought, a man would find hard to treasure. And at once felt the ghostly crack of Lisa's hand across the back of his head.

'Here they are, Ray,' she said, as if Malone and Clements had no name, no identity.

She stood aside and the two detectives went by her through a doorway into a large room that was apparently Brode's office. As he passed her Malone caught a glimpse of her full on for the first time. Under her dark hair there was a small sharp-featured face full of intelligence; her wide brown eyes had all the shrewdness of a veteran bookmaker. For some reason Malone saw her with Madame Tzu, someone who could hold her own with that formidable lady.

Brode sat behind a desk that looked large enough to be a converted pool table. Behind him three large windows, all barred, looked out on to a garden ablaze with colour. The colour was a contrast to the drabness of the room, the bars a barrier to it. Malone wondered if Brode ever turned to look out at it.

Brode didn't rise, but waved the two detectives to two chairs opposite him. 'Forgive me for not getting up — I'm not well . . . Thanks, Gwen.'

'Watch yourself,' said Gwen, and went out, leaving the door open.

Brode smiled weakly. 'She's my security guard . . . Well, what can I do for you gentlemen?'

'Do you need a security guard?' Malone bowled a bumper first ball, right at the head.

Brode frowned. He didn't look in the least unwell, but he was wary. Not of viruses but of questions. 'Why would I need someone like that? I was joking —'

'Mr Brode,' said Malone, bowling a little closer to the wicket this time, 'why did you lend your apartment in The Mount to Li Ping and the two young engineers from Olympic Tower?'

Brode looked at his desk as if measuring its largeness. Green folders covered most of it like sods of turf; a computer stood on one corner, its screen blank, secrets hidden. The room had a high ceiling and one of the light brown walls held a double row of framed certificates; Brode, it seemed, had been honoured for everything but innocence. The furniture was dark and heavy and Malone wondered if it had been left here by the original owner. The chairs in which he and Clements sat could have accommodated a Sumo wrestler.

'They told me they were scared,' Brode said at last.

'Of whom?'

Lisa always insisted on the difference between *who* and *whom* and he had fallen into the habit; or been dragooned into it. It made him sometimes sound a little prim, but there is not much difference between primness and an edge to the voice.

Brode gestured; he had big hands that moved like heavy birds. 'I don't know. Li Ping's brother was shot —'

'You knew she had a brother out here? Who told you that — General Huang?'

'General Huang?' Brode made a good pretence of looking puzzled.

'Come on, Mr Brode. Mr Shan.'

Brode all at once began to look unwell; he leaned forward as if he had a stomach cramp. 'How much do you know?'

'Enough.'

'What sort of answer is that?'

'I'm afraid it's all you're going to get.'

'Your wife works with me sometimes. Has she been telling you things?'

'Don't rile him with a question like that, Mr Brode,' said Clements as if he were the essence of patient behaviour. 'It's the Irish in him. We're gunna stay here till we get the answers we want, whether you're well or unwell. Do you have a gun?'

Brode sat back as if a gun had been presented at him. 'A what? You're joking! Jesus, if it was known a city councillor had a gun . . . During the gun amnesty, after the Port Arthur massacre, I gave speeches about it, about handing in all weapons —'

'So you did and we were glad to hear of it,' said Malone, who couldn't remember reading or hearing any word about the speeches. But at that time there had been a barrage of rhetoric and Brode wouldn't have been the only one unheard. 'Did you know about the money that was deposited in the accounts of General Huang's son and daughter?'

The random questions, coming at him from all angles, or anyway two angles, didn't appear to faze Brode; but then he had been a councillor, municipal and city, for twenty years. Life on Leichhardt council had been like spending Monday night in a shooting gallery.

He took his time, then said, 'Yes, I knew.'

'Who told you? General Huang?'

'Do we have to keep referring to him like that?'

'You don't like being linked with the Chinese

army? Righto, if you'd prefer Mr Shan —'
Remembering Greg Random's instruction.
'You'd prefer to keep the general's name out of
the media. Why?'

'I think it's better that way.' But didn't say
why he thought so.

'Because he was a sacked general? Did you
know he was army when he first came to you?'

'Who said he came to me?'

'We understand you were the one who got the
Olympic Tower project through council,' said
Clements. 'Were you to have had dinner with
Mr Shan and the others the night they were
shot?'

Malone held on to his head, didn't turn it at
this unexpected question. Where had Russ got
that one from?

'You see, Mr Brode, we've learned the
booking for that particular booth in which they
were killed was for five people. Les Chung was
the fourth, but he was talking to Inspector
Malone at the moment the gunman walked in
and let fly. Were you the fifth booking?'

'No.' No hesitation.

'Do you know who it might of been? Madame
Tzu? Jack Aldwych?'

'I have no idea. I never met any of them in restaurants after —' He had slipped and he knew it.

'After what?' said Malone, taking up the
bowling again. 'After you and the developers had
made the usual arrangements?'

'What arrangements are those?'

Malone refrained from rubbing his thumb and forefinger together; but the itch was there. 'We know, Mr Brode, that money changed hands.'

'Would you care to make that charge in public?' It sounded almost a *pro forma* answer: he had been accused many times and he knew the counter.

Malone stared at him: he, too, had played this game, but always as the accuser. 'Sure, we'll do that. You want to ring John Laws or Alan Jones? Talkback hosts love that sort of talk.'

Brode sat very still, one clenched fist resting on his desk as if he were about to lift it and bang it down; but he was too experienced for those sort of theatrics, this audience was too hard-bitten. He relaxed, spread his hand on the desk. 'Okay, there was an arrangement. The fucking project wouldn't have got off the ground if it hadn't been for me —' He was working up steam, in a moment he would be waving the flag of civic pride.

Malone held up a hand. 'Simmer down, Mr Brode. We're not here on council business. Sergeant Clements and I have seen so much corruption —'

Brode had simmered down; he actually smiled now, though it was more a smirk. 'In the Police Service you would have. Some of your guys had it down to a fine art, didn't they? At least councillors go in for honest corruption, we don't hustle hookers or drug dealers —'

'Don't let's get too moral,' said Malone wearily. 'Tell us, have you received any threats? Death threats?'

Beyond the barred windows, out in the garden a gardener had made an appearance, was leaning on a rake and talking to Mrs Brode. Or being talked at. She said something, then stalked back towards the house. The gardener looked after her, half-raised a hand to give the finger to her departing back, then looked towards the windows and dropped his hand. Mrs Brode, Malone decided, would give the finger to any death threat.

'I don't know whether they were meant as death threats,' said Brode. 'But yes, I've had a call. Les Chung told me I should take a holiday, get out of town for a while.'

'Les Chung? He gave you his name?'

'Well, no. But I recognized his voice.'

'When was this?'

'Yesterday morning.'

When you suddenly felt unwell? But Malone didn't ask that question; that would only put the secretary Rosalie and Lisa, too, on the spot. 'You didn't know we had picked up Li Ping and her friends at The Mount?'

'The manager rang me to say there'd been some sort of cock-up —'

'It was a balls-up, actually,' said Malone. 'But we sorted it out. We had quite an interesting talk with your young friends.'

He waited for a reaction from Brode, but there was none.

Malone went on, 'When did Les Chung call you?'

'About ten minutes after I got the call from the manager. Actually, it was Les who said there'd been a cock-up.'

'He was threatening you and he talked about a police cock-up? Come on, Raymond. Why are you putting Les Chung in the shit? I know Les, he wouldn't be stupid enough to make threats over the phone. If you want to work off some score against him, try something better than that. Les Chung and Jack Aldwych don't make phone threats. They'd call on you personally . . . Who made the call?'

Then Mrs Brode was standing in the doorway, giving orders. 'You will have to excuse my husband, Inspector. It is time for his medicine.'

He's getting it. But Malone didn't voice the obvious. 'We'll just be a few more minutes —'

'I'm sorry, it has to be now. Will you please leave?'

'If we have to, we'll be taking your husband with us. To Homicide.'

'Homicide?' Her face pinched.

'Didn't I mention we're from Homicide? Where did you think we were from? The Fraud Squad?' It was dirty, but he couldn't resist it.

It seemed to take some of the starch out of her. She stood very still for a moment, then with hurried steps she came into the room and stood behind her husband, one hand on his shoulder. It was probably unintended, but it looked like a posed statement: we are a team.

Brode put his hand up to cover hers. 'It's all right, love . . . Okay, Inspector, maybe it wasn't Les Chung. But it sounded like him.'

'So who do you think it was? Guo or Tong? They couldn't have called you after the balls-up. They were with us, being questioned. I think you're making all this up, Raymond.'

'No, he isn't,' said Mrs Brode. 'He's trying to protect me. *I* got the call. Here. Two nights ago.'

'So why did you try to lay it on Les Chung, Raymond?'

Brode didn't answer that, but said, 'Nobody has any reason to threaten us.'

Malone smiled. 'Raymond, if you've been taking handouts on Olympic Tower there are a dozen people who could threaten you. The Premier, the Minister in charge of the Olympics, the Lord Mayor — Yes, Mrs Brode?'

He had seen her hand tighten on her husband's shoulder. 'Yes, what?'

'I thought you wanted to say something?'

She shook her head, said nothing. Her husband reached up again and pressed her hand. 'It's all right, love, there's nothing to worry about. I don't think I can help you any further, Inspector —'

'Where does Madame Tzu fit into all this?' asked Clements.

Brode frowned. 'She's a partner in the project, that's all.'

'No,' said Malone, 'she's more than that. Who

paid you the initial bribe?'

Brode stared at him. His wife took her hand off his shoulder and reached forward — for the paper-knife on the desk? One of the paper-weights? Then she straightened up again, as if reason had taken control of her. Both husband and wife suddenly looked unwell, the medicine was the wrong dose.

Then Brode said, 'Madame Tzu. But you'll never find any evidence.'

'Was the money paid to you, Mrs Brode?'

She said nothing, but the answer was there in her face.

'How much? Half a million, a million? It doesn't matter — we're not chasing the money.' He stood up. 'But watch out. Let us know if you get any more threats, Mr Brode. These days people are killed for much less than a million —' He was laying it on. Petty spite can sometimes taste so good; even saints have savoured it. 'We'll see ourselves out —'

'No, you won't,' said Mrs Brode, and led them out of the room. Walking behind her Malone remarked that her stride was quick and firm again. She opened the front door, pushed out the security door, but barred their exit for the moment.

'My husband is a wheeler-dealer, Inspector. Some people are born accountants, lawyers or policemen — he was born a wheeler-dealer. It's what I fell in love with, am still in love with. I wouldn't want him any other way.'

'Thanks for your frankness, Mrs Brode,' said Malone, and meant it. 'Take care.'

'Oh, we'll do that,' she said. 'We've been doing it for twenty years.'

The two detectives left her and went down the steps and out the front gate. The postman had been and the mailbox was stuffed with what looked like junk mail.

The ambulance was drawing away from the house further down. Clements looked after it. 'I wonder if Brode was ever an ambulance chaser? He's got a law degree. It was there on that wall with all those other pieces of paper.'

'He'd have chased a buck wherever he could get it,' said Malone. 'This time I think he wishes he'd laid off.'

Chapter Nine

1

'Ms Feng is at her aerobics class.' The young Chinese girl had greeted Gail Lee and Sheryl Dallen at the head of the stairs, as she had on their previous visit. It was as if she had an antenna that picked up the arrival of strangers as soon as they entered the downstairs doorway. 'She will not be back for at least an hour. I'll tell her you called.'

'Better still,' said Gail, 'tell us where she goes for her aerobics.'

The young girl looked no more than sixteen, but she was already halfway to being the perfect secretary, the human picket fence. 'I don't think I can do that —'

'I think you can,' said Gail, and said something in Cantonese.

The girl flushed, then said, 'It is the Flower Girl gymnasium in Campbell Street.'

Out in the street again Sheryl said, 'What was that you said to her?'

'Cantonese. I used an expression I don't like to use in English.'

'You're an odd one, Gail.'

Gail smiled. She had come to have affection

for and reliance upon the other girl; they were going to be a good team. 'Half-and-halves often are.'

Sheryl nodded, though she would never know the problems that mixed-bloods had. She looked across the street to the Golden Gate. 'The scene of the crime is in business again.'

'I wonder if anyone sits in the back booth?'

'Of course. The world is full of morbid numbskulls. Splash some blood somewhere and in no time you'll have a crowd wanting to look at it.'

Gail nodded, then moved on. 'Let's try the Flower Girl gym. Do you know it?'

'Never heard of it. If their aerobics are anything like Chinese gymnastics, I don't want to know it.'

Campbell Street is a severed minor artery from Chinatown proper. Back in the 1920s and 30s it was a brothel area, sometimes with whole families in the trade; a nice girl was one who said *Thank you* after servicing a client. There have always been Chinese stores in the lower end of the street and they have now multiplied. The Capitol theatre, a derelict near-ruin for years, has been rebuilt and the 1920s and 30s are back with revivals of old Broadway shows. The occasional hooker is still to be seen, but too often she looks as if she has strayed out of the stage door of the past.

The Flower Girl gymnasium was above two grocery stores and approached by a narrow flight of stairs. As Gail and Sheryl went to go in, a man got out of a car at the kerb and approached them. Then he pulled up, recognizing them.

'Hello, Gail. You after Miss Feng?'

'Hello, Jeff.' He was a plainclothes man from Day Street. 'You still keeping an eye on her?'

He was young, eager for action, easily bored. 'It's a waste of time. Nobody's interested in her.'

'We are.'

He grinned. 'You're not dangerous. Go ahead, be my guests. She's up on the first floor.'

Gail and Sheryl climbed the stairs, pushed open a door and entered the gymnasium's main hall. At least a hundred people, men and women, old and young, were arrayed in rows, arms and bodies moving in slow motion as if they were all underwater.

'T'ai Chi?' said Sheryl.

'It doesn't raise much of a sweat,' said Gail, 'but it makes you just as aware of your body.'

'Do you do it?'

'Every Sunday morning. I go with my father and sisters. Dad goes to the rugby league matches on Saturday afternoon, watches all that biff-and-bash, then gets over it with T'ai Chi on Sunday morning.'

Sheryl looked at the group, most of whom were clad in tracksuits or tights and T-shirts. 'I think I prefer the sweaty approach. I like the shine of sweat on a thigh muscle.'

'Yours or some guy's?'

Sheryl just smiled, then nodded at the front row. 'Let's interrupt Camilla.'

Gail raised a beckoning finger and Camilla detached herself from the group and came towards them. She was not shining with sweat; she looked pale and tired. 'Yes? Did you have to come *here* for me?'

'Let's go somewhere quiet, Camilla. We have a few more questions.'

'Down there.' She nodded towards a far corner of the big room. 'T'ai Chi goes on for another half-hour.'

Down this end of the hall there was gymnasium equipment: weights, exercise bikes, three treadmills. Camilla sat down on the cushion of a press-bench and the two detectives sat on a wall-bench facing her. She was lower than they and Gail wondered if it were some sort of ploy. *Look, you're trying to beat me into the ground.*

'So why are you here again? I've got nothing to add to what I told you last time.'

'I think you might have, Camilla,' said Gail. 'One of our detectives has been looking into an insurance policy you took out some months ago on your father —'

Camilla looked around, saw a towel on a nearby bike and reached for it. She wiped her face, though there was no reason to; except that, for a moment, it was a blind to retreat behind. She looked away, like a Method actor in a movie, then back at Gail and Sheryl. 'So?'

'Ten million,' said Sheryl. 'Enough to get your father out of the trouble he was in. Then, conve-

301

niently, he is murdered.'

Camilla's eyes narrowed, but it was the only sign that she had winced. 'You're pretty brutal, aren't you?'

'We'll try not to be,' said Gail, 'if you tell us who suggested taking out the policy. Was it you or your father or someone else?'

'My father.'

'Did he discuss it with you?'

Camilla hesitated, then nodded. 'Yes.'

The T'ai Chi class behind her was still going through its slow motions. Hands and arms drew abstract patterns in the air; heads turned and profiles were sketched against the light from the windows at the end of the room. Silence prevailed; somewhere an ambulance siren wailed, a cry from another world. Sheryl, an energetic girl, felt out of place.

'There was also a policy taken out on Mr Sun's life. Who suggested that? Your father?'

'I don't know.' She retreated behind the towel again for a moment.

'Were there policies on the lives of Mr Chung and Mr Aldwych? Your father's partners?'

'I don't know.' She began to fold the towel, like a hotel maid.

'What about Madame Tzu?'

'Why don't you ask her? Ask Mr Chung and Mr Aldwych, too.' Her hands squeezed tightly on the towel. 'Look, the insurance policy was my father's idea — he didn't discuss it with me till after he'd taken it out.'

'Would he have had any ideas about suicide?' asked Sheryl.

Camilla looked genuinely shocked. 'Good God, no! You really have weirdo minds, haven't you?'

The two women gazed at her, said nothing.

Camilla squeezed the towel again. 'No, Dad wouldn't have thought of suicide — or *planned* it, like you're suggesting. He was an optimist, that was how he got into the mess he was in. Everything was always going to come up roses. He was a gambler.'

'Gamblers usually don't take out insurance policies, do they?' said Gail. 'Had your father had any threats? Was he afraid something might happen to him?'

Camilla thought for a moment. 'I don't know. If he had, he would never have told us. But yes, he might have had. He was acting — well, *different* over the past few months. It's difficult to explain, unless you knew my father. But he was *different*. He said something once — *never trust a stranger*. I asked him what he meant, but he just smiled and walked away.'

'Who were the strangers?'

Camilla shrugged. 'Mr Aldwych. Madame Tzu. Mr Shan — General Huang.'

'But not Chung and Sun?'

'No. Dad didn't know Mr Chung well, but they weren't strangers to each other. They'd worked together on a couple of charities.'

The class had stopped for a short break. All at

once the figures on a frieze became human, lost their grace. Half the heads turned to look at the three women in this far corner; lips moved but the gossip was silent. Camilla looked back over her shoulder at the class, then back at the two detectives.

'They suspect you're police.'

'How have they been treating you?'

'Sympathetically. Everyone in Chinatown knew Dad. He was very popular.'

'Camilla,' said Gail, 'who else knew about the policy on your dad's life? And the one on Mr Sun?'

'Darren and Troy knew — I don't know if they knew about my father's, but they certainly knew about their father's. They're the beneficiaries.'

'And that's all who knew? No one else?'

Camilla put down the towel, still neatly folded. 'My aunt.'

'Madame Tzu?'

In the background the class had begun to reform. Arms were raised, heads held still, the frieze frozen.

'Yes,' said Camilla, standing up. 'There's nothing she doesn't know.'

2

'There's been another homicide,' said Clements.

Malone sat back in his chair. It was late afternoon and he was ready to go home. There had been three more murders today: a security guard shot dead outside a suburban bank; a domestic in an outer suburb; a woman's head found in a hatbox on a riverbank at the foot of the Blue Mountains. He had taken Phil Truach off the Olympic Tower case and sent him to take charge of the hatbox murder; it would have him out in the open air for a few hours and he could smoke to his lungs' content. Out in the big room half a dozen of his men were finishing the paperwork on four solved murders, getting their notes together for future use in the courts, preparing their ammunition for use against the defence lawyers. Gail Lee and Sheryl Dallen had reported to him on their meeting with Camilla Feng and he had decided to leave her alone for a while on a loose rope; Day Street and Drummoyne were keeping an eye on her and she was their responsibility for the time being. Tomorrow morning, first thing, he would visit Madame Tzu again.

'Where?'

'Kirribilli.'

'That's not our territory. Let North Sydney take care of it.'

'It's Jason, the muscleman on the Olympic site. He didn't report to work this morning and a mate called in at the flat this afternoon and found him dead. A bullet in the head.'

'Bugger!' He sat up, feeling weary: no adrenaline this time. 'The body still there?'

'No, it's gone to the morgue. Crime Scene are still there, though. You wanna go over?'

Malone reached for his phone, rang home: 'Tom? Tell Mum I may be a bit late this evening. What are you doing?'

'I'm on the Internet. The market went up again today.' Tom had done two weeks' work experience in a stockbroker's office during his last holidays and ever since then had been running the country's economy. He was going to do Economics at university and already could see himself as a $300,000-a-year market analyst. 'You should've bought NAB when I told you.'

'I hope you're married and out of the house before I retire or my superannuation will just evaporate. Why don't you study to be a postman or a street cleaner? See you tonight.' He hung up, looked at Clements. 'He'll be a millionaire by the time he's thirty, shouting me first-class trips round the world.'

'You complaining? I hope Amanda grows up to be rich.'

Malone reached for his hat and jacket. 'You coming with me?'

'No, I'm going home to my wife and child. I've told John to go with you. That's all you've got on the Olympic case now — I'm stretched. John, Gail and Sheryl.'

'I used to be in charge of this place once. What happened?'

Malone and John Kagal drove over the Bridge to Kirribilli. The westering sun flickered on the harbour; a small yacht, red and yellow spinnaker curved like a large apple slice, ran away from the breeze. The peak-hour traffic streamed home-wards, drivers locked in their cars with their own secrets.

The streets of the tiny Kirribilli peninsula were lined with a mix of plane trees, jacarandas and Chinese raintrees; Malone remarked the last with a wry grin. The buildings were also a mix, with flats predominating. Those built in the last fifty years were either tall and ugly or, at best, plain and bulky; those surviving from pre-World War Two strove for some appearance of dignity and solidity. There were some private houses, but not many. Down on the point were Admiralty House, the Sydney residence of the Governor-General, and Kirribilli House, that of the Prime Minister. Both lent some tone to the area, though past residents of both houses did not always do the same.

Jason Nidop lived (or had lived) in a block of six flats on the northern slope of the Kirribilli ridge. It was not a luxury block, but it had a view over the narrow waters of Careening Cove, where a fleet of small yachts floated like sleeping gulls. Two police cars were parked in the street outside and a uniformed cop was just removing the Crime Scene tapes that blocked the entrance to the flats.

'Anyone still upstairs?' Malone asked.

The cop nodded. 'They're just about finished, I think.'

Going up the granite stairs to the second floor Kagal said, 'I never met this guy. Was he trouble?'

'I don't know. I thought he was only involved in a union battle.'

'Do unionists go around shooting each other in the head?'

'My old man would shoot *you* for suggesting such a thing. No, they were more rough-and-ready, guns weren't their thing.'

'You're talking about your old man. That's the past. Maybe things are different today.'

The flat was a two-bedroom unit, comfortably furnished but without any style. On the wall of the small living room were two large framed posters of two heavily muscled, scantily clad supermen: Mr World and Mr Universe. The latter looked slightly superior as if he knew his competition was bigger. A low bookcase held paperbacks, magazines and a row of videos. The latest decoration was the outline on the blue carpet where Jason Nidop's body had lain.

Two members of the Physical Evidence team were putting away their equipment. The young woman officer smiled at Malone and Kagal as they entered the room and Malone said, 'G'day, Norma. What've you got?'

'Not much. Some prints on the door. Maybe the guy in the bedroom will be able to tell you something.'

Malone and Kagal went into the main bedroom. This room was decorated with another poster, this one of Arnold Schwarzenegger in his more bulbous days. A slim good-looking man, not at all muscular, sat on the bed, head held in his hands. He looked up as the two detectives came in. 'Christ, not more cops —'

'I'm afraid so,' said Malone. 'You are . . . ?'

'Joe Zinner.' He gave his name as if it were a throwaway card.

'You worked with Jason?'

Zinner stood up, walked to the window and looked out; but it was obvious he saw nothing nor was he interested in what lay out there. Then he turned. 'We were partners.'

'Partners? In some business?'

Zinner's smile barely stretched his lips. 'No, we — we were friends. Lovers, if you like.'

'How long have you known Jason?' asked Kagal.

'A year. After he left the TV show he was on and came back to Sydney.'

'When did you last see him?'

'Last night.'

'You were both home all night?' said Malone.

'No.' He had turned his back on the window, was against the last light in the northern sky. The bedroom was not dark, but it had deep blue walls that threw off no light.

Malone looked for the light switch, turned it on. In the sudden illumination Zinner looked gaunt and pale, middle-aged, though he could not have been more than in his early thirties.

'So where were you last night?'

'Is it any of your business? Christ, I've just lost my — my friend, the guy I loved!'

'We understand that, Mr Zinner, but we're trying to find out why anyone would want to kill your friend.'

'You think I did it? Jesus!' He threw his head back, an almost effeminate movement. Yet, Malone thought, there was nothing — *sissy* about the man. And rebuked himself for the thought.

'Where were you last night?'

'We had a row — a terrific one. One like we've never had before.'

'What about?'

'It was personal. Christ, you really do pry, don't you?' Malone and Kagal said nothing and after some hesitation Zinner said despairingly, 'Okay, it was over another guy he's been seeing. We had the row and I stomped out of here and went home.'

'Home? Where's that? Your parents' home? Your own place?'

'Neutral Bay. No, I went home to my wife.' He gestured, a meaningless movement of his hands. 'Okay, I'm double-gaited —'

'Fluid,' said Kagal.

Zinner looked at him. 'You know the terms?'

'We learn them,' said Kagal, telling him nothing more. Don't complicate things, Malone told him silently. 'You stayed the night with your

310

wife? She'll verify that?'

'Maybe, maybe not.' He gestured again, but there was meaning to it this time: he was full of despair, his life had fallen apart. 'She hadn't any time for Jason.'

'Any time for you?' said Malone, and hoped he didn't sound cruel.

'What do you think? We have a little girl —' Suddenly he turned back to the window, buried his face in his hands and began to weep silently.

Malone said, 'Take care of him, John,' and went out into the living room. The second PE officer was just coming out of the second bedroom.

'G'day, Sam. Got anything?'

The PE man was in his forties, prematurely grey with a squeezed look to his eyes, as if a lifetime of peering at his trade had marked him. He collected the spin-off from a crime: the bullet in a wall, the dropped knife, the fingerprint, the shoeprint, the hair, the thread. He was the cluemaker and every detective paid his respects.

'G'day, Scobie. The bullet was still in the guy's head, it didn't exit. There didn't appear to have been any struggle, a fight or anything. Evidently he knew who killed him. There was no forced entry, he'd unlocked the door and let in whoever it was. The GMO said he'd been dead about eighteen hours, maybe a bit more. His friend Mr Zinner came by this afternoon about four and found him. So he was killed around ten o'clock last night, give or take an hour or two.'

'Any bullet casing?'

'No. It's possible the gun he used didn't eject any shells or he tidied up after himself. Some killers are born housekeepers.' He grinned.

'What's that you've got?'

Sam Penfold held up the large plastic envelope he was carrying. 'This was in a drawer in the bedroom. It's one I've never seen before.'

Malone took the envelope, looked at the gun inside it. 'It's a Chinese army Type 67.'

3

Malone had slept soundly, as he almost always did; but he was still tired. He had got up at six and gone for his usual five-kilometre walk down to and round Randwick racecourse. The horses, doing trackwork, went by him, all muscle and energy, the morning sun etching them in golden line. The trainers and strappers and the bookies' spies lined the rails in small groups, no excitement showing, just men at work. Malone had no interest in racing but he knew of the contrast between the silence, but for the drumming of hoofs, of morning trackwork and the roar of the crowd on Saturday afternoon. It was the comparative silence that appealed to him, that and the great grandstands as empty of sound as forgotten temples in the jungle. Here he got his mind into gear for the day.

He did his own trackwork, then went back up the hill, climbing into the sun towards home.

When he was leaving for the office Lisa had come out to him as he got into the car. 'I'll ride in with you and catch a cab from Strawberry Hills.'

He sometimes drove her into Town Hall, but this morning he sensed something different in her. He was in the mainstream of city-bound traffic before he said, 'What's on your mind?'

'When you were under the shower there was a phone call. I didn't tell you at breakfast, I didn't want to mention it in front of Claire and the others. It was a man. He said to tell you that we should all beware of accidents.'

'We?'

'That's what he said. We should all beware of accidents. Then he hung up.'

He said nothing for almost half a mile, trapped in the middle lane of traffic. He could not stop and turn round, though that was what he wanted to do. Cars hemmed him in on both sides; at one point there was a car on either side of him, both with four men inside, all laughing like a primed TV audience. One man turned to look at him, still laughing, and Malone was almost tempted to wind down the window and hurl abuse at him.

Another half-mile and his patience ran out. He put the blue light on the roof of the Fairlane, turned on the siren, flicked his indicator and squeezed his way through a gap on the inside lane and up on to the footpath. He drove along the pavement and swung round a corner into a side street and bumped back onto the roadway. It was the sort of caper he sneered at in TV cop shows. He pulled up, turned off the siren and pulled the blue light in off the roof.

'Spectacular,' said Lisa drily.

He was in no mood for dry wit; he was dry with fear for her and the family. 'What did he sound like?'

'What do you mean, what did he sound like? It was a man, that was all.'

'Australian? Chinese?'

'I don't know whether he was Chinese, but I don't think he was Australian. He was — *precise*. Careful with his words. He could have been Chinese, but I wouldn't swear to it.'

He said, careful with his own words, 'I may have to move you and the kids to a safe house, get you protection.'

'No.' She was adamant; he could see her stiffening. 'If we have to be protected, we stay in our own house. No,' she repeated, 'no, I'm not even going to allow that. I'll be careful, I'll keep an eye out, but I'm coming to work each day.'

'What about the kids? They don't break up till next week. We're going to let them run around loose? To let God knows what happen to them?'

She stared ahead of her. Suddenly the colour seemed to drain out of her face; her mouth thinned as she bit her lips, she looked older. This side street was lined with small factories and warehouses; cars and trucks went by, but there was little pedestrian traffic. She saw none of it; he had demolished her argument when he mentioned the children. At last she said, still not turning her head, 'All right, you win. Where do we go?'

'I'll have Russ round up the kids.' Claire was at Sydney University, Maureen at New South Wales and Tom at Marcellin College in Randwick. 'He can take you with him while he picks them up. I'll ring Greg Random and get permission to move you into a safe house they keep under the Witness Protection scheme.'

'Where is it?'

'Camden, I think.'

'Camden!' It was a semi-rural town that had been almost absorbed by the spreading outer suburbs of Sydney. 'Why not Tibooburra?'

Tibooburra was a family and Service joke: the most remote posting in the State, up in the far north-west where the only crims were old men kangaroos that went in for wife-bashing. 'I can arrange that for you, if you like.'

'Stop joking.'

He reached for her hand. 'Darl, I can't help it — I wish to Christ I could. I hate these bastards who try to bring my family into it . . .' A truck went by, back-fired; her hand jumped under his. 'I like my job. But I *love* you and the kids. If anything happened — anything . . .'

His hand tightened on hers; she almost cried out. She freed her hand, touched his cheek.

'We'll go to Camden. But the house had better be *clean* . . .'

He drove on in to Strawberry Hills, took Lisa upstairs and explained the situation to Clements. 'Collect the kids, Russ, then take Lisa and them home so's they can pack. Then bring them back here. I'll take them out to Camden.'

Clements was a mixture of anger and concern. 'This is getting outa hand. I think we oughta bring in everyone on our list —'

'Russ —' Malone was surprised by his own patience — 'we don't know that whoever is making these threats is on our list.' He kissed Lisa. 'I'll see you back here in about an hour. Tell Claire she doesn't need to take her entire wardrobe.'

'Stop joking,' she said for the second time, but kissed him in return. She wasn't angry at him: she knew the jokes were no more than camouflage for the anger and fear for them that he felt.

The detectives in the big room all stood awkwardly as Clements took Lisa out through the security door. They nodded or said just a word or two. All of them, with the exception of the two women detectives, had been the target of threats. But never their families.

Malone went back into his office, rang Greg Random and explained what had happened.

There was silence at the other end of the line; then: 'I could take you off the case.'

The offer was tempting; but habit was too ingrained: 'No, Greg. I'm going to get this bastard, whoever he is.'

'There might be more than one.'

'No, I'm staying on the job. Just get the permission for Lisa and the kids to move into the safe house.'

Random made no attempt to hide the reluctance in his voice; he valued his men, Malone above all of them. 'Okay. But you take care. Don't go playing bloody heroes.'

Malone hung up, looked up as John Kagal came into his office. 'Yes?'

'I went over to the morgue early this morning, got them to put Jason Nidop first on their autopsy list. They took the bullet out of his head and I had Ballistics come and collect it.'

Malone was impressed, but did his best not to sound too enthusiastic; Kagal would one day be Commissioner, but he should not be encouraged too much at this stage. 'Where do you get all this influence?'

'It's charm, not influence,' said Kagal, but his smile took the conceit out of it. 'Clarrie Binyan rang five minutes ago. The bullet in Mr Nidop's head came from the same gun that killed Mr Zhang out at Bondi, not the one in the drawer in Nidop's flat.'

Malone pondered this for a moment, then said, 'Go on, you haven't finished yet.'

'No, I haven't. That Chinese army gun, the Type 67, had been wiped clean, there wasn't a single dab on it that PE could find. Why would a hitman wipe his fingerprints off his gun before he put it away in a drawer? Unless he always wore gloves when using it. Was he wearing gloves when you saw him in the Golden Gate last Friday night?'

Malone shut his eyes, tried rescreening the memory of the murders. *Last Friday night: an age ago.* Then he opened his eyes and shook his head. 'I'm not sure. What I am sure is that Jason was not the feller in the stocking mask. He'd be — what? — six three, six four?'

'A hundred and ninety-two centimetres, the autopsy report said. Close enough to six-four or a bit more. A hundred and five kilos, according to the report. A big bugger.'

'No,' said Malone, closed his eyes for a long moment, then opened them. He was definite this time: 'The killer was slim, might've been six feet but I don't think so. Jason wasn't the hitman.'

'So the hitman plants the gun on him? Or was Jason minding it for him?'

'I don't know. If he planted the gun, hoping we'd tag Jason as the hitman, he wasn't very bright. But it wouldn't be the first less-than-bright thing done in this case. Planting that fifty-one million in those bank accounts wasn't very bright, either.'

Kagal nodded. 'Something fishy is going on here. Neither the bank nor Canberra have put out a statement. If the media are on to it, they've been told to keep quiet.'

'How do you keep the media quiet?' Like all cops he used the media whenever it was necessary, but, like all cops, he was suspicious of them. They were a necessary evil.

'By denial, I guess. Someone will run a story on it and the government will say it's just a furphy. All Kate can find out — and Fraud aren't in on it any more — is that once the story got to Canberra, it was buried.'

'Maybe I'd better see Mr Deng, their consul-general, again.'

'I tried to get him, but he's down in Canberra again at their embassy.'

Why didn't I guess you'd have already covered that point? Why don't I just retire and let you take over this chair right now? 'Keep me posted when he's back in town . . . What did you find out about this bloke Jason was supposed to be seeing? The one he and Mr Zinner had the blue about?'

Kagal looked at his notes; he had the case covered from every angle. 'His name's Harvey Smythe — S-M-Y-T-H-E. He's an actor, a young guy — he's a heart-throb in one of the soap operas. Friday he was up on the Gold Coast, he's got a part in a feature film. He was there Friday night. I rang the production company and he was in a night-shoot they were doing. He's in the clear.'

'Follow him up, he may know something. Is there a station at Surfers Paradise? What a posting! I suppose they wear bikinis and Ray-Bans. Ask them to question Mr Smythe, see if he can tell them anything about Jason.' He looked at his watch. 'I'm going down to the Olympic Tower site. Come with me. Gail can get on to Surfers.'

He wasn't sure why he had suddenly decided to take Kagal with him. Perhaps he needed re-assurance. The younger man seemed to have the touch of someone who believed that there was nothing that could not be resolved.

Out in the main room he told Gail Lee to get on to Surfers Paradise, then he said, 'If Russ gets back here with my family before I do, tell 'em I won't be long. What's the latest on Miss Feng?'

'Day Street and Drummoyne are still keeping an eye on her. Madame Tzu had dinner with the Feng family last night.'

'She doesn't hide herself, that lady.'

'The Empress Tzu was never shy.'

Malone looked at Kagal. 'I'm just waiting for the local feminists to find out about these Chinese empresses. We're done for, mate . . . Gail, has anything come through on the Hong Kong bank that sent out those dollars?'

'We tried getting the Hong Kong police to help, but nothing's happening. It's not like the old days, when the British were there — they're suspicious of us. Then we asked our consulate there what they could do. Nothing's happened.'

'Did China ever build a Great Wall of Silence?'

Gail smiled. 'I'll ask my dad.'

Kagal drove the unmarked car down to the Olympic Tower site, driving with all the skill and arrogant confidence of a professional. Is there anything this bloke doesn't do well? Malone asked himself. Sooner or later he would have to recommend three stripes for Kagal, but at the moment there was no place for another sergeant in the establishment.

The first person they saw when they pulled on to the site was Guo Yi. He came down the side of the structure in a work-lift, opened the gate, stepped out and pulled up dead as he saw them. The two detectives got out of the car and crossed to him.

'You shouldn't be on the site without helmets,' he said.

'Get us a couple, John,' said Malone, and Kagal went across to the shed by the gate. 'You decided to come back to work, Mr Guo? Who recommended it?'

'You did.' He was in slacks, white shirt and tie: a black tie.

Malone nodded at it. 'You're wearing that out of respect for the dead?'

'They were all older men. We respect age.'

'You don't respect me.' Guo just shrugged: *take it or leave it*. Malone went on, 'Mr Zhang wasn't old, but he's dead. So's Jason Nidop.'

Guo frowned as if the name meant nothing to him.

'The Allied Trades delegate here. A bullet in the head, night before last. You hadn't heard about it?'

321

'Oh, of course.' The recovery was quick. 'I just didn't know his name. I never had any dealings with him.'

'But you have dealings with Roley Bremner? Thanks, John.' Kagal came back with two helmets. 'You know *his* name?'

'Yes. A very aggressive little man.'

'A good many of our union men are.' Remembering Con Malone, who would have knocked down this uppity young Chinese without speaking to him. *Oh Dad, you retired just in time.* 'It's one reason why our workers are better off than they are in China. You find it difficult working with our unions?'

'Yes.'

'Enough to threaten one of the union men?'

'I told you, I had no dealings with Mr Nidop.'

'You remembered his name?' Malone waited, but Guo Yi did not bite. 'Just for the record, Mr Guo, where were you the night before last?'

Guo took his time. 'I was with Li Ping, at her flat in Cronulla.'

'Oh, you're back there? Glad to hear it. And Mr Tong?'

'He's back at his Bondi flat.'

'So the three of you are feeling safe again?'

Guo adjusted his helmet, as if it had slipped. 'We think so.'

'Even after we've told you about Mr Nidop's murder? He was killed by the same gun that killed Miss Li's brother, Zhang.'

Guo took off his helmet, fiddled with the

lining and put it back on. 'That's upsetting. You're sure?'

'Oh, very sure. We have one of the best Ballistics units of any police service in the world. The Hong Kong police used to call on them for advice.'

'Not any more.'

'No, I guess not. I suppose they're no longer interested in the finer points of forensics. Well, thanks, Mr Guo. Take care.'

As he and Kagal turned away the work-lift came sliding down, the gate was slammed open and Roley Bremner stepped out. Guo Yi looked at him, then turned his back and walked away. Roley gave his back the middle finger salute.

'Uppity bugger . . . Well, what can I do for you? As if I didn't know.'

'It's just routine, Roley. Would anyone you know have gone looking for Jason Nidop?'

'Like putting a bullet in him? Nah, no way.' Bremner held his helmet while he shook his head. 'We were losing members to him and his mob, but it wasn't that serious we hadda get rid of him that way.'

'Had you or anyone from your union threatened him?' Kagal asked.

'You kidding? We didn't go around throwing him kisses. Yeah, I suppose some of us did tell him to lay off or else.'

'Or else what?'

Bremner grinned. 'Your guess is as good as mine. But not else a bullet. Nah, look, you're wasting your time trying to lay it on us. I gotta be honest, I'm glad to see him go, but I wouldn't of done it that way. Neither would anyone from the union.'

'What about the two fellers down there, the foundation members?' Malone pointed at the ground.

'Before my time, mate. Look somewhere else, Scobie.'

'Where, for instance?'

Bremner shook his head again; this time he took off his helmet. 'What's that about the monkeys? Hear no evil, speak no evil, see no evil. Or whatever it is.'

Malone looked at Kagal. 'Another philosopher.'

'Confuckingfucious,' said Bremner, and walked off. 'Give my regards to your old man.'

Malone looked after him, then switched his gaze to Guo Yi, who had just come out of the administration hut. He paused by three men sitting on saw-horses having a smoke. He said something, then raised his hand and pointed a finger at them. Malone shut his eyes, then opened them again. Guo left the men and walked across to the work-lift. He got in, closed the gate and pressed the start button. The lift rose, crawling up past the floors that had already been clad by the outer walls, up until it was rising past the skeleton of the upper floors. Guo Yi looked down on the two detectives till the lift reached a height, still travelling, where the floor of it obscured him.

'He's the one,' said Malone.

'The one what?' said Kagal.

'The hitman. He did the Golden Gate job.'

'And Jason and Mr Zhang'?'

'Probably.'

'So do we go up there and tell him what you think?'

Malone began to walk back towards their car. 'What hard evidence have we got? We take him in and hold him and he just sits there, says bugger-all, and at the end of it what've we got to pass on to the DPP? They'd tell us we haven't got a leg to stand on when it comes to prosecution.' He got into the car, slammed the door with more force than was necessary. 'But we'll get him. If he's the bugger who threatened Lisa this morning, I'll get him!'

Kagal paused before getting into the car, stood back and looked up. High on an upper floor, there on a girder, someone in helmet and white shirt stood looking down at them.

'Jump, you bastard,' said Kagal.

4

Malone drove Lisa and the children out to Camden in the family Fairlane. The small town lies in the middle of what was the beginning of the nation's wealth, the wool trade. Now the city is reaching out to engulf it; soon it will be just another suburb and wool will only be something that politicians and used-car salesmen pull over people's eyes. It is a pleasant town, clustered around a central hill, and the safe house was halfway up the hill, on the street leading to the town graveyard.

'Very appropriate,' said Lisa.

'We'll never forgive you for this,' said Maureen. 'How long are we going to be stuck out here?'

'Don't let the locals hear you talking like that,' said Malone.

'Well, how long?' asked Tom. 'Geez, we're just about to start our holidays. It'd better be all over by Christmas. I start my work experience again the Monday after New Year's Day —'

'We'll have it all wrapped up by then. Come on, let's see what the house is like.'

'Who's here with us?'

'A policewoman disguised as a cook-housekeeper.'

'Can she cook?' asked Lisa.

'I don't know. If she can't, you can teach her.'

'Does she carry a gun?' said Tom.

'In the pocket of her pinny. For God's sake, I've never met the woman —' Then he calmed himself as they reached the front door of the old stone house. He noticed its windows were barred and there was a security door; just your normal abode in a sleepy country town. 'Look, I'll get you out of here as soon as it's safe. I don't like this any more than you do —'

'It's okay, Dad,' said Claire, and kissed his cheek. 'Relax. We'll do the same. Are we allowed visitors?'

'No.'

'Shit!' said Maureen, then looked at her mother. 'Sorry. I hope we're not going to spend *Christmas* here, that'll be jolly. The Commissioner playing Daddy Christmas.'

The front door opened. Constable Barbara Sherrard, in a pale blue sundress, no pinafore and no gun, stood there. She was tall and pleasant-looking; Malone immediately felt confidence in her. 'Constable Sherrard? My family.'

'Let's get off on the right foot,' said Lisa, putting out her hand. 'Lisa, Claire, Maureen and Tom. And I'm sure none of us is going to call you Constable.'

'Come in.' She appeared genuinely pleased to see them; keeping a safe house was evidently not a chore for her. She had a smile that seemed to take up the whole of her wide face. 'I'm just preparing dinner.'

'You like to cook?' said Lisa.

'Love it! I did a Cordon Bleu course once when I was running a safe house up in the Blue Mountains. I was minding a French canary —' She looked at Malone.

'I remember him. Sang like an aviary of canaries. He put away half a dozen heroin smugglers.'

'What are you cooking?' asking Lisa, keeping her priorities.

'I thought *coquillettes en pâté sauce Janik* might be a good introduction?'

'Go home, Dad,' said Claire. 'You won't be needed.'

5

Malone, however, stayed for dinner. Barbara Sherrard was unashamedly showing off; she confessed it. The *coquillettes whatever* was, to his taste, perfect; the *crème brûlée* that followed was as good as Lisa's. The safe house even ran to bottles of Hunter reds and whites.

'Is it always like this?' Lisa asked.

'I try to make it so,' said Barbara; then looked at Malone. 'Don't worry, sir. I've been ten years with the Service. I've been in three siege situations.'

'Inside looking out or outside looking in?' said Claire.

'Outside. But there's not going to be any siege situation here. I promise you.'

Malone kissed his girls good night, squeezed Tom's shoulder and took Lisa out to the car with him. 'I'll call every morning and night.'

'Every morning and night? How long is it going to be? Never mind.' She held him to her, kissed him passionately. 'Be careful.'

'Don't you or the kids answer the phone. Let Barbara do it every time.'

She looked at him carefully. 'You're afraid they may have followed us here.'

'No, I'm not. I went almost cross-eyed looking in the rear-vision mirror coming up here. It's just standard procedure — the protected personnel never touch a phone.'

'The protected personnel. Do we wear labels?'

He kissed her again. 'Stop joking.'

He drove back to the city through a night filled with stars and a scimitar of moon. Once a car, going the other way, passed him at high speed; a moment later a police car, lights flashing, siren wailing, went by with a whoosh that he felt through his open window. In Homicide, he comforted himself, you never had to risk your life in a high-speed chase after some hoons in a stolen car.

It was almost eleven o'clock before he pulled the Fairlane in before his house. He got out, opened the gates and pressed the remote control to open the garage door. He drove the car in, closed the door, then moved down the short driveway to close the gates.

At that moment the car, dark-coloured and without lights, pulled up opposite him. He saw the hand come out of the front window holding a gun; he dropped flat as the two shots hit the ironwork of the gates and zinged away. Then the car accelerated, went at speed up the street, disappeared round the corner with a screech of tyres.

He stood up, shivering with reaction. The shots had made little sound; the gun had been fitted with a silencer. Nobody came to any of the front doors; no lights went on in bedroom windows. Malone stood leaning on the half-closed gates, waiting for the bones to come back into his legs. Then he closed the gates and went into the house: the unsafe house.

Chapter Ten

1

The Premier liked to call early-morning conferences; it gave him an advantage over those whose minds didn't function till an hour or so after breakfast. This eight o'clock meeting had some very sullen people sitting in the Premier's office. Sports Minister Agaroff and Police Commissioner Zanuch were the two unhappiest-looking. Lord Mayor Amberton's smile might have been forced, but it was second nature to him.

'Give 'em the score, Roger,' said the Premier, hunched in his chair, enjoying his malevolence as if it were a second breakfast. Summer and winter, Gert, his wife, fed him the same breakfast: porridge with milk and sugar, two sausages and an egg, two slices of toast with her home-made strawberry jam. This second meal, of his visitors' discomfiture, tasted just as good.

Ladbroke would have been wide awake for a 6 a.m. meeting; he was long experienced in The Dutchman's ploys. 'You all read the papers this morning or listened to the radio. That guy who was shot at Kirribilli night before last worked on the Olympic Tower site. John Laws called it the

Jinx Site — he gave all his listeners a reminder of what happened there in the previous abortive development. Alan Jones did the same on his show. The talkback nuts started calling in right away. Is this to be a jinx on our Olympics, they wanted to know. Is it a warning from God — I dunno how He got into sports or hotel development — that we should never have bid for the Olympics?'

Amberton looked around, as if he had only just come awake. 'Why isn't anyone from SOCOG here? They're the organizers of the Games.'

'We don't need 'em,' said Vanderberg, who never felt the need of anyone who got more space than he did in the media. 'We handle this ourselves. How's the investigation going, Bill, on this latest murder?'

'It's in hand,' said the Commissioner.

The Premier wobbled his head, cackled softly. 'You oughta come into Parliament, Bill. You know how to look all dressed up and doing nothing. You mean the police haven't got a clue?'

Zanuch managed to look unruffled, but a *tsunami* was going on under the bespoke uniform. 'Not a clue, but a connection, something we haven't told the media. The gun that killed Mr Nidop, the corpse at Kirribilli, also killed the young Chinese, Mr Zhang, out at Bondi last Friday night.'

'So what does that prove?' asked Agaroff, bald

head shining in a streak of morning sun coming through the window behind the Premier.

'Nothing. But links in clues are like links in a chain. Eventually they lead somewhere.'

'Rupert wears a chain round his neck when he's all dressed up as Lord Mayor,' said the Premier. 'Does one link lead to another? Like in a circle?' He looked back at Zanuch. 'We don't want the police running around in circles, Bill. You better tell 'em to get their finger out. You're making haste in slow motion.'

That's a new one, thought Ladbroke, and I don't need to translate it.

Zanuch gritted his teeth. 'One of my men was fired on last night at his home — I got the report just before I came here. Detective-Inspector Malone, who's in charge of the case.'

'Holy Christ,' said Agaroff, and rubbed the top of his head, as if wiping off the sunlight. 'Do the media know about this?'

'No,' said Zanuch, 'and they won't. Not from my men.'

Your men? thought the Premier. My men, he thought, as Police Minister. He hated the idea of 13,000 police officers running around loose under someone else's command. 'There's another thing. Tell 'em, Roger.'

'I dunno,' said Ladbroke, 'whether you saw an item some weeks ago about millions of dollars being lodged in the bank accounts of two Chinese students — it was in a Cabinet report —'

'Then I wouldn't have seen it,' said

Amberton, aggrieved, and looked at Zanuch and Agaroff.

'I saw it,' said Agaroff.

'I got it in a secret police report,' said Zanuch.

Amberton was all at once the odd man out. His fairy wand as Lord Mayor of the biggest city in the nation was just a candy stick. He couldn't help the petulance in his voice: 'So what's the importance of it?'

'We thought someone at Town Hall might've explained it to you,' said Ladbroke. 'Councillor Brode, for instance.'

Amberton grimaced, waited while Ladbroke explained the situation. Then he said, 'What's happened to the students? Where are they, if everything's been kept so quiet?'

'One of them is dead,' said Ladbroke, and named Zhang. 'The other is a girl, Li Ping. She's to be picked up and deported.'

Zanuch raised an eyebrow and his ire. 'Who gave that order? We're investigating her —'

'The order came from Canberra,' said The Dutchman.

'What business is it of theirs?' Amberton was as jealous of parish power as the Premier, though he knew that here in this room he had no power at all. Sometimes in bed at night, his fabulous hair in a net (his dream cap, as his wife called it), he dreamed of Sydney becoming a Down Under Monaco, separate from and independent of the rest of the country, himself not as Lord Mayor Amberton but as Prince Rupert. Free of Premiers and Prime Ministers, ruler of the Emerald City, complete with its own casino just like Monaco. Monte Carlo no longer a biscuit but his domain. The hairnet sometimes shook like a stringbag full of sparrows. 'Who invited them in?'

'It's at a higher level,' said Ladbroke.

The others looked at the Premier, at this *faux pas* by his minder. They knew he recognized no higher level than himself; even the Pope, on his last visit, had found himself on a lower step than his greeter.

But, to their surprise, Vanderberg nodded and said, the words coming out of his thin mouth as if they were spiked, as if they were killing him, 'It's between Canberra and Beijing. Chinese politics.'

'China is all politics, isn't it? It's Communism.' Zanuch had thought Margaret Thatcher a neo-socialist.

'It's half-and-half now,' said Ladbroke. 'Capitalism is rearing its ugly head.'

'Who said it was ugly?'

'A figure of speech,' said Ladbroke, whose cynicism would have embraced anarchy if it had employed him to sell it. 'Anyway, the money is going back to China and so is the girl.'

'In the meantime,' said Amberton, still feeling he had been pushed out to sea without an oar, 'we're left with the Olympic Tower mess. All these murders. What do we do?'

'The same as we do in parliament and

council,' said the Premier. 'We establish a committee.'

'Who'll be on the committee?'

'Us,' said the Premier. 'And only me will make any statements.'

Here we go again, thought Ladbroke. Should I apply for a literary grant as a translator of gobbledegook?

2

Malone had had a restless night. At six o'clock he phoned Greg Random at home. 'Sorry to get you out of bed, Greg. I've got a problem —'

Random listened without comment while Malone told him of what had happened last night. Then he didn't explode, but his voice was cold: 'You're a bloody idiot. You know the drill —'

'I don't want Lisa and the kids to know —'

'For Crissake, Scobie, this is a major incident. A cop's been shot at —'

'I don't want the media to know, spreading the story all over —'

'Okay, we'll keep it as low profile as we can. But you stay out of it — let the investigating teams do what they have to . . . You understand? *You stay out of it.*'

'Righto, you win, Greg —'

'It's not a question of me winning — you know

the drill, it's got nothing to do with how you or I feel. Don't be so bloody pig-headed —'

He hated this friction between himself and Random. 'Righto, I'll get on to Randwick, to Physical Evidence —'

'I told you — stay out of it. I'll do it. Now pull your head in, stay out of the way and shut up.' Then the edge went out of his voice: 'You're okay?'

'Except for the way you've just kicked my arse.'

'You deserved it. I'll see you later.'

By seven o'clock there were ten officers on the scene. Uniforms and plainclothes from the local Randwick station, Phil Truach from Homicide, a woman officer from Physical Evidence and a young red-headed officer from Ballistics. Malone came out of his front door as a uniformed man was running out Crime Scene tapes.

'We don't need those, do we? I don't want the neighbours getting edgy.'

The officer, a young bulky man with an Italian name that Malone had forgotten and an Italian regard for the sensible, rolled up the tapes. 'Sure, Inspector. But we're gunna have to do some door knocking, case someone saw or heard something before you got home.'

Malone nodded resignedly. 'Try your luck — ask them not to broadcast it.'

'Are you kidding?' He was Italian through and through. 'Neighbours were invented for broadcasting. They were centuries ahead of Marconi.'

'Are you trying to make me feel better?'

Then the young Ballistics officer came in the front gate. He had a friendly face and Malone knew him only as Declan Something-or-Other. 'You might have a problem finding the bullets, Declan. If you have to go into the garden next door, tell 'em you're from the Water Board.'

Declan looked around, grinned ruefully. 'We could be here all day. What was it — a shotgun?'

'No, a handgun with a silencer. The car was out there, about five or six feet from the gutter.'

'Sounds like a woman driver,' said Declan. 'My wife always parks a short walk from the kerb . . . That'll cut down the area a bit. If it was a handgun, the velocity would be less. Okay, I'll start looking.'

Malone went back into the house and rang Clements at home, told him what had happened. 'Pick up Guo Yi. He'll probably be at work now, on the site —'

'Hold on, mate. Are you saying it was definitely him that tried to do you?'

'No, I don't. But he's my Number One suspect. Bring him in.'

'If it was him, he may already have shot through.'

'Not him. He's a smartarse, Russ. He'll be at work and he'll have an alibi for last night.'

'So what do we do? Bring him in and beat the shit outa him? Okay, okay,' as Malone started to protest. 'But if he's what you say he is, the

338

hitman, and he's after you, why's he doing it? Someone's using him. He's got no stake in Olympic Tower.'

'Then maybe if we beat the shit out of him, he'll tell us.'

'Don't come that one with me, mate. You've never come the heavy stuff — and don't expect me to, not this late in life. Have you told Lisa what happened?'

'No. And don't mention it to Romy, right?'

He hung up, went back out to the front garden. It was a beautiful morning; a wind-streaked cloud hung like washing in the sky. Malone walked under the awning of the camellias and Declan stepped in front of him and held up a scarred bullet.

'Bingo! A 32-calibre, I'd say. What's the matter?'

'It looks like it's been a busy gun. Two murders and an attempted one. The feller at Bondi, the one at Kirribilli and me.'

Declan slipped the bullet into a plastic envelope. 'We'll find the other one. You look disappointed.'

'Do I? Not disappointed, just bloody frustrated. It looks as if there might be two killers, not one.'

He looked at him sympathetically. 'Your family's in a safe house, you said. Maybe you should join them.'

'Not yet,' he said.

Ten minutes before Malone got his car out of

the garage Declan found the second bullet. 'In the main trunk of one of your camellias. We've found the cartridge cases, too, out there in the gutter.'

'Get them to Clarrie Binyan soon's you can, tell him I'd like a report yesterday.'

He arrived in the car yard behind Homicide just as Clements and John Kagal got out of an unmarked car with Guo Yi. He was in shirt and slacks and wore not a black tie but the vivid slash of an Olympic tie. For some reason he was also carrying his safety helmet, tucked under his arm like a football.

'This is insulting, Inspector.'

'It's not meant to be, Mr Guo. Let's talk upstairs. Why the helmet? It's not dangerous around here.'

Going up in the lift to the fourth floor Malone, standing behind the young Chinese, raised his eyebrows in query at Clements. The big man just shook his head, but Kagal ran his finger across his own throat. Mr Guo, evidently, was going to prove difficult.

Which he did in the interview room. 'Am I to be questioned again?'

'Yes.'

'About what? I've answered all the questions you can ask me.'

'Not all, Mr Guo. Where were you last night around eleven o'clock?'

Guo looked down at his tie, fingered it; mourning for the dead older men was over or he had suddenly become a Games booster. 'I was home in bed.'

'With Miss Li?'

'If it is any of your business, yes. Why, what happened last night?'

'Someone tried to shoot Inspector Malone,' said Clements. Only he and Malone were in the interview room with Guo. He flicked a finger against the helmet on the table, made a pinging noise. 'We think it might of been you.'

Guo Yi didn't try for inscrutability; he jerked his head back, went round-eyed. 'Me shoot him? Why? Why would I do something stupid like that?'

Clements shrugged. 'Maybe you don't like him? Or maybe someone told you to? You see, Mr Guo, we have a very short list of suspects in all these murders and, unfortunately, you're on the list.'

'I've heard an expression since I came to Australia.' Guo had recovered his composure. 'You're out of your fucking mind.'

'You're outa *your* fucking mind,' said Clements, temper just under control, 'if you think we're not gunna get to the bottom of all this. I think maybe you'd better get a lawyer.'

'Do you have a lawyer?' asked Malone.

'No.' Guo appeared to be gathering himself together, like a soldier strapping on equipment. As if he knew the war was no longer a phoney one. 'I shall have to ask a friend for advice.'

341

'Do that. Sergeant Clements will take you out to a phone.'

Malone stayed in the interview room; he was having trouble hiding his frustration and he didn't want to parade it. He looked up almost with irritation when Gail Lee came to the door.

'Russ has told me what happened last night. I'm glad they missed.'

'Thanks, Gail.' If nothing else, his relations with her were easier since this case had begun.

'Did he do it?' She jerked her head backwards.

'Guo?' He considered a moment, then nodded. 'I think so. He's claiming he spent the night at home with his girlfriend. I think we need to talk to her. You and Sheryl go out to Cronulla and bring her in. She's supposed to be a student — do you know where she goes?'

'UTS. She's doing computers.'

'Try the Cronulla flat first. You try to pick her up at UTS, you might have a students union protest on your hands. We're never in the right.'

She looked back at him as she turned away. 'I'm really glad he missed. We all are.'

He was touched by the concern, though he knew such concern for officers' safety was now endemic in the Service. There had been several recent incidents where cops had been in life-threatening situations and had responded, resulting in at least two civilian deaths. Public criticism of the police reaction had been loud and widespread, usually by people who had never been even close to such situations. The

Service had become resentful of the criticism, had closed ranks. Malone knew that cops were not always above criticism but, like all cops, he resented it from those well outside the danger zone.

Clements and Guo came back into the room. Guo sat down and drew his helmet towards him as if for safety. Malone said, 'Did the friend advise you on a lawyer?'

'Yes.' Guo had assumed the look of a man who had all the time in the world. 'He will be here as soon as possible.'

Malone glanced at Clements. 'Anyone we know?'

'Nobody's been named so far,' said Clements. 'Madame Tzu was the friend who's finding him a lawyer.'

'Aren't you the lucky one, Mr Guo, to have such a friend? Almost like a mother to you, I suppose.' Malone could taste the bile on his tongue. 'What other advice does she give you?'

'Only professional advice,' said Guo, elbows now on the table, fingers steepled together. He looked like someone about to *give* advice. 'After all, she and her partners pay my wages.'

Plus bonuses? But Malone kept the question to himself.

3

'Look, Charlie —'

Jack Aldwych would not have called the du Barry woman Madame, nor Mrs Chiang Kai-shek; madames were the women who had run his brothels and he had called them Ruby or Flo. He had had difficulty with the pronunciation of Tzu Chao and so, after their initial meeting, he had called her Charlie. She had accepted it with pained, amused tolerance, convinced yet again that the world was not yet free of barbarians.

'— we can't keep putting this off any longer. You've gotta come up with the money, that's final.'

He and Les Chung had come to the Vanderbilt for this meeting with Madame Tzu and General Wang-Te. They sat sipping tea, biscuits on the coffee table between them: Iced Vo-Vos this time. Aldwych had offended by asking for milk in his tea; Madame Tzu had instructed the maid to bring the milk in much the same sour voice that she might have used to call for yak butter. The atmosphere in the room was equally sour.

'A few more days,' she said defensively. She

was not accustomed to being defensive and it hurt. She looked at Wang-Te, who had sat silent so far. 'The general has been down to our embassy in Canberra —'

'What did they say?' Les Chung was as irritated as Aldwych, but showing it less. 'Once things get to Canberra, they get lost. Things down there go round and round, like their streets.'

Wang-Te nodded. 'A strange place. Full of ivory towers, someone at our embassy told me.'

'Like Beijing,' said Madame Tzu, and Wang-Te winced.

'Never mind the politics.' Aldwych belonged to a privileged class, the criminals who were above politics. 'What did you get out of your embassy?'

Wang-Te put down his cup, looked at Madame Tzu. 'We have to tell them.'

She wrapped her hand round her own cup, looked as if she might throw it at him. Les Chung said, 'Tell us, what?'

'The money is going back to China,' said Wang-Te. 'All of it. Nothing more will be said about it. The embassy told me it will become what you call an urban myth.'

'Fifty-one million dollars in solid cash?' said Aldwych. 'Some myth.'

'General Huang's son is dead,' said Chung. 'But his daughter is still alive. What if she talks?'

'She is to be taken back to China. She won't talk.'

'What if she won't go?' said Aldwych.

'Oh, she will go,' said Wang-Te. 'Your Federal Police have already picked her up, I believe. There is nothing to worry about,' he said with all the assurance of a man who knew how a mouth could be kept shut. It had shocked him to hear the clamour of mouths in a democracy.

Madame Tzu could contain herself no longer. 'Damn the embassy and its politics! Why can't the money stay here, be invested? Take the girl back, keep her mouth shut, but leave the money here. It will go back and what will happen to it?'

Aldwych sat back, studying her. He had had a certain morality as a criminal, forced on him by his wife, Shirl. She had known what he was, but she had turned a blind eye and a deaf ear to the bank hold-ups, the prostitution racket and the gold smuggling; they were honest, almost *decent* crimes, so long as no one was killed or hurt. She had known nothing of the murders he had ordered, believing him when he had told her he had been framed each time he had been charged, welcoming him back with open arms and legs when he had been acquitted. He had never gone into drug dealing, knowing that Shirl would have left him if he had. He looked at Charlie Tzu now and decided she had no moral values at all.

'The money will be invested in Hong Kong,' said Wang-Te. 'Or Shanghai,' he added with a certain quiet relish, knowing the latter destination for the money would be like sending it to Moscow, as far as she was concerned.

He had met her only twelve months ago when

346

she had invited him and two of his fellow generals to lunch in Shanghai. There had been no direct blatant approach on that occasion; she was just there, she had said, to give them her experience of the wider world. She had talked of the advantages of foreign investment, but always obliquely, never openly suggesting that they should consider the thought. She had spoken of the United States, where Wall Street money flew ever and ever upwards. But her real enthusiasm had been for Australia, where the locals had the long-range vision of bats and Chinese patience would reap a fortune. He had seen her only twice after that, at a reception in Shanghai and at another in Hong Kong after the British had left. They had been perfunctorily polite towards each other, but each knew what the other was: he an honest man, she totally corrupt. The other two generals, aided by book-keepers of lower rank, had fallen for the dreams she had painted. They were now in prison awaiting trial before an army court. Execution faced them, an act that would shorten *their* long-range vision.

'That's the end of your road then,' said Aldwych. 'Sorry, Charlie.'

It took a moment for her to get her fury under control. These barbarians, these *men* . . . 'What happens to what I've already invested? I have ten million in the project.'

'Your own or borrowed money?' asked Les Chung.

Hesitancy looked out of place on her; but it

was there. 'Some of it mine, some of it borrowed.'

'How much?' said Aldwych. 'Borrowed?'

Her words were slow, as if for the moment she had forgotten her English. 'Six million. From a Hong Kong bank that trusts me.'

Aldwych shook his head; it might have been mistaken for pity, except that he had never felt that emotion towards anyone but Shirl. 'Not enough, Charlie. If the bank forecloses on you, we get first crack at taking over the loan. We don't want any more outsiders in with us.'

'I'm an outsider?' She was affronted; the knuckles showed white on the hand that still held her cup. 'Me?'

'You've always been an outsider, Charlie. Les and me are the natives. Don't get het up —' He held up a hand as she started to rise. 'You'd of always got your fair share if you'd kept on bringing money in. But you didn't. You and General Huang got ideas of your own —'

'I had nothing to do with Huang's schemes!' There is a certain fire when an essentially dishonest person can be honest: it adds sincerity to them that they otherwise find difficult. 'The man was stupid — I don't know what he intended to do with that money — I know nothing about it —'

'He was going to push you out,' said Chung. 'He felt you were no longer needed.'

Even Aldwych looked at him at that. 'Where'd you get that from?'

'He told me last Friday night. Me and Sun and Feng, just before the three of them were shot.'

Aldwych sighed; it could have been a mixture of disgust and sadness, but no one would ever know. 'When I was in the game, before I retired, I never had any partners, I was on me own. That way I was never screwed by mugs I was supposed to trust —'

'Jack —' Les Chung was uncomfortable, but it barely showed. He had made two mistakes: one in divulging what Huang had said; two, in telling Madame Tzu. He rarely made mistakes; to make two at once was totally out of character. 'I'd have told you eventually —'

'Eventually? What the fuck does that mean?' The old cruel hardness was coming out in him.

The two outsiders watched this in stiff silence, Madame Tzu leaning slightly forward as if she might intervene at any moment. Wang-Te, the real outsider, sat back in his chair, content to be no more than a spectator. He took off his glasses, breathed on them, cleaned them with a handkerchief; none of this argument was going to touch him. He had been tempted, just for a very short time, by Madame Tzu's pleas somehow to keep the stolen money in Australia; he knew that temptation is an itch that everyone suffers from. To invest the money and maybe some day be rich, to never go back to Shanghai and the wife and her mission morality. The Baptists had been expelled by Mao, but they had left their corruption behind in her. Sin, which he had never known till she had educated him in it, had for the moment tempted him. A minor sin, of course, just theft: it was almost fashionable these days in China. But the temptation had not lasted. His honesty was a rope that bound him.

Madame Tzu, who had spent almost all her life watching and escaping from warring factions, was not impressed by the argument between — her partners? That was what she had thought they were; but now it seemed she had been only a means to their ends. Her own intended end had been to settle here in Australia, to sever her connections with Shanghai and Hong Kong, to become the Empress of Developers in this country of semi-barbarians and latent racists. She had met Les Chung two years ago in Hong Kong and after several subsequent meetings had made enquiries about him and found him sufficiently venal for her needs. He had introduced her to Jack Aldwych and she had instantly recognized that he had the same regal contempt as she had towards the suckers of the world, of whom there were billions. Everything, she had thought, was set for the future, *her* future. And now . . .

'You are not getting rid of me!' There was no mistaking her fierceness. 'I'll blow you all right out of the ground if you try —'

'How?' Aldwych had been threatened by women before, but they had been drunken whores who had rung him the next day to tell him they hadn't meant it, that they loved him and wanted to go on working for him. But this woman . . . 'How?'

Then the phone rang. She looked at it as if willing it to stop; then she stood up quickly, crossed to it and snapped into it, 'Yes?'

The three men watched her, all of them impassive, each with his own reaction to her threat to blow them out of the ground. Wang-Te had no ruthlessness in him, but he had seen so much of it over the past thirty years; he saw it now in the faces of these two silent men sitting opposite him. Madame Tzu had woven the rope for her own neck.

'How did you get yourself into this mess?' she said in Mandarin. Only Wang-Te understood what she had said. 'The best lawyer you can get for that situation is a man named Caradoc Evans.'

The name was all that Aldwych and Chung understood. They looked at each other like men who had heard a secret password; then Aldwych said, 'Caradoc Evans? How did you get on to him?'

'He's a lawyer,' said Madame Tzu, putting down the phone.

'He's a criminal lawyer. What do you want a criminal lawyer for?'

'*I* don't want him.' She was annoyed at the intrusion by the phone call. 'It's Guo Yi, one of our engineers. He is being held for questioning by that nuisance Inspector Malone.'

'Why's he being questioned?'

351

'Someone tried to kill Inspector Malone last night.' Her tone couldn't have been more casual; she wanted to get back to real concerns.

'Stupid!' Les Chung shook his head in disgust. 'When are you people going to recognize we're not in the backblocks of China?'

4

Cronulla is the bastardization of an Aborginal word meaning 'the place of pink seashells.' Aborigines lived and fished on the beach and the land back of it for several thousand years before the white men arrived; the seashells are gone, but a few Aborigines play in the local rugby league team, called the Sharks. They have been heard to remark that their ancestors had a much easier time fighting amongst themselves, though the pay was less. The beach lies 26 kilometres south of Sydney, at the end of a railway line, and the gunyahs of centuries ago have been replaced by restaurants, shops and apartment buildings.

'Li Ping doesn't do too badly for a Communist,' said Sheryl Dallen, looking up at the block of apartments; it was the sort of block where estate agents would never have used the words *flats* or *units*. 'I thought Communists were supposed to share the wealth? I wouldn't mind sharing a flat here with her.'

'I think the last thing Li Ping is is a Communist,' said Gail Lee. 'I doubt very much if she would have shared a toy at kindergarten.'

They went into the building and climbed the stairs to the first floor. The door to Li Ping's apartment was slightly ajar. Gail pressed the bell and the door was immediately swung back. A bulky man in a double-breasted suit stood there.

'You friends of Miss Li?'

'Not exactly,' said Gail and produced her badge. 'Who are you?'

The man produced his own badge. 'Agent Hurlstone, Federal Police.'

'Is Miss Li here?'

'Come on in.' He stood back to let them pass, then closed the door. 'In the living room.'

Gail and Sheryl went down the short hall and into the living room. A wall of glass looked out across a wide verandah to the beach. A second man, medium height and slim, turned back from a small desk he was searching, raised enquiring eyebrows at the bulky man.

'I think they're here for the same reason as us,' said Hurlstone. 'Agent Graveney.'

Gail introduced herself and Sheryl. 'We're from Homicide, we were to take Miss Li in for questioning. Why did you want her?'

Graveney closed the drawer of the desk, sat down on a chair and waved to the two women to sit. The furnishings of the room were standard rental, though of good quality: quality prints of beach scenes hung on the walls; shag rugs lay like pelts on the good-quality carpet. All that was missing was the suggestion that anyone had ever called the apartment home.

'I'm afraid you're out of luck.' Graveney had a soft voice, that of a man sure of his authority. 'Our bird has flown.'

'Back to China?' said Sheryl.

Whether Graveney was from the Sydney or the Canberra office of the Federal Police, he had the Canberra approach: he took his time. His speech was not only soft but slow and deliberate: one could almost hear the punctuation.

'If she attempts that, she will be picked up by Immigration. They have been alerted.'

'When was she last seen?'

'She was here in the flat last night.' He looked around the room, as if double-checking that she wasn't present. 'We checked with the people next door. They heard her go out about nine-thirty, but whether she came back they couldn't say.'

'You still haven't said why you want her,' said Gail.

Graveney looked at Hurlstone, who was sitting on a chair by the door that led out on to the verandah. 'They don't like us interfering, do they?'

'States' rights.' Hurlstone grinned and shrugged. His double-breasted jacket was still done up, stretched tight across his belly; the buttons looked as if they might fly off at any moment. 'They'd secede, if they could.'

'Yes,' said Sheryl, 'we would. But a little

co-operation might make us change our minds. We were here first, a coupla days ago —'

'Ladies —' said Graveney, and didn't appear to notice the stiffening of the ladies' spines. 'You will have to ask Canberra why we're here. The Department of Foreign Affairs, I think. This is no longer a police matter, we're into politics.'

'Bugger,' said Sheryl, and glanced at Gail. 'Say something shitty in Mandarin.'

Gail resisted the invitation. 'As my colleague said, we were here a few days ago. Li Ping and her boyfriend disappeared for a day or two, but then we found them.'

'We heard about it,' said Hurlstone. 'The cock-up at that block of flats in Chinatown.'

'You follow us in the media?' said Sheryl.

'All the time.' Hurlstone laughed, his belly expanded and a button flew off his jacket. It was his turn to say *Bugger!* as he bent down and searched for it in the shag rug.

'We found nothing when we searched the flat,' said Gail, 'nothing that helped us very much. Have you come up with anything?'

'Such as?' said Graveney.

'Such as a gun.'

Hurlstone had found his button. He sat back in his chair, then dipped into his pocket and pulled out a plastic envelope. 'We found these, they were under the bed in the main bedroom. Looked like someone had dropped them and didn't notice, as if they might of been leaving in a hurry.'

Gail took the envelope and looked at the pistol magazine loaded with five bullets; then handed it to Sheryl. 'Thirty-twos?'

'Yes,' said Sheryl. 'A seven-round magazine. I wonder what happened to the two that are missing.'

'Any significance?' asked Graveney.

'Two Thirty-twos were fired at our boss, Inspector Malone, last night,' said Gail. 'May we have these?'

'Why not?' said Graveney after a glance at Hurlstone. 'Since we're now into politics, what do bullets matter?'

'Are you kidding?' said Sheryl.

Chapter Eleven

1

Twenty-five years ago Caradoc Evans had alternated between playing scrum half and front row for the toughest, roughest club in Welsh rugby. He had learned how to head butt an opponent, to protect his balls from the groping hand in the opposing second row, to bite an ear that presented itself when the rucking got rough. Sundays he had sung in the chapel choir, his soul dark but his voice as light as a lark's; Monday to Friday he had gone to Cardiff University, where he had laid plans as well as girls. Graduating with a Law degree he had seen no future for a criminal lawyer in the valleys; the mines were closing and so was the soul, too embittered and exhausted to consider a life of crime. He had set out for Australia, where they played open rugby and where open slather was the credo of businessmen. He had fitted in amongst the con men and the rascally lawyers of the times like an indigene. Years later he had met Scobie Malone, recognized another Celt and introduced him to Gwyn Thomas, the sour Welsh humorist who wrote of the ills of the world and what it did to the voters. It was the one bond between them.

Many of the ills of the world have been perpetrated by criminals; Evans recognized a lucrative source of income, something Thomas never did. He had met Madame Tzu through a lawyer friend, sized her up for what she was but figured she was too smart ever to need his services. He had never met Guo Yi till now.

'Hello, Scobie,' he said, coming into the interview room, 'what persecution are we offering now? Mr Guo? I'm Caradoc Evans, your saviour and friend.'

'At five hundred dollars an hour,' said Malone. 'G'day, Caradoc. We're questioning Mr Guo about his whereabouts last night.' He explained what had happened last night.

'You were shot at? Someone tried to kill you?' Evans was incapable of looking shocked; but he looked genuinely sympathetic. 'It would have been a tremendous loss, Mr Guo. Inspector Malone is one of our more admirable policemen. Isn't that so, Sergeant?'

'Cut out the bullshit,' said Clements. 'We think Mr Guo might of pulled the trigger.'

Evans had remained standing, his briefcase on the table but with his hand still on it, as if he expected both himself and his client to be gone in a moment or two. Now he sat down, undid his jacket and prepared himself for argument. He was broad and bald-headed and beetle-browed; he had candid blue eyes that somehow told an opponent nothing. He was formidable, as Malone well knew.

'May I have a little time with my client?'

Malone and Clements got up and went out of the room. 'Ten minutes, Doc.'

Out in the main room Gail Lee and Sheryl Dallen had just come in. Malone looked at them and Gail shook her head. 'No Miss Li. She was gone, but we'd have been too late anyway. The Feds were already there.'

'The Federal Police?'

Gail gave him the bad news. 'They told us we're out of the game.'

'You've heard nothing, have you?' Malone asked Clements.

'We'd be the last to know, wouldn't we?' Clements' disgust was plain.

'If Canberra's got into the game —' Malone ground his teeth. Then he said, 'If anything comes in from Greg Random or Headquarters or anywhere, I don't want to know. Not till I've nailed Mr Guo to the wall.'

'You think you're gunna do that?' said Clements. 'Our mate Caradoc isn't gunna let him talk.'

Sheryl opened her handbag and produced the magazine of bullets. 'Two are missing, as you can see. Ballistics might be able to match them with the cartridge cases PE gave you this morning. Sometimes the magazine marks the cases as they slip up into the chamber.' Malone gave her an enquiring look and she grinned. 'I used to go out with a guy from Ballistics. Gun talk was his idea of foreplay.'

Malone laughed, glad of the momentary relief. 'You'll do me, Sheryl. But old fellers like Russ and me couldn't keep up with you modern girls . . . I'll show this magazine to Mr Guo, then send it to Ballistics. Maybe your boyfriend can help us.'

'He's no longer the boyfriend.'

'He wasn't sweaty enough,' said Gail, and the two girls laughed. It was nothing, an irrelevant moment of banter, but Malone was glad he had come out of the interview room. He needed the sound of a laugh or two.

When he and Clements went back into the interview room, Evans and Guo looked like old friends. They were sitting back relaxed, ready to play cards. Malone sat down, switched on the video recorder.

Evans looked up at it. 'What's that for? So soon?'

'Just to keep us all honest, Doc,' said Malone. 'I'll start with the bad news for your client. His corroborative witness, Miss Li, that he was home in bed with last night, has done a bunk. We can't find her. It may interest him, too, that the Federal police are after her. It looks as if she is going to be deported. That surprise you, Mr Guo?'

'No,' said Guo, bland as cream. 'Your government is always deporting people. For no reason at all.'

'Oh, I'm sure Canberra has its reasons this time.' Then Malone laid the magazine of bullets on the table. 'Recognize these?'

'I told you before. I don't have a gun.'

'Does Miss Li? A 32-calibre gun with a silencer, for instance?'

His gaze was as steady as that of a sightless man. 'Not that I know of.'

'My client,' said Evans, 'doesn't have to answer questions on Miss Li's choice of armaments.'

'Armaments? Come on, Doc. Who do you think you're representing here — Vickers? Let me tell you what we really think. We've had five murders in the past week, all of them, we think, connected. There were also the pot shots at me last night. Your client is high on our list of suspects in all those murders. Now we don't know how much he told you in your ten-minute confab, but I'll bet my bottom dollar he hasn't told you everything. Did you tell him about General Huang?' He looked at Guo. 'No? About Miss Li's brother being bumped off? No? You look peeved, Caradoc old mate. You're defending a client who hasn't taken you into his confidence. Or you're losing your touch, just like the Welsh rugby team.'

'Don't let's talk sacrilege. I can hear the keening in the valleys from here . . . May I have another few minutes with my client?'

Clements switched off the recorder and the two detectives stood up.

'Work on him, Doc,' said Malone. 'Impress on him he's on his own — his girlfriend has left him. And I wouldn't rely on his other friend Madame Tzu, not if I were him.'

Guo had been sitting with folded arms, head bent; but now he looked up. 'Where is Tong Haifeng?'

'You think he'll help you?' Malone shook his head. 'He's on our list of suspects, too. We're bringing him in now. Good luck, Doc. Don't let him show you how they built the Great Wall of China.'

Out in the main room Malone went across to Gail Lee and Sheryl Dallen. 'More work, girls. Go down to the Olympic site and bring in Tong Haifeng.'

'Why didn't we pick him up earlier?' said Clements behind him.

'Because I've been one-eyed. That bugger in there fired at least one of the guns that've gone off in the past week. But now — now I'm thinking there might be a conspiracy. Maybe someone has formed their own little Triad. Triad — isn't that a threesome?'

'Not in the way you think,' said Gail. 'And where does that leave Madame Tzu? If there's any conspiracy she'll be in it. Do we bring her in, too?'

'Not yet. Just get Tong —' He heard the phone ring in his office. 'We'll hold Guo till you bring in Tong.'

He went into his office, picked up the phone. It was Greg Random: 'Watch your language when you hear what I'm about to tell you —'

'I'm ahead of you, Greg. Canberra has shoved its oar in.'

'Not in. *Up*. Up your arse. Canberra doesn't care about the Olympic Tower schemozzle. They couldn't care a stuff about the murders. Good relations with China is all that counts — what's a few homicides against millions of dollars in trade? Trade, not love, makes the world go round.'

'Don't start quoting poetry or philosophy at me. I've had enough of that.'

'The girl goes back to China, the fifty-one million dollars goes back with her, General Huang doesn't get another mention and we quietly forget the murders of Mr Sun and Mr Feng and the kid out at Bondi and —' there was a rustle of paper as he looked up a name '— and Mr Nidop at Kirribilli.'

'And what about me? I nearly had my bloody head blown off last night.'

'Scobie —' Random had genuine concern for everyone who worked for him, especially someone as long as Malone had. 'Do you think I'm enjoying passing along all this bullshit? I know how you feel. But the message has come down the line — though it's not for general consumption. So don't go broadcasting it or you'll be in deep trouble. That's a personal warning from the Commissioner. He's just come from a session with the Premier. For once Macquarie Street and Canberra are in agreement — but for different reasons.' There was silence at Malone's end of the line; then Random said quietly, 'Scobie, do you hear what I'm saying? Lay off.'

Malone took his time. 'Yeah, I hear.'

'What are you doing now?'

'Nothing.' He hated lying to a friend trying to be helpful. 'Just tidying up some unfinished business. You remember what it was like when you ran this show.'

It was Random's turn to be silent for a moment; then: 'You're trying to screw me, mate.'

'Greg, I heard what you said. There'll be no charges laid. But I just have to ask a few questions of a bastard I've got here in the interview room. I think he fired the shots at me last night.'

The silences were growing longer. 'Okay. I'll log my call as half an hour from now. You can be a pain in the bum at times. Just don't do your block with whoever you've got in there.'

Malone hung up, stared out through the window-wall of his office at the main room. Half a dozen detectives sat at their desks, working on cases where there was no interference from higher up. Domestics, a bank customer killed in a hold-up, an old man bludgeoned to death for his wallet by a druggie: simple murders that never bothered Macquarie Street or Canberra. Nothing that would disturb the flow of trade. He spat into a tissue and dropped it in the wastebasket.

Clements came into his office. 'You look as if you've been shafted.'

364

Malone gave him the news. 'We've got half an hour to shaft young Mr Guo.'

Clements took a long moment to contain his anger, then he drew a deep breath. 'This is when I think the KGB had the right method.'

Malone somehow managed a grin. 'Let's see how our gentler approach works.'

'Trip him up and I'll accidentally fall on him. A knee in his gut might help.'

'Maybe we should ask Caradoc for some advice. He played rugby, he'd know all about legal mayhem.'

Evans and Guo, heads close together, were deep in conversation when Malone and Clements re-entered the interviewing room. They drew apart as the two detectives sat down and Malone said, 'Has your client decided to be sensible?'

'Ah, come on, Scobie old chum. Being sensible has never been a sensible defence. That would do us lawyers out of a job.'

Malone looked at Clements. 'You've got to admire him, Russ.'

'Criminal lawyers,' said Clements. 'You're half a crim, Doc.'

Evans smiled, unoffended. The Welsh had been suffering insults since the time of Owen Glendower; they had learned that coal dust and poverty took precedence as irritations. 'Every man to his talent, Russell old chum.'

'Do you still want Mr Evans to defend or advise you, Mr Guo?' said Malone.

'Yes.' Guo was bland and composed again. But he had taken off the Olympic tie and it lay, neatly folded, on the table in front of him. A flag to be surrendered? Malone wondered.

'He will say nothing,' said Evans, 'till he has seen his girlfriend, Miss Li.'

'So they can co-ordinate their stories? You've forgotten what I told you — Miss Li has shot through. Vamoosed. If she's picked up she's not going to be allowed to talk to Mr Guo or anyone, she's going back to China under escort. She's a Federal Police case now, not ours. You understand what I'm saying, Mr Guo? If Miss Li was involved in all this she's left you holding the can.'

Guo blinked, then bit his lip; all at once the composure was gone. He looked around, as if seeking escape; but the room had no windows, the door was shut. Then he turned to Evans, but was unable to say anything. His hand, of its own accord, reached out and crumpled the tie. The bright colours spread between his fingers like pus.

Evans took control: 'I notice you didn't turn on the recorder again, Inspector. Why?'

Malone had hoped the lawyer would not have been so sharp-eyed. 'I thought your client might feel less harassed. Are we harassing you, Mr Guo? All we want is the truth of what's been happening. Has Miss Li been more involved in this than we thought? Has she been playing you for a patsy?'

Guo was puzzled: 'A patsy?'

'A fool, Mr Guo. Women do that sometimes to men.' Glad that Lisa and Claire and Maureen couldn't hear him. And Gail and Sheryl. He leaned forward, feeling the adrenaline coming alive, a sluggish stream suddenly beginning to flood. 'Whose idea was it to kill General Huang and Mr Sun and Mr Feng? And Mr Chung, too? All four of them?'

'That's a leading question,' said Evans, putting a hand on Guo's arm. 'You don't have to answer.'

'I think he's already answered it.' Malone had seen the quick sidelong glance at the lawyer, seen the fingers tighten on the Olympic tie. 'It was all Miss Li's idea, wasn't it? Every one of the murders, including the attempt on me?'

Malone was aware of Clements' surprise; he was holding tight on his own. Li Ping had always been only on the periphery of his investigations; the margins of almost every crime were populated with shadows. He had let himself concentrate too much on the too obvious. He remembered a police profiler telling him about Occam's Razor, a fourteenth-century philosophy which, when applied to modern crime, meant that the obvious answer was usually the correct one. Well, not this time. The bloody obvious had let him down.

'Why did she get you to kill General Huang and the others? Who shot her brother, Mr Zhang, and Mr Nidop? Was she the one who tried to kill me last night?'

'I think it's time we closed up shop,' said Evans, gathering up his briefcase. 'You either charge my client, Inspector, or we walk out.'

There was a knock, the door opened and Andy Graham put his head in.

'Phone call, boss. It's urgent.'

2

It was Fadiman, the site manager from Olympic Tower, his voice a mix of excitement and exasperation. Obviously this was a project that was having more problems than the building of the Suez Canal; he sounded as if he was longing to be building a woolshed out the back of Tibooburra. 'Miss Li, Guo's girlfriend, is down here, bloody near berserk. When I told her Sergeant Clements had been down here and Guo had gone off with him, I thought she'd go off her head. A couple of our guys had to hustle her out of the office.'

'Where is she now?'

'Somewhere on the site. She's in the building somewhere, running around yelling for her other mate, Tong. She's got a gun —'

'Shit!' Malone signalled to Clements, who had come out of the interviewing room. 'Have you called anyone else?'

'No, I called you — you're the one who knows

what this is all about.'

'Don't call anyone — not yet. Not unless she starts shooting. We'll be down there in ten minutes, no more. Tell everyone to stay away from her — get your men out of the building —'

'Oh Christ —'

'What's the matter?'

Fadiman sounded as if he was already packing for the trip to the Outback. 'Madame Tzu has just driven in. She's got — wait a minute — she's got Mr Aldwych and Mr Chung and a Chinese guy with her —'

'Don't let them get near Li Ping!'

'How the hell am I —'

But Malone had hung up, was pulling on his jacket, shoving his hat on his head. He hurried out of his office into the main room, pulled up as Guo Yi and Caradoc Evans came to the doorway of the interviewing room.

'We're leaving, Inspector —'

'No, you're not, Doc. You can go, but we're holding your client.' He signalled to Andy Graham. 'Take care of Mr Guo, Andy.'

Guo frowned. 'What's happened?'

Evans patted his arm. 'Stay calm, Mr Guo. What are the charges, Scobie?'

'I'll let you know within the hour. We're bringing in his girlfriend, Miss Li.' He looked at the young Chinese. 'You'd better have another talk with Mr Evans. I'm afraid Miss Li is going to pour shit all over you for not being there when she wants you.'

369

Guo lifted his chin, not in defiance but like a man trying to keep it above water. He turned back into the interviewing room. Evans said quietly, 'How bad is it?'

'Bad,' said Malone. 'Talk some sense into him or he's on his way back to China.'

'And if he stays?'

'Point out to him we don't have the death penalty here. I believe there were five thousand executions in China last year.'

He let himself and Clements out of the security door. So far Clements had said nothing, but as they waited for the lift he said, 'Where is she?'

Going down in the lift Malone told him what little he knew. 'Gail and Sheryl will be down there now — I don't want them taking her on on their own.'

'Hadn't we better get the SPG guys in?'

'No,' said Malone emphatically. 'This is my case — *our* case — and we're sticking with it. If it develops into a siege situation, then we'll call them in. But for now —'

'If things go wrong and we finish up in the shit, how do we explain it to Greg Random?'

'We don't. I'll get fired.'

They were hurrying out to the unmarked car. 'And what happens to me?'

'You'll have been obeying orders from your superior officer and you won't have known about Greg's order to lay off.'

Clements got in behind the wheel, put the blue

lamp on the roof. 'Let's hope Miss Li comes in quietly.'

'She will,' said Malone, and hoped he sounded convincing.

With the light flashing and the siren wailing, with Clements twice pulling out to drive on the wrong side of the road, the drive from Strawberry Hills took six minutes. As they approached the Olympic Tower site Malone said, 'Righto, cut out the light and the siren. Let's arrive without fuss.'

Clements glanced at him. 'There's gunna be fuss whichever way we arrive. What are you gunna tell Greg Random?'

'I'll think of something.' But not now. Now, at last, he had his hands on the throat of the case.

They pulled on to the site, with Malone gesturing to the gateman to close the wide gates behind them. A cement truck was about to pull in, but the gateman waved it away. The truck stayed where it was, blocking the gateway, providing some sort of screen from the traffic passing behind it.

Malone and Clements got out of the police car and Gail Lee and Sheryl Dallen came towards them with Fadiman, the site manager. In the background, in the shadow of the tall building, over a hundred workers in their hard hats stood in a group, like a small field of tall toadstools. Outside the door of the site office stood the three partners and General Wang-Te, as unmoving as statuary. Beyond the gates, peering in beside the cement truck, a few passers-by had paused and looked in inquisitively: another strike? These bloody constructions workers were always demanding something . . . The clerks and the pensioners looked in sourly at the kings in their white crowns.

'Where's Miss Li?' Malone demanded.

Gail pointed up towards the towering building. 'Somewhere up there. With a gun, Mr Fadiman says.'

Then Roley Bremner detached himself from his co-workers and came towards them. 'She's up on the fourth floor, Scobie. Who let her loose? She's running around like a cut cat, yelling for Tong.'

'Where's he?'

'Christ knows. If he's got any sense, he's going nowhere near her. Get her outa there, mate, so's we can get back to work.'

'Did she threaten you with the gun?' Clements asked Fadiman.

The site manager shook his head. 'No. I didn't know she had one till one of the guys rang down on his mobile, said there was a dame on the fourth floor waving a gun and yelling for Tong Haifeng.'

Malone looked across at the crop of hard hats. 'Is everyone down?'

'Everyone except the guys right at the top, on the framework. She's not going to go up there.'

'What about Mr Tong?'

'He's up there somewhere — dodging her, I'd say.'

Malone looked upwards. 'What's the lay-out up there?'

'All the outer walls and inner walls are in place up to the twenty-third floor. No windows or doors. Above that it's all framework and floors laid as far as the fortieth floor. Above that just steel-and-concrete framework. Don't go up there, not unless you've got a head for heights.'

Malone continued to look upwards, then he lowered his gaze, eased the crick in his neck and looked at Clements. The latter said, 'Looks like we'll need the SPG.'

'SPG?' said Fadiman.

'The State Protection Group.'

'The guys with shotguns and flak jackets and Christ knows what. Holy shit!'

Malone stood stiffly, emotion flooding through him, crumbling the dykes he had built against disappointment. There had been disappointments in the past; he had seen murderers walk away free, their crimes hung round their necks like medals. But this was major; he had wanted to tie this one up himself. The threat to his family and himself had made it a personal vendetta: something no policeman should ever consider. But what the rules said and what the heart said too often ran on separate tracks. But he knew now that the rules were going to win.

'Get the SPG here, Gail.'

He left Clements and the women and Fadiman and walked across to the small group outside the site office. The crowd of workers had begun to disperse, clotting together in smaller groups as they looked for places to sit, to smoke, to drink tea or coffee and wonder again at the jinxes on this site.

'We're bringing in the State Protection Group,' Malone said.

'Men with guns?' said Madame Tzu.

'We all carry guns, Madame Tzu. But this situation needs specialists.'

'Don't cock it up like last time,' said Aldwych, and Malone looked at him pained. He waved a hand. 'I'm not being sarcastic, Scobie. This time they said the girl's got a gun of her own.'

'You think she's going to use it?' said Les Chung.

'She's already used it,' said Malone.

Madame Tzu had been looking up at the building, but now she turned her head quickly and looked at Malone. 'Used it? You mean she shot someone?'

'We think so.'

'Who?'

'You'll hear that when we make the charges. First, we've got to bring her down from up there.' He nodded upwards. 'Her and Tong Haifeng.'

Then Wang-Te spoke. 'I do not think I should be here. This has nothing to do with my government.'

'I think it has, General,' said Malone. 'Your government wants her taken back to China. That's why she's gone berserk. I'm guessing, but we think she wanted her boyfriend Guo to help her get away — I dunno where she thought they'd go. We've got Guo in custody, so I guess she's now looking for Tong to help her out. We want him, too.'

'What's he done?' said Aldwych.

'I'll let you know when we charge him, Jack.'

'I think I can guess. Jesus, I shouldn't of retired — I had less corpses when I was in the game.' Then he looked at Chung. 'We owe someone an apology.'

'Never apologize,' said Chung with a thin smile, 'never regret.'

'My sentiments exactly,' said Aldwych, smile even thinner.

Madame Tzu said nothing, but her look was expressive; she knew who was entitled to the apology. Well, well, thought Malone, maybe I owe her an apology too. But he knew none would be offered.

Clements came across towards them. 'They'll be here in ten minutes. We just stand around and wait.' His tone was bitter, even though it was he who had suggested the SPG should be brought in. 'It's an anti-climax, right?'

'It always is, isn't it?' said Sheryl; she and Gail had come across behind Clements. 'Whenever they're brought in.'

'Don't knock 'em,' said Malone but automatically. He had the same sentiments.

Then there was a shot. All activity on the building had ceased; there had been comparative silence. In the usual clamour a gunshot would have gone unnoticed, mistaken for no more than that of a ram-gun. But there was no mistaking this sound. Then, as if for emphasis, there was a second shot.

'Two?' said Clements, head turned upwards. 'She's done Tong Haifeng?'

'Or one in him and the other in herself.' Malone took off his jacket, handed it to Gail Lee, took out his gun. 'I'm going up.'

Clements was taking off his own jacket, said to Gail, 'Send the SPG guys up soon's they come. But tell 'em to look out for us — we don't want them to potshot us.'

The helmeted workers had all risen to their feet, were congealing again into larger groups. The tension in the yard spread; Madame Tzu put her hand to her throat. Chung and Aldwych looked at each other and the latter shook his head. The jinx was back.

Gail Lee said, 'You want me to come with you, boss? To interpret, just in case she's still alive . . . ?'

'No, Gail, stay here.' He was breaking the rule, endangering his own and Clements' lives; he wasn't going to compound the rebellion. 'Where do you reckon those shots came from, Mr Fadiman?'

'Hard to tell. Maybe the fourth or fifth floors. Go up on the work-lift, not up the stairs.'

Malone and Clements crossed to the lift, got in, slammed the gate and Clements pressed the start button. As they rose he said, 'We're doing the right thing, but how are you gunna explain it to Greg Random?'

'Let's get this solved first. Then I'll think of an explanation.'

'Thanks. I'll remember that when —' But Clements didn't finish, just looked out and down at the upturned faces, pale daisies in the mud of the yard, and the traffic crawling past in the street outside, their drivers oblivious of what was happening here on the Olympic Tower site. He was a fatalistic man, not afraid of dying, but all at once he reached towards the button, to stop the lift and then reverse it.

But the lift stopped of its own accord, at the fourth level. Malone flung up the gate and stepped out on to a narrow gangwalk. Clements hesitated, then followed him. They edged through a glassless window opening, moving quickly so they wouldn't be silhouetted against the light and flattening themselves against the inner walls. Their shoes crunched on grit and rubble on the concrete floor; they were in a wide corridor that stretched ahead of them into the gloom; there was a blank wall at the far end. They were on the eastern side of the building, but the sun had long gone from the window opening. Doorless rooms were open on either side of them as they moved cautiously down the corridor; another year and it would cost three or four hundred dollars a night to walk into the rooms. Graffiti were scrawled on the walls. *Join*

Allied Trades said one message; the answer was on the opposite wall: *Fuck Off!* Small heaps of debris littered the floor; a white hard hat looked like an albino tortoise. Soft-drink bottles were scattered round like landmines waiting for unwary feet to tread on them; a stale sandwich was curled like a seashell. There was a cold smell, of something still to come alive.

They had arrived at two doorways opposite each other; beyond them were stairwells, dark as pits. Malone edged round the opening, gun at the ready, shouted into the stairwell: 'Miss Li! Police! Inspector Malone!'

His voice boomed in the narrow shaft, died away as a whisper far above and below him. Then he heard footsteps coming up out of the darkness; he stepped through the doorway and on to the landing, pointed his gun downwards.

Then Madame Tzu, one hand on the wall as she felt her way, emerged slowly out of the darkness, as if coming up out of an invisible pool of water. A dozen steps below Malone she paused, breathing heavily; she was not accustomed to this sort of exercise. Leaning against the wall she looked to her right; there was no railing there, a misjudged step and she would have plunged four floors, perhaps even right through to the basement. She shook her head, then looked up at Malone, her face still as expressionless as a plate.

'I — I came to help —'

'Who let you in?' He was angry at this unwanted intrusion, this further complication.

'I slipped in — they couldn't stop me —' She climbed the remaining stairs, stood on the landing with Malone and Clements. She was still struggling for breath: 'I — I can help — Ping will listen to me —'

'Not if she's dead.' He looked upwards. 'We're going up to the next floor. You keep behind us. And don't go wandering off on your own, understand?'

Now she was here she all at once looked uncertain; she didn't bridle at all at being told what she had to do. 'I'll keep close. It's so dark —'

They went up cautiously, hugging the wall. They reached the floor above and Malone stepped through the open doorway into the dim corridor. He looked towards the far end, towards the oblong of light that was the window opening, saw the heap of debris in the middle of the corridor. Stepped a few paces towards it and saw that the heap was Tong Haifeng.

He kneeled down, peered closely, saw the large bloodstain on the back of the white shirt and the shattered back of the skull. He felt for the neck pulse, then looked back at Clements.

'Two bullets, both from the back. He's dead.'

Madame Tzu said something in Mandarin: it sounded like a curse.

'So she's still alive and somewhere around,' said Clements; then yelled, 'Miss Li!'

There was no answer but the echo of his voice. Then Madame Tzu shouted something in Mandarin. There was no reply for a moment, then there came a faint voice from a room at the far end of the corridor.

'What did she say?' said Malone.

'She told us to go away. She'll shoot if we don't —'

Malone faced down the corridor, pushed Madame Tzu flat against the wall and pressed himself against it. Clements had retreated into a doorway opposite.

'Miss Li! This is Inspector Malone — let me talk to you!' His voice echoed in the long empty corridor.

There was no immediate answer; then: 'Go away! I am not going back to China!'

'Miss Li —' Argument at a distance and with her hidden from his view was not easy. 'We are State Police — we're not going to send you back to China. Why did you shoot Tong Haifeng? Was he threatening you?' He knew that wasn't on the cards; but anything to keep her talking . . . 'Was it he who killed General Huang?'

A moment; then softly, difficult to hear: 'Yes.'

'Liar,' said Madame Tzu just as softly.

'So you shot him to avenge your father?' He was glad this interrogation was not being taped. She gave no answer and he said, louder this time, 'Were you paying him back for shooting your father?'

Another long pause; then: 'Yes.'

'Liar,' said Madame Tzu again and Malone motioned to her to be quiet.

'Then put down your gun, Miss Li. Come on

out — you won't be sent back to China —'

'How can I trust you?' Her voice was stronger this time.

'You'll have to trust me, Miss Li. There's no one else.'

Clements had come out of the doorway and begun edging along the wall, gun held out in front of him with two hands. He passed another doorway and suddenly something hit him on the shoulder; a bird careered off him, went flapping down the corridor as if on a broken wing, its shrieking bouncing off the walls. Li Ping stepped out of the far doorway, was silhouetted against the oblong of light behind her. The bird hit her squarely in the chest, she fell backwards, her gun went off. Two bullets zinged down the corridor; cement dust flew off the walls. She sat up, aimed the gun and fired; the bullet struck a chip off the wall above Clements' head. He dropped to one knee, took aim and fired. Li Ping, now on her knees, shuddered, then fell sideways.

Malone sprinted down the corridor past Clements, dropped to one knee and grabbed the gun from Li Ping's hand. She looked up at him almost sadly, shook her head, then died.

Malone got to his feet as Clements and Madame Tzu came up behind him. 'She's gone.'

'Stupid girl,' said Madame Tzu, but her voice had more pity in it than criticism.

'Did you know she was behind the murders?' said Malone.

But Madame Tzu was not stupid; she recognized a leading question. 'No.'

'Liar,' said Malone.

But said no more as the first of the SPG men came up out of the stairwell.

3

The Premier had never previously met Jack Aldwych or Leslie Chung. But he had known crooks, even criminals (if not sentenced) in his own party and that of the Opposition and he felt neither uncomfortable nor endangered. He had also not met Madame Tzu and General Wang-Te and he did feel somewhat uncomfortable with them. As he had said to Ladbroke, who arranged the meeting, 'The trouble with the Chinese is that they think they know everything but tell you nothing.'

Then you should feel right at home with them. But Ladbroke didn't voice the thought.

The Dutchman looked at his other guests. There were Sports Minister Agaroff, Lord Mayor Amberton, Councillor Brode and Police Commissioner Zanuch. They sat apart from the other group, like relatives of the bride and groom at a wedding. But then this was a marriage, of sorts. Everyone intent on keeping the name of the Games above reproach.

'You're probably wondering why I've got you all here. None of you has said anything to the media about it?' He glared at them, inviting them to be executed.

'Stuff the media,' said Raymond Brode, moderate in his language this time.

'Eight o'clock in the morning,' said Rupert Amberton, hair flat on his head as if still in its night-net. 'What sort of time is that for a meeting?'

'I haven't been up this early since I was in jail,' said Aldwych, and grinned at the Premier. He knew a gang boss when he saw one. He also knew, or thought he knew, why they were here.

'I've been in touch with Canberra,' said Vanderberg, sounding as if he had been in touch with Hell or one of its suburbs.

'Who needs them?' said Amberton, and Brode, for once, nodded in agreement.

'We all do,' said Madame Tzu unexpectedly, and everyone looked at her, especially General Wang-Te. 'Am I right, Mr Premier, in thinking you have made a deal with Canberra?'

Ladbroke waited. How much is he, who knows everything, going to tell them? The phone conversations last night had gone on till midnight.

The Dutchman evaded the question for the moment by turning his attention to Zanuch. 'The Federal Police have gone back to their cubbyhole. The murders are all yours now.'

'They were all along.' Though Zanuch's chair was only a foot or so from that of Agaroff, he gave the impression of being well apart. Perhaps it was that he was the only one wearing a uniform, but the real separation from them, even from the Premier, was in his face.

Vanderberg transferred his gaze back to General Wang-Te. 'Have you been in touch with Beijing since yesterday?'

'Yes.' Wang-Te was playing his cards close to his chest, aware that he was in a poker game where the cards, none of his, were marked.

'For Crissakes,' said Brode, exploding at last, 'what the fuck's going on?'

The Premier ran his eye over all of them; his smile had all the satisfaction of a vulture that had just eaten a buffalo. He held them all in the hollow of his claw: a politician could wish for no more. 'The young Chinese Guo Yi will be charged with the murders of Mr Shan, Mr Sun and Mr Feng. He —'

Madame Tzu interrupted. 'Mr Shan? General Huang's name will not be mentioned?'

Vanderberg glanced sideways at Ladbroke and the latter said, 'Oh, it will be mentioned, all right. The media will find out and it will mention it in headlines. But we'll deny any knowledge of it and it will be a three-day wonder. Beijing will also deny it, General?'

'Oh yes.' Wang-Te had his hands folded on his chest, as if hiding his cards.

'Canberra are gunna deny it?' asked Aldwych.

'Yes,' said Ladbroke. 'Foreign Affairs are very good at the cover-up. It's called diplomacy.'

'He's so cynical,' said the Premier, and

nodded in approval.

'So what happens next?' Up till now Les Chung had sat silent. He was out of his depth, but not neck-deep. 'What happens about the money Huang sent out to those two bank accounts?'

Vanderberg looked at Wang-Te. 'You going to tell 'em, General, or shall I?'

Wang-Te took his hands away from his chest; the cards had to be played. 'My government in Beijing has agreed that the fifty-one million dollars that were in the young people's accounts can remain here in Australia —'

'Wonderful!' Madame Tzu looked almost young.

'— a company will be set up in Beijing and will take over General Huang's — Mr Shan's — share of the partnership in Olympic Tower, with other investment of capital as it is needed.'

There was a gasp from Madame Tzu; she looked suddenly aged. 'Where does that leave me?'

'That will depend on your partners,' said Wang-Te.

They don't even tell each other anything, thought Ladbroke.

She turned on Aldwych and Chung. 'Well?'

'You'll need more money,' said Chung; he abruptly relaxed, back in his depth again. 'Can you raise it?'

'Yes, yes.' It was twenty years or more since she had showed such eagerness. Unfortunately it made her look older rather than younger. 'I'll leave for Hong Kong tomorrow — now everything is settled again —'

As if the murders hadn't happened, thought Ladbroke. And wondered at life in China, where amongst a billion people maybe murders dropped out of sight like a stone in a vast quicksand.

'So what happens?' Amberton was very much out of his depth. The usual shenanigans in council at the Town Hall suddenly looked like the Teddy Bears' Picnic. He couldn't get back there fast enough. He'd blow-dry his hair and clear his brain.

Agaroff spoke for the first time, rubbing the top of his bald head. The recent fashion craze for bald skulls had given him confidence in his looks; he looked in mirrors now almost as often as Amberton, the hairy one. 'If Mr Aldwych and Mr Chung agree to the new arrangements, we'll put everything of the past week behind us. The sole objective is that the Olympics —' he refrained from making the sign of the cross — 'go ahead without any hitches. Particularly in the accommodation area — we're having trouble there.'

'Five murders?' said Brode. 'You're going to hush all that up?'

'No,' said Commissioner Zanuch, and moved his chair further to one side.

'Bill —' The Premier gave him the basilisk eye. 'Least said, you don't have to mend anything.'

'Mr Premier —' Zanuch was no stranger to political chicanery, but he could see himself and his men carrying the can here. 'The police don't run the Justice system. We have a man in custody, Guo Yi, he will be charged and after that the Director of Public Prosecutions takes over —'

'I've talked with the Attorney-General,' said The Dutchman, which meant he had talked *at* the A-G. 'That young feller will be remanded till all the fuss has died down — say about six months' time —'

'You can keep him in custody all that time?' Amberton was the most innocent of all those in the room.

'There are ways and means,' said Aldwych, who knew from experience. 'Right, Mr Vanderberg?'

The old honest crook acknowledged another wise man. 'Like you say, Mr Aldwych, there are ways and means.'

'Won't his lawyer make a fuss?' asked Brode.

'He's a Welshman,' said Ladbroke. 'They know a roadblock when they see one — they live next door to the English. If he *does* protest, we just send Mr Guo back to China. What would happen to him there, General? You'd execute him, wouldn't you?'

Wang-Te shrugged, but said nothing. Nothing was enough.

The Premier looked at Ladbroke. 'Well, Roger, looks like we've cleaned up the mess.'

'You don't want a statement put out, do you?'

The Dutchman tried to look demure, but failed miserably. 'I wouldn't know what to say.'

4

Last night Malone had driven out to Camden to the safe house and picked up Lisa and the family. He had felt light-hearted, almost light-headed. It was a long time since he had been so glad to see the end of a case. For the second time on this road he passed a police chase of a stolen car. Both cars went by him like comets, the police car with siren blaring and the blue and red lights a swivelling glare. He had blown his horn in encouragement, on the side of law and order.

When he knocked on the front door of the house and announced himself over the intercom, Constable Sherrard, in a pinafore, opened the door. 'So it's all over?'

He nodded. 'They can come home.'

Which they did. They drove back to Randwick through a night that seemed to him to have music in it. I *am* light-headed, he thought. The suburbs lay on either side of them, tiled roofs covering a thousand agonies; but those were other people's and tonight he couldn't care less for other people. All he cared for and about were the four people here in the Fairlane with him.

Nobody asked how the case had been wound up; they knew he would tell them in his own time. They just knew he was safe, they were all safe.

In bed, in the capital city of the country of marriage, as Lisa called it, he wrapped himself in her limbs, felt the warmth and comfort of her that only she could generate. She said, 'You want to tell me about it?'

'No, not now. It'll keep.' He kissed her. 'I love you.'

'I know. Where's your loving hand?'

'On its way.'

Then this morning a uniformed Harold Boston, brand new sergeant's stripes bright as neon on his shoulder, came to collect him at Homicide. 'The Commissioner wants to see you. Now.'

'How come he sent you?'

'I volunteered.'

'Why did I ask?'

Boston looked sideways at him as they got into the Headquarters car. 'He's going to kick you up the arse.'

'It was worth it, Harold. That's something you'll never understand.'

And now he and Greg Random were in the Commissioner's office and Zanuch was reading the riot act. 'The SPG were on their way — why the hell couldn't you have waited? Have you blasted him about this, Greg?'

'Not yet, sir. I was going to, but you got in first.'

Zanuch eyed him; then looked back at Malone. 'I don't know why I'm letting you sit. You should be standing at attention with a poker up your bum. Why didn't you bloody well wait for the SPG?'

Malone had never seen the usually imperturbable Commissioner so irate. It didn't worry him, however; if Zanuch had been going to sack him, he would have been cold and distant. 'There were two shots, sir. I assumed Li Ping had shot Tong Haifeng and then committed suicide. The site manager had told us she was berserk, off her head —'

'She might have been. But that was no reason for you to risk your own life and that of Sergeant Clements and the Chinese woman, whatshername —'

'Madame Tzu. She wasn't up there on the fifth floor at my invitation. She slipped into the building and came up of her own accord — I'm not sure what she thought she could do —'

'I've had her up to my office,' said Random. 'She had some influence over Miss Li — or so she thought. She had some idea she could run those three youngsters and all the time they were laughing at her.'

'She told you that?' Malone was incredulous.

'No, that's my own guess. Chinese kids, some of them, don't respect the old the way they used to — she as much as told me so. Sir, this case has been a helluva mess —'

'You're telling me? I've been in political swill

up to my neck. What did you get out of this young bloke, Guo Yi? Has he confessed to anything?'

'Scobie talked to him yesterday afternoon —' Random looked at Malone.

'He committed the first three murders, at the Golden Gate. He was the hitman in the stocking mask, the feller I saw. Li Ping had been told by General Huang that the money would be coming into her account. That was why she had been going to the bank for several days before it arrived. She was going to transfer five million of it to another bank as soon as it arrived in her account. Then she was going to do a bunk to the United States, lose herself over there under another name. She promised to take Guo with her if he would kill General Huang — she hated the general's guts. She just didn't know about the Cash Transactions Reporting Act. Neither, it seems, did General Huang or the Hong Kong bank executive who arranged the transfer. Li Ping found out, too late, that the man in Hong Kong had come from Beijing, he was new and he didn't really know what went on in the rest of the world. I guess there are rules and regulations in Hong Kong, but it seems money still passes in and out of there like it did in the old days. Except that the old Hong Kong hands are wiser than the Communists who have come in.'

'Where did Guo get that Chinese army gun?' asked the Commissioner.

'It was General Huang's — maybe he'd used it

on some of his mates. Li Ping stole it from him. She shot her adopted brother, Zhang, because he squealed to his father what she had intended to do — take that five million. The general was going to take her back to China with him when he went. I don't know where she got the gun that killed Zhang, but she knew how to use it. She used it on Jason Nidop, too. And she tried to drop me.'

'How did Nidop get into the act?'

'Because he was the first one she approached to do the hit on General Huang. She had some idea that because he was so tough about the union business, he could be bought. He couldn't but he made the mistake of trying to blackmail her. In the end it was Guo who did the Golden Gate murders.'

'But why kill Mr Sun and Mr Feng?' asked Random.

'Les Chung was on the list, too. The idea was that if all four of them were done in, we'd cast a wider net of suspicion. At one time we were thinking it might have had something to do with the Triads. If it had been only General Huang, the first two we'd have looked at would have been his son and adopted daughter.'

'Jesus!' Zanuch looked at the ceiling, as if Himself might have been hovering there. 'How callous can these Chinese be?'

'Sir —' Malone put his neck out. 'Li Ping thought she had been done out of five million dollars. She wanted to escape China, get away

. . . I've arrested Aussie women — and men — who've killed for much less than that, a few dollars and cents.'

'Are you telling me I'm prejudiced?'

'No, sir. I've got enough of my own — I've been battling them all through this case —'

'I think, sir,' said Random, coming to the rescue, 'Scobie had more to put up with in this case than in ordinary circumstances. We all have.'

Zanuch didn't forgive easily; but he was not a vindictive man. He nodded. 'All right, you've made your point. I was at a meeting this morning with the Premier —' He didn't elaborate; he still had the sour taste of the meeting in his mouth. 'From now on we all salute the Olympic flag. You understand?'

Malone's tongue, true to form, got away from him. 'What if someone takes pot shots at the flag, sir?'

'Look the other way,' said Commissioner Zanuch, and actually smiled.

Chapter Twelve

1

While Malone had been caught up in the five-ring circus, stock markets around the world had put on their own act; stocks melted in the sweaty hands of panicky investors. On exchange floors everywhere dealers shouted, gibbered and flung up their arms like drowning swimmers. Apes at Taronga Park zoo, watching the scenes on the TV sets in their cages, looked at each other and shrugged. 'That's evolution? You think we oughta send 'em some bananas?' Tom listened to the gurus, all of whom had a different opinion; then he decided he would be an airline pilot, where going up and down was an everyday affair. Malone, a man of the long view, just hoped that the day he drew his superannuation, the market would be airborne.

Guo Yi was charged and remanded in custody. His trial somehow kept slipping back on court schedules; six months passed before he went to trial, was found guilty and sentenced to life imprisonment. He is now in a top security prison, keeping abreast of advances in engineering in the prison library and through magazine subscription; he is waiting stoically for his

394

release in his early forties. On the wall of his cell the prison governor has allowed him to do a coloured chalk vista, pale as a Chinese scroll, of the Great Wall of China. In the distance, a visual anachronism, is the outline of a skyscraper that bears a resemblance to the Olympic Tower: a mockery or a dream? He doesn't know, or has chosen to ignore, that fifteen to twenty in prison doesn't qualify one for Australian citizenship.

General Wang-Te retired from the army and now makes regular trips to Sydney as a director of the Chinese company that is a partner in the Olympic Tower consortium. He always comes without his wife and is a regular visitor to the Quality Couch, a top brothel where they accept his American Express card and in the interests of international relations, give him frequent bonus points. He has discovered the pleasures of sin and other positions besides the missionary one.

Camilla Feng collected her father's insurance payment and paid off his debts and was accepted as a minor shareholder in the Tower consortium. Ron Fadiman asked her out to dinner and she went, but the date came to nothing. She kissed him good night and goodbye. She has bigger fish to hook.

Madame Tzu still flies back and forth between Hong Kong and Sydney, bringing more and more money each time she arrives. She appears regularly in the Sunday social pages, cool and dignified amongst all the inane smiles, still seeing herself as an empress amongst barbarians.

Jack Aldwych and Leslie Chung, pillars of respectability, go their own quiet way. They have been invited to visit Beijing as guests of the Chinese government and will probably go. Jack Aldwych, retired gangster, only regrets that he has been too late to meet the Gang of Four. He could have taught them a lot.

2

'I hope it's going to be quieter than last time,' said Claire.

'Don't even mention it,' said Lisa.

'We never did get that French champagne,' said Maureen. 'How about it, Dad?'

'I think I might try some,' said Tom.

Malone felt his credit card beginning to curl. Then looked up as Les Chung appeared beside their booth. 'Good evening, Mr and Mrs Malone. And, of course —' He bowed to the family. 'I'm glad you decided to honour us again. Dinner is on us. I can recommend the Peking Duck.' He smiled at Claire; he had a Chinese memory: 'The champagne is on its way.'

He went away and Malone looked after him. He paused by the back booth, which was empty, a red rope across it. Nice touch, Les, thought

Malone. But you can't put a rope round memory.

Lisa put her hand on his, said softly, 'Forget it. It's all over.'

Kirribilli   August 1996-August 1997

We hope you have enjoyed this Large Print book. Other G.K. Hall & Co. or Chivers Press Large Print books are available at your library or directly from the publishers.

For more information about current and upcoming titles, please call or write, without obligation, to:

G.K. Hall & Co.
P.O. Box 159
Thorndike, Maine 04986 USA
Tel. (800) 257-5157

OR

Chivers Press Limited
Windsor Bridge Road
Bath BA2 3AX
England
Tel. (0225) 335336

All our Large Print titles are designed for easy reading, and all our books are made to last.